N FALCONER

"On [...] want to read everything he has ever written."

—*Crystal Book Reviews*

"Falconer's grasp of period and places is almost flawless . . . He's my kind of writer."

—Peter Corris, *The Australian*

"If you haven't read one of Colin Falconer's novels, then I promise you are in for a real roller-coaster ride of never ending intrigue."

—*History and Women*

"Each chapter ends with a gripping cliff-hanger that makes the book irresistible and unputdownable."

—Mirella Patzer, Historical Novel Review

"I enjoyed his storytelling voice so much that, had this book been say, set in modern times, the intriguing main characters would still have been able to pull it off."

—*Bookbag*

"Falconer demonstrates exceptional characterization."

—*Bookgeeks*

"Provides action, romance, and beautifully descriptive writing by the cartload."

—Des Greene, *Novel Suggestions*

"Living history at its best, fictionalized yet immensely believable."

—Alan Gold, *Good Reading*

"Beautifully written in typical Falconer style with plenty of snap and sharpness, and wonderfully researched, I enjoyed every page of this book."

—*History and Women*

"Falconer's descriptive narrative is exquisite at times. Each short chapter opens with a flowing brush of words that paint precisely, yet mellifluously, in a manner that is almost poetic."

—Historical Writers Association

"It is the richness of the prose itself that truly made this historical era come alive."

—*Historical Novel Review*

"A page-turner."

—*Booklist*

"Plausible and engrossing."

—*Woman's Day*

"Moves along at a cracking pace, the narrative fraught with action and tension at every turn."

—Historical Novel Society

"Colin Falconer is one of those historical fiction authors that takes a subject and not only researches it thoroughly but also has the talent to take you to the heart of the matter whilst making you feel that you're seeing history being made at the time of the events . . . Add to this top notch prose a wonderfully almost cinematic feel to the story and of course a lead character that you can really get behind and all in it's a wonderful read. Great stuff."

—Dros Delnoch, *Falcata Times*

LOVING
LIBERTY
LEVINE

LOVING
LIBERTY
A Novel ## LEVINE

COLIN FALCONER

Published by Lake Union Publishing, Seattle

www.apub.com

Amazon, the Amazon logo, and Lake Union are trademarks of Amazon.com, Inc., or its affiliates.

ISBN-13: 9781503904002
ISBN-10: 1503904008

Cover design by Shasti O'Leary Soudant

Printed in the United States of America

This book is dedicated to my two beautiful daughters,
Lauren and Jess.

AUTHOR'S NOTE

Any errors in the representation of historical facts are mine and mine alone. And yes, the term *skid row* was not used until 1931. I claim poetic license on that one.

PART 1

1

Tallinn, Russia, Winter 1912

Sura wanted to love her husband more than she did. I should be wailing too, she thought, as she watched Micha peel his mother's arms from about his neck. There was a part of her that was terrified she would never see him again; another part of her wished him gone forever so that she could one day become a mother.

You are so lucky, her sisters told her. Soon you will be millionaire rich! They shovel the gold off the streets over there in Golden Medina. But she didn't want to leave Tallinn, didn't want to follow him to America and a better life. What was wrong with this one?

Gelt, what of it? Can Micha buy me a baby with it? Can money buy me my very own family, like they have?

The sailors scurried about the deck of the iron ship, getting ready to cast off for the first leg of the journey to New York. Will it be warmer over there, she wondered. This winter's day was so bitter, the wind had frozen the sea spray into icicles through the sedge at the waterline. Her nose was stinging with cold above her scarf, her feet numb.

Just go, Husband, so we can all get out of this wind.

What a terrible person to think such shameless-wife thoughts! Poor Micha, trying only to make a life for himself, for her, trying to become a proper *mensch.*

"Sura," he said, and wrapped her in his big bear arms. There was ice on his wool coat, and it melted against her cheek. "Stay well, *bubeleh.*"

"*Zol zion mit mazel,*" she said.

"I will send you a ticket as soon as I have the money." He hefted his cardboard suitcase, all tied round with string, and put his other arm around his mother. "It's all right, Mama," he said to her. "I will see you soon, in America."

"You go over there, you will lose all your Jewishness."

"I won't lose my Jewishness, Mama."

"Look at you. I can see the Jewishness coming out of you already."

The captain of the ferry gave a blast on the horn; the sailors threw the heavy ropes off the bollards. It was time to go. Micha ran up the gangway, and Sura helped his mother back to the wagon. She was afraid the old woman might faint—and such a weight she was. If it wasn't for Sura and Ruth, Micha's sister, she would have sunk to her knees right there in the snow.

"You'll see him soon in America," Sura said to her. "You heard him, he promised you."

"No, I won't ever see my son again," the old woman moaned. "What do I want from going to America?"

"But you told him a hundred times you would go. I heard you say it!"

"Got as much use for telling as I got use for America. Never going to see my boy again. What am I going to do now?"

The ferry pulled away from the dock. In minutes it was plowing through the gray sea. The first stop was Stockholm, he had told her, in a country called Sweden. *From there, I will get a boat to New York, then I will start shoveling up the gold. I hope I have not left too late, and there is some left for me!*

She saw him holding on to the stern rail with one hand, waving the other high above his head. The frost in his beard will be frozen like glass by now, she thought. My poor husband. Everyone says he is so good; he deserves a better wife, one who is not always wishing other women's babies belonged to her.

When he gets to America, he should forget all about me.

2

"How do you know it is because of Micha you can't have babies?" Etta said.

"He told me, that same night we are married. Right then, I cannot make any sense of it. It is the wedding night, what do I know from these things? How do I know what a man is supposed to look like down there?"

"What did he look like?"

"I don't know. Like normal, I guess. Like a horse."

"Like a horse?"

"Well, same like a horse, only smaller."

"Thank God."

The sled bumped on the rutted ice. Sura saw elk tracks in the deep snow beside the trail. The jangle of the reins was the only sound in the darkening forest. Shadows were deepening between the crooked bog pines. Etta had kept them late at the market trying to sell the rest of the potatoes, and they would be lucky to get back before dark now.

"Micha was married before, and his wife didn't have a baby."

"You shouldn't say bad about the dead," Etta said.

"I'm not speaking bad of her. I am just saying. Five years they were married and nothing to show."

"You've only been married two years, Sura. Not even two years."

The sled bounced on another deep rut, and Etta gasped and clutched at her belly. Easy for her to say, Sura thought. Barely married a year and already her first on the way. No such problems for her.

No problems for any of my sisters, only me.

"Don't be having it now," Sura said.

"Not having my baby in the forest."

"That's good, because you start pushing now, I'm leaving you here." Sura flicked the reins to hurry Ivor, their old horse.

"You miss Micha?" Etta asked her.

Sura felt a guilty flush in her cold cheeks. "Sure, I miss him. He's my husband."

"You never talk about him."

"Doesn't mean I don't miss him."

"He's a handsome man, your Micha."

Very handsome man, she wanted to say. But what good is a handsome man when he can't give you handsome babies?

"Soon you will be going to America too."

Sura didn't say anything.

"Don't you want to go?"

"When I go to America, when will I see you and Zlota and Gutta again?"

"It's got to be better than here. Who ever gets to be a proper human being in Russia?"

Another flick of the reins. Old Ivor was getting cranky and slow these days. A wolf was baying somewhere in the forest. Sura didn't like how dark it was getting.

"Sura, you and Micha, did you, you know, do it a lot?"

"Sure, we did it a lot. What do you think?"

"To have a baby, Yaakov says you have to do it a lot."

"Well, sure, Yaakov's going to say that. He's a man, what else is he going to say?" Sura glanced at her sister. There was something wrong with her. She looked red in the face, and she kept blowing out her cheeks, like she couldn't get her breath. Please not now, she thought. Miles to go before we get home. Please don't let it be now. "Etta, you okay?"

But Etta ignored her. "Why did Micha think he couldn't, you know?" she said.

"He had an accident."

"What kind of accident?"

"He fell off a horse when he was a *boychick*. Onto a pine stump. They had to take him to the hospital, in Tallinn. He said one of his you-know-whats, it was the size of a potato. Etta, I don't like the look of you. What's wrong?"

"I think maybe the baby's coming."

"You think what?"

"I've been having these pains."

"Since when you been having pains?"

"Since we left the market."

"Since the market? Why didn't you tell me?"

"I thought maybe I was imagining."

Sura stared at her little sister. She was trying to look brave, but Sura could tell by her eyes Etta was really scared. She gasped as the sled jolted, and gripped Sura's arm. "Sura, I think it's happening."

"No, it's not happening. It can't be happening. Take a deep breath."

"What good will it do, a deep breath? What do you know from stopping babies?"

"You can't have it out here!"

She flicked the reins. Don't panic, Sura, she thought. Not far from the village, if Ivor can keep up this trot. Just a little faster, old boy. Get us home.

Etta gasped again. Sura felt her fingers tighten around her arm, squeeze all the blood out of it. Should have left her home this morning, but she said she had weeks yet. Should never listen to your little sister, Sura, you know that. Never had any brains this one, just like their *vati* said.

Suddenly the sled lurched and skewed, and they nearly tipped all the way over. Etta screamed as Ivor crumpled to his knees in the snow. The old boy was keening down in the traces and slumping onto his side; only the trunk of a birch tree kept them from toppling all the way over.

Sura was lying on top of Etta, who was moaning softly. Sura jumped out, and straightaway she could see what had happened. In his hurry Ivor had put his foreleg in a bog. He was struggling to get up, whimpering all the while.

Sura pulled Etta clear of the sled.

"I'm all right," Etta said. "How is Ivor?"

Poor Ivor, he had pulled their sled between the village and the city for as long as she could remember, but maybe today was the last time. A close look told her the worst: his left leg was snapped. She could see white bone and a streak of bright-red blood. She knelt down, stroked his old head, all the good it would do. Nothing to be done to help him now.

One moment we are talking about having families, she thought, next we are lying in the snow with a crippled horse and Etta is having a baby. She looked around: deepening forest shadows, Etta moaning in a bundled heap on the ground. Sura could see the first evening star above the black tips of the pines.

She crouched there, listening to her sister's gulping moans. Etta's breath froze on the still air, each puff a little condensation of pain coming faster and faster.

What was that there, in the dark? Oh, okay, just a squirrel. It watched for a moment, then darted between the trees, leaving tiny tracks in the snow. Her muscles felt frozen. She didn't know what to do.

Well, Sura Levine, you have to do something, cannot sit here feeling sorry for yourself. Your fault you are in this mess, now you have to mend it.

She scrambled over to Etta, grabbed her hands, and sat her up.

"How is Ivor?" Etta said.

"He broke his leg."

"Poor Ivor. Oh, listen to him, Sura."

"Cannot listen to him before I listen to you. Is it coming?"

"I don't know. I don't know!"

Sura fetched some of the empty burlap sacks out of the back of the sled and put them underneath Etta. She took off her gloves, blew on her fingers, then started to drag down her little sister's drawers.

"What are you doing?"

"Got to see if the baby is coming. What, you too modest to show me? I'm your big sister, nothing you got I don't got too." She pushed Etta's knees apart. There was a smear of blood and mucus on the sacks, a sticky black mop of a head right there. Took her two other sisters almost a whole day to have their first—here is Etta out in the snow, and she has almost pushed out this little *schnorrer* just with a few grunts, sitting on the sled. Not enough sense to feel any pain, Vati would say.

"Have to leave me here," Etta said. "Run and get someone."

"I am someone."

"I'm scared, Sura."

"Nothing to be scared of. I can see the head. You're nearly done."

"You can see the head?"

"You must have been laboring all the while we were at market. How could you be so quiet about it?"

"I thought it was just normal. I'm not due till Purim."

"This little thing don't have a Jewish calendar in there, Etta."

Oh, not here, little one, not here! Already Sura's fingers were so numb, she couldn't feel them. Her mother and her aunt had helped when her big sisters had their babies, made her run for hot water and towels. She had watched what they did over their shoulders, but she had never had to do it herself. And what did she have for the birth cord?

Just the string from the potato sacks and a rusty old knife in her belt she used for cutting them open.

"Run for help," Etta said. "Run for help, it's coming, oh my baby, my baby, everything's *fakakta*!"

Never even thought she knew that word, Sura thought. Etta screamed again, and Sura watched wide eyed as the crowning head swelled, then withdrew. "It's almost there," she said.

Poor Ivor, poor Etta, both of them growling in pain. I can help only one of them, she thought, if I can help at all.

It was getting darker. How late was it? When would someone wonder why they weren't home and come looking for them? The crown of the head was still there, all glistening with blood and dark hair between Etta's legs. "Push," Sura said.

"Can't have it here!"

"Got no choice. Push!"

Suddenly the head was out; the baby's face was blue and smeared with greasy vernix.

"What is it?" Etta gasped.

It's a goblin, she wanted to say, ugly as a forest troll. "I can't see yet. When you get another pain, push hard!"

Etta's next cry echoed through the gloaming, and something hot and slippery slithered into Sura's hands. Vapor rose in a little cloud. She almost dropped the tiny thing into the snow. Etta gasped and lay back, mouth open like she had just died.

Sura bundled the infant in a rough piece of burlap. Oh, it wasn't crying yet; it was blue and quiet. She cleared away the slime from its tiny mouth and nose with a finger, tapped its bottom, put her lips over its tiny face, breathed life into it. "Wake up, bubeleh, wake up."

A drop of fluid leaked from the heart-shaped mouth, and it gave a trembling cry. "It's a girl," she said.

Etta opened an eye, then held out her arms and took the child from her, Sura reluctant to give her up.

"Feed her," she said.

"How?"

"Put her on your breast, *yotz*. It will help deliver the rest."

Her aunt had told her what to do with the liver-looking stuff when it came, what to look for. She wished now she had paid more attention. She tied the cord in two places with the rough string, sawed through the cord with the knife. She looked at the bright splash of blood in the snow. There seemed so much of it, but with the child feeding, at least the rush of it had stopped.

The sky was cold and gray as gunmetal, the sun had sunk out of sight now below the birch trees. They could die out here. Poor Ivor was still whinnying in pain, his great flanks twitching.

Her little sister was white like candle wax. How much blood you got in one body, she wanted to ask. Over Etta's shoulder she saw a fox watching them, its red fur stark against the winter white. You can't stay out here, it seemed to be saying. Got to get your young back to the burrow, like I did.

"Get up," she said.

"What?"

"Get up."

"I can't."

"Got to, Etta. We can't stay here."

"No. You take the baby. Go ahead. Get help. It will be quicker."

"Can't leave you here."

"I got to sleep first."

"Get up." Sura took the child from her, held the wriggling bundle tight to her chest, put her other arm under her sister, and hauled her to her feet. "Stand up."

"I'm trying."

"Stand!"

"So tired. Let me sleep for a minute, then I'll do it."

"Stand up, Etta!"

Sura almost fell getting her upright—they dropped to their knees in a drift of snow—but finally she had her on her feet. The ice crunched under their boots.

All they had to do was follow the track, she thought. Easy enough to do in the day, but not now. She gripped under Etta's arm, made her start walking, holding up her weight like she had held up Mrs. Levine the day her Micha got on the ship. The little girl had fallen asleep in the fold of sacks under Sura's other arm, like trudging through a dark forest when you were just born was the most normal thing in the whole world.

"Can't do it, Sura."

"What are you *kvetching* about, you can't do it. It's only walking, one foot in front of the other."

"I'm going to faint."

"Not going to faint, Etta! If you faint, I got to stay here with you and then I'll freeze and this little mite will freeze too. Is that what you want, that your little baby dies out here?"

"Don't make me walk, Sura."

"Got to make you walk. You know how to walk, one foot, then the other foot. Do it, Etta."

But soon it was too dark and she couldn't see the track and they kept staggering into snowdrifts. The infant started making mewling noises, and Sura propped Etta against a tree and told her to try and feed her. But again Etta said she couldn't. She was too tired, and she had no milk.

Sura peered under the makeshift blankets. Look at the poor thing crying, her pink toothless mouth wide open, eyes screwed shut. Shush, now, shush, not my fault it's so cold and we're lost out here and your mother's nearly dead. You want to get born in Russia, you have to get used to bad luck.

For the first time it occurred to her that they might really die out here. She wondered what Micha would say when he heard about it. It was Micha who was supposed to be in danger, sailing on the boat all the way to America. Funny how life is.

She sank to her knees. Etta had wrapped her scarf around her face, and all Sura could see of her was her eyes. "She doesn't want to feed, Sura. I think she's cold." She was shivering too hard to hold the baby. Sura had to help her.

A full moon hung over the forest, wolves were howling somewhere, she heard something big lumbering through the forest close by, an elk or a roe deer, a wild boar perhaps.

"You should have gone ahead," Etta said.

"Never leave you, Etta, you know that."

"Such a good sister, Sura."

"I'm not good."

"Sure, you are good. How can you say it?"

I should tell her now, she thought. What does it matter now, no one is going to come and save us, going to die out here. I can tell her what a bad good sister she got. "I always wanted to marry Yaakov."

"What?"

"Ever since I was a little girl, I wanted to. So jealous when Vati arranged the wedding for you."

"Oh, Sura."

"It's true. I'm sorry, Etta."

"But Micha is a good husband. Such handsome man! You are going to America to be rich."

"Every night since he left, I wish his boat will sink so I can marry someone else and have a family like you and Gutta and Zlota. Everyone thinks I am so good but I'm not. And that is why poor Ivor broke his leg and we are stranded out here. God is punishing me for my bad-wife thinking."

Etta reached for her, grabbed her coat, pulled her close. "You look after my little girl."

"Why I should look after her, Etta? Is your baby."

14

"You look after her, never mind what happens to me."

"Don't you do that, Etta! Don't you go to sleep!"

Sura was shaking so hard she felt like her bones would break. She wanted to lie down and rest, but lying down was like dying now, and she made herself get up.

"Have to keep walking, Etta. There is enough moon now, I can see the track."

"No, Sura, can't walk anymore," Etta mumbled.

Sura took the child from her, tried to shake her awake, but Etta would not stir anymore. Has lost too much blood, Sura thought. She could see spots of it still in the snow, in their footprints. Perhaps if I walk on, she thought, I can still save the baby.

But how could she leave her little sister? Have to drag her, then, she thought.

She took hold of one of Etta's hands, pulled as hard as she could, dragged her two feet through the snow, perhaps three, before she lost her footing and stumbled, landing hard on her hip to protect the bundle in her arms.

She lay there, gathering strength to try again, when she heard something in the forest, thought it was the wild boar for sure now, it sounded so big, but then she saw a light.

"Etta, they're coming," she said, but Etta did not answer.

She waited and listened. There it was again, people's voices, and now she could see the light clearly, a torch flickering through the trees. She tried to shout, but her voice was no more than a croak.

She tried again, took a deep breath; the air was so cold it was like fire in her lungs, her shout came out just a hoarse whisper. But then the baby joined in, her cry unmistakable in the forest dark.

"Etta, they're coming," Sura said again.

But Etta was slumped onto her side and didn't stir.

3

Haapvinni, near Tallinn, Russia

It was not yet light.

Dawn inched its way through the door, reluctant to begin the day. All that Sura had out of the blankets were her nose and her eyes; the ashes in the oven underneath her only a little warm now; it needed more wood. The baby was still asleep. She felt her angel breath on her cheek, the whisper of her still there, despite all she had been through.

Etta lay on the other side of her. Sura strained in the dark to watch the blankets move, knew from the heat of her that she was still alive. She could see the shape of their mother sitting there in her chair, piled over with blankets, must have been watching them all night, but now she had fallen asleep.

Sura stared at the dark, wanted to hold on to the night, stop it slipping away. Nothing decided yet, nothing done. Right in this moment I have everything I ever wanted, she thought. An infant, warm and pink, under my arm, something living I brought into the world. This is my life, done right here, but when morning comes and Etta is alive, it will all be gone.

But then, what if Micha never sends back for me? What if something happened to him on the way to America? If the ship sank on the big ocean?

Oh, what kind of a no-good wife thinks things like that, Sura Levine?

Yes, but if it did, is all I'm saying. If Micha never reaches America, will Vati let me marry someone else? If Etta doesn't wake up, then this little baby will need a mother, and Yaakov, he will need a wife.

She got to stop these thoughts. No one else can hear this bad-wife, bad-sister voice in her head, but God hears, her vati and the Reb said God could hear every silent thought as loud as if it was a Cossack shouting out new laws in the square outside the church.

Last night was a dream. It never really happened.

But it did happen. When she woke up, it would be real. They had found poor Ivor, not even a mile away from where they had walked, already dead from cold when her vati and the other men got there. Her fault the old horse had died, he was too old to gallop so fast in the traces in such weather.

The child stirred, soon she would be howling for Etta's milk, but she had no milk to give her yet, she didn't even have blood in her to keep herself alive, nothing left over for the baby. They had sent for their sister Zlota, her with her three-month-old, she would feed her until Etta was better.

Until then, Sura thought, I shall lie here with everything I ever wanted, hold on to time slipping, have to make this my forever time.

"That was a good thing you did," Vati said.

Sura didn't know what to say. It was the first time her father had ever praised her this way. Overwhelmed, she nodded and concentrated on her stitches, the buttonholes for a new suit for the Reb Jacob Rabinovitz. She was the only one of her sisters her father allowed to work on the suit. When he had told her to tailor the buttonholes, it was like God coming to earth and saying she was Chosen before all other women. It was that big an honor.

It was still dark. The candle was almost burned down to the stub, and he lit another, then blew on his fingers to warm them. He squinted, pushed his broken glasses farther up his nose, peered at the stitching on the lapels. She knew his eyesight was failing him, but he was too proud to say. She would have to check his work herself later, after he had gone to *beth midrash*.

"So you are going to America."

"Yes, Vati."

"What will I do when you are gone?"

Well, her heart stopped right then. She waited to hear him say that he would miss her for her laugh, for her spirit, for her company.

"You are a better sewer than any of your three sisters," he said. "You are a better sewer than anyone in the *shtetl*. You have the eye. I show you a dress, you can make it; I show you a coat, you can cut it, just from memory. Never did I have even half your gift!"

He's going to persuade me to stay, she thought. He won't make me go away.

Instead he shrugged and shook his head. "If only you had been a boy."

He peered closer at the chalk marks on the suit trousers. Nothing but perfect would be good enough for their Reb.

"Perhaps Micha will get to America and forget all about me."

"Why would he do that?" He glanced up at her, the look on his face, he knew what she was thinking. "Then what would we do with you? What kind of buyer you get for a secondhand suit?"

"What good is being a wife when the husband I have cannot give me what I want?"

"Children come from God's design, Daughter. You can make a tapestry, a nice suit for a rabbi, a nice dress for Mrs. Klas. But you cannot tell God what to do."

"All my sisters have families now. Why not me?"

"I don't know why not you. I don't know why God took all my sons when they were still in the cradle. I don't know why God gave me instead a daughter with such quick and nimble fingers and such a fast brain. What good is it? But I don't ask. I just pray. That is what you should do too."

Sura heard the clatter of boots on the planks outside the house, the men making their way to the beth midrash. From out back she heard milk squirting into a tin pail as her mother milked their family cow. Light leaked through the wooden shutter, she could smell cooking smoke, a whiff of Rivka Lotman's bagels.

Her father stood up, straightened his frock coat, reached for his hat. "Time I was to prayer. Have the buttonholes finished by the time I come home," he said to her, and went out.

4

Some days in the winter there was so much ice around the water pump you could break your neck on the cobblestones, but today it was all melting to slush. The old women sat around the benches to gossip. They watched her as she sat down with Etta and her little baby, Bessie, smiling big toothless smiles at them.

Etta was getting stronger every day. Sura watched the women coo over her Bessie, and felt a real pain inside. It felt as if Etta had stolen Bessie from her. I was the one who saved her that day in the forest, she thought. I was the one who held her and kept her warm.

More bad-sister thoughts. What is wrong with me?

Sura's two other sisters were there too, Zlota and Gutta, chattering away with the other women. Already Sura felt like she did not belong. I don't got no husband anymore, no children. They all know soon I will be going away, everyone in the village looking at me now like I am a stranger or I don't know what.

Zlota looked at her, so smug she was, there with her two little boys at her feet, another at her breast, and a clever husband; her Ari would be head of the *yeshiva* one day, or so her vati said. And Zlota younger than her! Why hadn't Vati married *her* to Ari? During the *kest*, while he was at his studies, her father could have taught her to take over his tailoring business, then it wouldn't matter that she wasn't a boy. Why did it have to be Zlota to stay behind? She had two hands full of thumbs, even Vati said so himself.

And there was Gutta, her belly swollen with yet another baby. Her Benno was a carpenter. He was away all summer building roofs. In winter he was at the beth midrash every day. Gutta said he only ever bothered her at night, and then for only a couple of minutes. Not a bad life.

Sura was the one with the nimble fingers, and now she would have to go to America, where no one cared about her clever stitching. This was God's plan, according to Vati. Some God, some plan.

"Have you heard from Micha?" Etta asked her.

Sura shook her head. Nothing, and it was nearly two months now.

"Perhaps his letter got lost. Have you spoken to Mrs. Levine?"

"I saw her the last time I was to market. Nothing."

"Do you think something has happened?"

Sura was scared to say that it had, scared to say it hadn't. She just shrugged.

"Don't worry. Everything will be all right. He is a clever man, your Micha. Soon you'll be in America and you'll be rich."

"He was supposed to be rich right here, not in America. Since his great-grandfather's time, his family has their leather shop right next to the Raeapteek. What more rich does he want?"

"You must trust your husband."

"What if he never comes back, Etta?"

What if Micha never comes back; what if he never sends me a ticket? This she had wondered every day even since he announced he was going to America. Even her own *mutti* had been shaken, she wasn't like Vati, not so sure of God's divine plan, she had not stopped questioning God's reasoning in this ever since Micha left. It was all supposed to be so different when Vati had arranged the marriage. Micha was supposed to be their pot of gold; she hadn't expected him to go to Golden Medina looking for his own.

Sura carried the water back through the yard to their house, trying not to slip on the planks. The frost had turned to slush, and the rutted tracks to mud—it would just be muck like this now till summer came. She could hear the little kids chanting in the *chaider*.

"Do you believe what they say?" Etta asked her.

"About what?"

"About America. That the roads are paved with gold."

"And the czar is a rabbi! I would be happy to live anywhere the roads are paved with anything." She put down the buckets, stopped to rest a moment.

She supposed she should be just thankful for living after what had happened. Everyone treated her like she was queen of the shtetl after she had saved her sister. Perhaps Etta was right; she was lucky, lucky to be alive, to have a husband with the *chutzpah* to go to America and try and be rich. Just think on that.

Look at this place: the lopsided houses with the wooden shingles; Mr. and Mrs. Gutnik with their handcart loaded with onions and horseradish, stuck in the mud; a raven sitting on a leaning fence, jeering at them. Why would a girl not want to go to America?

But she had liked it well enough in the town, living above the leather shop, until Micha got this idea in his head to leave. He said New York was ten times bigger than Tallinn. *"It is the best city in the world, Sura!"*

Sometimes she thought her clever husband was maybe just a little bit of a dumbhead.

There were more running boards over the big puddle in front of their house. She went across very slowly so she didn't step in, stopped halfway over when she saw her vati standing outside the front door, waiting for her. She knew what it was as soon as she saw him.

He held the letter out to her in his broad brown hands. "It's for you," he said. "It's from Micha."

She sat down at the table. News like this you couldn't read standing up. There were three pages in Micha's careful hand on onionskin paper. She read it through quickly, a word here, a word there, looking for clues.

"What does he say?" her mutti almost shouted.

"Come on, girl," Vati said.

She read it out loud to them. Micha had a job now, he was manager of a big hotel in New York, America. He was going to be very rich very soon. He said other things that could not be true, about how many motor cars there were, and buildings taller than Toompea Castle, trains that ran in the air.

"He wants me to come to New York," she finished. "He has sent me a *shifcant*." She picked up the envelope and shook it, and the ticket dropped onto the table, and they all stared at it, like it was alive and poisonous.

"When?" her mutti said.

She picked up the ticket and stared at it. "Next week," she said.

Her mutti sat down hard on a chair and started to wail. Etta gripped Sura's arm like she was holding on for her life. Her vati went to the synagogue to pray. Even little Bessie started to cry. One by one her neighbors came by to pay respects. They talked to her mother, to Etta and her sisters, but her they didn't talk to. She was a ghost. No one who went to America ever came back.

While everyone howled and prayed, she leaned over and stroked the baby's tiny head with its down of black hair. "I'll miss you, bubeleh," she whispered. She had helped her into the world, kept her safe on her first terrible night on earth, and now she would never even see her grow up. Somehow that hurt her more than anything else.

But there it was, nothing more to be done.

Stop it, Sura, she told herself. Micha needs you in Golden Medina. Got to go help him shovel gold off the street.

She listened to her mutti and Etta crying, but she didn't have any tears left for herself. You're a woman, Sura, got to go and do whatever a man tells you that you got to do. That is just the way it is.

5

The Grand Central Hotel, Park Avenue, New York

Micha had never seen such a place; it wasn't a hotel, it was a palace. A wonder in a city of wonders. Every day he spent stumbling around in a dream.

There was no gold lying around in the street, like some people had said, but then he had never believed those stories anyway. But how could he explain in his letters this place where he worked? Perhaps only the czar himself would not be amazed.

The hotel was granite and cast iron and red brick, tall as the tower of Saint Nicholas's Church in Tallinn, with great columns either side of the entrance. But it was what was inside that made a person catch their breath: marble on the floors, and not just one color—it was red and pure white, with blue-and-gray veins, like nothing he had ever seen, ever imagined. There was a stairway of mottled-gray marble and chandeliers of polished brass studded with crystals that glittered as if they were made of diamonds. And they were lit with electricity, not candles. And no one here even stared at them as he did, as if it wasn't the most extraordinary thing they had ever seen. There were gilt-framed mirrors and carmine plush chairs and even a stone fireplace the size of a kitchen, where the guests could warm themselves, the snow melting off their boots onto the slate.

He glimpsed these glories only through cracked doorways, of course. His uncle Max told him that a janitor's job was to keep things spotless and be invisible. *"They want to see everything clean,"* he had said to him his first day. *"They don't want from seeing you clean them."*

For now, the front of house was an impossible glory, but one day perhaps, Uncle Max said, when there was an opening, he would get him a job as a bellboy or perhaps waiting tables in the restaurant. But first, he had to learn him English. "Work hard at night school. Then we'll see."

Micha also saw parts of the marvel that the guests didn't see: the ladies' entrance, as Uncle Max called it, on Fortieth Street, where certain ladies came and went; and, of course, the alley at the back, where the food carter and the laundry van made deliveries, and where the rubbish stank in the bins just like it did for poor people.

For now, that was his domain, the dirt. Maybe he was a somebody back home, but in this New York, his job was to mop floors, clean spills, take out the trash.

The only people he ever talked to were the Polish laundry driver or the kitchen hand from Minsk. So that one day when he saw a girl in a blue velvet coat and button-up boots, smoking a cigarette, leaning against the wall among the trash cans, he supposed she had come out the ladies' entrance. Well, that was none of his business. He lowered his head and got on with emptying the trash.

She said something to him, and so he said to her, "Sorry, I don't have English," like he said to everyone, thinking she would go away, but instead she held up her cigarette and signed to him that she needed matches.

Micha shrugged and shook his head.

"Oh, I get it. You don't speak English, right?"

Micha felt his cheeks flush hot. He wasn't supposed to talk to the hotel guests, especially female ones.

"What are you? Russian? German? Oh God, why am I even asking you that? You don't speak English, so you don't know what you are."

He could feel her watching him. American women scared him, a little. They were not like the girls in Russia. They smoked cigarettes, and they looked right at you instead of down at the floor, like a good girl should.

"I guess I shouldn't be down here, right? You probably think I'm a working girl. It's all right, I won't bite."

Micha remembered her now. He had seen her the day before, in the corridor on the top floor. She had checked in to the hotel with a man in a fancy fur coat, and they had so much luggage they needed two bell-boys to fetch it all. She had been carrying a baby in a wicker bassinet.

"He doesn't like me smoking, so I come down here," she said, and tossed the unlit cigarette in the alley. He watched it skitter behind one of the cans. "Oh sorry, I guess I just made you more work."

She turned and gave him a look. He looked down at his boots.

"Jesus, men. They all want to tell you how to live, what to do. I thought this one was different. But men aren't different, are they? They're all the fucking same. I can say *fuck*, right? I mean, you don't know what *fuck* means, so you won't get offended."

Something scurried behind one of the trash cans. A rat, he supposed. He dared a glance back at the woman. She was very pretty and very young, not much older than his Sura, with a bruised plum of a mouth and eyes it hurt to look at. She looked as if she was halfway between laughing and crying and couldn't decide which.

"I better get back to the kid," she said. She lowered her voice to a mock whisper. "He thinks I'm not a very good mother." She startled him by reaching out a hand and giving his cheek a playful squeeze. "Don't look so sad. America's not such a bad place when you get used to it. Watch out for the girls, though, they're all crazy. And thanks for listening. What's your name, anyway?"

He stared at her.

She pointed at herself. "Clare. *Clare.*"

"Micha," he mumbled.

"Okay. Well, have a nice day, Mickey. Don't do anything I'd do." And then she was gone.

Haapvinni

Everyone in the shtetl came out to say good-bye. There was a procession right along the street, all come to see off the brave girl who had saved her sister and her baby and was now going to a better life in Golden Medina. For this one day, she was as famous as the czar.

With Ivor gone, her vati had to borrow a neighbor's horse and wagon for the ride into the city. He stopped there on the road at the edge of the shtetl, so much crying and kissing like she couldn't believe, Sura hugged good-bye to neighbors she had said barely a word to all her seventeen years. Even Mr. and Mrs. Gutnik waved their handkerchiefs and scarves and shouted *mazel tov*. Her sisters and her mutti cried and cried and wouldn't let her go, neighbors had to tear their fingers off her coat. Etta fainted in the mud, and her husband had to carry her home.

Then it was over, and her vati grabbed her arm and dragged her up onto the running board, and they set off for the long bumpy ride into Tallinn. In the distance she could see the black steeple of Saint Nicholas's church and the white smoke pouring from the new power plant. Her vati sat there beside her, stone-faced. Not a word.

She realized that Yaakov, love of her life, had not even looked at her, had eyes only for Etta. That is the way it should be, she thought.

That is the way it always was.

The ferry was waiting down by the dock, the same ship that Micha had sailed away in. There was a small knot of other families already there, saying their good-byes too. Sura stood there with her little bundles, the potato *latkes* her mother had made her for the journey, a feather mattress bundled up and tied with stout rope, a little brass samovar.

"We will say the *Tefilat Haderech*," her father said, and he got down on his knees there in the wet mud, and they said the wayfarer's prayer together, side by side.

She kissed his hands. "Good-bye, Vati," she said. "Be good to Mutti."

He had always looked larger than life to her, but suddenly he looked so small, standing there in his black brimmed hat and threadbare coat. She waited for some other word from him, and when there was none, she turned and made her way toward the gangway.

"Sura," he said.

She turned expectantly.

"Send money when you can."

"Yes, Vati," she said, and that was the last she ever saw of him.

6

The Grand Central Hotel

Uncle Max said there was a problem with a window up on the ninth floor, right at the top of the hotel. The service elevator was broken again, and they didn't let him use the one for the guests, so he had to walk all the way up there, the third time that day. What did he know from fixing windows? Still, he would have to learn if he wanted the job. Better get this done, or he would be late for night school again.

He kept his head down. How many times did his uncle Max tell him: *"You stay away from the guests. If you see them, you don't talk to them. If they talk to you, be polite, keep your eyes on the ground. Like they are a Cossack, or one of the czar's soldiers."*

He found the room, 908, got out his skeleton keys, but the door to the room was ajar, and he could hear a baby crying inside. It was *her* room, he realized. He knocked, and the door swung open wider.

Such a beautiful room it was: the carved oak chairs upholstered in stamped leather, beautiful carpets, the velvet hangings on the walls were the color of burnished gold. There was a marble mantel, even frescoes on the walls, like in a palace.

The door to the bedroom was wide open, and she was sitting on the end of the bed, all hunched over and smoking a cigarette. There were tears running down her cheeks onto her dress, but she wasn't paying them any mind, and not to the baby either, who was crying and kicking her little legs in the bassinet in the corner.

She looked up and saw him, and he took a hurried step back. She was tearstained and bright eyed, such a look on her face, it scared him.

"Mickey," she said.

He pointed to the window, pantomimed trying to open it. She nodded, as if she understood.

"Oh, the window. That's why you're here. I thought you must have heard the poor little Yankee trollop crying into her baby's crib."

He looked past her at the infant. Not right to let a baby cry like that, he thought. She followed his gaze and turned around. "The cause of all my problems," she said, and went over and scooped up the child. Straightaway the sobbing stopped. She patted the infant's bottom and held her to her cheek. "I know what you're thinking. But I do love her. I'm all she's got now." She gave a bitter laugh. "All she's got. I guess that's why she cries all the damned time."

Micha understood barely a word. Suddenly she crumpled, sat down hard in the middle of the floor, the baby in one hand and her cigarette still poised in the other like she was at a cocktail party. He didn't know what to do, just stood there. He couldn't run away, he couldn't touch her, he couldn't do anything. She was a woman, she was a guest.

The baby started up her crying again.

"You don't understand a thing, do you? Not a damned thing. Because if you did, I wouldn't be telling you."

She hurled the cigarette across the room, still lit. He scurried across the room to retrieve it before it burned a hole in the carpet.

"He's left me, Mickey. Just walked out and left. Because men can do that, see? That's part of the deal."

Micha stubbed out the cigarette in one of the onyx ashtrays. The tip was smeared with bright-red lipstick.

"I can't go back to Boston. Can't go back home neither. I'm a married woman, not Pa's responsibility anymore. And I can't stay here after the end of the month, because that's all we're paid up to, and I don't have any money. So here we are, me and baby, all dressed up and no place to go. Who's going to want me now, Mickey, a rich man's tart with a kid to support? We'll be out on skid row."

Micha backed out of the room. He wished he understood more of what she was trying to tell him, but she was using too many English words and her accent was different from his teacher's. He knew a tart was some kind of cake. But where was skid row?

She wiped her face with the back of her hand and sniffed. "My God, what am I doing? Sniveling on the floor in front of the help. George would be horrified. *'Clare dear, what on earth do you think you're doing?'* I think you'd better go, Mickey."

Micha shut the door. He hurried away down the corridor. He felt sorry for her, she was so young to be so unhappy. He hoped his uncle Max didn't find out what had happened. He mustn't lose his job, with his Sura arriving next week.

He must remember to ask his English teacher where skid row was and what a rich man's tart tasted like. Oh, and the window, he had forgotten about the window. He would come back tomorrow and try and fix it.

7

Sura woke from a black and bottomless sleep to shouts and screams. She thought the ship must be sinking. She threw herself out of her bunk, turned right around on the spot, trying to remember where she had put her clothes. Everyone was clambering over each other to get to the companionway.

Some of the people were laughing. Why were they laughing if the boat was sinking?

She put her sheepskin coat over her nightdress, let herself be carried by the press of people along the narrow aisle between the rows of bunks, then up the companionway to the third deck. It was still dark, and the bitter cold took her breath away. There was fog all around, and the water was oily and flat. Everyone was standing at the rail, pointing at something in the distance.

Then she saw it too, a speck of light in the distance. As they got closer, she could see it clearer: a woman with a spiky crown, her hand outstretched and holding a torch.

"What is it?" Sura said to the woman beside her.

"It is the Liberty statue," she said. "It is New York!"

"What is the Liberty statue?"

"It is gate to America," someone else said. "It says underneath that everyone is welcome."

"And welcome to have an opinion, also!"

"Even poor people."

"Even poor people?" Sura said.

"There's no poor people in America," a man in a black sheepskin hat said behind her. "Everyone is rich!"

"It is the place where dreams come true," a Polish woman said.

As they got closer to the harbor, it was like the whole sky was lit up for miles.

"America," people said; impossibly bright, impossibly big. It was cold and she did not have on enough clothes, but she stayed up on deck anyway, glad to be away from the fug of people and smells, not wanting to miss anything about Golden Medina.

Already people were streaming back up the companionways with their bundles and bags, eager to get there. There was music playing on the upper decks, the rich people dancing. Soon I will have music to play too, Sura thought. Soon I will dance and drink yellow sparkling wine.

Here I am, at last, in the place where dreams come true.

Micha had not meant to fall asleep. He had finished his work for the day and gone into the little cupboard in the basement, where he kept the mops and buckets and brooms, to change out of his uniform. When he was dressed, he sat down on a wooden stool and closed his eyes for a moment—so good to take the weight off his feet. He had never worked so hard in all his life like he worked in America.

He woke with a start, for a moment he couldn't remember where he was. What time was it, how long had he been in there? He jumped to his feet, fumbling for the door handle. His first thought was how late he was going to be for his English night class. Then he remembered he had promised Max he would fix the stuck window in 908 before he went home. He had better do it first, late or not. He picked up his little box of tools and stumbled up the stairs.

At least the service elevator was fixed. As he rode it to the top floor, he leaned against the grille and closed his eyes. These long hours were really knocking him out.

The elevator juddered to a stop. Micha pushed open the gates, then took a step back again as if someone had pushed him in the chest. He couldn't see anything out there; the whole corridor was full of smoke. He fumbled for a handkerchief in his pocket to cover his mouth and his nose.

The fire alarm was going off. He took a step into the hallway, saw shadows running about, carrying dogs, bundles of clothes, and suitcases. A woman was screaming. How could there be a fire? Uncle Max said that the owners had boasted to him that the building was fireproof.

He was buffeted by people running for the stairs: a businessman clutching a carpetbag, who went leaping down the stairs three steps at a time, like he was trying to fly; a man wearing a derby hat and striped pajamas, making a plaintive whining noise, his wife trying to follow, clutching the hands of two terrified children; a fat man in a dressing gown, a lit cigar clutched between his teeth.

Where was the fire, where was all this smoke coming from?

Micha was about to follow everyone down the stairs, he didn't dare use the service elevator again. But then he thought: No, the right thing is to make sure everyone is safe. So he ran down the now-empty hallway, banging on all the doors. "Fire! Fire! Wake up, wake up. Get out." There was the clang of fire trucks in the distance.

He reached 908, banged on the door, couldn't believe when he heard the baby crying, still inside. How could she still be in there? He tried the door handle. Locked. He fumbled in his pocket for his skeleton keys, remembered they were still downstairs in his overalls. He banged with the flat of his hand, then his fist. "Fire!" An English word he knew, not so different from the Yiddish.

He heaved his shoulder against the door, no good, so he kicked with his boots until the lock splintered. The smoke was getting thicker now; he really couldn't see a thing. Hurry, Micha, get them out and get out yourself.

He pushed his shoulder against the door and it flew open.

It was easier to breathe inside the room; there was not as much smoke as in the corridor. He called out for the lady, couldn't see her, only the little baby screaming in the bassinet.

The smoke was getting thicker, pouring in along the ceiling, flowing like water. He heard timbers in the wall cracking, splitting from the heat. A part of the ceiling came down in the passage right outside the door; flames were licking toward him along the walls. It was like a live thing, this fire. How could it move so fast?

He yelled out again. Where was the woman, where was she?

He scooped up the baby, ran out into the corridor. There was a fire escape right outside, through the window. He heaved on the latch, forced it open enough so he could squeeze himself through and onto the landing. He looked down, eight floors of shaking iron between him and the ground. The baby was screaming now, eyes squeezed shut, her legs and arms held out rigid from her body. "Shush, *beibi*," he said, for all the good it would do.

He hesitated, one leg over the sill, the rest of him still in the corridor. Should I go back and try once more to look for the lady? A blast of heat hit him in the face. He panicked. She isn't here, Micha, get yourself out of here before it's too late.

Another part of the roof came down, and he yelped and started down the fire escape, leaping from one step to the other, one hand on the railing, the other clutching the baby to his chest.

He was halfway down when he heard someone screaming somewhere above him, up there on the top floor. Straightaway he knew it was her. He looked up, but it was too dark to see anything, and there was so much smoke.

How could she still be up there? Micha looked down into the alley. There was no one down there to help, smoke was even pluming out of the windows underneath him. If he went back up, they could all die— him, her, the little baby. But he had to do something.

He started back up the fire escape, his boots clanging on the iron. Up to the seventh floor, breathless, shouting for someone to come and help all the way. He saw her, for just a moment, fighting with her bedroom window, but it was jammed shut, the same window he was supposed to fix.

"The fire escape," he shouted up at her, but she couldn't hear him, and what difference could it make now even if she could? There was black smoke pouring out of the window he had come out of, flames as well, roaring like a train going past, scorching the bricks black. The fire escape gave a lurch under him as a wall collapsed inside. Any moment, the whole building would come down.

He turned around and clattered down the fire escape as fast as he could.

Hoses snaked across the street. Micha splashed through the pooled water, stared in numb astonishment at the fire trucks skewed across the street, the policemen holding back the crowds that had gathered along Park and Fortieth. There were people milling all around him, sobbing and crying.

He looked up. Pillars of thick smoke poured into the night sky; there were flames roaring out of all the windows above the fourth floor, even as he watched another section of wall crash down into the street. A policeman grabbed him and pushed him away. "Get the hell out of here! What do you think you're doing? Can't you see the damned place is about to come down?"

Micha started to run. Once he had started running, he couldn't stop. He stumbled along block after block, people streaming past him the other way, toward the fire, eager not to miss the spectacle, but Micha ignored them, hugging the baby tighter to his chest. He ran and ran and didn't stop until he reached Delancey Street.

⟢

"And what have you got there?" Tessie Fischer said when she saw him.

"Do you have milk, please?"

He saw over her shoulder a gaggle of children. How many was it, four, five? He could never remember, and all in one room not much larger than his. She sniffed, could probably smell the smoke on his clothes. "What have you been doing, Mr. Levine?"

"I seen trouble tonight like I couldn't tell you."

She peered in at the bundle he had in his arms. The little girl mewled and wriggled. "And what is it you're doing with that little thing?"

"I found her."

"Found her?"

"In the street."

Tessie frowned, had heard of such things, of course; plenty of working girls in the ghetto threw their babies out with the dirty water.

"My wife arrives from Russia tomorrow. We can look after her." She stared at him as if he had gone mad. Perhaps I am mad, Micha thought. Saying it out loud, I sound like a crazy person. "She always wanted a baby," he said, as if that made every kind of sense.

Tessie's husband was shouting at her from inside, "Who's that you're talking to, come back in here, woman." So the man next door has found a baby, he could see Tessie thinking; with so many children in the world, why make it my business? "Wait here," she said.

She went back inside, came back a moment later with a little bottle of milk. "Don't let Moishe know I gave away some of our milk," she said.

"What do I do?"

"Remember to warm it. Not too hot now. And I hope your wife's not as *meshugga* as you are," she said, and shut the door.

<hr/>

He had nowhere to put the little girl to sleep but next to him on the mattress on the floor; he had nothing to change her with but some old towels and a sheet that he tore into strips. What did he know from babies?

He started shaking all over, shaking so much he couldn't help it. He had to wait until the shaking stopped before he could give her the milk, then he walked grooves in the floorboards trying to get her to sleep.

It was hours before she stopped her fretting, but even when she was finally quiet, he couldn't sleep. He lay beside her in the dark, listening to the sound of her breathing, but he could still smell the stink of the smoke on his clothes, and when he closed his eyes, he saw the woman's hand pressed against the window, banging on the glass, the last thing she ever did before she died.

How was she still in the room? He should have looked better, maybe she was in the other room asleep on the bed, maybe drunk, or perhaps she was in the bath and didn't hear the alarm. He supposed he would never know, no one would.

I could have saved this little mite's mother for her, he thought. If I had been a little braver, not just stood there in the room for so long, like a *schmuck*.

Or if I'd fixed that window, maybe she could have got out and climbed down the fire escape. He burrowed the heels of his hands into his eyes, tried to stop himself seeing it all again, tried to stop himself remembering. If only he could have those few moments back, do it all over again, but this time do it better.

8

Ellis Island, New York

The ground felt as if it were still swaying beneath her feet, and her head was dizzy with fresh air again, the clean salty air. Now everything smelled so good because the boat had smelled so bad. She had been poked and prodded by men in uniforms and white coats ever since they landed, and there were people everywhere shouting in languages she did not understand. But at last she was ready, she had her samovar and rolled-up feather bed, and her precious landing card was pinned to her coat.

She hesitated at the top of the stairs, stared out the window at the bigness of Mrs. Liberty, so green she was. Left stairs for New York, everyone said. Right stairs for everywhere else. And middle stairs? Oh, you don't want to go down the middle stairs, girl.

He'll be waiting for you at the "kissing post," someone told her. And they were right; he was, down there in the Great Hall. Like a different man he looked, only just after Hanukkah when she saw him last, on the dock at Tallinn, but now it was like hugging a complete stranger. He looked thinner, his nice suit was crumpled, his black hat battered and ragged at the rim.

This is your new life now, Sura Levine, she thought. Better make the best of it you can.

Battery Park

What is the difference between being terrified and being so excited and amazed a girl cannot think or speak, just stares openmouthed like a simpleton or I don't know what? Not so much difference, Sura thought, holding tight to Micha's arm as he pushed his way through the crowds outside the pier.

She had never seen so many people, so many horses, so many carriages. And motor cars, so many it made her head spin, all polished and black-painted. But they were nothing compared to the train that ran through the air, the one that Micha had written her about in the letter. So it was really true. He called it the Third Avenue Elevated.

They even rode on it. It rattled along, high above the people, the wheels shrieking and grinding, the carriage shaking and twisting so she was sure it would crash down into the street. And such streets! Micha had not lied to her. Everywhere there were buildings taller than the castle tower in Tallinn, so that even though it was afternoon, she could not see the sun in the sky.

"You like it?" Micha asked her.

She couldn't answer him. How to like or not like? She could be astonished, only. It was like nothing she had ever imagined. She wanted to shut her ears and her eyes so she could get her breath. But she couldn't, because everywhere there was something new to stare at: people with black skin like coal; long carriages full of people drawn by horses; the sun glinting in the windows of buildings, so many windows it hurt the eyes.

They got off the railway at Delancey Street. There were so many people, like she never saw in one place before in her life. It was all pushcarts and noise and hustle-bustle. She was shoved every which way, held tight to Micha's arm or she would have been swept away, like in a flooded river. There were a thousand smells in the air, a million. And all the different languages all around her: Russian, German, English, even the Yiddish they spoke a hundred different ways, so many accents and ways of speaking.

"Here is home," he said to her.

They walked up so many steps that by the time they got to where they were going, she was out of breath. Their apartment was on the fifth floor, Micha told her. She had never been in a building so high.

And such an apartment it was. After Micha's letter, after everything she had heard about Golden Medina, she had expected at least a palace. But when she walked in, it was just a dank little room with a tub for washing and two little windows with a view of iron stairs.

And no furniture, only a mattress on the floor for sleeping and some old wooden crates for sitting. Walls so thin she could hear everyone in the whole building, all shouting like nobody's business. And the noise from the street, like an army of Cossacks having a battle down there.

For this, she had sailed halfway around the world in a rusty, stinking old ship. She wanted to sit down and cry.

"I have something for you," Micha said.

He looked so excited. Be a good wife, Sura, she told herself, like you promised yourself. Smile at him, look to your husband like you're happy.

He went out, crossed to the door on the other side of the landing, and gave it a knock. A woman came out and handed him something, a bundle wrapped in a blanket. She was not much older than Sura, but she looked wrung out, like an old rag that had been washed too many times.

Micha came back with the bundle, nudged the door shut behind him. He had such a look, like it was a million dollars he was holding. She had never seen his face shine like this.

"Don't you want to see what I got for you?" he said.

She went over, moved aside the folds of the blanket.

"She's asleep," he said.

Sura was too astonished to say anything.

"This is what you wanted, isn't it?" he said.

"It's a baby."

"I wanted to make you happy, Sura. All I ever wanted was to make you happy."

9

Back Bay, Boston, Massachusetts

George Seabrook was interrupted in the middle of his morning's correspondence by his butler, Frankston. There was a gentleman at the door to see him, Frankston said. By the name of Turner.

"Show him in," George said, and put down his pen. He blotted the letter he was writing and laid it aside.

Alfred Turner did not look like a private detective; an accountant perhaps, with his wing collar and pince-nez. He stood on the other side of George's desk, fingering the kettle curl of his gray homburg.

George invited him to sit.

"What do you have for me, Turner?"

Turner unfastened the buckles of the battered leather satchel on his lap and took out a sheaf of notes, written in a bold copperplate hand with blue ink, and laid them on George's desk. George picked them up and leaned back in his chair to peruse them. The leather creaked under him.

He read them through quickly. "New York?" he said.

"As you see from my notes, she and her . . . companion . . . were briefly in Concord. They checked in to the Grand Central Hotel on the eleventh of this month. Their reservation is until the thirtieth."

"The child?"

"She has the infant with her. It appears to be in good health."

George laid the report back on his desk, covering it with the flat of his hand as if he was shielding it from prying eyes. "And her companion?"

"He has recently left the hotel, boarded a first-class compartment on a train bound for Philadelphia. He had another lady with him. They seemed . . . comfortable with one another." There was a long silence, punctuated only by the loud ticking of the German carved oak clock on the mantel.

"Can I be of further service to you, sir?"

George had almost forgotten he was still there. "No, Turner," he said. "Thank you. You have done very well. You have my gratitude, for your sterling work, and your discretion."

"Thank you, sir." He buckled the briefcase, bowed, and took his leave.

George Seabrook stared at the handwritten pages fanned out on the blotter in front of him. Finally, he crumpled them in his fist and hurled them across the room. Damn you, Clare. Damn you to a hundred kinds of hell.

"So you found her? Found her in the street?"

"Yes, a foundling," Micha said. "In a doorway, down an alley. I heard crying. What can I do? I cannot leave her there. What hard heart would do that? Tessie told me it happens a lot. There are loose women here, jezebels, harlots. A child is an inconvenience to them."

The baby stared up at her. Oh, look at those beautiful green eyes, Sura thought. Even if we keep her, with such eyes, how could anyone ever think she belonged to us? "The poor little darling," she said. "What must she be thinking?"

"I guess she is thinking: At last there is someone who will take care of me."

"We have to get her milk, and cloths for diapers. What have you been doing to her? Do you know nothing, Husband?"

"Tessie gave me milk and a bottle. She has had lots of babies."

"So the poor little thing has been passed around like old fish." She held her, sniffed at her. Oh, the new-baby smell of her hair. She remembered that smell from the night she brought Bessie into the world. "No one is going to pass you around anymore, bubeleh. What place this is, America, a woman leaving babies in the street like potato peelings."

What a place, yes. Nothing in America was as she thought it would be; never such big buildings, never so smelly, never so many people, never such poor, never such rich. And all living together.

And this place her husband lived. Nothing like his mother's big house in Tallinn with so much bedrooms and the shop downstairs and the nice furniture, all comfortable and nice smelling.

But then, like a miracle, here was Micha with something better than gelt, better than a big house: a baby that was hers, just for herself. It was everything she had prayed for to the God she thought had been punishing her for thinking so much like a bad wife.

"Do you really think we should keep her?" she said.

"Look around you, bubeleh. Children are everywhere. No one wants her. If we take her to the police, she'll be in the end an orphan. You want that for her when she can have a good home with us?"

"She's so beautiful. Are you sure she was left? There is no mother out there in the street looking for where it is she left her baby?"

"You don't leave a baby like you leave your dog tied up to a post. What mother does such a thing?"

Sura stared at the tiny little thing in her arms. "We should wash her. Did you give her her bath?"

"Maybe Tessie gives her, I don't know."

"Tessie is not her mother," Sura said. She took a deep breath and said the words she had always wanted to say. "I am."

———◆———

Micha heated water in a kettle over the hearth and filled up the wooden tub on the rickety stool in the middle of the room; only one wooden tub he had for his dishes and his clothes.

Sura bathed the child in it, stared at the fine down of reddish-blonde hair at the nape of her neck, the fuzz of curls on her head. She's a *shiksa* baby, all right, no doubt about it. But I don't care.

I'll love her to the end of my days like she's my own. Elohim, hear me, that's my promise to you. Perhaps not part of your grand design, but now you have relented and given me this miracle, don't you dare try and take it away again, not now.

"We will have such a good life together," she whispered into the little girl's tiny pink ear. "You are going to be so happy. I will make sure. I am going to love you like you are my very own. You wait and see."

She dried her with a ragged towel—all Micha had—and pinned a new cloth for a nappy, felt growing in her a purpose, where for so long there had been only a kind of numb despair. She felt Micha's eyes on her, watching. She smiled at him for doing this for her even though there was a part of her that wondered if perhaps this was too good to be really true.

But she mustn't think about that. If no one really wants this baby, why not us?

"Look at you," Micha said. "Your face is shining, just shining. You were born to be a mother."

"It's everything I ever wanted. This makes everything . . ."

"Complete."

"Complete, yes."

"What will we call her?" he said. "Why not we call her Rachel, after my mother?" When she didn't answer him, he said, "What do you want to call her?"

"What about Liberty?"

"Liberty? What kind of name is that?"

"It is a not-Jewish name is what it is," Sura said. "Look at her! Everyone can see she is a shiksa, she should have a name that is not Jewish, and not *goyim* either."

"Liberty?"

"After the Mrs. Liberty statue in the harbor. The goddess of the poor people. She can be Liberty Levine."

"Liberty Levine," Micha said, and nodded. "All right. What do I know from names anyway? So long as you are happy."

"Liberty," Sura said. How many times had she held little mites like this? Bessie, still slick from her birthing, Zlota's two little boys. But now she had a baby of her own to look after and to love, like she had always wanted. She had lost her family and her shtetl, but now she had a new purpose.

She warmed some milk on the little stove and made sure it was not too hot, then fed it to her from the glass bottle that the woman Tessie across the hall had given them. As she suckled, the little girl's eyes never left her face. Sura thought about little Bessie lying beside her in the bed that night their sled turned over on the way back from Tallinn. This time I do not have to give you back, she thought.

Afterward she lay down on the mattress with her, started gently nibbling on her nails as her sister Zlota had taught her, to soften them and keep them short so she didn't scratch herself with them. She stroked the baby's face with her fingers, fought down the panic stirring in her, something inside her warning her to hold back.

She's not yours, she thought. How can you be so sure the Americans will not come and take her away? What will happen when she grows up and everyone sees she is a shiksa? What will you do then?

No, she is mine now, my Micha told me so. A tear dropped onto the baby's cheek, and she wiped it away with her thumb. "Now look what you did," she told her. "The first time you make me cry."

She started to sing her a lullaby, the same lullaby she heard Gutta sing to her own little ones.

> *Shlof mayn kind, mayn kroyn, mayn sheyner,*
> *Shlofzhe, bubeleh.*
> *Shlof, mayn lebn, mayn Kaddish eyner,*
>
> *Bay dayn vigl zitst dayn mame,*
> *Zingt a lid un veynt.*
> *Vest a mol farshteyn mistome,*
> *Vos zi hot gemeynt.*
> *Vest a mol farshteyn mistome,*
> *Vos zi hot gemeynt.*
>
> *Sleep, my child, my crown, my beauty,*
> *Sleep, my darling.*
> *Sleep, my life, my only Kaddish,*
>
> *By your cradle sits your mother,*
> *She sings a song and weeps.*
> *You'll understand some day perhaps,*
> *What is on her mind.*
> *You'll understand some day perhaps,*
> *What is on her mind.*

"Look, she's sleeping," Micha said. "It's like she knows your voice already."

"The nonsense you talk," Sura said, but she was secretly pleased.

Micha lay down on the mattress beside her. "Did you miss me?" he said.

"What a question."

"I missed you," he said.

"You're my husband. What kind of husband does not miss his wife?"

"I am sorry for this apartment. It's not like the house we have in Tallinn."

"At least it doesn't have your mother in it."

He laughed. "How is my mother?"

"I don't see her since you left. She doesn't even talk to me in the street. She blames me for you leaving. She says you only come to America for me."

"Perhaps it's true. You are the most beautiful girl in the whole world. I would do anything for you."

The light went out. Micha told her he didn't have a nickel for the machine. It was a gas meter, he said, like a machine that told a person how much light they could have, but you had to keep feeding it little coins to get more. Micha said he had no more coal for the stove, so the only thing to do was sleep.

Even in the shtetl we lived better, she thought. At least we had the wood stove to sleep on when it was cold, and candles for light, even in winter.

"So, I suppose you're going to tell me now that the streets in America are not paved with gold," she said.

"You can see for yourself, some of them are not paved at all. I think it's why they want us here, so we can pave them for them."

"What do you know from paving streets? You have a leather shop like your vati did."

"I don't have money to buy a shop. That's why I asked my uncle Max to get me a job."

"But you got a job, that's good. When we save enough money, then we will buy you a shop. You are already the manager of a big hotel."

"Not anymore."

"What are you saying, not anymore?"

"The hotel is gone. There was a fire."

"So you don't have a job? But what will we do?"

"Uncle Max will look after me."

"Who is this Uncle Max? What can he do?"

"Well, he's not really my uncle. He's my landsman, an old friend of my father's. He's been in America a long time. He worked at the hotel too. He was what they call here a concierge. So now he doesn't have a job either. But my uncle Max, he knows everybody, he will soon get another job, and he will get me one as well."

Sura cuddled up on the mattress with the baby, trying to keep warm. Her first night in this America, with all the new smells and the new sounds. So noisy here at night in America, not like in the shtetl.

Micha tried to touch her under the blankets, but she wriggled away. "You'll wake the baby," she told him.

"But Sura, it's been so long."

"I'm so tired, Micha." It was true, or partly true anyway, she was exhausted. But even as tired as she was, she could not get to sleep. Whenever she closed her eyes, she would wake herself up again to make sure little Liberty was still there, still breathing.

It was hours until she finally fell asleep, a black sleep with bright and mad dreams. She woke the next morning to the rumbling of milk wagons, the clatter of bottles and cans, the cries of peddlers setting up down in the street, the screaming of other babies in the building, and little Liberty gurgling and kicking beside her. "Such a beautiful sound it is," she said, and turned and laughed over her shoulder at Micha, and he laughed back, and for the first time she thought: I could really grow to love him.

Little Liberty and Micha and me, we will make a real family right here, right here in this America.

10

Boston

George Seabrook ate his breakfast alone in the salon, as he did every morning; bacon, toast, eggs, maple syrup, and coffee that Frankston brought in on a tray along with a neatly folded copy of that morning's edition of the *Boston Globe*.

He took a sip of coffee and opened his newspaper, flicking the pages to unfold the creases. He stared at the front page and murmured a blasphemy under his breath, something he would never usually do, even when alone. The coffee spilled and burned his hand. He gasped and leaped to his feet, dropping the cup on the floor, where it shattered.

He stared at the headline.

TWENTY DIE IN HOTEL FIRE

Dozens trapped in ten-story building perish or hurl themselves to death

Underneath were pictures of crumpled bodies lying on the sidewalk, beside a photograph of a blackened and gutted building.

"Grand Central Hotel," he murmured, reading the paragraph below the photograph.

The door opened, and Frankston ran in to the room. "Is everything all right, sir? I heard a crash."

"Get my car ready," George said. "I have to go to New York."

11

The Gouverneur Hospital, Lower East Side

George Seabrook removed his derby and followed the nurse along the ward, the grim green-and-off-white-painted walls matched his mood. His nose wrinkled at the strong smell of antiseptic.

Max Beerschaum lay propped up in the iron-framed bed, his bandaged hands and arms resting on pillows. Only the tips of his fingers were visible. He appeared to be asleep.

"This is Mr. Beerschaum," she said. "Shall I bring you a chair?"

George nodded, and she hurried off to find one. Max opened one eye. He took in the three-piece sack suit, the burgundy silk tie, the club collar, and walking cane, and blinked in surprise.

"Do I know you, sir?" he said.

"I don't think so," George said.

The nurse returned with a chair. George sat down, crossing his legs but taking care with the pleats of his trousers. He leaned the cane against the wall and placed the derby on his lap.

"You don't look like a reporter," Max said. "There have been reporters in here asking me about the fire."

"I'm not a reporter. My name is George Seabrook, one of the Boston Seabrooks." Max blinked at him. That meant nothing to him, clearly. "The reason I'm here is that I believe my wife and daughter may have died in the fire at the Grand Central Hotel."

"Oh. Oh, my condolences, sir. I don't know what to say."

George nodded and continued to stare at Max, who waited, embarrassed and a little intimidated by the other man's unblinking gaze.

Finally: "I believe you were the concierge at the hotel."

"Yes, yes I was. As you can see, I was lucky to get out with my life."

George looked at the bandages, then back at Max. "What happened?"

"One of the bellboys. A metal stanchion fell across his legs. Me and the desk clerk helped lift it off him."

"You were burned."

"The pain, I can't tell you. White hot, it was."

"That was a very brave thing to do."

"He was just a boy, he was screaming. Some of the things that happened that night—" Max stopped. "But this, you don't want to hear."

"I wondered if you could help me."

"Me, how can I help a man like yourself?"

"I wonder if you remember my wife. You see, the police have recovered what they believe is her body. But, as you can imagine, because of the fire . . ."

Max nodded vigorously. He had seen some of the bodies for himself, laid out on the sidewalk among the tangle of firemen's hoses, not something he ever wanted to see again, not if he lived to be a hundred.

"They still haven't found my . . . my daughter."

Max fidgeted in the bed. What was he supposed to say to the poor man?

"Do you remember my wife, Mr. Beerschaum? I rather imagine you would. There can't have been many women staying at the hotel with a babe in arms."

"Yes, I remember her. They . . . she arrived maybe two weeks before the fire. She had a suite on the top floor of the hotel."

"There is no need for delicacy, Mr. Beerschaum. I know she wasn't alone."

Max swallowed hard.

George leaned closer to the bed. "I can rely on your discretion?"

"Discretion is my middle name. Nine years I was concierge at the Grand Central. You can ask anyone. Max Beerschaum is the prince of confidential."

"Good. You see, as I said, I am aware that she was not unaccompanied, at least, when she arrived at the hotel."

Max lowered his voice to a whisper. "The desk clerk, he tells me that this fellow pays for the room three weeks in advance. Top floor, a suite, they don't give it for nothing, you know? It's a lot."

"I understand."

"Well, a week later he sees the man jump into a cab in the street, with his suitcase, and that's it, he never comes back. The lady, she doesn't come down from her room for days. My nephew, he says she just sits in her room and cries."

"Your nephew?"

"Well, he's not so much my nephew. He's the boy of a schoolboy friend of mine, from back in the old country."

"Your nephew spoke to her?"

"He never meant no harm, sir. He's got a soft heart, that boy, that's his trouble. I told him once, I told him a thousand times, not to speak to the guests."

"He talked to my wife before the fire?"

"That's what he said."

"And she was crying?"

"I don't want to get him in any trouble."

"He's not in any trouble, Max. You don't mind if I call you Max? All I want is to find out what happened to Clare. My wife. Do you think I could speak to your nephew? What's his name?"

"Micha. But like I said, he won't know anything. He was just the janitor."

"Micha," George said.

"Mr. George, I am sorry for your loss. But I don't understand how this is going to help."

"Perhaps it will help me understand her frame of mind. It is one thing to bury a body, it is another to bury the past. I would like to know if perhaps she regretted what she did. Do you understand my meaning?"

Max nodded.

"And there is the matter of . . . my daughter. I still cannot be sure what happened to her. Perhaps the gentleman who accompanied my wife to the hotel returned to collect the child before the fire. Perhaps that might explain why they did not find the body."

"Well, Mr. George, a fire like that, and her just a little *maideleh* . . ."

"I have to be sure she is gone."

"Perhaps you should talk to Joe on the desk, he—"

"I have already spoken to every other member of the hotel staff who was on duty that night. You are my last hope."

He recrossed his legs and waited.

Max nodded. "Micha, Michael he calls himself in America, he's working down at the docks now. When I get out of here, I'll find him something better. It's just for now."

"You can arrange for us to meet? I'd like to talk to him."

"He doesn't speak English so good. But the doctors say they are letting me out of here tomorrow. Maybe I can take you to see him. Translate."

"Thank you, Max." George reached into his pocket and took out his wallet. He put two banknotes in the bedside drawer. "I very much appreciate your help and discretion in this matter."

He picked up his cane and left.

Sura made her way through the *toomel*, the chaos, on Delancey Street, holding Liberty tight in a sling around her neck, keeping her warm under the shawl. A summer like a Russian winter, a dirty drizzle coming down, everything gray and dripping.

She had never seen anything like this New York, all the jostlers and scavengers and sleeve tuggers and barterers. There were pushcarts all up and down the streets, hundreds of them, thousands, as far as a person could see, everything splashed and muddy. Here you could buy anything you could ever want, from collars to shoestrings, if you had a few cents in your pocket to buy them after you paid the rent. What is it you want? A tablecloth, a tin fork, a curtain, a pair of eyeglasses? There was someone to sell it to you. You needed half a parsnip for the nighttime stew, or a lady's intimate garment, it's all laid out right there for everyone to see.

And the stink of it all. So many flapping, glistening fish, the sea must be empty, and all the live chickens and rabbits panicking in tiny cages.

Little urchin girls pushed among the street vendors, selling matches, toothpicks, cigars, and flowers, others scavenging for wood in the alleys and in the gutters. Not for one day, my little Liberty, Sura thought. This won't be her life.

"Look at all this, bubeleh," she whispered to her. "Ever you see anything like? You see those yellow things there? Here they call such things banana. First time your papa give me, I think I am going to be ill. Hope you never taste such a disgusting thing. And look you how the people here are chewing, always chewing. No, you mustn't stare, bubeleh, they get angry here in America if you stare. Like cows they are over here. Gum, they call it. And you see that one? First, I think there is something wrong with his skin, but they are born that way. All different colors of brown they have here. *Schvartzes*, they call them here. But only the white ones chew, the ones with brown skins, they don't chew so much. No, don't stare bubeleh, didn't I just tell you?"

Such a street it was. The houses, they would have been fine houses once, pretty houses. They had fancy tin moldings, beautiful wrought-iron fire escapes. She couldn't believe how pretty it must have been once. But now there were too many people and too much poorness.

Along Hester Street she went, under the Third Avenue Elevated Railway—the El, Micha called it. Another wonder, she thought, but when she looked up, she got an eyeful of soot. The steel girders were all black with dirt. And that was America, she thought, from a distance it was a wonder, with pretty buildings and railways in the air; but up close you saw the rats and the children in their bare feet and rags, and the railway made you choke. And everybody was all bent over with their poorness, their hands veiny and blue, their collars pulled up round their grimy faces.

"We're not going to be like that," she whispered to Liberty. "This is not going to be your life, bubeleh. Your daddy and I, we are going to make you like a queen. I promise."

She stopped outside the kosher butcher down on the corner. She stared, imagining the good taste, the feeling of fullness inside. A long time since she had felt that way. "Tomorrow is *Shabbas*, we got to have a nice meal. You know what is Shabbas? It is the special holy day God gives us so that we can rest. We light all the candles in the house, and we get nice things to eat. Oh, I know we don't have much, but we got each other. We got each other, and no one is ever going to take you away."

She hoisted Liberty up to her shoulder, loved how she fitted into the notch of her neck and her chin, the ticklish warmth of her breath on her skin. She felt the child's arms tighten reflexively around her neck. She looked down at the little girl's eyes. She could look forever into them. Such adoring, such trusting.

She had heard her sisters talking about the love they had for their husbands. Etta said it was like a real thing to her, an ache inside her, in her belly, not in her heart like the songs said. And now Sura felt it too, watching the child, looking into her eyes she felt this same twisting inside.

For a moment, it was like the hawkers all up and down the street had gone quiet, the press of people and pushcarts and dirt and noise disappeared; there was just her and her little baby, and nothing else existed in the whole world.

What was she to make of this, this newfound happiness, happiness like she had never known? It was a miracle.

Her little Liberty, she was a gift from heaven; in this big press of strangeness and people and loudness, she was hers, a nest of happiness and belonging snuggled against her, and the smell of her was sweeter than anything else in this whole big America.

⇒≫

There was rust bleeding all down the sides of the freighter. A mist of rain drifted across the wharf. The foreman had formed them into a long chain, teams of two men snaking from the dock to the warehouse to heft the burlap sacks of brown sugar up from the hold. A week now, and Micha dreaded every load. Every sinew in his back was raw and screaming. Cannot keep doing this, he thought. But if I don't, what will little Liberty and my Sura have to eat for Shabbas?

Still another hour before the final whistle, someone said. Most of the others were bigger men than him, Irish and schvartzes; they laughed and called him a skinny Jew at first, and other things he didn't understand, but now they gave him a sort of grudging respect for the way he kept at it. Most of what they said he didn't understand, even though he studied English hard at night school. The foreman said to him, don't you understand plain English, but it wasn't plain English, not the way they said it.

But here they went with the sacks now: one, slide the hook in; two, lift; three, swing it around; four, toss it to the next man. Up they went, in a rhythm, no time to rest again until the last sack, or the big schvartze he worked with would swear and kick at him for being too slow.

He had to break Shabbas to keep the job. But what was more important, his Sura and his baby having something to eat or what the Reb would say about him? Uncle Max had told him he would find him something better as soon as he was out of the hospital. He had to hold on until then.

What a place he had come to, his hands raw with cuts and blisters, chapped red and numb. But not always will it be like this, he told himself. Already he was learning some English, and Uncle Max promised him one day he was going to be a somebody, a mensch, like the ones he saw driving a motor car.

At last the whistle sounded, and the other men headed for the bars on Tenth. Lately they had taken to asking him along too, but he always said no and caught a horse car across town to the new Grand Central station and then took the El home. But today, instead of going straight to the Elevated, he walked a block to where the old hotel used to be. It was a blackened shell now, boarded up to stop the hobos getting in. He could still smell the burned wood, even after all these weeks.

The fire escape was still there, swaying in the wind, the back wall all that was still standing. If he closed his eyes, he could see it all happening again, feel the iron stairs buckling underneath him, hear her screaming. Whenever he played it over in his head, as he did every night when he got into bed and closed his eyes, he remembered looking up, seeing her hands beating at the window. Had she been in the bedroom all along? Perhaps she had been in there all along, asleep, or perhaps even drunk? Why hadn't he gone in to look for her?

He put his collar up against the rain and walked, head down, toward the station. He put his aching bones on the Third Avenue Elevated and stared out the window as it rattled back down this brown brick of America. She's dead now, and you have her baby. What sort of a man are you?

He walked a little faster down Delancey because he knew Sura and Liberty would be waiting for him at home.

Home: the top floor of a tenement with line upon line of laundry flapping between the fire escapes. Not so much washing today, though, just a few weary rags hanging sodden in the wind. He and Sura lived right at the top for the cheaper rent. Micha stopped at the foot of the dank stairs to gather his strength for the long climb up. Such creaking and shouting coming from up there; the Irish and the Italians didn't know about quietness. Everything was shout, shout, shout.

He took a breath and started up, pausing to catch his breath again at every landing until he got to the top floor.

He threw open the door. For all his tiredness, how could he forget to smile when he saw them, Sura there sitting on a wooden crate, feeding their baby her bottle. Such a wonder it was to see them.

And what she had done to the apartment since she had come from Russia. She had scrubbed it top to bottom, washed the grime from all the windows, pasted down the wallpaper where it hung down, put up pictures from the newspapers over the holes in the plaster.

She had even persuaded Tessie Fischer next door to give her an old spring mattress, had put it over four empty herring pails she got from the street, so now they had a proper bed. Then she found a potato barrel, put some clean newspaper over it, and they had a table. What a lucky man he was to have a wife like this. He had worried that she would be gloomy when she came to America and found this same dirt and poorness and hard work, just like in Russia; but no, he had never seen her so happy. It was because of Liberty, of course. Whenever Sura looked at the baby's face, her eyes shone with happiness.

"Bubeleh," she said when she saw him. "How was your day?"

"Today I shoveled ten sacks of gold off the street."

"Only ten?"

"I could have got more, but I wanted to leave some for your brother-in-law Benno when he comes."

"Sit down, I made some latkes for supper, and my *gefilte* fish you like so much."

As he ate, she talked about the price of the baby clothes in the stalls; everything was so much gelt in this America, so she had bought herself needle and thread and some cotton and wool to make their clothes herself, like she did at home, while their little bubeleh was sleeping. If she had a fancy sewing machine, she said, she could make clothes for everyone in the street.

"A sewing machine is expensive," he said.

"It can pay for itself."

"Now it's nonsense you are talking. Nothing pays for itself! We will wait and see. Perhaps when Uncle Max finds me a new job, we will have enough money then."

"Until then I will use needle and thread, like at home. It is what our Zlota does while her Ari is at his studies at the *yeshiva*. You know, here in America, lots of other families work in their apartments sewing clothes. That Tessie Fischer sews shirtwaists, and you should see, she is nothing at it. You cut all my fingers off, I could sew better."

"Is it that you don't think I can give you what you want?"

"You gave me Liberty," she said. "You gave me everything I want." She put a hand on his. "I don't mind you are not millionaire," she said. "We are the richest people in all America!"

He smiled at her, felt something he had not felt in a long time, something he had never felt since he had come here to this America.

He felt proud.

Afterward he heated water on the little coal-burning stove, and Sura gave Liberty her bath. As she dried her off, he read the newspaper,

though he always had one eye on his wife and his daughter—his little daughter—because it made him feel like the king of the world.

"Why you always got your head stuck in the newspaper?" Sura said.

"I'm learning me the English. It is important I learn fast so that Uncle Max can get me a good job."

"So, what did you learn last night?"

"Well, it's not just the words you learn, you must also learn how to say them, because they say everything backward in America. Like if you want to say *what*, then the teacher tells me first to say 'ooh what,' or otherwise it comes out 'vhat.'" He pointed to his lips to show her the difference. "If you say 'vhat,' they make fun. If you remember to say 'ooh what,' like this, they still make a little fun, but not so much."

"So everything they spell with a *w*, you have to say 'ooh' first."

"It is hard, some words sound so much the same. Like the number three. In my class, we all say 'tree,' but in English, 'tree' is like what you get apples from." He showed her with his tongue. "You have to say like this: 'th-ree.' And spelling. Don't start me on the spelling."

"You talk English good. You learn everything so fast, Micha."

"When I talk English perfect, then I will be happy."

Sura finished drying Liberty off with a raggedy towel she had bought that day off one of the pushcarts on Delancey. Micha went back to his newspaper to practice his reading. There was a grainy photograph of a rich man wearing very nice clothes. He read the words *fire* and *Grand Central Hotel* and sat up a little straighter.

He felt the blood drain from his face.

He laid the newspaper aside and stood up. "I must go to night school." He looked around, turned a complete circle in the middle of the room. "Where is my coat? I can't find my coat."

"It's right there, in front of you."

"Ah, who put it there?"

"You did, bubeleh. Are you all right?"

"I'm all right."

"Nothing will go wrong, will it?" Sura said.

"What's that you're saying, bubeleh?"

"Nothing can go wrong, can it? Not now. Promise me."

He forced a smile. "I promise."

"You will have a big shop, like in Russia, and we will have a motor car and a nice house for Liberty to grow up."

"Yes, yes. Everything is going to be all right."

She beamed. "Good," she said.

He kissed his wife on the head and went to the door. Sura lifted Liberty's hand in hers and waved to him. He forced another smile and waved back.

He hurried off to night school, his head spinning. *Everything is going to be all right.* He wished now that he hadn't read the newspaper. If he didn't read about it, would it all go away?

Of course it will all go away. No one knows anything about the baby, I am the only one who knows, and I will tell no one the secret, not even Sura. If someone really wanted little Liberty, then why did they let her mother cry like that all alone in the hotel?

No, he would just forget all about that night, and then everything would be perfect, and no one would suffer or be angry with him.

Just forget.

12

Micha woke in the middle of the night, rolled over to check that the baby was breathing, put his face close to her mouth, not satisfied until he felt the flutter of breath against his own cheek. It frightened him, this devotion; he had never loved anything like this, not even Sura. And it had happened so quickly.

His baby girl.

He dressed in the dark and kissed little Liberty on the head, then his wife. Sura murmured and rolled over and wrapped her arms around his neck so that he had to pull himself free. He was gone, then, down into the dank street. Already the pushcarts were there, the hawkers shivering and smoking cigarettes and arguing and *schmoozing*.

He walked, head down into the wind, toward the Elevated. His back ached, his muscles screamed. He didn't think he could face another day at the dock, but he would—he had to. He would do it for Sura and for Liberty; for them he would do anything, anything.

Dearest Vati. Dearest Mutti. I am writing to you with such gladness in my heart, I cannot tell you.

She stared at the words she had written. But what could she say? No one could know, not yet. Little Libby—that was what she called her now—lay on her back on the bed, gurgling and trying to suck her toes. Such an adorable baby. Sura smiled just from looking at her.

She could not tell them all the truth, that she was a foundling, have them all think of her little girl as a whore's castoff. Well, Etta wouldn't, but her vati, not so sure. So before she told them anything, she would have to think carefully, would need to write everything down so that she did not forget. Etta had given her a journal before she left. *"This you must keep,"* she had said. *"Write in it every day so that when I come to America, you will not forget anything, and you can tell me it all."*

There were only two entries in it so far; she had started writing on the boat when she left Tallinn, but then she got seasick and forgot.

She ripped out the pages she had written in and licked her lips. This will be my private and secret diary, she thought. On this left side I will write everything she does; and on this side I will write about the pretend life she will have, the life I will make up, the life I will tell everyone else.

So I do not forget.

This is what I will do: I will write in here today's date. And three months from now, I will write to Vati and Mutti and tell them I am going to have a baby. By the time they come from Russia, Libby will be all grown, so no one will ever know that there is a year missing.

It will be our secret, Micha and mine.

⟨◆⟩

The end of another day.

One of the schvartzes lingered after the whistle, leaning against the sugar sacks. He lit a cigarette, offered one to Micha, and he took it. Sura didn't know about this, the cigarettes. She didn't need to know. It was all part of learning to be American.

They smoked in silence. Micha closed his eyes, almost groaned aloud at the ache in all his muscles. But he had done it, he had got through another day.

"You'll get used to it," the schvartze said. "Takes a while is all."

The man crushed the stub of the cigarette under his boot heel and wandered off, hands in his pockets. Micha took his time to finish his cigarette, too tired even to go home. But finally, he tossed his butt in the oily water and began walking toward the gates.

There were two men standing there; one of them was obviously a boss, by his suit and his frock coat and derby. The other was his uncle Max, his hands still in thick white bandages.

"Micha," Uncle Max said. "How are you, *boychick?*"

"Getting by, thanks, Uncle Max."

"There's someone I'd like you to meet." He turned to the man in the frock coat, who leaned on his cane and offered him a curt nod. His face was familiar.

"This is Mr. George Seabrook. He wants to talk to you about the fire. Shall we have a drink somewhere?"

⟞⟞⟞

The tavern smelled of stale beer. Hard faces turned and stared at them as they walked in. This was a working man's bar, not a millionaire's place. Men in overalls and flat caps drank stout and ate hard-boiled eggs, dropping the shells on the sawdust floor.

The bartender didn't look pleased when he saw them, and Micha wondered if he would throw them out, until Seabrook put a note on the bar and said to him, "Keep the change." The man nodded then and jerked his head toward a little alcove at the back.

They pushed aside a curtain and went through. The alcove was warmed by a cast-iron stove in the corner and reeked of tobacco and spilled liquor. There were photographs of longshoremen on the walls.

They sat down. George Seabrook removed his gloves and dropped them in his derby. The barman brought them a pitcher of stout and drew the curtain shut behind him as he left.

"Can you do it, my boy?" Uncle Max said. "I can't hold anything yet."

Micha poured from the pitcher, handed the millionaire his glass first. Then he held his breath and waited. The man sat there, legs crossed, holding the derby in one hand, jiggling the silk gloves. Micha could almost see his reflection in the man's boots. At home, he probably had a dozen schvartzes to polish them for him.

"I told Mr. Seabrook you were there the night the Grand burned down."

Micha nodded and said nothing.

"No one else you tell about this," Uncle Max added.

Micha picked up his stout, then put it down again. "What's this about?" he said to Max, switching to Yiddish.

"Mr. Seabrook's wife was in the fire, my boy. She was the one on the top floor with the little babe in her arms. You remember her?"

"Sure I remember, Uncle Max. But what do you mean, his wife? She was with another man, a real *momzer*, I remember."

Uncle Max swallowed so hard his Adam's apple bobbed in his throat like a cork in a bathtub. He looked at the millionaire type, then back at Micha. "Not all wives are good girls like your Sura," he said so softly Micha could barely hear him.

"What has this got to do with the fire?" Micha said, thinking all the while: I was never good at this, they must see the lie written right here on my face.

"They didn't find the baby's body. This poor man, he thinks, you know, that she might still be alive."

"I am sorry for that. But again, what has that got to do with me, Uncle Max?" He looked at this George Seabrook. They were still talking in Yiddish, sure, but still he had not spoken, just sat there. It made him sweat, the way he was looking at him.

"Mr. Seabrook wants to know if you saw anything," Uncle Max said, talking American again. "If there is anything, you know, that can maybe help him find her."

"Like what?"

"Like anything. They didn't find the poor little baby's body after the fire, see? Could the other man, the one she was with, could he have come back and taken her?"

"I was just the janitor, Uncle Max," he said, in Yiddish. "How would I know?"

"But you said you saw her crying one day. You told me."

"What's he saying?" George asked, in English.

"It's like I told you, Mr. Seabrook, the boy doesn't remember anything more than what I said."

"Can he at least tell me why my wife was crying?"

"He wants to know why she was crying," Uncle Max said to Micha.

"Because the *momzer* left her."

"That's why?"

Micha stared at Max, then at the millionaire. I have to do something to make this stop, he thought. He leaned forward. "Look, Uncle Max, you got to tell him, the baby is dead. I heard her crying inside the room the night of the fire, but the door was locked, from the inside."

"Where was Mrs. Seabrook?"

"I don't know. I tried to get in, I really tried, Uncle, but I didn't have my keys, and I couldn't open the door, couldn't even kick it open. I tried and tried, and then the smoke and flames were so thick." He shrugged. "What could I do?"

"Why didn't you tell me this before, my boy?" Uncle Max said, and put his big hand on his shoulder.

"I only wanted to forget about it," Micha said, and covered his face with his hands so the millionaire could not see how much he was sweating.

Uncle Max translated what Micha had said. George fumbled in his coat and brought out a silver cigarette case. He tried to take out one of the cigarettes, but his hands started to shake, and he dropped them onto the floor.

He squared his shoulders and took his gloves out of the derby and started to put them on. "I can see I have been wasting both your time. I apologize. Enjoy the rest of the stout. I shall trouble you no further."

He got to his feet, put the derby on his head, and, with a nod, left the nook.

Micha stared after him.

"Poor man," Uncle Max said. "How I should hate to be in his shoes. To lose your wife and your daughter like that. Such a life he has now."

Micha picked up the pitcher of stout and poured some into his glass. He drained it in one swallow.

"Are you all right, my boy?"

"I still dream about that fire, every night. This just brought it all back."

"The things we've seen, eh? No one can know."

They finished off the pitcher, and Max ordered another. When it was all gone, they went back outside, unsteady on their feet now. Rain drifted under the orange arc of the gaslights. But Micha didn't even button his coat. His whole body felt numb.

"How are you doing down at the dock?"

"It's hard work, Uncle. I do my best."

"I'll see if I can find you something better. Which way are you getting home? You want to catch the trolley car with me?"

"I think I'll walk for a bit on my own."

Uncle Max nodded and patted him on the shoulder. Then he turned up the collar of his coat and dashed across the street.

Micha watched him jump on board the car.

Micha walked south to the wharf. He went as far as Fortieth, where the big freighters were, big as buildings and bound for Cape Town and London and Buenos Aires. On Pier 57, there was a Cunard liner ready to sail to Southampton, brightly lit and ready for boarding, horse carriages and limousines and checkered taxicabs blocking the streets in both directions. It gave two mournful blasts on the horn, the echoes reverberating around the vast stretches of the Hudson and the far Jersey shoreline.

He retched into the gutter.

When he was done, he walked out to an empty pier, leaned against one of the pilings, stared into the oily black water. The dark silhouettes of warehouses crowded the waterfront, the tall buildings of America piled up behind them. He imagined people standing at all those lighted windows up there, all the way down the island to the Battery, watching him.

We saw what you did, America said. You can hide it from your uncle Max and from the millionaire whose baby you stole, but you can't hide it from us.

"I didn't mean for it to be like this!" he shouted into the rain and wind.

What do you all want? That I should give the baby to some goy millionaire, someone who will give her to his schvartzes to look after, someone who could never love her like my Sura will love her? I saw her, with my own eyes I saw, how her mother was crying alone in the hotel room. Such a hard heart he has. How could he be a good father to our little Libby?

But she's not your daughter, America shouted back at him. Who says who gets to decide?

"I say. That's who! Micha Levine says it! That's the end of it!"

But he knew America did not believe that to be the end of anything. He could feel it in his bones. There would be a reckoning. And when it comes, he thought, let the sins fall on my shoulders, not on Sura's.

PART 2

13

Broadway and Fifth, August 1917

The press of people on the sidewalks was impenetrable. Fifth Avenue was bright with red-white-and-blue American flags, even Libby joined in, waving her little Stars and Stripes as she sat on her father's shoulders to watch the parade go past. She squirmed with excitement as the band passed in the middle of the street, followed by the National Guard in their khaki, the brass shining on their belts and badges, rifles at slope.

"I want to see, I want to see!" she squealed, though up there on Micha's shoulders, she was perhaps the only one in the crowd who could see anything. The noise of the band and the cheering was deafening. Micha reached up and held her as high in the air as he could.

"What are they doing, Papa?" she squealed.

"They are going off to war, bubeleh."

"What's war?"

Micha looked at Sura.

"It's when men fight each other with guns," Sura said. "It's all *meshuggaas.*"

"Will Daddy go to war?"

"No, Daddy doesn't have to go. Daddy has to stay here and look after us. Isn't that right, Daddy?"

"That's right, bubeleh. Daddy isn't going away."

Libby laughed and waved her flag as high as she could. When they got home, she said it was the best parade she had ever seen and marched around the room the rest of the afternoon pretending she was blowing a trumpet.

⊰—⊱

Dear Vati. Dearest Mutti. Our little darling is three years old today. You would not believe how much she has grown! She loves her mama's kugel, and at suppertime she is always at the window listening for the lemon-ice man ringing his bell, and nothing will do but for Micha to go down and get her one. Everything now she must do herself, and she is a little mimic, she makes cries like the hawker she can hear from the street, like you think someone is selling herring right there in the living room. And the stories, I cannot tell you. Every night, Micha must read her a story. She likes the one about the little brown duck best.

Sura looked up. Micha was in his favorite chair by the window, so hot today, tonight they would have to sleep again on the roof, she supposed. Libby was playing there at her father's feet with her doll and a little wooden donkey, talking to her toys in a singsong chatter, like Sura talked to her when she was in the bath. She couldn't help but smile at her.

I wish one day you will see her. She is such a lovely little girl, and never any trouble. We are so lucky and so blessed that God brought her to us, a miracle it is. Here is a drawing she made for you. Michelangelo, she will never be.

Today we took her to see the big parade, the first American soldiers were leaving New York to go to France. America is full of the war, it is all anyone talks about in the street and in the newspapers. We came here to get away from such troubles, but trouble is everywhere. They are telling all the young men they must be ready to be soldiers. My Micha does not have to go, of course, it is only for men with wives who can work, and I have to stay home and look after little Libby.

We have moved to a new place in Cannon Street, by the Williamsburg Bridge. It was so dark where we lived before, and crowded, like I couldn't tell you. Our new place has four rooms, on the corner of the building, so it is really light. There is even electricity, you switch on and switch off, like magic. Libby has her own bedroom now, and it has a bathtub in it. Every Friday afternoon we all have a bath, ready for Shabbas. It is like kings we live now.

There is even a separate kitchen and a sink with running water, and even a room just for sitting in, with a pattern wood floor they call here parquet. Our apartment is on the fifth floor, so it is still a long way to walk up and down, but so much better we have it now.

Micha has a good job, in a big store that sells just clothes for women, like you never saw. He is manager of dresses, now, only three years he has been there, can you imagine. When he starts he is only lifting and carrying, but now already they give him his own office. One day he will be manager of the whole store, and then America better watch out! He talks like a proper American, but I ever see him chew gum, I swear, I will kill him.

Micha put down his newspaper and stood up, restless, jingling the coins in his pockets. He went to lean over her shoulder to see what she was writing. "What is this you are doing?"

"You know what it is, I told you. It is a letter to my mutti and vati."

"What's this? Why are you sending this drawing? I never seen this before. It's just scribble. This new one she made for us, why don't you send?"

"Micha, they think she is three years old."

"So, let them think she is a prodigy, or I don't know what." Again with the coin jingling.

"What's wrong, Micha?"

"I worry. What if they come here tomorrow, then they will know! Just one look. Look at her, the red hair she has, and those green eyes. We might as well have a schvartze for a baby."

"They say they will come, but they won't come. We don't have to worry about it. You are the only one in our whole shtetl that is brave enough to leave."

"The last thing I am is brave." He picked up her journal and thumbed through the pages. More of Libby's drawings fell out and fluttered to the floor. "What's this? You keep a diary? I didn't know you have a diary."

"It is so I remember. Everything I tell them must be later than when it happens."

"You keep a book for this?"

"Of course."

He tossed the book back on the table. "I wish we didn't have to lie like this."

"Bubeleh, what is wrong? It's all kvetch, kvetch, kvetch, ever since we got back from the parade. Never I saw such a sad-sack person. Where are you going?"

"Out for a walk."

"Micha!"

"What, I can't go for a walk now? I work hard all week. If I want to walk, I'll walk." The door slammed behind him.

Libby looked at her mother and then at the door and started to cry. Sura went to her, scooped her up in her arms, and held her as she sobbed. "Papa!" Libby shouted, and reached out a hand to the door.

"Papa will be home soon," Sura said to her. But it took a long time to soothe her. Papa's little girl now.

Why does he have to carry on so? In Russia, he would never shout and slam like that, would never go for a walk without her. God had given them good luck, and now he didn't want it. They had a nice apartment, he had a good job, they had their little miracle. How many times had she prayed to God when she heard of a little child in the street who had died from scarlet fever or diphtheria or she didn't know what, when every baby on all Delancey Street was sick and crying, please God not our Libby, and what happened?

Not even a sniffle.

Other mothers and fathers lost their little treasures, but Libby was still here and growing. Never mind whatever happened back then so long ago, who could remember? It was plain, God meant for them to have her and love her, anyone could see that.

Why couldn't Micha let it be?

14

In Tallinn, Micha could never have imagined such an emporium as this; his father's leather shop was one of the biggest shops in the town, and everyone thought Micha was *meshugga* to give it up to be a nobody in America. Well, if they saw him now, they would not shake their heads and mumble into their beards anymore. He wasn't a greenhorn now, he was a proper mensch. He had even outdone his uncle Max.

As Micha came out of his office, he stopped for a moment to look around, admire the alabaster planters and brass sconces and polished mahogany walls. A spiral wrought-iron staircase led to the second and third floors, where they sold handbags and gloves and woman's underthings. Department stores, the Americans called them, and this one was the cat's pajamas. Sura was right, he must stop thinking about everything that had happened in the past. How can they have such good luck if God didn't want it that way?

Micha made his usual round of the floor, making sure the salesgirls weren't reading magazines or putting on makeup, checking that all the hangers on a rack faced in the same direction and the price tags were tucked away.

He stopped to look at the mannequins near the canopied entrance, dressed this morning with the new fall fashion; this season the department stores were telling their customers that at least one dress in every woman's wardrobe should be khaki, for America's sake. He aimed to make this gabardine street dress with matching satin and braid their biggest seller.

Next to it was a beetroot serge dress with gray trim, calf length, with one of the new tiered skirts; also a shirtwaist of blue satin with a daring V neck.

He knelt down to adjust the hem. He supposed later that was why the two women did not see him there.

They were regular customers; he knew them both by name. One had a monthly account at the store; the other, her husband's father was a friend of his uncle Max, very respectable, worked in a savings and loan.

"Well, my husband certainly isn't going to shirk his duty to his country," one of the women was saying. "He was one of the first in the queue at the draft office. He's proud to serve America."

"What will you do if he goes?"

"We shall manage. I can always find work in an office, I shouldn't wonder. What about Frank?"

"Well, we have no children, so hell or high water wouldn't keep him away." There was a pause. "Not like some."

Micha felt his heart beat faster. If I get to my feet now, he thought, they will see me, and I will not have to eavesdrop.

He stayed where he was.

"I don't think it's right how some men are going to stay at home while our husbands risk their lives for our country over there. Extreme hardship exemptions! You know what I call them? Cowards!"

"Oh, Jean."

"Well, it's not right." Dropping her voice to a whisper. "You know that Mr. Levine is one of them."

"You mean the nice man in the office over there?"

"You know that nice man in the office is a Jew?"

"Well, I knew that, but—"

"Do you think it's right that he stays behind while our men go off to fight the battle he ran away from? That's why they came here, you know. To get away from fighting the Germans. Yellow, I call it. I've thought of taking my business somewhere else."

Micha got to his feet and walked back to his office, didn't care if they saw him or not. He shut the door behind him, leaned his back against it, took two long slow breaths to compose himself. He shut his eyes, was suddenly back on the swaying fire escape. He could smell smoke.

"Yellow, I call it."

He stumbled to his desk and slumped into his chair. One of the salesgirls was knocking on the door, saying something about a customer asking for credit, could he come and discuss it with her. He gripped the edge of the desk, felt like he was on top of a tall building. He broke out in a cold sweat, thought he was going to be sick.

What really happened on that fire escape? If he hadn't hesitated, if he'd gone back up there straightaway, could he have saved her? The truth was, he couldn't really remember anymore. The more time had passed, the more jumbled it all seemed in his mind.

If she had been still in that room, then he must have had time to save her. He imagined himself standing in front of all the other men in the shtetl, trying to explain what had happened, how he had no choice; they all just shook their heads and muttered into their beards.

Yellow, they'd call it.

―⟶―

That night as he walked down East Broadway, he tried to ignore the newspaper boys yelling about the latest news of the war, and the "Wake Up, America!" posters, and the "Liberty Bond" signs mushrooming now in every shop window.

He proceeded down Broome Street, his head down. The city was seething in the heat. It was Friday afternoon, and all the housewives were out on the street buying for Shabbas. He had to use his elbows to get through the bedlam of pushcarts and people. He just wanted to get home.

Sometimes he found a comfort in it, all the signs in Russian and German, hearing Yiddish shouted from the street and the shops, the miles and miles of pushcarts, the sun beating down on the shimmering rows of herring, the stink and the shove of it. What do you want— apples, potatoes, eggs, collars, a tablecloth, a tin fork?

But today he wanted only to be alone.

He saw a sign painted on a window: "Lager Bier." He smelled the stale stink of hops. It looked so dark and cool inside. He went in. Let them all push and yell out there. He would go home in a little while, when he felt better.

⸎

A boiling day to be in the kitchen. Oh, this New York! Never had she been so hot. Sura had her sleeves rolled up, her hair pinned so she could feel some coolness on her neck. She dropped the bones and tails and heads of the whitefish in the boiling water and started to slice the carrots. Libby clung to her leg, demanding to see.

Sura bent down and lifted her up onto the wooden bench beside her. But first she pretended to drop her, and the little girl giggled and screamed. "You are such a big girl! I cannot believe your heaviness. How much you are grown!"

She picked up the knife again. "You see what I'm doing? It's your papa's favorite. Next we throw in the onion and the carrot and the beets. Are you watching? Because this is my special recipe, one day you must learn."

"Why, Mama?"

"You got to learn about your Jewishness so you never forget."

"Papa says I have to be all-American."

"Sure, you have to be that too, we can't be all our lives just green-horns. When you grow up, you will make for yourself a proper person, drive a motor car and live in a nice house, wash your blankets with Ivory soap and eat special food, like canned pineapple. Not live in an apartment like this, everything will be the bee's pajamas for you."

Libby wanted to help her chop the carrots. Sura let her put her hand on top of hers as she did it, but then Libby yelled, "No, me do it, Mama," and tried to grab the knife, and screamed when her finger got sliced along the blade.

Sura dropped everything and held the little girl in her arms, gently sucking on the cut finger. "There, little bubeleh, there, it's only a little cut, you're all right, baby, you're all right."

She danced her around the kitchen, pretending she was a prince and Libby was the princess, like in one of her stories, until she stopped crying. Oh, my little precious, she thought, you scare me so much. You are so much of what we have, and such happiness is like a paper scrap, any strong wind and it is gone.

Tessie Fischer, she thought, she looks sideways at her husband, and she is pregnant. So many children she does not know what to do. Micha and me, we have only our little foundling, and if anything happens, just nothingness then.

"Mama, you're hurting," Libby said, because she was squeezing her so tight.

"I'm sorry, bubeleh," she said. Together they examined the cut finger. "You see, it's all better now."

"I been in the wars," she said.

By the time she had made the dinner, Micha still wasn't home, so she changed out of her cooking things, put on the new shirtwaist she had made from a pattern in the *Ladies' Home Journal*, and brushed out her long hair. She stared into the cracked mirror. So tired she looked these days.

"One day when I grow up," Libby said, "I want to be beautiful like you, Mama."

"You will be much more beautiful, my bubeleh."

"Promise me?"

"I promise."

It was almost dark when Micha got home, and straightaway she could smell the drink on him. He said he didn't want the gefilte fish she had made, even though it was his favorite. "I want to go out," he said. "I don't want to stay in here in this stinking hot."

So they went to Katz's, and nothing would do but he ordered them all franks and beans to eat with napkins on their laps, like real Americans. For Libby he ordered a chocolate soda as a special treat. She started chattering about her day, how she made him gefilte fish all by herself, and how she cut her finger, and there was blood, and how she and her friend Etta went to visit Zayde and Bubbe in Russia.

"Who is this Etta?"

"It's her little friend," Sura said.

"I didn't know from such friends."

"Well, she is special make-up friend. She only comes when her mutti and vati aren't around. Doesn't she, bubeleh?"

She thought she would see him smile. He always did when Libby told one of her stories; but no, he was staring out the window and chewing on a hangnail. The smell of drink was still strong on him.

"What is it?" she said.

"It's nothing."

"You always say nothing."

"Because you never like what it is I say. So, what do I do? I tell you, you say don't talk about it."

"Aren't you happy with us?"

The look he gave her, like a man trapped in a room with a debt collector.

"What we did, Micha, it was a good thing."

He was about to say something, but then he shook his head and looked away.

"Why is Daddy so cross?"

"He's not cross, baby. Drink your soda."

"I hurt my finger, Papa," she said, and showed him where she had cut her finger.

"My little bubeleh," he said, and he kissed it and mussed her ginger curls. "There, it's better now."

Libby sucked on her straw but kept the finger held out, the little cut her peace offering.

"She thinks you're mad at her."

"I'm not mad at her. Why would I be mad at her?"

"Do you like my new hat? I made it myself. A dollar ninety was all it cost." It was pale gray crepe with a rolled brim. She turned her head left, then right, so he should have a good look at it. "See how I get all gassied up for you."

"Gussied. You say 'gussied,' not 'gassied.'" He closed his eyes. Why did he always close his eyes like that? What was there in the world he did not want to see? "I should have been a better man to you, Sura."

"How can you be a better man? You done everything for us."

"Yes," he said. "Yes, I did everything for you."

Two men came in, in uniform. She saw him look at them and wince.

"We need you, bubeleh," she said to him, because she knew what he was thinking. "Me and Libby, we need you."

Later, back in the apartment, she watched him read Libby a bedtime story, her favorite, the one where the little brown duck grows up with the wrong family, but one day it turns out she isn't a duck, she is a big white swan. Lots of storybooks they had, but that was always the one she wanted.

When she was asleep, instead of coming out and sitting in his favorite chair to read the newspaper, he went out on the fire escape. She waited awhile, and then she followed him.

"What are you doing out here?"

"It's too hot in there."

It was true, the city was breathless, it was hard to get enough air. There were people out on their fire escapes up and down the street. Out here was better, never mind the stink of the street, the noise and shouting of kids on the stoops.

"Maybe we should take the mattresses and sleep up on the roof tonight," she said.

"Maybe."

"What is it you're not telling me, Micha? Is it another woman? Tell me it's another woman. Another woman I can handle."

"As if there is any woman in all America better than you." He started rolling a cigarette. In Russia he never smoked, now he smoked all the time. He licked the paper, tamped in a plug of tobacco from a tin. "I want to be on my own for a while."

She stared at the glow of his cigarette in the dark, wondering what to do. Then Libby started fussing, and she went in to quiet her, and when she came out, he was still out there. She wished he would tell her what it was. Or perhaps he was right, she never really wanted to know it all.

When Micha finally went back inside, he found Sura asleep on Libby's bed. They were curled around each other. Libby's damp curls were stuck to her forehead, it was so breathless hot in the tiny room. He thought of waking them and taking them all up to the roof, but then he thought: Well, they are sleeping now. What is the point?

He stared at the little girl's face. How beautiful she was, but how different, with her green eyes and red-gold hair. How old would she be before she started looking in the mirror and asking questions? Already he was worn down by it, strangers staring at them in the street, in shops: *"Is that your baby?"*

He went into the bedroom, turned on the light. He reached under the bed and took out his cardboard suitcase, unlocked it with a key he kept on a chain at his waistcoat, took out the old tin box inside, and opened it. There was a newspaper cutting, curling up at the edges now and yellowing with age. He unfolded it carefully and stared at the grainy photograph of George Seabrook. He read the words under the photograph, his lips moving silently, though he knew it by heart well enough by now.

What was he going to do? He hated it now whenever Sura or Libby looked at him with so much adoring in their eyes, like he was such a good man. He couldn't stand it, couldn't abide how much they loved him. It made him think only how happy his life could have been, if only he deserved it.

15

Sura was in the kitchen—it was another sulfurous day—she was using tongs to push dirty sheets into a boiling tub. He held out the papers to her, and she looked over her shoulder at them, wondering what it was he was showing her.

"What have you got there?"

"Look."

Impatient, she dried her hands on her apron and took the piece of paper from him. She stared at it, not really understanding all the words. The blood drained from her face. This couldn't be true.

"I leave next Wednesday," he said.

"What?"

"We go to Camp Dix in New Jersey for training first."

Sura sagged against the counter. "Oh, Micha, what have you done?"

"It won't be for long. I'll be back before you know it."

"But . . . what about Libby?"

"I've saved a little money. I'll send you my pay. I won't be needing it over there. You can take in a little sewing perhaps."

"You did this without even talking to me?"

"I don't need your permission, woman!"

She screwed up the draft paper, threw it in his face. She tried to hit him, with both fists, but he caught her hands. She screamed and screamed in his face.

"Mama, Mama!" Liberty ran into the room. Sura scooped her up in her arms, but the child would not stop crying.

"Sura—"

"Go back, tell them it is a mistake."

"It's too late to change my mind. I have signed the papers."

She was shaking so hard she was making Libby scream all the more. She turned her back on him. "Get out."

"Sura—"

"I'll never forgive you for this," she said. "Get out!"

"You don't understand. I have to do this."

"Get out!"

Micha left, leaving the enlistment papers on the counter. When he came home, it was very late, and Sura and Libby were asleep. He stared at their silhouettes, thinking how once this was everything he ever wanted. But he couldn't have it. It wasn't his to have.

Two months later Private Michael Levine, his khaki uniform freshly pressed, his duffel bag over his shoulder, marched up the gangplank of the cruiser anchored in the Brooklyn shipyard. When the whistle blew, they broke ranks and surged toward the railings to wave and blow kisses at their wives and sweethearts and mothers gathered on the quay below.

Sura watched the ship's four screws churn the murky East River, driving the massive gray hull toward the Liberty statue. Smoke from the three funnels trailed into a cloudless sky. Sura watched it, dry eyed, until it was out of sight, Libby clinging to her neck. Then she turned and headed for home.

16

The captain knocked the ash out of his pipe and looked over. "Always writing, Levine. Always writing."

"Yes, sir."

"Who are you writing to?"

"My wife, sir."

"Married, are you? You look too young."

"Sura and I, we have been married eight years now. It was arranged for us, but we are very happy. She is the perfect wife."

"The perfect wife? You're a lucky man. I wish I had the perfect wife. Where are you from, Levine?"

"Russia, sir. We've been fighting Germans all our lives over there."

The captain tamped tobacco into his pipe and lit it. The crackle of the tobacco sounded somehow soothing over the distant rumble of the artillery. Every now and then a shell would land very close; Micha felt it rather than heard it—it shuddered through the earth and into the bones.

They were resting up in a vaulted cellar in what the captain told them used to be a seminary. They had been caught in the open on the road from Château Thierry, and several of the men had been hit by shrapnel and now lay on the floor covered in bloodied bandages, smoking cigarettes. Only one of them, a sergeant, was badly hurt; he lay on a stretcher, turning gray, making grunting noises in the back of his throat.

Micha took a dog-eared photograph from his shirt pocket and handed it to the captain. He held it under the nub of a candle and peered at it. "Not only perfect, she is also very pretty."

"Thank you, sir."

"Let's hope we can get you back to her in one piece."

Micha took back the photograph and returned it to his pocket. "We have a little girl."

"How old is she?"

"She was five years old in March."

The captain sucked on the pipe. "I've always wanted a family. Before all this, I always assumed I would have one, one day."

Micha folded the letter he was writing, slipped it into an envelope, and pressed it into the captain's palm.

"What's this?"

"If I don't get back, if something happens, can you make sure my wife gets that?"

"I'm sure she'd rather have you than a letter. Best thing is to try and look after yourself tomorrow."

"I'll do my best. But it's a war, who knows what will happen? And there's things . . . she should know."

The captain frowned. "If it's another woman . . ."

"No, it's nothing like that. Since I married Sura, I never looked at another woman. But all the same, it's important. Very important."

"All right, Levine," the captain said, and slipped the envelope inside his coat.

In that moment, Micha felt like he had when he'd finished a shift at the docks. There, no more loads to shift. He was done. He fumbled in his pocket for a cigarette, his hands shook as he lit it from the candle flame. He peered out at the street through a broken window. He heard the muffled voices of the sentries, saw shadows moving along the walls, the moonlight frosted by the mist.

Some men had hauled down a huge wax candle from the chapel above them; it was the size and shape of an artillery shell. When they lit it, it was like when he put another nickel in the gas meter in Delancey Street.

They could see the room better now. It was clear the Germans had been there before them. There were vile pictures drawn on the walls next to the pictures of Catholic saints, and a pair of muddy and worn-out German boots protruded from a pile of green vestments. A torn missal lay next to a piece of black rye bread, hard as a brick.

Micha found a postcard on the floor, the king of Saxony peered out between two draped flags in one corner of it. The king looked a lot like Uncle Max.

"What's going to happen tomorrow, sir? Will we see action?"

"Looks that way."

Micha couldn't stop his hands from shaking. That was the worst thing, he thought, not the dying, but having all these other men see him piss himself, or cry, or hide. That was what he was really afraid of.

"Can I ask you something, sir?"

"It depends what it is, Lance Corporal Levine."

"What's the worst thing you ever did?"

"What a strange question. I'm not sure I could answer that." He puffed out his cheeks and thought about it. "I stole two dollars from my mother's purse once. I wanted to take a girl to a dance."

"That doesn't seem so bad."

"Thing is, if I'd asked her, she probably would have given it to me. What about you, Levine?"

"Same. I stole something."

"What did you steal?"

"Someone's whole life."

A hiss, as the captain took a deep breath. "Goddammit, Levine. What did you do, kill someone?"

"I wish it was that simple."

"What the hell are you talking about, son?"

"I didn't set out to steal, sir. You think at the time that there is no choice, and you think of all sorts of reasons and excuses, but then this thing, it keeps turning over in your mind night after night, day after day, year after year. In the end, you just want to forget. But you can't."

"Look here, Levine, I don't think you should tell me any more. I'm going to turn in. Try and get some sleep. You'll need your wits about you tomorrow."

"Yes, sir."

The captain moved away, and Micha lay down, huddled inside his greatcoat, and tried to sleep, like the captain said, but he couldn't.

Cold for summer. He couldn't stop this shivering.

⸻

The barrage began just before dawn. Micha woke with the cellar floor shaking underneath him, the whine of shells overhead. They sounded like a train going over on the Elevated right when you were underneath and then collapsing right on top of you. Men screamed, thinking that the cellar was going to collapse.

The captain shouted to one of the sergeants to close the iron door at the top of the stairs to keep out shell fragments. The earth lurched again, and dust fell from the cracks between the stones. Some men put hands over their ears and shrieked with terror. Micha was surprised how calm he felt. He had supposed he would be shaking and yelling along with the rest of them.

He even raised his head long enough to peer through the shattered window, saw houses along the street collapse in clouds of dust. The smell of gas and explosives made him choke. He fumbled to put on his rubber mask.

The barrage went on and on until dawn, which came with a creeping of greasy light over what was left of the houses. When it stopped, there was a stunned silence. Through the ringing in his ears, he heard someone sobbing in the back of the cellar.

The beam of a flashlight flickered around the walls. For the merest second he saw the Christian Jesus Christ nailed to a wooden cross, men huddled together underneath. They looked like they were covered in snow, then he realized it was plaster dust from the ceiling.

The captain shouted at them to get ready to move out.

"Lance Corporal Levine! Get everyone out of here."

He went around dragging men to their feet, kicking at boots, so icy calm he wanted to laugh aloud. He knew what he had to do now.

The men followed him up the stairs and into the street. The ring of their iron hobnails on the stone pavement seemed too loud. He wondered about snipers.

They clattered in a long line past the Hotel de Ville, the clock and the mansard roof ruined from the shelling. Then the captain led them down a path toward a partly demolished steel mill. Beyond that lay the railroad, piles of coal sitting beside the tracks, wreathed in early morning mist.

Men trooped down in a thin line to the river. There was the stab of rifle fire and the steady punch of machine guns from somewhere very close, but, because of the mist, he couldn't make out if it was coming from behind them or in front.

The captain took him and several other NCOs aside. Their orders were to take up positions on the hill on the other side of the river, he said. From there they could halt any advance into the town itself. "Get your men into position as quickly as possible."

My second chance, Micha thought. This time I won't panic; I won't try and save myself first; I'll prove to everyone how brave I am. Then

I can go back to America, to my Sura and my little Libby, and know I deserve them after all.

A shell had struck the bridge halfway across, blowing away half of the roadway and leaving stones from the coping scattered about. There was a section no more than two feet wide for them to cross. The captain led the first platoon over himself. As they ran over, Micha looked down into the river at a snarl of blackened bricks and wire. Like being on that fire escape again.

The Germans started shelling, columns of water and mud reared up around them. The enemy was trying to destroy what was left of the bridge. Micha shouted at his men to hurry and followed the captain up the hill.

There was a wall halfway up the slope, and he headed toward it. It was only knee high in places, and in others it was just a pile of stones, but it would provide them with a little cover from the trench mortars. He threw himself down behind it and urged his men up the hill after him.

As he watched, they started to jerk and scream and fall. He felt the jackhammer tearing of the machine-gun bullets in the air, scything back and forth over the muddy slope. He twisted around this way, that way, trying to see where the fire was coming from.

There was a farmhouse about fifty yards farther up the hill, and bullets were punching deep holes in the stone walls, sending slates slithering off the roof. He saw two men run toward it, thinking to find cover, and the bullets tore them apart.

He saw the captain signaling furiously at him, and he crawled over. "They're behind us!" he shouted. "Get the men on the other side of the wall and tell them to stay down!"

Even as the captain said it, Micha saw two more of his men jerk backward, and blood sprayed behind them up the stones. He jumped the wall and screamed for his men to follow. He couldn't believe it, how few of them were still left.

He heard the thump. Trench mortars. The Germans were in front of them as well as behind. They had been led straight into a killing field.

Men were tearing open their first-aid packages, trying to staunch other men's wounds, were holding their mates as they lay screaming at the sky. Others had curled into a ball and just lay there, not doing anything. Stone chips were flying everywhere. He felt a sharp sting on his face, he put up a hand, and it came away bloody.

He crawled toward the captain, who lay propped against the wall, white faced.

"We have to do something!" he said.

The captain stared right through him like he wasn't there.

"We can't stay here!"

The man's mouth opened and closed, but no sound came out.

"Captain!"

The hammer of the machine gun was deafening. Perhaps he couldn't hear him. He grabbed him by the tunic and shook him. That seemed to do it.

"Sir, we have to pull back."

"We have orders to take the hill."

"The Germans are all around us! We need to go back."

"Yes, yes, of course." He seemed to shake himself, peered over the wall. "We can't go back, Lance Corporal, not without covering fire."

"Someone has to get back to town, let the colonel know what's happening."

"How? They'll get cut down before they go ten yards."

Micha pointed away to the right. "There's a drainage ditch over there, it runs down to the river. A runner could use the bridge as cover to get across to the far bank. They'll be almost at the town by then."

"All right, you'd better call for a volunteer."

"I'll do it."

"It's suicide, Levine."

"No, I can do it, sir." This is it, Micha thought. This is my moment.

"You really think so?"

Micha nodded.

"Good luck, then. Godspeed."

Micha turned and started to crawl along the wall, down the hill toward the ditch, the machine-gun bullets whipping the air above his head. The mortar barrage was getting heavier; twice, shells exploded close enough to send him a foot into the air, the concussion deafening him.

He closed his eyes, his face pressed into the mud, fought the urge to get up and run, run and never look back. Isn't that what you did last time? He looked up. He could have walked to the village in five minutes on a clear day; now the white houses looked as if they were miles away. Even the battle seemed to be getting farther away; he thought that the Germans had finally stopped shelling, but then he saw another gout of dirt spurt into the sky and realized the last explosion had deafened him.

He forced himself to keep crawling. At last he reached the ditch and threw himself in. The smell of gas was cloying. Even his hands were stinging. He fumbled for his mask and put it on.

What if he didn't get back to America? What would Sura and Libby do without him? Just stay alive, Micha. Stay alive and get back to New York, and after this you won't ever have to think about that woman's hands trying to pull up the window through all the smoke. You'll have made amends.

He fixed his helmet farther down his head and started to crawl.

⊷⊶

The ditch was dry at first; it got increasingly swampy the closer he got to the river. It took him half an hour to reach the bank.

He started to wade, then swim across. He knelt on a tangle of submerged barbed wire. He tried to get free of it, but only got more caught up. Soon his hands and legs were bleeding. He fell backward into the water, and his mask filled with water and he almost choked. He threw it aside in frustration, finally managed to tear himself free of the wire and scramble on, never mind the pain. He had to find the command post and give the colonel the coordinates of those machine guns, give the captain and the men covering fire so they could get off the hill.

There was a pontoon downriver from the bridge. He used it as cover, crossing hand over hand along the boards. When he reached the far bank, he lay there in the mud and water, exhausted, his lungs bursting. His eyes still burned, but the river had washed off most of the gas. He vomited.

He raised his head above the bank. He could see the command post a hundred yards away, behind the Hotel de Ville, at the top of the cobbled street.

The street was littered with bodies. He counted them off. They all had red armbands, couriers like himself. One, two, three, four, five. None of them had made it farther than halfway. There must be a sniper.

He slithered back down the muddy bank. He was safe there if he did not move.

You don't have to do this, Micha. Think about Sura, think about Libby. They need you.

He dared another look up the street. He saw the face of the dead runner closest to him, the look on his face, he looked so surprised. I suppose everyone feels surprised when they die, he thought. No one ever thinks it will happen to them.

"Yellow, I call it."

He launched himself to his feet. He had almost reached the last dead runner when the sniper's bullet hit him in the back of the head, and his helmet went spinning across the cobblestones. He was dead before he even hit the ground.

An ambulance stopped in front of the dressing station. The air was hazy with black smoke and the gag-inducing odor of high explosive.

The captain stopped when he saw the medics carrying out the bodies. A blanket fell away from a man's face, and he realized he knew him. "Levine," he said. "Goddammit."

He felt in his jacket and took out the letter the man had given him the night before. What was it he had said about stealing? He couldn't remember. But he said the letter was for his wife, that it was important. He would write to her as soon as he got a moment, tell her she should be proud. Levine was one of the bravest men he had ever served with. He must have known he couldn't make it to the command post with snipers everywhere.

And in the end, it didn't matter a damn anyway. The colonel had figured out the situation for himself, their artillery had taken out the machine-gun post.

He heard the whine of a shell overhead. He looked up, almost with a smile, as if it was a rocket at the Fourth of July. Perhaps he had heard too many shells for one war. He was numb to them by now. He had survived so much that day, and he felt, well, immune. He wasn't going to get killed by some stray shell. Hell, the Germans had been trying to kill him all day, and here he still was.

It was only at the last moment that he realized that the round was going to land almost directly on top of him. "Goddammit," he said, and a moment later he vanished in a plume of flame and smoke. His body scattered over the entire stretch of the street, and the letter he held in his fist drifted through the air as burning specks of ash, and then vanished on a breath of the evening wind.

PART 3

17

Garment District, New York, Spring 1922

The bell rang—another quarter of an hour until they could finish. Sura—Sarah Levine, please, I'm not a greenhorn anymore—had three more sleeves in her pile. She could finish them by five o'clock if the thread didn't break or the belt on her no-good Wilcox didn't come loose again. She could not wait to get outside, away from this stink of oil and clatter of noise, and into the fresh air, if this New York air you could call fresh. That Mr. Schonberg wouldn't open the windows, said they were too stiff.

What kind of person wouldn't fix a window when it was too stiff to open?

He stood up from his desk in the corner, where he had finished reckoning the slips for the week. She had earned nine dollars and forty-five cents, by her own count. A good week.

It would be a fatter pay packet than the other girls, but not everyone could be a sleeve cutter. You had to work fast, and you couldn't afford to make mistakes. She had the good skills her father had taught her, and now she had put them to good use. She earned her money.

Schonberg went down the row of benches, dropping the little brown packets in front of them. When he got to her, he stopped and gave her a sly grin, waited until she looked up before he put it down in front of her. *Schmendrick!* She tucked the envelope in her stocking and kept working; she wanted to finish these last sleeves in her pile before she went home.

The bell went off, and everyone started packing up to go home. Sarah worked a few minutes more to finish her sleeve before she got up and went to the cloakroom to check her pay packet. Seven dollars and ninety cents.

When she came out again, Schonberg was writing figures into a ledger. I can do these same tricks, she thought. She stood in front of his desk until he looked up.

"This is wrong," she said.

"It is good money," he said. "You are lucky. That some of these girls should get as much."

"Should be nine dollars and forty-five cents."

"How do you know how much?"

"I know how to figure. You think because you are a man, you can count better than me. I am short. Count my slips again."

"I throw away all the slips when I finish. Go home."

"You are counting crooked."

The chair creaked as Schonberg leaned back, his fingers steepled in front of him. Such a greasy man, with that wiry red beard and no-good teeth. "You want to earn a little bit more money," he said. "I show you how."

Sarah looked around. Everybody was gone, even Kohn on the door, the old man who checked their bags at closing time to make sure they weren't stealing scraps. Foolish girl, she thought. How can you let this happen? Never be alone with Schonberg, wasn't that what they told her from the very first day?

But he owes me a dollar fifty-five cents, this little *putz*!

She was afraid, but she was also angry. What she could do with so much money at the butcher!

Schonberg got up and took two one-dollar notes out of his pocket. He put them on the desk and shrugged off his suspenders. "You want a bonus? You can earn it."

She turned away, but he grabbed her wrist and dragged her back. "You think I can't get another sleeve cutter? Plenty of girls out there in the street. I only have to put up a sign, and I have a hundred girls line up."

"Let me go!"

He pulled her back toward the desk. "Teasing me all day. I should teach you."

Teasing him? All I do is stitch sleeves and try not to faint from the smell of the oil and the squinting in this bad light! She tried again to pull away, but he wouldn't let her go. Well, never mind the one dollar fifty-five cents. She had to get out of here.

They heard someone coming, and Schonberg let her go. One of the cutters, Max, came in and saw them. He stopped, his mouth open in surprise; he knew straightaway what was happening. "I forgot my glasses case," he said, and hurried over to his workbench.

"Hold the elevator for me," Sarah said.

She rode down with him. Neither of them looked at each other. When she reached the street, Sarah walked as fast as she could the six blocks to the Third Avenue El, not looking at anyone, her cheeks on fire, so ashamed, so scared, and so angry. Take her husband, take her family, take her money! How much more this life going to cheat her?

It was shoulder-to-shoulder on the platform for the Elevated, the conductors in their green caps shoving and shouting, and the train wheels shrieking as the next train pulled in and the doors opened. She crammed into a carriage, everyone in so tight she could not move, so hot and breathless in there, and after everything that had just happened to her, she thought she was going to faint.

She hung on to one of the straps as the train moved off. She closed her eyes, trying to shut out Schonberg, that look he gave her, greedy little eyes like a pig he had. If Max the cutter hadn't come back, he would have started pawing at her, or worse.

It was as if she could feel his hands squeezing at her.

At first, she thought she was imagining too hard, but then realized it was real, someone really was touching her, squeezing her bottom. She tried to squirm away, but there were too many people, she couldn't move, not even her arm. The carriage swayed around a bend, she tried to look over her shoulder to see who was doing it to her, but she couldn't see for sure, got a glimpse of an old rabbi in a *yarmulke*, next to him a swarthy man with slicked-back hair, a bald goy in a nice suit.

Which one of them? Maybe all of them, she thought. I am just a bit of meat now for the whole of America to feel up.

I should shout out, she thought. But then what would happen? All the world looking at me, like Schonberg looked, even the women, all thinking: Well, she must have asked for it. Everyone knew, even in the shtetl she had heard her father say, *"Men only touch a girl who wants it."*

When people got out at the next station, the touching stopped. She looked around the carriage, wondering which of the men had done it to her. What was the use? It was the way of it. A girl wasn't safe until she was married, that was why her father had married her and her sisters off so young. But she was a widow now. She had no one to look after her, and she had to go to work so she and her little baby girl didn't starve.

She got out at Rivington and walked fast through the crowds. Today she didn't look at the bearded rabbis in their skullcaps and silkaline coats or into the tiny dark shops with fabrics all spread across the tables, not a glance for the children in their dirty clothes playing in the gutters.

Felt up, cheated, treated like a whore. This America. What a place she had come to, what a place to bring up her daughter.

She vowed her Liberty would never have to live like this. Wherever you are, Micha, help me. I have to do better for our little girl.

The Florence Nightingale public school was across the road from their tenement, and Frankie and Libby were supposed to go straight home after the bell, but they never did. By now they knew every inch of Delancey and Hester, and they wandered farther and farther every day, sometimes right up to where the Irish lived. They always walked arm in arm, or with their arms about each other's waists, like the girls did around here. They looked an odd pair: Libby with her home-chopped red hair and green eyes and Frankie with her dark eyes and coal-black braids. They horseplayed all along the street; there was never any rush.

"Joey Robbins said he'd give me a penny for a kiss today," Frankie said.

"He never."

"He did."

"What did you say?"

"I said I'd do it for a nickel."

"I wouldn't kiss any boy, even for a dime, even for a whole dollar," Libby said. She wished only that Joey Robbins would ask her so that she could say no, but no boy ever did. Frankie was the prettiest girl in the class, everyone knew that. The one whose pigtails they always liked to tug on in class to make her turn and look.

Libby wished she looked more like her mother, with her beautiful dark eyes and long black hair, not long and skinny with this stupid red hair. Her mother kept it cropped short, but everyone could see what color it was. Other kids made jokes about her, called her a goy and told her she was adopted. She never told her mama about it, but it hurt just the same. She looked more goy than Frankie herself, whose father was from a place called Dublin.

Frankie told her to pay them no never mind and punch them with a fist if they kept it up. Sometimes she'd do it herself. "Don't you say that to my Lib," and whack! A real friend, was Frankie.

"Joey wanted to show me his weenie," Frankie said.

Libby laughed like she was being sick.

"I said, what do I want to see a weenie for? I said, I've seen a pink little worm before, my daddy baits his line with them when he goes fishing at Canarsie."

Where the Irish lived didn't look so different from Hester and Delancey if you looked up at the tenement buildings; feathered mattresses hung out of the windows like raggedy tongues gasping in the heat, and rags of every color were strung on the poles and hanging over the street like bunting, or draped over the fire escapes.

It was the streets that were different; there were no pushcarts or men in yarmulkes or shops selling candlesticks and pickles and *challah* bread. And the smells were different too; no sour rye bread baking, no tang of herring. Libby would have known Delancey Street even if she were blindfolded.

Up ahead there was a gang of kids on the footpath playing skully. They all had had their summer haircuts, clippers taken to the lot, some of them with scabs where their mothers had been careless with the shears. They wore long shorts and filthy caps at all angles on their heads, their older brothers, too old for the game, standing on the corners with their hands in their pockets, watching and looking for trouble. Some of them even had cigarette butts dangling from their bottom lips, even though they were not much older than her. She supposed they had filched them from the gutter. Their mothers would kill them if they ever found out.

One of them called out—she heard him say "Jewboy" and then shout the usual insults, sheeny and kike and she didn't know what.

"How do they know I'm Jewish?" she said to Frankie.

"They don't. It's me they're calling out to."

"You?"

"Sure, me. Which one of us you think looks more like a Jew? You're the one with the red hair."

There was a piece of coal lying in the gutter, and Frankie picked it up and threw it at them. "Go across yoursel', ya gobdaw dryshite!" They glared at her but shut up, confused.

Libby grabbed her arm and dragged her away. "What did you say to them?"

"It's something me daddy shouts at the people on the stairs. I've no idea what it means, but it always works for him."

They were almost at Rivington when Libby saw the penny gleaming in the gutter, and she dashed out and grabbed it; another kid had seen it too, but he was too late. She held it up triumphantly to Frankie. "Look what I got!"

The boy stepped out into the street in front of them and held out his hand. "That's my penny," he said.

"Well, it's not, because it's in my hand," Libby said.

"I said it's mine, now hand it over."

He was bigger than her, a big goy, perhaps twelve years old, a red-faced and piggy-eyed kid. She'd seen him before; he would stand outside the bathrooms at school and demand dimes from little boys to use them. Most of them didn't have a dime and couldn't hold it and ended up wetting their knickerbockers in the class.

"Go take your nonsense somewheres else, you pig-faced gombeen," Frankie said.

"What's a gombeen?"

"It's someone who's not getting my penny," Libby said.

"Would you be after hitting a girl now?" Frankie asked him.

"That's not a girl."

"Well, it is."

"Her hair's too short for a girl. She looks like a carrot."

Well, that did it for Libby. If she was even a tiny bit scared of him before, she was only mad now, and she bunched the penny in her fist and hit him as hard as she could on the nose.

He put a beefy hand to his face and seemed surprised by the trickle of blood on his fingers. He swung his other fist and took Libby on the side of her head and sent her sprawling. Frankie threw her arms around the bigger boy's neck and jumped on his back.

He twisted this way and that, trying to get her off. Libby jumped to her feet, kicked him in the shins, then in the groin, and finished off the fight by poking him hard in the left eye with her finger. He shrieked. Somebody shouted for a policeman.

They ran off.

It wasn't riches, but it wasn't to be wasted; a penny was a penny after all. They walked down Hester like ladies in furs walking along Broadway, staring at all the pushcarts and shops and trying to decide what to do with it. There were lots of hawkers selling balloons and penny whistles. But why spend their penny there when those were things their mothers might buy for them anyway? They felt sorry for the crippled soldier on the corner of Columbia, with one arm of his jacket pinned to the breast pocket, but they had no use for a necktie even if their solitary penny could buy one.

Finally, they stood outside a store on the corner of Willett Street; Libby looked at Frankie to see what she thought, but she just shrugged, undecided.

"You like pickles?" Libby said to her.

"I don't mind 'em," she said. "My daddy likes them with his beer, and sometimes he gives me one."

She went in. The man behind the counter had a dirty silk yarmulke and a long white beard. Libby was terrified of him; when she had first come in the shop with her mama when she was four years old, she had thought he was God, he looked so severe and bad tempered.

She put her penny on the counter.

The old man took it and held it up to the light, like he was sure it must be tin or a soda bottle top, then turned his scrutiny her way. "What happened to your eye?"

Libby touched her cheek with her fingertips. It was hot and swollen where the bigger boy had hit her. She would have a shiner in the morning.

"I walked into a door."

"Little pasty-faced *schlemiel* like you, you can't afford no bruises," he said. He picked up his big wooden fork. He stirred his vat of spiced vinegar and brought out a fat green-yellow pickle and slapped it on a piece of brown paper and handed it to her.

"*Dank!*" Libby shouted as she ran out. Outside, she tore the pickle in half and gave a piece to Frankie. Sucking on their pickles, they ran across the street and headed back toward the Williamsburg Bridge and home.

18

Sarah was shaking when she got home. She knocked on Mary's door. Mary took one look and led her into the front room and sat her down on the green plush parlor chair. "Whatever's wrong?" Mary said.

Sarah shook her head, not trusting herself not to cry, she wouldn't do that, not even in front of Mary.

"I know what you need," Mary said, and she went to the kitchen and came back with two teacups, half full. Sarah took one, almost gulped down what was in it, but then she smelled it and realized it was whiskey. "Dan won't miss it," Mary said. "Go on, have a sip, girl, it'll do you good. Now tell me, whatever's wrong?"

Sarah told her about Schonberg, about the man pinching her on the El. It was about then that they heard the girls on the stairs. Mary went to the door and told them to go off and play, it was too early for their dinner.

"I should go out and see her," Sarah said. "I've been gone all day."

"Lib and my Frankie are just fine. Now you drink your special tea and calm your nerves, girl."

Chevrons of light angled in through the blinds on the narrow windows; up here on the sixth floor, the noises of the street were muted, almost comforting. Sarah watched motes of dust drift in the yellow sunlight.

Mary stood there in the middle of the carpet with her hands on her hips, shaking her head.

"It's a stupid girl you got here, it's what you're thinking."

"No," Mary said. "What I was thinking was, it's a waste we got here. To be honest with you, I wouldn't mind a man pinching my behind on the El, but those days are long gone. Dan would rather have a beer than have me."

"Mary!"

"Well, it's not that I mind. Five kids is enough for me. But I miss him looking at me that way sometimes. I was never the beauty that you are, mind."

"I'm not a beauty, Mary. It's men that are the problem."

"It's men that are the problem around *you*, or have you not looked in a mirror lately?"

"I have, and what I see is a worn-out widow with chilblains." She held up her hands and noticed the rag on her finger where she had put a needle through it. She had quickly wrapped it with a scrap of fabric so she could keep working and not bleed on the goods.

"I'm twenty-six years old, Mary. What's the matter with these men?"

"Well, I know you're not a girl, but you're hardly an old crone either. I should love to have looked like you do at twenty-six when I was a colleen."

The door flew open, and more of Mary's kids came tumbling in, yelling and fighting, and she went out and shouted at them to be quiet and take themselves off back to the street and not to come back till suppertime.

When she came back, she said, "You should do something with those looks of yours before it's too late. How long has your husband been gone?"

"Four years only in July."

"That's long enough to be a widow."

"What's the use? Every man who comes around here, courting me, just wants someone to cook and clean for him. And what choice I got? Stan Kronsky, works in a hardware store. Moishe Brodsky, a furniture salesman. Sam Aaron! They don't got more than what I got. Besides, no decent man wants used goods."

"You're not used goods, Sarah."

"Where I come from, a man sees you new in the shop, you're worth new price. After that, he wants discount." She stared at the marble-topped table in the middle of the room, the framed photograph of a younger Mary in her wedding dress standing next to her husband, all proud of his big shoulders and big moustache. That was the way it was supposed to be, getting older together, not getting shot all to pieces and not even a body to pray *shibah* over.

She swallowed half the whiskey, enjoyed how it burned all the way down. "When I come to America, I dreamed I was going to wear beautiful dresses, not slave every day making such *schmatta* for someone else. You know what he does, that Schonberg? He pretends he can't figure, so when he adds up my slips, he always makes mistake, and at the end of the week, I am a dollar short. Always."

"Maybe you should find a job somewhere else."

"Where somewhere else, Mary? What if there is no somewhere else? Even one week and no money, Libby and me, we don't eat."

"You know, a woman like you, you should be a millionaire's wife, I've said to Dan over and over."

"No millionaire life out there for me. I do only what I got to do, every day, for Libby's sake."

Mary got up and went out. While she was gone, Sarah stared at the wallpaper, dark brown with cream stripes. It reminded her of the waistcoat jacket Schonberg wore every day. That disgusting man! How could she go back, how could she face another day?

Mary came back in holding a long and wicked-looking stainless-steel hat pin. She gave it to her.

"What is this?" Sarah asked her.

"It's insurance."

"Insurance?"

"First of all, Sarah, you got to learn to stand in the train without holding on to the strap. Keep your hands free every second, no matter where you are. And if that doesn't work, keep this in your hat. If you feel a man's hands on you, stick him good and hard with that."

Sarah stared at the pin with its gleaming point. "I couldn't use that," she said, and tried to give it back.

"Keep it anyway. And never say you couldn't do it, because you don't know yet if there's anything that can happen that's worse than having a man's hand on your bottom. All right?"

⟢

Frankie's mother bribed them a whole nickel to go off and play, and that gave them another problem: how to spend it.

They went back down to the street, lingered for a long time outside the bakery, staring through the window at the icebox cakes with their candied cherries and whipped cream, but they would need more than a nickel for one of those.

Then they heard the banana man wheeling his pushcart down the street, the fruit covered with a quilt to keep off the hot sun. "Ba-nan-as, ripe ba-nan-as, if you no got the mu-nee, you no get the bun-nee, ripe ba-nan-as!"

Libby knew they were a dime a dozen, but they bargained with him for six, three for Frankie and three for her. They went up onto the roof of the building to eat them, so pretty up there, all the sheets of washing like sails straining at their wooden clothespins, the overalls and dresses dancing in the spring breeze.

The iron of the Williamsburg Bridge cast its shadow over the river. They watched the trains and trolley cars inching over it, the sprawl of

Brooklyn on the far side, brown tenements huddled together just like theirs. Somehow up here, life didn't seem like such a jumble, it seemed like there really was a pattern to the chaos down there.

"Your ma was crying," Frankie said.

"My mama never cries."

"I saw her through the door."

Libby looked at her sidelong, not sure whether to believe her, felt a bit scared that perhaps she was right. "Why would my mama be crying?"

"Perhaps she's missing your da?"

"My papa died years ago."

Frankie was quiet, thinking about this. "What happened to him?"

"He died in the war."

"Was he a hero?"

"Of course he was a hero. He killed thirty Germans with his bare hands, Mama said."

Frankie finished her banana, started to peel another. "My da didn't fight in the war, because he had us to look after." When Libby didn't answer, she said, "Do you remember your daddy?"

"I remember him carrying me on his shoulders once. At a parade. But every day he gets a bit further away, and I think, maybe I'm remembering, or maybe I'm just making it up. Mama says he was at work a lot."

"Was he rich?"

"I guess not."

"Our da works all the time, but we're not rich. Last night I heard Ma call him a gombeen, and an eejit. She says we could all buy a house on Long Island with the money he spends on the drink. I'd like a house on Long Island. I'd like a house anywhere, I guess. It'd be nice to have a rich daddy, instead of a gombeen. What would you do if you had a rich daddy?"

Libby finished her bananas and wiped her mouth with the back of her hand. Down below, people were coming out to sit on their stoops: women with babies; men with their cigarettes and pipes; little kids running in and out of doors with a few coins clenched in their fists, running home again with little newspaper-wrapped bundles from the grocer's and butcher shop.

"What I want," Libby said, "you can't buy with money."

"And what's that?"

"I want to be beautiful," she said. "Like my mama."

⟞⟝

The sun was already set when Libby went downstairs to the apartment. Sarah took one look at her and shook her head. "And what is it you've been doing? Look at the dirt on you. And where do you get that bruise on your face?"

"I fell over."

"Been fighting again you mean. What was it this time?"

"I wasn't fighting."

"You fight in the street like I don't know what, then you lie to your mother. What am I going to do with you? Look at you. You need a bath. Anyone think I got myself a schvartze for a daughter, the color of you."

Libby hated baths. The bath was soapstone with a hinged wooden cover, and the bottom of it was so rough it made her bottom sore, and she could never get in or out of it without giving her back a good whack on the faucet. The one thing she remembered about their old place in Delancey Street was the wooden tub on the floor; even though it was tiny and you had to heat the water on the stove, at least she wouldn't get out of it with welts on her back and a sore behind.

But she did as she was told and sat there while her mother washed her face and hair with soap. Her mama was angry with her and so she was rough, not like usual. Libby winced as she pulled her this way and that.

"What were you doing after school?"

"Frankie and me, we went up to East Village. We watched some Italians playing this game in a park with like cannon balls, and then we saw a man shoeing a horse in a garage."

"You never thought to come home and help out with the washing and ironing? You're old enough now. I have no one to help me after I come home from working all day."

Libby looked up at her mother, tried not to get soap in her eyes. Frankie was right, something was wrong. Her mama's eyes were red, like she'd been rubbing them, and there was this hard look on her face, like the rabbi got when he talked about God's commandments. Still, she was right, she hadn't given any of that a thought.

"You can finish washing yourself, and then it's time for bed."

"Will you read me a story?"

"Not tonight. Now go on and hurry up."

"Mama."

"What?"

"It wasn't Papa's fault."

"What wasn't his fault?"

"He didn't mean to die in the war. Don't be mad at him."

"I'm not mad at him. What made you think that?"

Libby shrugged.

"No, bubeleh, it wasn't his fault. He always tried to do right by us. Now hurry up with you."

Libby got out of the bath, forgetting about the faucet and scraping her back as she always did, and then took herself to bed.

⟩⟨

Next morning she woke up early—it was still dark—even too early for the pushcart sellers. She tiptoed out the door and down to the street, went searching through all the ash cans and picking out pieces of unburned coal and putting them into a tin bucket. Then she went over to the spare lot on Broome Street and found a few pieces of scrap wood for the boiler. It would provide coal for the stove, for cooking only, but that would be enough in such hot weather.

Sarah was just awake when Libby crept back into the apartment. She sat up in bed, startled. "Libby? What time is it? Where have you been?"

Libby showed her the half pail of coal she'd collected and the wood for the boiler. When Sarah saw it, she hugged her so hard she couldn't breathe. She was crying, Libby could feel the wetness on her neck.

"You silly girl!"

"I'm sorry I didn't do the ironing, Mama. Don't be mad at me for forgetting."

"It's all right, it's all right. Forget only the ironing! You're just a little kid, bubeleh! That you should ever go out in the dark morning like that again. Promise me."

Libby promised. Her mama. She couldn't never work her out.

⋯⋯⋯⋯

It was a Sunday, no work, no school. Sarah sent Libby off to play with Frankie and then sat by the window, staring at the Williamsburg Bridge, listening to the church bells ringing, all the Italians and Irish off to church. Frankie'd go off to Mass with her brothers and sisters soon, so when Libby came back, she promised herself she would make her a good breakfast, perhaps spoil her and take her to Katz's, buy her a chocolate soda.

She had a biscuit box on her lap, the one she had found under the bed with the rest of Micha's private things when he didn't come back from that stupid war. "Holmes and Coutts," it said. "Famous English Biscuits." She opened the box, took out the newspaper cutting that

Micha had kept in it with his other private things. It was yellowed and creased now, and she was careful not to tear it.

She stared at the grainy photograph of George Seabrook, read all the words underneath—she could read and write English as good as any American now.

WANTED

$5000 (five thousand) REWARD

BABY GIRL

Missing since 3rd March, 1913

MR. GEORGE SEABROOK

of Lexington House, Boston, Massachusetts

offers $5000 for any information leading to the whereabouts of missing infant.

Following the fire which destroyed the Grand Central Hotel on Park Avenue, New York, no bones of the missing child were found in the ashes and ruins. Her mother, Mrs. Clare Seabrook, was identified among the deceased, but no trace of the baby was found.

If you are in possession of any information regarding this event, please communicate with the undersigned.

George R. Seabrook

She didn't really need to read it; she knew it all by heart.

Why did Micha steal that man's baby? She supposed she would never know. Whatever he had done, the secret had died with him.

Five thousand dollars! A fortune. Why hadn't anyone claimed it? The date on the cutting, it was two months after the fire, but no one in her block could read the English papers, and even if they did, how would they know? Only Tessie Fischer, from the tenement. She had looked after the baby that night. She was the only one who might have worked it out, and not a word from her. Had she suspected? Who knew, she was dead now from the consumption, not long after her Micha was killed in the war, so there was no one but her who knew about it, she supposed.

Micha, Micha, what did you do? Almost four years she had lived with this. Every morning, since she found the box, she had woken up and thought: I must write to this George Seabrook. I must tell him what has happened. But every day she thought: Not today. One more day with my beautiful daughter. I'll tell him tomorrow.

"You're never going to tell him, are you?" she said aloud. What kind of woman, what kind of person, does such a thing? This kind of person, that's who.

How could she give her back? Libby was a part of her now. What a mother I am, such a woman. My Libby, she should be living in a fine house, going to a nice school, with servants and nice things, not living in this dirty tenement with a smelly toilet in the yard and noise from the street all the day and night.

She knew they all talked about her down in the street, at the water pump, and up on the roof, putting out the washing and gossip, gossip, gossip. *"That Sarah Levine,"* she imagined them saying, *"I heard her husband, that one that died in the war, he was a shtetl Jew just like her, and have you seen her daughter? How do you think they got her?"*

She rehearsed in her head all the time what she would say, *"Yes, there are Jews with red hair. She's a gingit. What's wrong with that?"* What about Esau, what about David, the greatest Jew of them all? They had had red hair! But how will you explain the green eyes to them, Sarah?

All that time, Micha said not a word to her. But what if he had, that very first night? What would she have done? She could pretend: Oh, I would have told him, *"You must tell someone about this. We cannot keep the baby."* But what you think you will do, what you really do, these are two different things.

She put the cutting back in the box and closed her eyes. "Oh, Liberty, if you can only forgive him for what he did," she murmured. "For what we both did. You're going to have good life, the life you should have had, only better. I will make it up to you, bubeleh. You see if I don't."

19

All that week Sarah took care never to be alone with Mr. Schonberg.
She could feel his eyes on her, but she made sure never to look back.
It was not until Thursday, close to finishing-up time, that he stopped
by her bench. He waited there, looking down at her until she had no
choice but to look up at him.

"Come and see me when you finish," he said.

This is it, she thought. He will fire me now. She didn't know if she
was happy or terrified.

When the bell went off, the clatter of the sewing machines stopped,
and it was quiet except for the scraping of stools as the rest of the girls
got up from their benches and went to the cloakroom for their hats and
bags. Sarah stitched her last turn and then went over to Mr. Schonberg
at his desk in the corner. It was hot and stuffy in the workroom, and
her dress was damp against her back.

Mr. Schonberg pushed a note and some coins across the desk.

"What is this?" she asked him.

"It is a dollar and fifty-five cents. Didn't you say you were good at
figuring?"

Sarah hesitated.

"It's what I owe you, girl. Go on, take it."

"Why did you make me wait?" she said.

"I could ask you the same thing," he said, which made no sense to her.

This is a no-good thing, she thought, but she snatched the money off the desk and hurried to the cloakroom. She didn't want to be too far behind the other girls.

She got her hat and her bag and hurried toward the door. The last of the girls were clustered around the elevator doors just as they were opening. If she hurried, she could catch up with them.

Kohn put out a hand to stop her. "I have to check your bag," he said.

It was like this every day, a company rule, make sure you did not steal any scraps for yourself. The misers, the skinflints! She waited while he took his time looking in her bag.

"I will miss the elevator," she said, and tried to push past him.

"Your pockets," he said.

"I never touch anything, you know that."

"Your pockets."

The elevator doors were shutting. The girls' chatter was suddenly shut off.

"I don't have pockets on a shirtwaist! I will miss the elevator."

"Elevator is out of service."

"Out of service? But I saw it right then."

"You have to use the stairs," he said.

She tried to shove past him, but he wouldn't budge.

"The stairs," he said. "No elevator today."

She looked over her shoulder. Mr. Schonberg wasn't at his desk. She felt her heart start to race. "How much did he pay you?" she said.

Kohn shook his head and pointed to the door. "The fire stairs," he repeated.

She felt herself start to shake. What could she do? She looked back at the elevator, praying that Max or one of the cutters would come back, like last time. Kohn almost shoved her toward the stairs. "Go home now," he said.

She found herself out on the stairs. The door slammed behind her. She looked down. It was quiet and gloomy, six floors of staircase echoing. Go down quick as you can, she told herself. You can see the bottom from here; you can do it if you hurry.

She started down, her heels echoing on the stairs. She had reached the landing on the fifth floor when Schonberg appeared right there in front of her from nowhere, he must have been waiting in the alcove. He had a look on his face, like he hadn't eaten for days and he was desperate. His cheeks were shining and his eyes too.

He didn't say anything, just grabbed her. She screamed and tried to twist away. But she knew there was no one to hear her, only Kohn, and Kohn had been paid not to hear anything.

Schonberg's arms went around her and held her tight. He was strong for such a schmendrick of a man. "You know you want it. The way you tease me, you think I don't know what you like?"

She felt his hardness against her bottom, his hands tearing at her shirtwaist. All she could think was: If he tears it, I won't be able to go home. Can't get on the El if he tears my dress.

"Don't," she said.

He pulled up her skirt and dragged her down to her knees. He was trying to pull down her drawers while he held her with the other hand. She pushed his hand away, then reached over her shoulder to scratch his face. He was grunting like a pig the whole time, and she could smell his bad breath, the reek of rotten teeth and the onions from his lunch.

She remembered the pin that Mary had given her. He had knocked her hat on the ground when he grabbed her, but it was right there, just within reach; she pulled it toward her with her right hand and found the pin and pulled it free. She thought he must see what she was doing and stop her, but he was too busy undoing his belt, getting out his hard thing, making a noise almost like he was crying.

There was a moment then that she might have done worse, if she had wanted; she had the pin in her hand, she could jab back hard into his belly, or his eye, maybe she would kill him. Bad enough what she did, she supposed, a quick stab back into his groin, he was not expecting, she heard him scream high and shrill like some animal scalded with boiling water.

He let her go straightaway, and she scrambled to her feet, grabbed her hat and bag, and lifted up her long skirt so that she could jump past him. Schonberg lay on his side on the ground, all curled up and kicking, both his hands between his legs. His mouth and eyes were wide open, but he was seeing nothing except his own pain.

She didn't stop to see what she had done. She ran down the rest of the stairs and out onto Thirty-Fourth Street, and in a blink she was rushing away toward the Elevated. She expected to hear someone shouting after her, police whistles maybe, but there was just the usual rush and hurry of after-work crowds. Whatever happens, she thought, I will never be coming to work here again. Even if tomorrow is payday.

He can have my seven dollars and welcome to it. But he's cheated me for the last time.

<hr />

"Did you kill him?" Mary asked her.

"I don't know," Sarah said. "But I think I done him a terrible damage."

"Well, serves him right, then," Mary said, and she went to fetch the whiskey and the teacups.

"What am I going to do?" Sarah said. "All week I work for that schmuck and what I got? I got *bopkes* is what I got! Always it is like this. The rich they don't have to worry, the poor they got to prove they're alive!"

"Why don't you do your sewing and stitching yourself?" Mary said. "Everyone needs clothes to wear."

"I tried this before, after Micha died. How do I ever make enough money? I can't. That is why I go to work for Schonberg."

Mary chewed her bottom lip. "Well. There are other employers, not only this Schonberg." Mary lowered her voice, like the whole street might be listening to them. "I've got a friend works at the New Amsterdam Theatre."

"The Follies," Sarah said, with a little frown to show she didn't approve.

"She works there as a dresser. She helps the girls in and out of their gowns."

"I heard they don't wear gowns," Sarah said. "They wear whatever God gave them, plus a tassel."

"It's a lot more glamorous than you think. The thing is, my friend says one of the girls in the seamstress department is leaving, and they'll need a new girl."

"Me?"

"Job's made for you."

"Sewing little bits onto another girl's little bits? That's a job?"

"Sarah, you sound like my grandmother. It's only a show. It's not like working in a bawdy house. And you're a wiz with a needle and a bit of cotton. Look at all the dresses you made me, they're as good as anything you'd find in Macy's."

Sarah sipped her whiskey. Her hands were still shaking. She thought about Schonberg, wondered if she'd killed him with that pin in his you-know-whats. Any minute the police would come beating down her door and take her away to the big house. Why was she worrying about a job?

Then what would happen to little Libby?

"He's starting a new show," Mary said.

"Who is starting a new show?"

"Ziegfeld. So look here, my girl, I want you to get yourself down there first thing in the morning. Now drink up your whiskey. Time to celebrate a new start."

Sarah finished her whiskey, eyes screwed shut to the taste and the burning. All right, if she woke up in the morning and she wasn't in the big house, she'd take herself downtown to Broadway and talk to this Mr. Ziegfeld about sewing him new dresses.

What did she have to lose?

20

The New Amsterdam was up Broadway on West Forty-Second. A tall, skinny building, it looked like it had popped out of a toaster; only the massive Candler Building a few doors down stopped it from looking totally ridiculous.

The front of it, from a distance, looked like a slice of wedding cake, and the entrance like the doors of some enchanted castle, with all the statues and pillars and carvings, which is what she supposed Mr. Ziegfeld liked about it.

There was a long queue of girls outside, it went right around the block, some of them tearing at each other's hair and swinging their bags. All the mad pushing was so bad that there were three burly policemen with wooden clubs trying to keep all the girls in line and waiting for their turn.

Sarah had never seen so many big-bosomed long-legged women in one place. They couldn't all be here for the seamstress job.

She pushed her way to the uniformed man at the door. He shoved her aside with his elbow. "Get to the back, sister."

"Do I look like a dancing girl, you big *yok*? Ilsa, the seamstress, needs a girl who can sew good."

He looked her up and down. "You can sew?"

"What else you think I can do?"

He grinned. "I don't know, sister, you look like you can do plenty." He saw the look on her face, and he jerked his thumb over his shoulder. "To the left and down the stairs. Watch out, she bites."

"So do I," Sarah said. The girls at the front of the queue squealed in protest when he let her through. Sarah breathed a sigh of relief. Such craziness! After all this time she still didn't believe this America, where women would scratch and scream for a chance to take off their clothes in public.

The inside of the New Amsterdam looked like an expensive hotel, with its plush carpets and fancy pilasters and painted ceilings. She went down a long corridor, like the man at the door had told her, saw two older men coming toward her in nice suits and waistcoats, smoking cigars. One of them stopped and pointed at her. He was dapper; she noticed the cut of his suit first, hand-tailored, and such stitches. He had a long nose, thick lips, big personality, like if he wasn't boss of the world, then he was at least floor supervisor. "You!"

She froze.

He walked straight up to her and looked her up and down; but he didn't look like Schonberg looked. It was like he was pricing her by the yard. He nodded, puffed on his cigar, and said to the other man: "Get her on a contract." Then he walked away, toward the auditorium.

Sarah didn't know what to make of it. The other man puffed out his cheeks and shrugged. "I guess you're hired," he said.

"Don't I talk to Ilsa first? Let her see how good I can sew?"

"Sew? What do you want to sew for?"

"For the job."

"You from Kansas?"

"Russia."

"That explains it. This way, sweetheart."

He led her up some stairs to a cramped first-floor office. He sat her down and closed the door behind them. Sarah felt for the hat pin, just in case.

But he didn't want funny business. Instead, he opened a drawer in the desk and took out a pile of contracts and a fountain pen. He asked her for her name and her address. He filled in the spaces on the paper, then pushed it toward her. "Read it through if you want, but it's a standard contract. Mr. Ziegfeld doesn't change them for anyone. Only the performers ever get to negotiate."

"You want me to sign a contract to be a seamstress?"

They stared at each other.

"You want to be in the Follies, right?"

"The Follies?"

"That is why you're here?"

"I take off my clothes for my husband, even then, strictly in the dark."

He shook his head, like he was not hearing right. "You see the line of girls out the front? Any one of them would give their right arm to have Flo pick them for the Follies, lady."

"I need my right arm to sew with."

He took back the contract. "Well, if there's somewhere else you can earn seventy-five a week, you better hurry over there."

"Wait," Sarah said. "Seventy-five? Dollars?"

"Sure, seventy-five dollars. What else you want to get paid in, ice pops?"

"Wait with the contract. Give me a minute."

"I don't have a minute."

"But, mister, I can't dance to save my life."

"You won't be in the chorus line. All you have to do is walk. You can walk, can't you?"

"I can, but I'm not expert." She pulled the contract back across the desk. "Mister whatever your name is—"

"Brown. Fred Brown."

"Mr. Brown. You want I should take off my clothes in front of everyone in New York?"

131

"No, not everyone in New York. Not everyone in New York can afford a ticket. And we don't ask any of our girls to take *all* their clothes off. That would be distasteful to Mr. Ziegfeld." He jabbed a finger on a page in the contract. "That only happened at the Frolics, and Mr. Ziegfeld has dropped the midnight show this year."

"Seventy-five dollars. Every week?"

"That's standard."

"For walking."

"Miss . . ." He looked at the contract to remind himself. "Levin."

"Levine."

"Levine. You're not getting paid for walking. You're getting seventy-five mazumas a week for looking like the perfect woman."

"According to who?"

"According to Mr. Ziegfeld. He's the world's leading authority."

Sarah stared at Fred Brown and then back at the contract. She thought about what she and Libby could do with seventy-five dollars every week.

"Lady, you just happened to be in the right place at the right time, and there's something about you, I don't know what it is he wants, but you must have it." He put his elbows on the desk and leaned forward. "You don't have to sing, you don't have to dance, you're not Fanny Brice or Lilly Lorraine. You're a stage prop, that's it." He held up the contract. "You want me to tear this up?"

She snatched it out of his hand, unscrewed the pen, and scribbled her signature at the bottom before Mr. Ziegfeld or Mr. Brown could change their minds.

He blew on the ink and put the contract in the drawer. "One thing. Don't go spending the whole seventy-five on champagne and diamonds. The contract stipulates you gotta look like a Ziegfeld girl twenty-four hours a day. That means you don't take the trolley to work, you don't go into restaurants or even walk down the street without gloves and a hat and heels. A Ziegfeld girl is never ever off stage. You understand?"

"I'm a Ziegfeld girl now?"

He checked his fob. "Anything else? I have to get back to work. Mr. Ziegfeld has to hire a chorus line today."

"And now a girl to help out in the costumes," Sarah said.

"Yeah, looks like it."

When she left, there was still a mob of girls outside the theater. She walked away in a daze. What's a good Jewish girl doing taking a job in just her birthday suit and maybe a hat? What would her vati say if he ever found out?

She should be ashamed. But she didn't feel ashamed. What she felt for the first time in her life was rich.

Seventy-five dollars a week!

⟞≡⟝

Sarah made the long slow climb up the tenement stairs. Most days she got to the top with her lungs on fire and her legs shaking like they were made of Jell-O, but not today. Today she was laughing when she reached the top landing. She had seventy-five dollars a week. She could have run to the top of the Liberty statue.

She stopped laughing when she saw Libby slumped against the door to the apartment, her head on her knees. "Libby," she said and bent down to see what was wrong. "Lib, what is it, bubeleh, are you hurt?"

"It's nothing," Libby said, and wiped her nose on her sleeve.

"If this is nothing, what is something? You having a bad time at the *shul*? Is it your teacher?"

"I like my teacher."

"The kids, then. What they saying to you?"

Libby, her little green-eyed, flame-haired little Liberty, looked up at her and said: "Why don't I look Jewish?"

"Who's saying to you, you don't look Jewish?"

"You want the name of every single kid in my school?"

"You don't take any mind to such stupid talk. Of course you are Jewish."

"But I *don't* look Jewish, Mama, do I? I don't look like you!"

"You got your father's Jewishness."

"Do I?"

Libby glared at her. Sarah knew that look, that prove-it-to-me look. Well, what did you think, Sarah? Did you think she was never going to ask? "Come inside," she said. "Good little Jewish girls don't talk back to their mamas out on the landing, where everyone can hear their business. Even good little Jewish girls with not much Jewishness."

Sulky, Liberty got to her feet and followed Sarah into the apartment. She slumped into a chair in the tiny kitchen, hugged herself with her arms, her eyes on the cracked linoleum floor.

"Why are there no pictures of Papa around?" she said.

"I don't like to be reminded."

"You mad at him?"

"I'm not mad," Sarah said. "All right, maybe still a little bit mad. Why did he have to go away to the stupid war? You think it is easy, bringing up a kid all by myself? This isn't even my country. Russia is my country."

"Doesn't mean you can't have a picture on the wall, on the mantel, somewhere."

Sarah went to the big dresser in her bedroom, sorted through the carved wooden box where she kept all her private things, and took out a tiny black-and-white photograph: Micha, sitting down, in his soldier's uniform, her beside him, scowling at the photographer, Liberty in a smock on her knee, one hand stretched out, like she was reaching for the camera.

She gave it to Libby, who stared at it for a long time. Years since she had last seen it. "He doesn't look like me."

"Sure, he looks like you."

"Why doesn't he have red hair?"

"What do you know from red hair when the photograph is black-and-white? Sure, your vati had red hair. He was Ashkenazi."

"What's that?"

"It's a kind of Jewish person that has red hair. He had green eyes too, just like you. I put you in a uniform and soldier hat, no one will ever tell the difference."

"Was he nice?"

Sarah felt as if she had swallowed a stone. How to explain Micha to her? Half the things her husband had done, she didn't know that he had, or why he had done them. Was he nice? Good question. "He loved you like nobody's business," Sarah said.

"Can I keep this?"

Sarah was about to say, but it's the only picture I have of all of us, but she stopped herself. "Sure, you can have the picture," she said. "Put it wherever. Now, enough of this crying. You want some good news? I got a new job today. So how about you get your friend Frankie, and we'll all go to Katz's to celebrate."

❦

"You can have anything you want," she told them. They stood on the corner, looking at the fat salamis hanging in the window. Frankie looked up at the "Katz's That's All!" sign painted on the bricks and asked Sarah what it meant, and she told her she didn't know.

"What's that she's eating?" Frankie said, pointing to a woman sitting at one of the tables near the window.

"Bagel and lox," Libby said.

"What's a lox?"

"It's fish," Sarah said. "Fish in a sandwich."

"Have they got any normal food?"

They went inside. It was full of people on their way to the theaters on Second Avenue. Libby thought she saw Ludwig Satz.

"What do you know from Ludwig Satz?" Sarah asked her.

"He's a famous actor."

"I never heard of him," Frankie said.

"He's Jewish," Libby said.

The waiter came. Libby stared at her menu. "You can have anything you want," Sarah said.

"Really anything?"

Libby and Frankie looked at each other with suspicion.

"Can we have a chocolate soda?"

"What else you want?"

"Mama, you said you lost your job."

"Well, I got another one."

"What kind of job?"

"It's in the theater."

"Will you be on stage with Molly Picon?"

"Not the theater here. On Broadway."

"Are you going to be an actress?"

"No, not an actress. I'm just helping with the play."

"What do you mean?"

"Don't worry what I mean. Means I will be out at night, but at the end of the week, there will be more money for us. We don't struggle anymore."

The girls did not look convinced. They read their menus like they were studying the Torah, and finally decided on franks and beans. Some night out, Sarah thought. Living like royalty we all are. In the end it turned out what they both really wanted was an icebox cake from the baker's on the way home.

When Sarah tucked Libby into bed that night, she told her what a life they would have, a millionaire life with real cloth tablecloths on the table and a marble bathtub, not a sore-bottom one, and hot water already in the tap so they wouldn't have to heat it, and they could take a bath whenever they wanted, and even new towels, fluffy white ones like they saw in the Broadway department stores, not old rags.

There is good luck on us now, she told her. There is coming good times. Just wait and see!

21

If this was millionaire life, then she would rather have a pushcart in the street. Already she worked longer than she had for Mr. Schonberg in the shirtwaist shop.

Twelve-hour days she worked, and this was only rehearsal. Mr. Ziegfeld made them rehearse a hundred times until it was perfect, and only when it was perfect, they must rehearse a hundred times more.

But before they could even rehearse, they had to get into their costumes. And such costumes they had. Even though it was nothing much, it would not do but the nothing much they wore must be designed by big-shot designers like Lady Duff Gordon. Every new number they would have a new costume, all chiffon and pearls with a glittering headdress. Even naked was no good on its own. Mr. Ziegfeld said a woman's leg looked more naked in a silk stocking than for-real naked. That was the way he was.

Go figure.

So even when they had to go out wearing just a bit of fluff, the fluff had to be right. He would fuss over every girl. Should this piece of chiffon go over the right or left shoulder, no not like that, I can see too much of your bubbies that way, you will get us all arrested! You have to make them wonder, you can't let them *see*.

This Mr. Ziegfeld, he had an eye for a beautiful girl, she thought; and such figures some of the girls had, from as young as seventeen they were. She didn't know what they were doing with an old woman like her, but she must have something, she guessed, even if she didn't know what it was.

And there were all sorts of girls: the ones fresh from Kansas, she could still see the hayseeds in their ears; schoolteachers tired of screaming at brats and getting chalk under their pretty painted nails; cashiers cashing in on themselves.

There was nothing to what they did, sitting on cardboard cutout moons or walking down stairs. But a certain way they had to walk. Mr. Ziegfeld told them over and over, you arc showgirls, not chorus girls. You don't have to touch your noses with your knees, only walk; well, some of those blonde girls from Kansas, Sarah thought, that was challenge enough.

He made them walk with their arms out, like they were trying to fly or she didn't know what, and it wasn't as easy as it looked, not with feathers and pearls piled on her head like a person would need an elevator to get to the top of it.

He taught them the Lucile Slither that he learned from Lady Gordon, and then there was the Ziegfeld Walk, a way to come down stairs and look like you were going on your wedding night at the same time.

"Don't smile," he shouted at her. "Don't laugh. Don't even think. You must look aloof, like you won't even give Rockefeller the time of day."

So she pretended to herself that she had eaten too many potato latkes and her stomach was hurting, and Mr. Ziegfeld shouted, "Yes, like that. You got it." So that's how she always tried to look when she was on stage, pretending she'd eaten too many latkes.

She didn't know how much he spent on the show, but she figured it was more than the czar spent to throw a grand ball at the palace in Saint Petersburg. He spent money to make money, he said, a big lesson in life.

And he could spend like nobody's business. Some of the old hands said he had three gold telephones on his desk and his own private railcar. His favorite dinner was liver and onions, like her Micha, only Micha's knife and fork weren't made of twenty-four-thousand-carat diamonds.

The girls also said he didn't sleep until he'd *shtupped* each and every one of his leading ladies, but to her and the rest of the showgirls, he behaved almost like a rabbi.

All the day she spent learning to be glamorous, but by the time she was finished, there was no more glamorous left in her. She got home late at night, climbing the tenement stairs in the dark with a coat buttoned up over her silk stockings and almost-nothing dress. More and more, Libby wasn't even there to kiss good-night—she started sleeping next door in Frankie's bed—and she didn't see her sometimes for days. But she told herself: For seventy-five dollars every week, I can manage.

＝＝＝

The show opened in June with some big-name stars; there was Will Rogers, a real gentleman, and Mary Eaton, a looker with her blonde Marcel wave. There was Mr. Gallagher and Mr. Shean; they were the big-hit act—two funny guys who could sing and spiel like nobody's business. And there was that Gilda Gray, shaking her shimmy and making a sensation of herself.

Sarah peered between the curtains before the show started, staring at all the men in their dinner suits, their women glittering with diamonds. At least no one from Delancey Street out there to see her and call her *kurveh*.

And what a theater, full of rich people and all lit up. The seats were all red velvet plush. Puffy clouds were painted on the ceiling, like heaven would look while you are waiting to see God. There were peacocks made of marble and big as houses, all watching from between the balconies and the fancy pillars. Maybe the czar himself could see such a place and not think it remarkable, but for a girl from Tallinn, she could not believe life had brought her there.

And then it started: first there was a number that made fun of all the latest revues with schvartzes, "It's Getting Awful Dark on Old Broadway"; and then there was a girl, Evelyn, she could cross the stage on one leg while wagging a disapproving finger at the other—which she had raised above her head. You think the men didn't like that?

Such different theater it was. No shouting at the stage and no drinking and no eating and no babies crying like in the Jewish theaters on Second. And the music was so catchy. She always liked the songs by that Mr. Berlin.

And then it was her turn.

That first time was the hardest. Mr. Brown came around backstage and gave them their final instructions while they waited for the curtain to go up. They were all dressed in not much more than a few rosebuds and spangles. They would all have got arrested on Coney Island. "Lean," he said. "Pose," he said. "Don't move," he said. "If you even so much as wiggle one of your bazoomas, you're fired."

As if I am going to wiggle a bazooma, Sarah thought. I'm a good Jewish girl. I shouldn't even be anywhere near Broadway this time of night, let alone be here with my bazoomas.

But when it started, it wasn't so hard. In the glare of the footlights, she couldn't see anything, so she thought only of the bad-potato-latkes look that Mr. Ziegfeld liked, and the seventy-five dollars at the end of the week, and no one from the Lower East Side out there, just fancy people who would never even know her in the street. They would never ever be in any street she would walk down anyway.

It was bright lights and singing and clapping and music, and that was it. The rest of the night, all she had to do was walk up and down stairs in a cardboard fruit salad with a battleship on her head made from silk and lace.

Her first night on Broadway. She was a Follies girl.

✦

Sure, she worked harder than she had for Schonberg, but at least she didn't have to squint in the bad light, and no one pinched her bottom or clipped her wages. In the mornings she made Libby her eggs for breakfast, then wrapped her lunch in brown paper and sent her off to school. She had time only to get dressed and take a taxicab to the theater.

Rehearse, get dressed, do the show. Afterward many of the girls got presents delivered. There were so many long-stemmed roses in the dressing room, she could have opened a flower shop. Other girls got little velvet boxes with diamonds in them. Sarah knew what a girl did to get presents like that, and it wasn't wash and iron.

She made a friend, Evie; she had been a Follies girl for three years. She knew the ropes, kept asking her to go out with her after the show, but Sarah always said no, she had to get home. She went scurrying back to the Lower East Side, there in the shadow of the Williamsburg Bridge, like Cinderella hurrying back to the rags and the scullery mice after the ball.

22

"Look," Evie said to her. "The seventy-five a week will only last as long as the show runs. Then what you gonna do? You're back to the grindstone, girl. If you're smart, you want to trade in your chips for a long-term investment. You with me? You better get used to the idea that you don't stop work when the curtain closes."

"I'm tired."

"You can be tired when you're old and fat. We're all tired, honey. But this won't last. You have to find yourself a more permanent position."

"What are their names, these more permanent positions?"

"Wilson and Dewey."

"They sound like vaudeville, they should be spieling up on stage."

"This vaudeville act are two of the most eligible bachelors in New York. They both run banks on Wall Street."

Sarah pulled off her headdress, and when that was done, she had hardly anything more to change out of. She put on her step-ins and reached for her new dress. She had made it herself to save money; she told everyone it was from Bergdorf, and to her astonishment they all believed her. It had a long hem, because that was the latest thing, and was made of chiffon and silver spangles she had found in a shop on Hester Street. It was sleeveless, of course, and it had a plunging back. If her vati could see her, he'd tear out his beard with his fingernails. Well, what Vati never knew would never hurt him.

She didn't need much else except some bangles; she didn't need to strap up like some of the other girls; she was a perfect shape for the new fashion. Once, no one would look at a girl if she didn't have big bubbies. Now everyone did.

"So what do you say?" Evie asked her.

"I say dokeyokey, let's do it."

"Good girl. And it's okeydokey. Okeydoke?"

⟨≡⟩

It was a sweltering night on West Forty-Second Street. The usual fancy-schmancy cars were parked outside, their coachwork shining under the electric foyer lights: a mustard-yellow Rolls-Royce, a Duesenberg, a royal-blue Peugeot convertible. The doormen were shouting the owners' names: Guggenheim, Vanderbilt, Hutton.

Most nights Sarah charged out the door, past the hordes of men waiting there with flowers, all looking for a Ziegfeld girl to escort to a party out at Great Neck or a club on the Upper East Side.

Tonight, as she strolled out arm in arm with Evie, she thought: Okeydoke, don't feel so guilty, girl. Remember what Evie told you: you are still working.

Two men in white scarves and tuxedos called to them.

Evie waved back. "All set," she said to them. "Sarah, this is Wilson, and this handsome gentleman is Dewey. Okay, boys. Let's show this showgirl a good time."

⟨≡⟩

Down dark basement stairs in an anonymous row of brownstones, from somewhere Sarah heard the faint sound of drums and a trumpet. Dewey tapped on a beat-up door, and when it opened, the noise from behind it was suddenly deafening. They crowded inside.

The speakeasy was all red velvet curtains and ornate chandeliers and bare brick walls. The foursome was escorted to a table with two curtained-off couches and dirty white lamps with strings to turn them on and off. Wilson ordered champagne. It would just be apple cider and cost the same as Taittinger, but at least they wouldn't end up in the hospital—Evie said the gin in some of the smaller places was pure moonshine and could kill you quicker than arsenic.

Sarah looked around. There was a stuffed antelope head on the wall right above them, in between a raccoon and a bear wearing a bowler hat. Only in America do bears have bowler hats, she thought; in Russia, lots of bears. Never seen one with headwear.

Straight off it was plain to her that Evie had a crush on Wilson. She claimed him first, putting her arm though his and snuggling up on the banquette. It looked like Sarah's date was going to be Dewey. He ordered an Alexander.

"Your friend doesn't say much," he said to Evie.

"She don't speak much English," Evie said, which was such a big lie.

"Where is she from?"

"She's Russian," Evie said, answering for her. "Her cousin was a countess."

Sarah listened to this wide eyed. Her cousin milked cows and sold potatoes at the market in Tallinn, same as she did.

"A real live countess," Wilson said, and whistled, easier to impress than his pal Dewey, who just shrugged, like being a countess was bargain basement.

Sarah studied their dates. Their single-breasted tuxedos had thin-notched lapels, with two buttonholes on either side held together with coat links. Wilson, who looked a lot younger than his companion, was a real goy, with fair hair and a fat money clip that he liked to show off. He looked like he bathed in banker's drafts.

The other one, Dewey, he didn't say much. He was shorter and stockier, and he had wire-rimmed glasses. With his snappy little polka-dot bow tie, he looked more like a bank clerk than a bank president.

Sarah tried to brazen it out, listened while Wilson talked about the parties they had been to out on Long Island, the fancy yachts they took sailing, and animals she had never heard of that they had shot at, tramping in the woods. She sipped her champagne and remembered Follies lessons: think about too many latkes and look like you're too good for them.

When they had finished their drinks, both men looked at their watches and said it was time to go to a party on the Upper East Side.

I can't do this, Sarah thought. I can have a bare tushy on stage every night, but this I cannot do.

"I have to get home," she said to Evie.

"She talks!" Wilson shouted, laughing and nudging his companion.

"Leave the girl alone," Dewey said. "Maybe she's shy."

Sarah pushed away from the table.

"You're really going?" Wilson said. "But we just got started. The night is young."

"Me, I'm not so young. Feels like half past four in the morning at my age."

"You can't go," Evie whispered in her ear. "Are you crazy? These are live ones."

"No, I have to go home."

"First, let's go and see a man about a dog," Evie said, and she led Sarah off to the powder room.

But when they got there, there was no man and no dog. This English, Sarah thought. Every time you think you know it all, there is something else to learn.

Evie rounded on her. "You can't go, sugar. That Wilson, he told me he thinks you are the cat's pajamas."

"He's with you."

"If that's what he wants, he's yours. There's plenty more fish in the sea."

"Evie, I don't got no fishes, no cats. What I got is a daughter home in bed, waiting for me."

Evie stared at her. "Why didn't you tell me you had a kid?"

"Does it matter?"

"Sure it matters. If you want to land yourself a millionaire, believe me, sugar, it matters."

"I got to go," Sarah said, and she went out to the street and called a cab and didn't even say good-bye to her date. Mr. Rockefeller, she was sure he would get over it.

23

Ilsa, the seamstress, was fussing around her, uttering curses through a mouthful of pins, trying to get the chiffon to reveal enough of Sarah's breast to please the audience but not too much to displease Mr. Ziegfeld. And Sarah's headdress, it had more wire and modern engineering than the Williamsburg Bridge. Ilsa hurried to fix it to her hair, still muttering through the pins in her mouth.

This was supposed to be my job, Sarah thought. I wonder how much she is getting for all this work, when all I have to do is stand around?

Evie watched her in the mirror as she finished putting on her lipstick. "Pity you had to leave the other night. We had a swell time. Didn't get home till four. Nothing like seeing the sunrise over Manhattan."

"I seen sunrises before. It's like when it goes down, but the other direction."

"The boys wanted to know where you'd gone."

"I told you, Evie, I leave my daughter on her own long enough."

"That Wilson is sweet on you. He says he'll be by after the show to take you to dinner."

"I got a date already. She's nine years old. Don't got a polka-dot tie, otherwise she's perfect."

"How old is this kid of yours?"

"I told you, she is nine."

"Don't mind me saying, but you don't look old enough."

"Where I come from, we start young."

"You want my advice?"

They looked at each other in the dressing room mirror.

"You are a real looker, sweetheart. But looks, they don't last forever. This kid, she's going to spoil your chances, and when they're gone, they're gone."

"What are you saying?"

"I'm saying, don't you have an aunt or someone you can send her to for a while? She's going to queer your game."

"Gentleman caller!" one of the other girls shouted.

They both looked up.

"He wants Sarah!"

Evie smiled. Sarah bit her lip.

She got up, made her way through the racks of sequins and feathers and chiffon, clambering over hatboxes and shoes. It wasn't easy with the headdress that Ilsa had just finished pinning—the Eiffel Tower or she didn't know what, all in gold spangle.

Some of the other girls looked around. She could see on their faces they were jealous. Evie was right. This was the real game for the show-girls, not the Follies.

Wilson was waiting in the corridor, a bouquet of flowers in hand, peering in through a crack in the door, though there wasn't much more to see that he and half of moneyed New York hadn't already seen up there on the stage. Sarah was wearing only a chiffon wrap and her slip-ons. She forgot she was near naked until she opened the door.

Wilson didn't know where to look. He mumbled something at her nipples.

She took his handkerchief out of his jacket pocket and pretended to wipe his chin. He flushed and straightened. "Did Evie tell you? I came to ask you out for dinner after the show."

Sarah had told little Libby that tonight she would be home early. Promised her. But then she thought: What if the show finishes tomorrow? Evie's right, I have to find a husband, and the clock is ticking. I'm twenty-six years old. Not too many more Follies left for me.

"Okay," she said. "Let's do it, Wilson."

He beamed, took one more look through the door to satisfy himself there weren't any girls he liked better, and then left. He turned back to give her the flowers.

"I almost forgot," he said.

"Mama said she would be home hours ago," Libby said.

She heard someone down in the alley sorting through the garbage, trying to find something to eat. She should be grateful to be up here, she thought, on the roof with her best friend, safe and with something warm in her belly.

It was her new routine. She ate dinner with the Donnellys every night, and then played with Frankie until it was time to go to bed. She knew her mama was paying Mrs. Donnelly to look after her while she was at work, but it didn't really feel like that. It was like having another family, and most nights now they let her sleep over on the floor next to Frankie's bed or up on the roof, with Frankie's brothers and sisters, where it was cooler.

The only thing about the roof was the airshaft. You could hear everything through it; there were rats in there; the things that went down that chute was nobody's business, as her mama liked to say. The smell that came out of it was vile, especially on muggy summer nights like this.

They could also hear people going up and down the stairs, tripping on the torn linoleum, and there were babies crying all night long. But after a while she got used to it. She lay there next to Frankie and listened to Mr. and Mrs. Donnelly talking. Frankie's dad was saying that Sarah was aiming to marry some rich man.

Was she? Is that what she was doing every night when she said she was on the stage on Broadway? Is that why she would never let her go and watch?

She wished her papa was still alive; she wished they had a family like Frankie did. She didn't want her mama marrying some millionaire. Not having any money didn't worry her. It was only her mama who cared about all of that.

"Do you think she'll leave me, Frankie?"

"Who?"

"My mama."

"Don't be daft. She loves you, ya eejit. She'd never leave you."

Libby curled up on her side. She wanted to believe her. Frankie might be right, but what Libby really thought was that she was like the plain brown duck, only in reverse. Her mother was a swan, and Libby was so obviously the duck who had been found in her nest by mistake. Perhaps one day she would fly away; she was just a nuisance, and an ugly one at that.

⊰⊱

The Red Hen

Wilson's limousine pulled up outside the club, and a uniformed valet in hat and tails opened the doors for Sarah. I could get used to this, she thought. At Katz's you just shoved the door open with your shoulder.

She had never been to the Red Hen, and when she first walked in, she didn't think it was so much. There were framed cartoons on the walls—she had seen better—and the tables and chairs weren't much better than Katz's. It was the goyim that made the difference. They looked like they owned a block of New York each.

The men all wore tuxedos and topcoats, and the women were dripping with diamonds, all of them dressed like they were going to a coronation. She could feel them all looking at her, and she thought somehow they knew her from the show, but then she realized they were staring because she was the youngest woman there. If only they knew I have a kid nearly ten years old at home, she thought.

The maître d' led them to a table and delivered the menu. It had more words in it than the holy Torah. But Wilson saved her the trouble of reading it all and ordered for her.

"We'll have the lobster tail," he said. "And a bottle of shampoo, please, Arnold."

The menu was snatched out of her hand again. Well, she didn't mind. If Wilson was going to pay, she would eat whatever he wanted her to eat. She was never hungry after a show anyway.

She let her shawl slip off her shoulders. Everyone was looking anyway. Give them a show like Mr. Ziegfeld always wanted. She had on a beaded tulle dress with sequined paisley, the hem a little higher than she had ever worn before. The men of course were looking at her arms and her bare back; the women all were looking at the dress.

"That looks expensive," Wilson said.

"Got it today at Bergdorf," she said.

A lie. What if I told him it is an original Sarah Levine, she thought. Wouldn't he be surprised then?

There was an awkward moment. He didn't seem to know what to say; she had already figured he liked looking at her more than he liked talking to her.

"You're very beautiful. Have you never been told that?"

"Never think much about it. I suppose Mr. Ziegfeld must think so."

"There's something about your face. When you're on stage, I can't take my eyes off you."

"When you have Miss Gilda Gray to look at?"

"Not every man is looking at her, you know." He leaned in. "You're rather mysterious, aren't you?"

"Am I?"

"Your friend Evie won't say much, other than you're Russian and that you have blue blood."

"Blue this year. Next year I'll go with the fashion."

He smiled, almost like he knew it was a joke. He took out his cigarettes, a silver case with monogrammed initials: "WB."

"Do you like it here?"

"It's nothing on Katz's."

"Katz's?"

"Doesn't matter."

"Have you never been here before?"

She shook her head. "I'm not a girl that gets out a lot."

"I'm sure I could show you around."

She wondered what that meant. He had that look on him, she thought, he was like Schonberg but without the onion breath. If I was pastrami, he'd be licking his fingers right now and already thinking about what to have for dessert.

"My family has a house out on Long Island. You should come out."

"What is it you do out there, Wilson?"

"We have a yacht. Most weekends in the summer, we go sailing out on the Sound or go on picnics. There are some rather fine parties out there. All of New York is there in the summer."

"Thanks, but I don't think Mr. Ziegfeld will like it."

"Surely he can spare you for one day?"

"If he can spare me for one day, he can spare me for a whole season is what he says."

"You like working for Mr. Ziegfeld?"

"It's okay in the summer, but I'm figuring in the winter, it could get a bit chilly. But reading the papers, I say it beats bolshevism hands down."

He smiled. He was one of those men, she thought. He had a way of smiling that made you feel uncomfortable, like there was something crawling on you. "You're not really a countess, are you?"

"If I was a countess, I wouldn't be walking around on stage with the Eiffel Tower on my head."

"So what are you, then?"

"Just a girl trying to get by."

"You see, I could probably help you with that." He put his hand on her knee under the table. Where's a hat pin when a girl needs one, she thought. "It's hard being all alone in the world, isn't it?"

"I'm not alone. I got my Libby."

"Libby? Who's that?"

"She's my daughter."

"You have a daughter? You don't look old enough."

"That's what Evie said. What can I say? Where I come from, you can walk, you're old enough to get married."

"Where's your husband?"

"Not to be fancy about it, he's in a ditch in France, last I heard."

"I see. I'm sorry. Evie never mentioned a daughter."

"Sorry about my dead husband or my daughter?"

He called for the check and signed it. "It's getting late," he said.

"No lobster?"

"I've rather lost my appetite. I'll call you a cab."

"I'll call my own," she said.

24

A sultry summer night a week later, and the crowd was pouring out of the theater onto the street, which was already five-deep with taxicabs. Sarah pushed through the after-show crowd, ignoring the laughter and lighted cigarettes, the men in their silk scarves and tuxedos, the women with scandalously bare arms and flashy diamond bracelets. Suddenly Wilson's friend Dewey was behind her, waving a bouquet like a baton. He had followed her all the way from the stage-door entrance.

"Wait, Sarah. Please."

She stopped and wheeled around. "Please go away. I have to get home."

"I'm not like Wilson," he said.

"And what is Wilson like?"

"He only wants one thing."

"You want more than one thing? What other thing do you want? Only so many things I got."

"I know about your daughter, and I don't care. In fact, I think it's wonderful."

"What is wonderful?"

"That you're not just another good-time girl. That you're looking after her."

"What else would I do?"

"Come with me for a drink."

"What about Evie?"

"Never mind about Evie. Just one drink."

She stood there trying to make up her mind, and while she hesitated, he took her arm, to protect her from being buffeted by the tide of people maybe. He was shorter than she was, and even the bespoke cut of that beautiful double-breasted suit couldn't hide the potbelly. The steel-rimmed spectacles made him look old enough to be her father.

Yet there was something else, something, well, almost boyish about how ardent he was in his pursuit, like a beau with his first crush. Well, she thought, why not?

"One drink," she said.

He beamed at her.

His car was waiting there at the curb, a powder-blue Bentley.

No matter how long she'd lived in New York, how many times she'd walked up the fancy-schmancy stretches of Broadway, there was something about such millionaire cars. If you want to get from one end of town to the other, you catch a cab. But getting around town was not why these stage-door Johnnies had such automobiles and someone with leather gloves and a uniform to drive them.

The shape of the fenders over the whitewalls, like a woman's hip lying on a chaise; the gleam of the paint like marble in a palace. Such a car is like the lamp in the Aladdin story, she thought. Rub the coachwork, and its master could make a girl's dreams come true.

She climbed in.

They didn't drive downtown to Greenwich this time. Dewey told his driver to head for the One-Thirties. She'd heard some of the girls talk about Jungle Alley, but she'd never been up there. When she heard where they were going, she felt a thrill of excitement despite herself. It was like she was going to a foreign country.

North of the Park the avenues seemed broader, and the brown-stones didn't hug the sidewalks as tight as they did downtown. There were a lot more schvartzes in the street too, standing around the street corners, outside basement speakeasies with red awnings over the doors. Suddenly they were in the Alley, and there were shiny Franklins and Pontiacs parked bumper-to-bumper along the curbs, just like Broadway.

"Have you been up this way before?" Dewey said to her. His eyes were shining. Somewhere on the way uptown, he'd changed. He didn't look like a banker anymore.

She shook her head. "No, I never been."

"It swings to beat all hell up here." He leaned forward and slid aside the glass partition. "Stop here, Nelson."

It wasn't like any speakeasy she'd been to before. At the Red Hen and the other clubs in the Village, the only schvartzes were playing on stage; here, she saw them sitting in the dark, drinking and smoking along with the whites from Midtown. Dewey led her to a table with a checkered tablecloth, near the back.

A torchy-voiced singer, sweat gleaming on her skin like molasses under the lights, was urging her lover to "take your time with what you do, make me cry for more of you." She was accompanied by a Brylcreemed mulatto with a pencil-thin moustache and sweat-stained white jacket, playing a beat-up upright. The back of the piano was missing; she could see the hammers moving. Somehow, he made the old eighty-eight sound like an entire orchestra.

Dewey the banker spread his arms over the back of the chairs either side of him and looked right at home. He ordered two top-to-bottom cocktails and took a silver cigarette case from his coat jacket. "You look—I have insufficient superlatives."

"Thank you."

"You like it here?"

He put a cigarette between his lips and lit it. It looked different from a store-bought cigarette, like he'd rolled it himself. The smoke had an acrid, slightly sweet smell to it.

"Marijuana," he said. "Nelson gets them for me. Two for twenty-five cents. Better than bathtub gin and a lot cheaper."

"That a millionaire type like you should worry about money."

"A banker always watches his bottom line."

This was a different Dewey, she thought, without his pal Wilson there watching him. She looked around the club. There was a cop sitting in the corner, still in his uniform, eating fried chicken and waffles. A waiter came over and put a beer and a brown envelope on the table next to his elbow. The cop took a deep swallow of the beer, wiped the froth off his moustache with the back of his hand, and slid the envelope into his pocket.

Next to him two schvartzes in spats and loud ties were tapping their feet in time with the music. The piano player was playing solo now, pounding out a barrelhouse ragtime.

"Never imagined you in such a place," Sarah said.

"Nobody is everything they seem to be," he said. He blew a stream of blue-gray smoke toward the ceiling and grinned at her.

Their drinks arrived. Sarah took a sip at hers and winced. This is why Dewey prefers his marijuana cigarettes, she thought. Such cocktails could clear a drain in a slaughterhouse. She shuffled hers to the side.

She looked around, nodded toward a man sitting in a dark corner. He looked to her like a gorilla squeezed into a double-breasted suit. He had a fancy girl with him, in a too-short skirt.

"You know him?" Dewey asked her.

"Sure, got a pushcart on Hester Street. He sells hats."

"That's Umberto Valenti. He's a shooter for one of the Italian mobs."

"Then why he sells hats?"

Dewey laughed and shook his head.

"Thinks he's tough. Tell him he should try selling hats on the Lower East Side. Look at the girl. Got more crust on her than a *piroshki*. I can see her tushy before she even sits down. I'm ashamed for her, and I show my tush professionally."

Dewey shook his head. "Jesus Christ, quit staring. I'm not kidding, that guy she's with kills people for a living."

"I always wondered, do they charge by the bullet or by the pound?"

"I have no idea."

"And you tell everyone you're a banker."

He was an easy guy to talk to, and he didn't look at her in the hungry way, like Wilson did. He was content to schmooze. They talked about entertainment things, about Gloria Swanson and Babe Ruth, and then later, because she asked him, he told her his life story.

Which was this: He was from Boston, he said. He went to the same prep school as his father, and the same university, Brown. When he graduated, he went to work with his father in the family firm on Wall Street. When his father died, Dewey inherited the same desk and the same secretary; though in a break with tradition, he didn't sleep with her on Wednesday afternoons like his old man did. The older members of the firm saw it almost as an act of rebellion.

"You must be real smart to be so big-time," Sarah said.

Dewey shook his head. "Just lucky I was born in the right clan. Having the right family, that makes all the difference in life."

Sarah reached for her cocktail.

"I thought you didn't like the drinks here," he said.

She shrugged.

Dewey kept talking. "The old man said that when they were handing out the brains, I was selling the tickets at the door, which was fine with him. Told me the only books a man ever needed to read were the accounts ledgers and his Bible. I left a bookmark on page three of Genesis when I was eleven years old and never got back to it. These days the only thing I ever read start-to-finish is ticker tape."

He had a hunting lodge in the Adirondacks, he said, an apartment in the West One Hundreds, and what he described as a weekend shack on Long Island.

He finished his cigarette. He leaned back in his chair, glassy eyed, tapping his feet in rhythm with the ragtime.

"What is it you do at your papa's firm?" Sarah said to him.

"Actually, it was my great-granddaddy's firm. *He* was the smart one." Dewey polished his glasses on his paisley-patterned silk vest. "Brokerage. We deal in government bonds and public stocks and some handpicked financial securities."

"I see your lips move, but what I hear is jibber-jabber. What does a girl like me know from banking. Explain me."

"Well, I help people buy a little bit of a company. When that company does well, they can sell their bit of the company for a bit more or use the profit they made to buy a part of another company."

"I thought you were a bank. You sound like you sell saucepans door-to-door."

He laughed. "Nobody else would dare say it to me, but between you and me, that's exactly what I do. Only I'm the kind of salesman where the customer puts his foot in my door, not the other way around. You got to have a lot of money before I can sell you something."

"So you own a fancy pushcart where rich people come to buy more money."

"I guess."

"That's a very nice business you got."

"Well, my granddaddy thought so. That's why he gave it to my old man. Now you know all about me, and I don't know a thing about you."

"What is it you want to know?"

"Well, you sure you didn't grow up in New York?"

"I grew up in Russia. You know Russia? It's like winter, only it lasts all year."

"Is that where you started in show business?"

She laughed. "Show business. You mean where I first started to show my business? Sure, it was at the Winter Palace. You think the czar didn't like a little tushy on the side?"

"Hey, I don't want Jewish theater. The truth."

"The truth?" For the truth, she thought, I need a drink. She dared another sip at the cocktail. It made her eyes water. "Dewey, let me tell you. I didn't have no hunting lodge, no shack for Shabbas. I grew up in a village not much bigger than this basement. My father railed at God every day for giving him four baby girls and no sons living. Before I came to America, I knew from milking a cow and selling potatoes and a little bit of tailoring, nothing else. I did what my vati said and what Elohim said and my husband told me. And you know what? They all let me down. There, that's the truth."

"Did you come to America with your husband?"

"Sure, I did. I didn't have no choice. He says you come. I come."

"What happened to him?"

"He died and went to Jewish heaven."

"How?"

Another gulp of the gin and wine. The room started to spin. "Got himself shot in the war. A war he didn't have to go to, never mind. Left me with little Libby."

"You're still angry about that."

"He gives me my precious daughter, then he goes away himself, and what for? For nothing. Sure, I'm angry. But what you going to do? Nothing you can do."

"Where is your daughter now?"

"My daughter? She's at home."

"On her own?"

"Got a good friend who sees after her. My friend, she has a husband and five kids, and she says, 'What is one more?' I pay her to look out for my Libby until I get home. What else am I going to do, without a husband?" Listen to me, she thought. Why is he still sitting here with me? I don't even sound to myself like someone I want to know. The drink was making her talk too much. She grabbed her Saks handbag and stood up. "You got to excuse me. I have to powder my nose."

They were two-deep at the washbasins in the ladies' powder room. A girl in a flapper dress came out of one of the cubicles, unsteady on her feet with white powder on her nose. Most of the other girls in there looked like gangster molls to Sarah: too much lipstick, not enough skirt. But what am I to judge. I take off my clothes for money and leave my little girl home on her own every night.

"Is that Bill Dewey you're with?" one of the girls said to her, addressing her in the mirror.

Sarah nodded.

"How did you hook him? He doesn't even want it when it's free."

"You know him?"

"Not in the biblical sense," the girl said, "but I tried. They say he's loaded."

"He's only like the bank of America," another girl said on the other side.

When she got back to her table, Dewey had just lit his second cigarette. His red-and-yellow foulard was loose, and there was cigarette ash on his white linen shirt. He had his feet up on the empty chair. He gave her a lazy smile.

"I got to go home," she said.

"So early?"

"I got to look out for my little girl."

"I'll get Nelson to drop you off."

"It's fine," she said. "I'll get a cab."

He laughed again. "I'll be at the show tomorrow night. I'll pick you up afterward."

"Really?"

"Yes, really."

"I got to ask you. Why me, Dewey?"

"That's a big question after one bathtub gin."

"Lot of showgirls Ziegfeld has, most of them easier than me. I'm twenty-six years old, I got a nine-year-old kid. I got inconveniences, like your friend said."

"Well, Sarah, let me tell you something. When people look at me, they see what they want to see. My guess is you feel the same way."

She shrugged.

"You see? We have a lot more in common than you think. I'll see you tomorrow night."

25

Two Months Later

George Seabrook hurried along Broadway. He heard faint organ music as he crossed onto Wall by the Trinity Church. Gulls wheeled over the dark Gothic spire above, their seabird cries out of place here on Wall Street. He didn't come down to the city very often, and it was years since he had been down the money end of Manhattan. There was something corrupt about it, he thought; it wasn't where the honest dollars were made.

He passed the massive edifice of the National City Bank, with its soaring marble columns. The buildings on the street looked more like fortresses than banks to him. He spared a glance for the limousines parked outside The Corner, their liveried chauffeurs buffing the coach-work of the Rolls-Royces and Bentleys at the curb. A lay preacher on a podium draped with Old Glory and crude and gaudy pictures from the Bible harangued him as Seabrook walked past.

Dewey was sitting in a booth at the window of a diner at the other end of the street. Damn the man, he could have thought of a hundred better places to meet. It was oppressive inside, not even any fans to move the air.

Dewey grinned when he saw him. "George! Great to see you."

"You too, Billy," he said, and they shook hands.

George sat down, put his homburg on the table. "Thought we'd be eating at one of your fancy clubs."

"They're so stuffy," Dewey said, and nodded to the waitress, who brought them two coffees. "I prefer this place. There's less eavesdropping."

"Why, are you going to be telling me trade secrets?"

"No, just one of my own."

George raised an eyebrow, but Dewey just shrugged and smiled. All in good time with Dewey.

"So," Dewey said, "what brings you to Sodom and Gomorrah?"

"I'm thinking of investing. An import-export company, textiles mainly. The pup who runs it is a damned fool. I knew his old man, and he was a different stripe. His boy has practically run the business into the dirt, so I've made him an offer. He'd be crazy not to take it."

"Import-export. Branching out? Not like you, George."

"It's that or retire, and I'm a little young for that."

"Why don't you invest in the market? You could make a lot of money with the right advice."

"I'll leave the market to people who know about these things."

"Knowing about these things is how I built my business."

"Thanks, but I like to see what I'm buying. Fooling around with bits of paper, that's not for me."

George could smell coffee, the real thing, not the mud they were drinking. It was coming from a group of men in suits behind them.

Dewey leaned in. "Coffee importers. Their house is a few doors down. Like fish, you can't get the smell of it out of your clothes, they say."

"Like the smell of money."

Dewey grinned.

"Haven't seen you for a while, Billy."

"I don't get back to Boston very often these days."

"It looks like New York agrees with you."

Dewey patted his belly. "I have a cook. Stole her from the Doorans. They were miffed with me for a while."

"So, what have you been doing?"

"This and that." He lowered his voice, though as far as George could tell, no one was paying them the slightest attention. "Thing is, I'm thinking of getting hitched."

"At your age?"

"Comes to all of us sooner or later."

"I thought you were married to the bank."

"You should never mistake an arrangement for a marriage."

"Who's the lucky girl?"

"You won't know her."

"Interesting. What's her name?"

"Sarah."

"Sarah . . . ?"

"Levine. Sarah Levine."

"You're right, I don't know any Levines." George raised an eyebrow. "Jewish?"

"Hmm."

"And that's not going to be a problem?"

"Nothing we can't sort out."

"Where are her family from?"

"Russia."

"Yes, of course. But where did they make their money?"

Dewey sat back, a wry smile on his face. "She doesn't have any."

"Any what? Money or family?"

"Either. Well, she has family, but she hasn't seen them in years. She has a daughter, though. She's nine."

"What does she do?"

"Plays with dolls, I suspect."

"Funny. The mother. What does she do?"

"You'll like this part. She's a Follies girl."

George stared at him, couldn't believe his ears. He tried to keep his expression flat. "Is this a joke, Billy?"

"Why would I joke about this, with you of all people?" A flash of a smile. "Everyone knows you don't have a sense of humor."

"Well, you never cease to astonish. What the hell are you doing, Billy? If you want to get yourself a Follies girl, why not some long-legged Okie with no complications. This woman, what's her name again?"

"Sarah."

"Sarah. You're telling me she has no connections, no influence, and no breeding. She can't help you in any way. My God. What would your father say?"

"My father would have a heart attack if he hadn't had one already, may he rest in peace."

"Your future wife is penniless, Jewish, and she's a showgirl. Is that what you're telling me?"

"Not quite penniless. She's getting seventy-five a week through the season."

George slumped in his seat. He couldn't think of a single thing to say. Finally: "Have you lost your mind?"

"In a way, I suppose I have."

"When is this . . . going to happen?"

"Well, I haven't asked her yet. She might say no."

"From what you've told me, I very much doubt that."

"Women can be quite unpredictable."

"I think you overestimate women."

"Thing is, I haven't told anyone else about this yet."

"Why are you telling me?" George said.

"We've been friends a long time, George. In fact, even though we don't see each other very often, I'd say you know me better than anyone."

"Thank you, Billy. I happen to feel the same way. Look, I know you can be a little . . . different . . . at times, but I find it utterly incomprehensible that you should be thinking of marrying so far beneath yourself."

"She's not beneath me, George. If you met her, you'd understand. She may not be an heiress, but she's not beneath me."

"She must be damned good in bed." He turned and signaled to the waitress. She brought over the coffee pot.

As she refilled their cups, Dewey said, "I haven't bedded her yet, George. That's the whole point. I admit she's a very beautiful woman, but it's not about wrecking the sheets."

The waitress gave Dewey a sharp look and moved quickly away.

"Marriage is about making connections, Billy. It's a social contract. If you don't want her as a mistress, and she can't bring good breeding and social standing to the table, then what the hell do you think you're doing?"

"I think I love her."

"Did you say *love?*"

"You know what I'm talking about."

George looked away. His cheeks were burning, Goddammit. "Yes, I know what you're talking about. You damn well know I do. And what good did it do me, Billy? Tell me that."

"It doesn't always have to end badly."

"No, and the dealer doesn't always win at blackjack. But most card players still end up sleeping on the street and lucky to have the clothes they stand up in."

Dewey dropped two sugar cubes into his cup. "You had your moment of rebellion, didn't you? I never did."

"It wasn't rebellion."

"Wasn't it?"

"Is that what this is? You're marrying a showgirl so you can relive a youth you think you never had?"

"If it's self-indulgence, at least I can afford it."

"But why take on a child as well?"

A shrug.

"You're going to ride in like a knight on a white charger and save a fair maid and her helpless *kind* from the dragons. Is that it?"

"After the bell goes off at the Exchange, my time is my own. I've decided to use it doing things I want to do, not what my father would have done."

George opened his mouth to answer him, then thought better of it. He wondered, for a moment, if perhaps his old friend didn't have a point.

"What was it that made you marry Clare?" Dewey said.

Clare. A long time since anyone had spoken her name aloud to him. His waistcoat felt suddenly too tight. He put his finger to his collar and cleared his throat.

"I'm sorry," Dewey said. "But I have to ask."

"Clare." He closed his eyes for a moment, allowing himself to remember, something he had not done for a long time. "There was just something, every time I saw her, I felt quite—breathless, I suppose. I can't explain it. She was different from any woman I'd ever known."

"You see? You do understand."

"But does she love *you?*"

"I'll make her love me."

"That's what I said about Clare."

"Perhaps I'll be luckier than you, George."

"Yes," George said. "Yes, perhaps."

26

Dewey picked Sarah up outside the New Amsterdam, as he always did. Most nights they went downtown to a speakeasy or up to Jungle Alley. He had still not tried to sleep with her. Sarah wasn't sure whether she felt relieved or insulted.

"You sure he isn't a pansy?" Evie had asked her one night as they were changing after a show.

"You think he likes . . . men?"

"That's what I'm asking."

"Why would he want to take me out?"

"So nobody knows he's a pansy, dummy."

Sarah had never thought of that. I must be the least worldly showgirl there's ever been, she thought. "How would I know?"

"Some guys, it's not always easy to tell. You don't get around much, do ya?"

Sarah shrugged.

"Well, my advice, until he asks, you won't really know. But when he does ask, make sure you say no. Once you sold him everything in the shop, why would he want to come back to look at the empty shelves?"

Nelson opened the car door for Sarah, standing to attention in his cap and leather gloves as if she was royalty. She almost expected him to salute. She settled into the leather upholstery. Dewey smiled at her from the other end of the seat. The back of the Bentley was almost as big as the living room in her apartment.

"Where to?" she said.

"Why don't we do something different?"

"Different like how?"

"Actually, I'd like to meet your daughter."

She stared at him.

"We can't keep putting this off forever, Sarah."

"Why not?" she said with a little laugh.

He leaned forward, pushed the glass panel aside. "Lower East Side, Nelson. Cannon Street. It's near the Williamsburg Bridge."

"You know where I live?"

"I know a lot more about you than you think."

They set off downtown, through the chaos of taxicabs and limousines. This must be how Cinderella felt, Sarah thought, on her way back from the ball. Wait till he sees where I live. When the clock struck on Delancey Street, she would turn from a princess back to a scullery maid. At Union Square, she could almost hear the clock chiming down to midnight.

The Williamsburg Bridge loomed ahead, stark against the night sky. She could make out the glow of the oil-drum fires under the approaches, the bums settling in for the night.

Nelson pulled up outside their tenement. She looked at his face in the rearview mirror. He was inscrutable, as always; she supposed that was what Dewey paid him for. He reached under the dashboard and passed his employer a box wrapped with pink tissue paper and a white ribbon.

"Thank you, Nelson."

"You sure you want to do this?" Sarah said.

"Shall we go up?"

Nelson came around to hold open the door. She could feel eyes watching them from the fire escapes—all the mattresses up there, the only place to be on a hot night on the Lower East Side.

He didn't seem to mind the climb up the five flights of dark steps, and at least he didn't trip over any rats. The rancid summer smells would have knocked over a horse, but Dewey, gentleman that he was, never even mentioned it.

She knocked on the Donnellys' door. It opened, and there was Mary, her jaw falling open when she saw Dewey standing there in his homburg and his fancy suit with the trouser cuffs and embroidered waistcoat. A warning glance from Sarah, and she recovered quick enough. "I'll get Libby," she said.

Libby came to the door and stared. Sarah could see the rest of the Donnelly family behind her, peering out in a sea of red cheeks and snotty noses. Even Mary's husband, Dan, was there watching, rubbing his walrus moustache like he always did whenever he was perturbed.

"Libby," Sarah said. "This is my friend Mr. Dewey."

She led him across the hall into their apartment. What must it look like to him, Sarah thought: moth holes in the little lace curtain she had put up around the sink to hide the pipes, rotten boards on the window sill, broken plaster on the walls. At least there was a new white oilcloth on the table and the cheesecloth curtains on the windows, she had bought them new just last week.

If Dewey was bothered, he gave no sign of it. He crouched down so that he was eye-to-eye with Libby. "I've been wanting to meet you, young lady," he said. "Your mother has told me so much about you."

Libby hesitated a moment, then reached out, fingered his tiepin and the jacket, feeling the quality like a good seamstress's daughter.

Sarah wanted to say, don't do that with your smudgy fingers, but she didn't because of the way he was smiling at her. "Your mama says you're very clever."

Libby shrugged and kept her eyes on the carpet. Sarah had never seen her daughter so shy.

"Here, I've brought you a present," Dewey said.

Libby tore open the pink paper wrapping. Inside was a book of fairy tales. It had color illustrations as good as the paintings Sarah had seen once in an art gallery, and it was printed on shiny white paper, expensive. It was the most beautiful book Sarah had ever seen.

"Your mother said you like to read."

Libby nodded.

"Say thank you, Lib. The cat got your tongue?"

"Thank you," she said, her voice barely audible.

"I'll make you tea," Sarah said.

"Do you have anything stronger?"

She shook her head.

He nodded toward the little girl. "I suppose that's very commendable. Setting a good example, I mean."

Sarah went into the tiny kitchen. When she came back with tea in her two best cups, he was sitting on the sofa with Libby, who had her dirty bare feet resting on his pressed gray trousers. He was flipping through the pages of the book. They had found the story about the brown duck and the white swans, and she had persuaded him to read it to her.

Dewey grinned at Sarah.

"Well," he said. "Isn't this nice?"

It was as he was leaving that he turned at the door and told her what a beautiful daughter she had. "When she grows up, she's going to be a real head-turner."

"You think?" Sarah said.

"Where did she get those amazing green eyes?"

"They are Ashkenazi eyes. Her father, he was Ashkenazi."

"What's that?"

"It's a Jew that has green eyes."

"I didn't know Jewish people had green eyes."

"Sure they do. For a smart man, you don't pay much attention."

Dewey laughed.

"What's so funny?"

"There aren't many people who dare to talk to me like you do."

"How do they talk?"

"Like they are either afraid of me or licking my boots, hoping I'll give them money."

"You don't scare me, Dewey. And your boots? Look at them, looks to me like they are shiny enough."

"You should ask me back sometime. I'm a good storyteller. Just ask your daughter." He put on his homburg, touched its brim, and kissed her on the cheek. "Good night, Mrs. Levine."

She closed the door behind him. "Good night, Dewey," she murmured. She went in to check on Libby, make sure she was asleep. As Sarah closed her door, she heard Libby say: "I liked him."

27

Dewey picked Sarah up on her day off. This time there was no Nelson; Dewey had decided to do the driving himself. Sarah thought they were going out to his house on Long Island, but he stopped at a general store a few miles short. There wasn't much around: a low whitewashed fence; the glare of a few dusty, open fields; a billboard advertising building lots with easy terms.

It wasn't much of a store either: a couple of diesel pumps; a sad-looking office; and a run-down bungalow out back, where the owner lived, she guessed. Dewey left his car in the forecourt, threw his jacket in the back seat, and walked up.

The owner seemed to know Dewey pretty well. He shuffled out from under the car he was working on, wiped his hands on a rag, and shook hands with him. Dewey introduced him to her as Mike. "This is Sarah," Dewey said, and Mike touched a finger to his forehead.

"Want a beer?" he said to Dewey.

Dewey nodded and followed him into the office. He shucked down his suspenders and sat down on a wooden box while Mike went into the back to fetch a chair for Sarah.

"You want a lemonade?" Mike asked her.

She shook her head. Mike took two beers from the refrigerator and handed one to Dewey, who raised it in a toast and drank straight from the neck of the bottle.

"How's Betty?" Dewey said.

"Much the same. Thanks for asking."

Dewey put his feet up on a crate. "Business all right?"

"Can't complain." Mike turned to Sarah. "Sorry about this place. I guess a fine lady like you ain't accustomed to this kind of mess."

"Fine lady like me grew up helping my mother milk cows and sleeping on the stove. It's Dewey that tiptoes through puddles."

Mike liked that and dug Dewey in the ribs. The two men talked about cars and about the new lots being built down the road and how that might help turnover. Mike rolled two cigarettes and handed one to Dewey, and then a car pulled in, and he went outside to pump gas.

"How do you know him?" Sarah asked.

"Used to be my chauffeur, before Nelson," Dewey said to her. "His father worked for the old man for near on twenty years. He was with me for another five until his wife got sick."

"Does he own this place?"

"Kinda," Dewey said, and she realized that it must be Dewey's place and that Mike worked it so he could look after his wife and still make ends meet. She wondered how much of the action Dewey took for himself and guessed that it probably wasn't very much.

He and Mike talked some more when he came back, and then Dewey said he had to be going, and they went back out to the car. They drove out to the Sound, and he stopped by the shore. They had a good view of all the houses along the water from there. Dewey got out and sat on the hood. Sarah came and sat next to him, and they watched a yacht beat against the wind, the whitecaps breaking over its bows.

"Practically grew up here," Dewey said.

"Nice."

"Maybe."

She gave him a look.

"Loneliest time of my life," Dewey said. "Milking cows and balancing on duckboards doesn't sound so bad if you got company. Fact is, been lonely a lot of my life." He reached into his trouser pocket and took out a Tiffany's box. He gave it to her. "Well, go on, open it. Not going to bite."

"Is that a diamond?"

"I sure hope so, or I was seriously overcharged."

"Is this for me?"

"I don't see anyone else out here. This is not too romantic, I guess, but I'm not good at things like that."

"It's beautiful," she said, and she felt like she had a stone in her throat.

"I want you to marry me, Sarah."

"Marry?"

"Well, where else did you think this was going? I'm a serious guy; I'm not like Wilson. I don't take Follies girls out every night of the week."

She picked up the ring and held it in her hand, couldn't think. This was what she wanted, wasn't it? Her second time a wife, but this time she would have a choice.

"You're the nicest girl I ever met," Dewey said, which showed what kind of judge of character he was, she thought.

"You can't marry me, Dewey."

"I can do what I damn well please. If you'll have me."

"Dewey, I hardly know you. This is so fast for me. You sweep me off my feet like nobody's business. One minute you are in the dress circle, staring at my tush, the next you want I should be wearing white gloves, shaking hands with Mrs. Rothschild?"

"When you know, you know," he said.

"But, Dewey, I don't think . . . I don't love you, not in that way. I mean you are such a sweet man, and I like you, a lot. But . . . I don't know."

She supposed it was his being rich that confused her. She did like him, but was she liking him for herself, or did she like him for Libby and the fine life he could offer her? It was all mixed up in her head.

"Well, I don't pay no mind to that," Dewey said. "I know I'm no Rudolph Valentino. Just liking me, maybe that's enough for me right now. Maybe you'll come to love me in time. At least you're honest about it."

"Why me, Dewey? What I got that you need? I can walk in high heels; I can sew; I can bargain for herring. What good is all that on your West Side?"

"High heels and herring are much in demand. You ever been to one of J. P. Morgan's parties?"

That made her laugh.

"I like it when you laugh," he said, and he picked up the ring and put it on her finger. "Tight fit," he said, and grinned. "You'll have the devil of a job trying to take that off now."

⟩⟩⟨⟨

Sarah and Libby stood side by side and stared at the Bergdorf Goodman window. The new season's fashion was in, and the window designs had been themed with fairy tales. Libby was disappointed there was nothing about her favorite swan story, but she had been drawn to the Cinderella window.

Cinderella wore a black lace evening dress by Jean Patou. It seemed her fairy godmother had given her a Marcel wave, a long pearl necklace, and silver drop earrings. Her coach was a gleaming red Fiat roadster, and four mice sat around the hood looking up at her with expressions of sheer adoration.

Prince Charming waited for her in a tuxedo and two-tone wing-tips. He was holding a silver satin T-strap. Behind a ragged curtain, Cinderella's three sisters looked on, dressed in rags.

"So you like Mr. Dewey?" Sarah said.

Libby nodded her head.

"Is he a millionaire, Mama?"

"Yes. He's very rich."

"Is that why you like him?"

"No, it's not why I like him."

"Then why do you?"

"Well, it's not the only reason."

Sarah waited for more questions. Libby stared at the glass, the lights from the window reflected in her huge green eyes. So hard to know what she was thinking anymore. And she had been such a chatterbox as a child!

"He's asked me to marry him."

Libby was quiet for a long time.

"What will happen to me?"

"Nothing will happen, bubeleh. We'll all go and live with Mr. Dewey. We'll be a family together."

"What about Frankie?"

"Frankie?" Sarah squeezed her daughter's hand a little tighter. "Frankie will have to stay with her family."

"But where will we be?"

"I told you. We'll live with Mr. Dewey. He has a nice apartment up near Central Park."

"That's a long way away. Can I still see her?"

"Sure, you can see Frankie if you want to."

"When are we going away?"

"Soon. Mr. Dewey wants to get married straightaway, but I said I would have to talk to you first."

Sarah had hoped Libby would be excited by this promise of a better life. But the look of sadness she had, Sarah hadn't expected that.

"Things are going to be so much better for us now. It's no more than you deserve, this millionaire life."

"I like my life just fine, Mama," Libby said.

Sarah bent down, took Libby by the shoulders, looked right into her face. "You mean everything to me," she said. "Don't ever forget it. Everything I've done, I've done it for you."

"You don't have to marry him for me, Mama."

"I'm not marrying him for you, bubeleh."

"Aren't you? You hardly know him. How long have you been stepping out with him?"

"You are still at school, bubeleh. What do you know from stepping out?"

Sarah stood up again, looked at Cinderella in her new season's gown and her new season's man. The perfect fairy-tale ending. Or was it? Would the scullery maid in the story really have married the handsome prince if he didn't have a castle and a red Fiat roadster?

But what was it Dewey had said to her? *Just liking me, maybe that's enough for me right now.*

She did like him. She liked how he knew which jazz clubs to go to and where the best speakeasies were, but he could shrug off his jacket and his suspenders and sit down on a wooden crate and drink beers with men called Mike. She liked that he smoked strange-smelling cigarettes and didn't care that she knew how to milk a cow.

How did you know if you loved someone, anyhow?

"Is the fairy godmother real?" Libby said.

"Sure she is," Sarah said. "You take my word."

***

Long Island

Bill Dewey threw a long shadow on the rolling green lawn. With his hands in the pockets of his white flannels, he strolled to the water's edge and stood there watching the sun flick golden spangles across the surface of the water.

The neighbor's kids were splashing and yelling around their jetty; a motorboat sliced through the water farther out, throwing up a moustache of foam. Dewey took off his tennis shoes so that he could feel the warm sand between his bare toes. This was all so nearly perfect.

But not quite.

He heard the Bentley's tires on the gravel drive, and he put his shoes back on and headed back to the house. When he got there, Nelson was unloading the Seabrooks' luggage from the trunk of the car. George's young son, Jack, was squabbling with his father about whether he could go straight to the lake or whether he should change first. Dewey told the maid to fetch lemonade. Jack negotiated a truce on refreshments first and went inside.

Dewey shook hands with George. "Good to see you again," he said.

"Thanks for inviting us. And for sending Nelson to pick us up from Grand Central. It's bedlam down there."

"You're just in time for a cocktail."

"I hear congratulations are in order."

Dewey clapped his friend on the shoulder. "You don't mean that."

"I'd like to mean it."

Nelson came back to get the rest of the suitcases.

"Nice place you have here," George said.

"You've not seen it before?"

"You know damned well I haven't."

"I bought it a couple of years ago. Needs doing up a bit."

"I should put on an extra wing if I were you. What is it, twelve bedrooms? Not nearly enough for a bachelor."

Dewey smiled. "Not for much longer."

"I hope you're not planning on filling the place with your offspring."

"I need at least a son and heir. Come on, we can't let the ice melt in the gin."

Dewey led the way through the marble hallway. George stopped and glanced at the silver-framed photographs on the wall: Dewey's grandfather staring dourly at the camera in his dark suit, his fob watch on a chain; Dewey's father at the helm of the family yacht; one of Dewey's sisters with her first pony.

"What do Emma and Susan say?" George asked him.

"The same as everyone else."

"Which is what?"

"Pretty much what you said—don't do it."

⎯⎯◆⎯⎯

They sat on the deck, the lowering sun striking gold on the beach. Dewey snapped his fingers while he waited for the help to bring the gins.

"Nervous, Billy?"

"Of course not. Why?"

"You always snap your fingers when you're nervous."

"Nonsense."

"Are you afraid this is the last flicker of the candle before it goes out?"

Dewey threw back his head and laughed. "You're the only one of my friends who would have the effrontery to say something like that to me."

"I'm the only one of your friends who doesn't owe you money. When do I get to meet the lucky woman?"

"Probably not until the big day. You will come?"

"I wouldn't miss it for anything. Would you like me to speak the eulogy?"

Dewey toyed with the mint leaf from his gin glass. "No, but I would like you to be the best man."

"Me?"

"You're my oldest friend, George. Well?"

"I'd be honored."

"Good."

Dewey took a long swallow of his gin and tonic.

"Did you buy that firm you were looking at in Union Square?"

George nodded.

"So you're going into the rag trade now?"

"I saw an opportunity."

"You should have come to me. You'll get better returns on the market."

"I told you, Billy, that's not for me. I like to buy real things with my money, not bits of paper."

Jack came bounding down from upstairs. Dewey looked up. "How old is he now?"

"Twelve."

"Growing up fast."

"He already thinks he knows it all too."

"The apple never falls far from the tree," Dewey said, and grinned. "Look at him. He's the spitting image."

That much was true; there was no mistaking whose son he was, with those piercing blue eyes and mop of fair Waspy hair. Dewey got to his feet as the boy bounded in, dressed for action in his tennis shoes and Fair Isle sweater. "How about a twilight sail before dinner?" George said to him. "We can take the cat out on the water before dinner."

"Can we, Uncle Billy?"

"Let's do it." Dewey led the way down the lawn. Must be good to have a son, he thought. Perhaps I really should get one myself.

28

Lower East Side

Libby was sleeping up on the roof with Frankie again. Those girls, like Siamese twins they were. It was a shame to tear them apart. Sarah would try to get Frankie to visit them when they moved up to the One Hundreds. It still seemed unreal to even think of starting a new life up there, in the America her Micha had dreamed of, the Golden Medina he had left Russia to find.

Sarah reached under the bed and pulled out his old biscuit box. She took out the bit of paper, unfolded the receipt:

> *Dear Madam,*
> *Forwarded herewith, the personal effects of the late Lance*
> *Corporal Michael Levine, 4th Infantry Regiment, as per*
> *inventory attached. Kindly confirm receipt of same by*
> *signing and returning the enclosed slip.*

She used her index finger to sort through what was in the tin: his wristwatch, stopped at 10:37; a French five-franc note; a postcard with German script.

And there it was, underneath the useless mementos of his life, the ancient cutting from the *New York Times*. She stared at it still folded. She would not open it as she was afraid it would tear. Besides, she knew what it said by heart.

"You knew, Micha," she murmured. "But you never told me. How did it happen? How did you bring this miracle into our life? Well, I have done what you wanted. I have got our baby girl what she was born to. We are not cheating her anymore."

⟨※⟩

The summer was almost over. There was a bite to the air tonight. Libby and Frankie wouldn't be sleeping out on the roof together many more nights. They curled up side by side on the mattress, and Libby showed Frankie the book that her mama's new friend had given her. They read until it was too dark to see, and then they huddled under the blankets listening to the Kohns shout at each other in the apartment next to Frankie's, and the family of mice scamper on the roof by the air shaft.

Libby rolled on her back and looked up at the stars and tried to pick out the Great Bear. Suddenly, Frankie said, "Are you going away?"

"Who told you that?"

"My ma said. She said your mother's going to marry a millionaire, and you're away to live in a fancy apartment, and we're never going to see you again."

"I'll still see you just the same as always. I promise. Even if I have to walk a hundred blocks every night."

"No, you won't, not once you're a fancy girl. You'll forget all about us down here, and I don't blame you."

"I won't forget about you!"

"Of course you will. Don't look so sad about it. You're right lucky, you are. You'll be able to have icebox cakes whenever you want."

"Even if I do, it won't be the same if I can't share them with you."

"Well, don't forget us forever. Come back at Christmas and Saint Paddy's Day, and I'll forgive you."

Libby didn't know what to say to her. She didn't want to leave, not for all the icebox cakes in the world. Of course she would come back.

They heard Frankie's brothers and sisters yelling downstairs, her ma and her daddy having another row, the sound of a plate smashing. Someone was drunk on the stairs; a big rat poked its whiskers around the gutter right over their heads.

"If it was me, I'd never come back here," Frankie said. "Not for anything. And you won't either. You'll see."

29

Long Island

Sarah thought about the times in her life when she had wondered if she could face another tomorrow—in the stink and gloom of the third deck on the boat out from Russia; when the soldier came to her door in the tenement in Cannon Street and handed her the brown envelope with all that was left in the world of her husband.

But she had never felt quite as desolate as this. I am supposed to feel so excited, she thought. Today I marry a rich man. This is the day all my dreams for my daughter come true. It's the end of the fairy story, the moment the shoe fits.

Why do I feel like this?

Dewey had hired extra help to get everything ready. All week his staff had mopped and scrubbed until the marble and parquet shone like glass; his gardeners had been busy with shears and lawnmowers, working the privet hedges and borders into geometric precision.

It was so nearly perfect.

She stood on the front steps of the house as the white Rolls-Royce made its way toward her along the gravel drive. She looked down at Libby. The flower chaplet could not hide the unruly red curls. Was there ever a girl that looked less like her mother? But despite her skinny bones, she looked as lovely as Sarah had ever seen her in the shimmering white satin.

"It's going to be all right, bubeleh."

"You're shaking, Mama."

"Shaking with happiness."

Libby frowned, wasn't buying it. "What happens afterwards, Mama?"

"After, there will be a big party, with lots of nice people."

"At the church?"

"No, here at our house."

"It's not our house, Mama." Libby was squeezing her bouquet of flowers so hard, Sarah thought she would squash them before they even got to the church. She reached down and smoothed her curls, tried to settle her. "I've never been into a church," Libby said.

"You've been in the synagogue. It's like that."

"The Reb says that marrying a goy is not really a marriage, and God will not be happy with us."

"I don't care what the Reb says anymore."

"Will there be other children at the party?"

"I don't know."

"I'm thirsty."

"You can have as much ginger ale as you want when we get back from the church."

"Will we live here after we're married?"

"No, I've told you a hundred times. We're going to live up by the Park. Mr. Dewey has a nice apartment there."

"Will I sleep on the roof?"

"No, you'll never have to sleep on roof again. I promise."

The Rolls-Royce crunched to a stop in front of them.

"I liked the roof," Libby said.

One of Dewey's maids helped Sarah adjust her veil and handed her a bouquet of lilies. Libby helped push the yards of silk on Sarah's train into the back of the Rolls-Royce, then got in beside her.

It was only a short drive to the church, a small wooden clapboard affair painted a duck-egg blue. As they pulled up, a shower of rain swept in from the sea. They waited in the car. Finally, a bolt of sun coaxed a rainbow from behind a lead-dark cloud.

Nelson came around and opened the door, and suddenly the noise of the bells seemed deafening, or perhaps the din was just all the shouting inside her own head. Dewey had said he had arranged to keep the photographers away, but she heard flashbulbs pop as she stepped out of the car.

She was shaking so hard by the time she reached the wooden porch, she was afraid her legs would not carry her down the aisle. She glanced at her daughter and found her strength there. This is for you, little bubeleh.

A hundred faces craning to see her inside the church, all of them strangers. There was no one to give her away; she had decided to walk up the aisle alone. She felt Libby walking in time behind her, never missing a step.

As the organist picked out the first notes of the wedding march, Sarah took a deep breath and took her first step toward the flower-banked altar. She tried not to think about what her vati would say if he could see her marrying a rich goy.

Never mind what he would say. He wasn't here, and he didn't have to live her life. From now on, she would stitch her own way.

—◆—

Chandeliers blazed in every room of the house, throwing bright splashes of light onto the dark sweep of lawn. Staff in white jackets whirled around the rooms with cold and hot hors d'oeuvres on platters; jeweled fingers plucked a champagne flute or a canapé from a tray without even a glance at the help.

Sarah moved in a dream from room to room, overwhelmed by the glitter of silver and crystal, the scent of a hundred bouquets. Dewey must have bought every flower in Manhattan. She tried to mingle, her juniper and tonic in hand. *I must be the loneliest bride in the world,* she thought. *The only person here who does not know everyone else.*

Laughter and conversation filtered through the French doors from the terrace, where silver-haired bankers and brokers in black ties and flappers in fringed gowns flirted with each other in the shadows. A twenty-piece orchestra played Mozart in a room somewhere out of sight. Dewey had told her that he had a black blues quartet coming in from Harlem later to play ragtime. *"When the stuffed shirts have gone home."*

She came upon a room piled almost to the ceiling with boxed presents meticulously wrapped and beribboned. In another, there was a table covered with a white linen tablecloth and on top of it an artfully arranged pyramid of champagne glasses. A thickset man with oily hair and a white jacket two sizes too small for him was pouring French champagne into the topmost glass so that the liquid flowed in a cascade down to the glasses below.

The Volstead Act was merely an inconvenience for men like Dewey. He told her he had organized for crate loads of French champagne, eighteen-year-old Scotch whisky, and spiced gin for the party, all arranged from a reliable source he had. He didn't tell her where.

But now she recognized the man pouring the champagne, from a club they had been to in Harlem. He kept ducking below the table to take nips from the whisky bottle itself. She told Dewey, but he shrugged it off. "If I complain, they could skedaddle and take all the booze with them," he said.

"But they're stealing from us."

"We never use that word on Wall," he said. "Let's just say they're paying themselves a commission. Don't worry, darling, let's mingle."

Dewey introduced her to the Sharkeys and the Walkers and the Rochfords and the Whitneys and the Weirs. As they circled the room and she listened to the gossip, she started to realize how far out of her depth she was; Dewey's guests talked about the currents in Shinnecock Bay, "that damned Kennedy fellow," how dull it was in Kennebunkport in the winter, the best place to ski in California, the scoop on RCA's new prospectus. Had she heard that Gretel was enrolled at Radcliffe next year?

Gretel who? she thought. And what was Radcliffe?

How could she ever host parties for these people? How could she even find things to talk about? What did she know from mergers and share prices and summer in Maine and winter in Palm Beach?

She started at a terrific bang from outside. The crowd exploded into laughter, no one seemed concerned by it. They poured out the French doors onto the lawn. There was a whistle as another rocket arced up in the sky and then exploded into an orange shower of sparks.

She tugged on her new husband's arm. "I'm going to find the powder room," she said.

⸻

Such a bathroom it was; and her new husband had four of them just in this one house. All glazed white tiles, floor to ceiling, and a mirror almost the length of one wall with a shelf underneath filled with soaps in fancy packets and little bottles of sweet-smelling stuff for the hands and hair and face.

In Cannon Street, they had two wooden outhouses downstairs for every schmuck and his wife. They stank like nobody's business in summer and froze over in winter.

She didn't really need to pee, she just needed to be alone. She went into the cubicle, locked the door, and sat down. She put her head in her hands. What have I done?

Everything had happened so fast. Every few years there is a new me: first, Sura Muscowitz, then the widow Sarah Levine, now Mrs. Sarah Dewey?

She heard the door open and close and heard voices. Someone tried the cubicle door. Sarah thought they would go out again, but no, they decided to fix their faces in the mirror and wait.

"Isn't this place the bee's knees," a woman's voice said.

"Dewey must be rich as Croesus," her friend said. "Excuse me, but what is he doing marrying that little trollop? Did you see her? She hasn't a clue. I heard this time last year she was digging up potatoes in Poland."

"Guess she gave up potato digging for gold digging."

"You know the flower girl is her daughter?"

"You are joshing me! I thought she was a showgirl?"

"The girl must have been showing it before Ziegfeld found her, I guess."

Sarah felt the acid of her own bile in the back of her throat. Too much champagne, too much humiliation. What if Libby heard these people talking about her like this? Libby—where was Libby? She hadn't seen her since going upstairs to change out of her wedding dress.

"She's a Jew, you know."

"They can smell money, those people."

"She sure sniffed out a bargain this time."

Sarah opened the door. One of the women was bent over the washbasin, repairing her mascara in the mirror, her well-rounded bottom papered in taffeta; the other, with bobbed hair and a knee-length fringed dress, was fidgeting with an earring.

They stared aghast at her in the mirror.

"It wasn't Poland, it was Russia," Sarah said. "And us Jews, not true what they say. We can't smell money, only trash." She stepped up to them and sniffed, took one of the perfume sprays off the shelf and squirted it at them. "There. That's better."

I won't let them see me cry, she thought as she walked out. I won't. Now I must find my Libby.

She clenched her fists at her sides and made her way back down the hall toward the garden.

"The new Mrs. Dewey."

A man in a beautifully tailored topcoat and striped trousers stepped in front of her as she made her way down the hall from the bathroom. It was George, Dewey's best man. Her cheeks still felt like they were on fire. What did he want? She didn't need anyone else telling her she was trash.

"A word?" he said. He put two fingers on her upper arm and gently guided her through a door into the kitchen and kicked the door shut behind him. She saw the cooks look up for a moment, but when they saw who it was, they quickly put their heads down again, went on with their clattering of saucepans and skillets, throwing purple lobsters into pots, arranging desserts on silver trays. And shouting, everyone shouting at each other. Like being back in Hester Street, it was so much din.

"I promised him I wouldn't say anything," George said.

Sarah waited. The look on his face—she had seen bailiffs looking more friendly.

"Billy said I shouldn't. But I find I can't help myself."

"What is wrong?"

"Sarah. You don't mind if I call you Sarah? Sarah, you are what is wrong."

"You too, huh? Everyone is entitled to their opinion. I got to find my daughter." She tried to push past him, but he stood his ground.

"The thing is, you don't know him, do you? Not like the rest of us. How long ago did you meet him? A month, was it? Two?"

"Three months."

"Three months." A chill smile. "He probably told you about inheriting a bank and going to an Ivy League college and having a shack on Long Island. Must have been irresistible."

"What is it you want?"

"Did he tell you—I mean, knowing Billy, he wouldn't have—his firm was almost bankrupt when he took over from dear old Dad? I know he makes it sound like he was born with a silver spoon in his mouth, but it wasn't like that. He spent the last twenty years making good on his father's mistakes. Did he tell you he had a brother who was born"—he tapped his forehead—"let's say he wasn't quite right. He spent his whole life in a nursing home. Billy took care of him. I don't mean just paid the bills; he went to visit him every day for fifteen years."

"No, he never told me."

"No, of course he didn't. He wouldn't. Something else he didn't tell you: when I lost my first wife, it was Billy who stopped me throwing my life away. I mean literally. I was going to throw myself off a bridge. Billy talked sense into me, got me back to work, stopped me drinking, made me see a purpose in things again."

"Why are you telling me all this?"

He stepped closer. "Just reminding you that for all his eccentricities, Billy has a lot of friends, powerful friends. You've done well for yourself. Well, good for you. But don't you ever hurt him. Do you understand?"

The door to the kitchen burst open. One of the waiters stood there, wide eyed, and said, "Is Mrs. Dewey here?"

Sarah looked around. George shook his head and smiled. "He means you."

Of course, of course. "What is it?" Sarah said.

"You should come, Mrs. Dewey. There's trouble. Your daughter."

Sarah pushed George aside and followed the man out the door.

30

Libby sat in the dark on the lawn, beyond the line of shadow, listening to all the people talking and laughing, watching the millionaire types with their pretty wives and girlfriends, all fancy-schmancy, and wished she was back on the roof with Frankie, listening to the Kohns fighting and the mice scuttling in the air shaft.

She saw a boy walk onto the lawn past the white marquee tent, coming right toward her. She kept very still. He fidgeted with the fly on his pants, then she heard him start to pee. She couldn't help it: she started to giggle.

"Holy crap!" When he saw her, he did himself up again and took a step back, into the light. "What are you doing there?"

"I'm just sitting here," Libby said. "What are *you* doing?"

"What does it look like I'm doing?"

"You're not allowed."

"Hell, Uncle Billy won't mind. A few brown patches on his lawn; he's got acres of the stuff." He stepped closer, peered at her face. "You're a girl."

"Top of the class, boy genius."

"Are you Mrs. Dewey's flower girl?"

"I'm her daughter."

"Her daughter," he said, and something about the way he said it, she didn't like.

"What of it?"

"What are you doing creeping around here?"

"I don't know anyone."

"Big surprise."

Libby stood up. She thought she could take him on her own, but she wasn't sure, not without Frankie there to help her. "What's that supposed to mean?"

"Nothing."

"Sounds like it sure means something to me."

He squinted at her. "You don't look much like your mom, do you? I mean, she's a real good-looking dame."

"Are you saying I'm not?"

"Well, you're not going to be in the Follies when you grow up, not with a monkey face like that." It wasn't just what he said; it was the little laugh he finished off with. She guessed he wasn't expecting to get hit, not by a girl. But that was one advantage of growing up on the Lower East Side. She didn't know much about where the silver went on the table, but she sure knew how to take a bigger kid by surprise and make it count.

<hr />

When Sarah reached the lawn, she heard her daughter yelling. There was a little crowd gathered around, and when she pushed her way through, she found Libby wrestling with a bigger boy. She had him in a headlock, and his nose was bleeding. Sarah grabbed her daughter and pulled her away, still wriggling and yelling. Sarah had never seen her so mad.

She guessed the boy was two or three years older than Libby. He wanted to carry on with it as well; but then that George, Dewey's best man, suddenly he was there, and he took the boy by the arm and spun him around.

"What the hell's going on? Are you fighting? Explain yourself, young man."

"She started it!"

"You're fighting with a girl?"

"I didn't hit her, she hit me!"

"Well, if she hit you, you must have deserved it." He looked directly at Libby. "Please accept my apologies for my son's behavior," he said to her. "Rest assured, he will be reprimanded." And he dragged the kid away, back inside the house.

Sarah stared after him, trying to square the man who had threatened her in the kitchen with the man who had just told his son that a woman was never to be harmed in any way, no matter the provocation.

Dewey appeared, a champagne glass in his hand. He was smiling as if the whole thing was part of the amusements.

"Heard there was a bit of a to-do. Has George sorted it all out?"

"Yes, everything is fine now."

"That's good, then. Good old George."

"What is it that is so good from old George?" she muttered.

"Are you all right? Just kids being kids." He winked at Libby, then looked back to Sarah. "Don't worry about it, darling."

"Who is this George?"

"My fault. I should have introduced you properly. George and I grew up together. Probably the oldest friend I've got."

Something about him, she thought, was oddly familiar.

"And this George, what is his other name?"

"It's Seabrook, George Seabrook."

31

There was a fine glaze of light along the sky, dawn not far off. The sand along the shoreline was cold under her bare toes. She looked back at the house still blazing with light through the mist, wondered if all the guests were gone, if it was safe to go back.

She heard a foghorn somewhere out on the Sound. It reminded her of the troopship that took Micha away from her. I should have loved him more, she thought.

A green light burned on the end of the dock. I should have loved him more. Will I be saying that one day about my new husband?

"There you are," a voice said. It was Dewey. "A fine way to spend your wedding night."

"Have they all gone?"

"Just the servants clearing up."

"Where is Libby?"

"She's tucked up, asleep." Dewey had taken off his shoes and socks, stood there in his suspenders and shirtsleeves, a brandy snifter in his right hand. He offered it to her, and she took it and gulped at it, felt it burn all the way down. She shuddered.

"What's wrong?" he said.

Tell him, she thought. Tell him everything. If you don't, you are going to have to lie for the rest of your life together. Tell him about his friend George Seabrook, that you stole his daughter from him, that Libby is his blood and bone.

Say it, Sarah. End this now. It's your fault you are in a mess again. Now you have to fix it.

"He threatened me," she said.

"Who? Who threatened you?"

"'Good old George.' He said I should never hurt you, or else I would be in trouble."

"Did he?" He took the snifter back and swallowed the rest. When he spoke again, his voice had taken on a hard edge. "I'm sure he didn't mean it."

"Do you see him very much?"

"Not often. He lives in Boston now. We go out to lunch whenever he comes to town, maybe three or four times a year."

Three or four times a year, she thought. That's not a lot, especially if he doesn't come to the house, just goes to Dewey's club downtown.

"I'm sure he didn't mean to scare you. He's a teddy bear, really, don't take any notice. Come back to the house. It's our wedding night. We should be tucked up in bed by now."

Sad, sweet Dewey, still wanting to protect her over anything. She felt a sudden wave of affection for him. She supposed right then she felt a lot better about him than she did about herself. She smiled and took his hand and walked back with him across the lawn.

<hr />

She woke up a few hours later in the large white bed on the top floor of the house. She reached out for her new husband, but he wasn't there, the bedsheets on his side thrown back, the pillow still warm. She sat up. It was morning. The French doors were open, and the white net curtains billowed in a soft salt breeze. Out on the Sound the scalloped sail of a yacht luffed in the wind as an ancient cedar-hulled schooner reached back toward the land.

She put on a dressing gown and went out onto the landing. The servants were still clearing up after the party. She heard Dewey's voice, leaned over the bannister, and saw him murmuring into the telephone.

⋙

"Billy," George said down the line. "You're up early. Thought you'd still be sleeping it off."

"Wanted to catch you before you headed back to Boston."

"I was about to go down to breakfast. What can I do for you, Bill?"

Dewey watched two of the servants carrying boxes of empty bottles out to the truck outside. He wondered how many bottles of French champagne his guests had gone through last night. He wasn't looking forward to getting the bill.

"Heard there was a bit of a set-to last night."

"You mean Jack and your stepdaughter? I wouldn't worry about that. I handled it."

"No, not that. Sarah said you two had words."

There was a long silence on the other end of the telephone. Finally, George said: "Sorry, Bill, but you know me, if something needs to be said, I say it."

"And what is it that you think needs to be said, George?"

"For God's sake."

"I know what you think of her. You've made that clear enough."

There was a crash from the kitchen: one of the maids had dropped a plate. Dewey hissed "Keep it down in there!" as one of the juniors ran to fetch a dustpan and broom.

"I'll call you next time I come to town," George said.

"I guess," Dewey said, and hung up. Something made him look up. He saw Sarah on the landing. She was there only for a second, and then she dashed back to the bedroom. He hadn't meant for her to hear, but he supposed it didn't matter that she had. He wanted her to know she was his wife now, and she didn't have to take bad-mouthing from anyone. Even George Seabrook.

PART 4

32

Arlington Apartments, Upper West Side, New York, August 1929

Sarah woke to the sun streaming in through the tall windows. She slipped into her gown and velvet slippers and went out onto the terrace. Central Park was bathed in sunshine all the way to Harlem. The sound of traffic from below was muted. New York already up and about its business, making more gelt than it could ever spend.

Seven years, and still not a morning she didn't look at this view and think about Delancey Street. Back in those days, she was lucky ever to see any blue sky between the tracks of the Elevated and the tangle of fire escapes. Up here there were eggs scrambled in a pan for her whenever she asked, brought to her on fine bone china along with an ironed newspaper; a maid to fetch pickles instead of buying them from a pushcart; no hiding under the stairs from the rent man; here she had the smell of coffee and not the reek of the outhouse in the yard and the stink of yesterday's herring going stale.

Dewey was already dressed in his banker suit and polished banker shoes, sitting at the breakfast table reading the financial pages of the *New York Times*. He murmured a good morning to her from behind the newspaper. The maid asked her if she wanted breakfast.

"Just coffee, Constance," she said.

"Not hungry?" Dewey said to her.

"I didn't sleep good." She stared at the stack of mail on the table beside her plate and winced. "Is Libby up?" she asked Constance when she returned with the coffee.

"Not yet, ma'am."

Still in bed! Sarah thought. Home from her fancy school almost a week, and she had hardly seen her.

Another glance at her mail: invitations to parties and dinners. Why she should care for such things? She read the front page of the *Times* as Dewey held it, his hand reaching from behind it occasionally to grope for his coffee cup.

On the bottom corner of the newspaper was a photograph of a man with a ridiculous moustache standing on a big podium, crowds all around. Adolf Hitler again. Another rally, this time Nuremberg or someplace, him spieling about "unwanted populations"—He means the Muscowitzes and the Levines, she thought, the Jews. People like me. She thought again about Mutti and her father and her sisters in Tallinn. Will they be safe? Will they never stop hating us, those people? Perhaps Micha was right to bring us here.

Dewey put the paper down.

"Can I see?" she said.

He passed her the newspaper, and she pointed to the picture of Hitler. "Should we be worried about this *meshuggener?*"

"It's nothing to do with us here in America. We have other things to worry about."

"What about my sisters in Tallinn?"

"Estonia isn't part of Russia or Germany anymore."

"What do Russia and Germany know from borders? They will just swat them away like they are nothing, like always."

"It is all Poincaré's fault."

"Who is he?"

"He was France's prime minister until a few weeks ago. He wanted the Germans to pay back every cent of their war reparations debt."

"Why shouldn't they pay?" Sarah asked him.

"Whether they should or shouldn't is irrelevant. But by keeping the Germans on their knees, they're feeding the popularity of this Hitler and his National Socialists. When it comes to money, you have to be practical. Always. They don't seem to understand that." He glanced at the mail by her sleeve. "What have you got there?"

She tore open the first one. "The Charltons, their oldest daughter, she is getting engaged at the Ritz. We are invited to the party."

He made a face.

"Do we have to go?" she asked.

"Afraid so."

"Was a time you said we're not going, and that was that."

"Things are a bit different right now," Dewey said. "It will give me a chance to . . . what do you call it?"

"Schmooze."

"That's it. Schmooze."

"What do you need from schmoozing? You told me once, your customers, they put their foot in your door."

"Times change."

"So, this summer, we are going out to Long Island?"

"I don't think so."

"But every year we go in August. So hot in the city now."

"This isn't every year. Usually, the market's quiet and everyone's away. But it's still crazy right now. Have to make hay while the sun shines, as they say."

"We don't have enough hay?"

"You can never have enough hay, darling."

"But we don't need to worry, yes?"

"Worry? Whatever do you mean, worry?"

"We got enough hay for when the summer ends."

"But that's the whole point, sweetheart. In America, the summer never ends."

"No, Dewey, something I know for sure. Winter, it always comes."

She saw the look on his face, that flash of uncertainty, then it was gone. The old Dewey wasn't like that, she thought. He never talked about hay and summer back in the old days.

But what did she know from such things? All his life he had worked in this money business. He knew from dollars and cents like her papa used to know stitches. If he said not to worry, then there was nothing to worry.

She could hear the muted chatter of the radio in the kitchen, the morning prayers finished, so time for the stock report. These days everyone listened to it, even their cook owned shares on the market. She heard her talking to Constance about AT&T prices when she was preparing dinner.

Sarah said to Dewey: "Jane Pargetter told me their butcher's boy came to see her the other day, wanted her to ask her husband if the latest turndown was the end of the bull market or readjustment only."

"Downturn not turndown. And I think she made that story up."

"She swears it is true."

"Because someone says something is true doesn't mean it is true. A friend of mine told me yesterday that Saratoga was cutting out all races over five furlongs because the jockeys didn't like spending so long away from the ticker in the clubhouse. Swore on his mother's life. But it's all nonsense. I'm sure our old friend Will Rogers will be having a lot of fun."

"So what do I say to the Charltons?"

"We'll have to go, we can't avoid it."

"Do we take Libby?"

"She's of an age now. I don't see why not." He glanced at his wrist-watch. "I'm late. I'd better go to work." He drained his coffee cup and stood up, told Constance to call down for Nelson. He picked up his leather briefcase and hurried out the door.

After he had gone, Constance came back in with the silver coffee pot and poured Sarah a second cup of coffee. Sarah idled through the newspaper, looking at the advertisements; that fancy-schmancy British woman Lady Grace Drummond Hay wanted her to know she smoked a Lucky instead of eating sweets; an Austrian baron smiled at her, insisting that a bond release she'd never heard of assured the future of all his estates in Salzburg; an Italian count was recommending a rival issue while he watched the sun rise over the Mediterranean from the terrace of his villa.

This was the America her Micha had told her about: gold on the footpath waiting to be shoveled up. He should be here to see all this, she thought. She looked through the entertainment guide and told Constance to book three seats for Eddie Cantor's *Whoopee* for tomorrow night. Libby would enjoy that.

Sarah lingered over her coffee. The day stretched out in front of her, endless, like when she came from Russia on the boat, nothing to do but look at forever-flat sea.

She hoped Libby would get up soon. There was this nameless ache inside. What was this thing? She had done everything as she had promised Liberty she would. But having everything perfect should feel more perfect than this. She had thought Dewey would give her another baby to look after, but seven years now and nothing. She knew for certain now, there would be no more babies, not ever.

All those years she had blamed Micha for no family. But maybe it wasn't Micha, maybe it was her all along. Two husbands now, and still no babies. Maybe Micha falling off his horse when he was a boy, that was all just *shtus*. All that time she had wished herself a new husband, and what it was, poor Micha had got himself a barren wife. Maybe her vati was right: God had made a different plan for them, a no-baby plan, until Micha had decided to change it.

She went into her study, took out her pen and her writing paper, and wrote a long letter to her vati and mutti in Tallinn, as she had done on the first of every month since she arrived in America. She worried about them all the time these days. The last she had heard, Mutti had been very sick. And this news from Germany, this Hitler person, it made her worry for all her sisters: Etta, now with two boys as well as young Bessie; Zlota with a real brood; Gutta, her own tribe (or that was Etta's private joke to her). Sarah had tried to persuade them to leave, but no. Etta had written, "Everything is going to be all right. We are our own country now. Estonia they call us. No one will harm us here."

Everything is going to be all right. How many hundreds of years had Jews been saying that? She finished the letter, and before she licked the envelope closed, she folded a fifty-dollar note very tight, and slipped it inside the pages, like she always did. She hoped it would get there safe. So many hands it had to pass through before it arrived in the smoky little shtetl of Haapvinni.

⚊

The captains at the Plaza had long red coats with brass buttons. They reminded Sarah of the footmen in the Cinderella story that Liberty had loved as a child. One of them blew a whistle to summon a horse-drawn carriage to the foyer for one of the guests, another saluted her as she climbed out of the car. A uniformed bellhop swung the revolving door for her.

It was palatial chaos inside: guests checking in, their luggage and mistresses and pet poodles scattered among the potted palms, the sound of a string quartet played somewhere in the lobby hidden by the pink-and-gray-veined marble pillars. An enormous chandelier hung from the ceiling, bigger than the sled she used to ride to market on as a child. She never told anyone, but she never liked the Plaza, even though she came here almost every week. To a little girl from the shtetl, it looked only vain and vulgar.

Like so many of my friends these days, she thought.

Most of the club members were already there: Jane Pargetter, smoking a Turkish cigarette from a long ivory holder; Beatrice Charlton, floating across the carpets in a fug of Chanel perfume, wearing one of the new high-low hems; and Diana Richmond, what was she wearing? Sleeveless, shapeless chiffon, and all that décolletage! So much gelt, and what did she know from elegance? With her, everything was about dollars. If it cost a lot, then she must have it.

But, then, nobody cared about day wear, about evening wear anymore. There were frocks for everything: shopping frocks, traveling frocks, dancing frocks.

Yes, why not stock frocks?

One of the Plaza's assistant managers, dressed in a herringbone morning suit, greeted them all good morning and escorted them into the elevator and up to the suite the hotel had reserved for them. Inside, there were ticker machines and bottles of champagne in ice buckets and canapés all laid out on a linen-covered table. Jane Pargetter had a waiter pour her a glass of Taittinger and lit another cigarette. Instead of a chocolate tartlet, Sarah thought. Watching her figure, like Lady La-di-da from England.

Sarah read the latest ticker tape, by now she knew all the symbols as well as any of the other ladies: ATT was American Telephone and Telegraph; SAL was Seaboard Airlines. She had made almost fifty thousand dollars since she'd joined the club and started trading, almost a year ago. Not bad for a girl from Delancey Street.

Jane Pargetter plumped down in the leather chesterfield beside her. "Did you hear on the radio?" she said to Sarah. "The Graf Zeppelin is taking off from Lakehurst today. It goes back to Germany first, then flies all the way to Tokyo *nonstop*. Imagine."

"Over Russia?"

"Yes, over Russia. If you were on board, you could be waving to all your old friends out the window this time next week."

Sarah smiled and thought about putting Jane's ivory cigarette holder where the sun didn't shine.

"They say in ten years, you'll be able to fly from London to New York like taking a train to Boston."

Sarah remembered what Dewey had said about the Saratoga races and decided this was just another of Jane's fancy stories.

"Oh look, it's Katya," Jane said. "That's Henry Garret's new wife. Katya!"

Sarah thought she saw a look of dismay on Katya's pretty face, but perhaps she was imagining only. Whatever it was she saw, the look was quickly replaced with a smile. She came over.

Katya was young, early twenties, a pretty little thing in a trompe l'oeil bow sweater and a pleated skirt.

"Love what you're wearing," Jane said.

"It's Elsa Schiaparelli."

"Bee's knees! Katya, do you know Sarah Dewey? Sarah's from Russia too. Came here to get away from those dreadful Bolsheviks. Lost all her estates, like you did. Where was it you lived, Katya?"

Sarah recognized a look of panic on the young woman's face; this time she was not imagining.

"Just outside Saint Petersburg. Well, they call it Petrograd now."

"Sarah is from there. Aren't you, Sarah? What was your Russian name, Katya? Perhaps you two knew each other!"

"I don't think so," Katya said.

"Annenkov. That was it!" Jane lowered her voice, as if she was imparting a secret. "Katya told me her maternal great-grandfather was Pyotr Zavadovsky. He was secretary to Catherine the Great. Katya says he provided other services as well." She gave Sarah an exaggerated wink. "Were you often at court, Katya?"

"No, not often. Our estates were some distance away."

"Wait a moment," Sarah said. "I remember as a child my father talked about Annenkovs. They are a very famous family in Russia, Jane."

"Isn't that nice," Jane said, and drew on her cigarette, "to be remembered. Even after you've lost everything."

"Yes," Katya said. "It is."

Sarah excused herself and went to the ladies' powder room. To her surprise Katya followed her. They studied each other in the mirror.

"Thank you," Katya said.

"For what?"

"For what you just did," Katya said, and Sarah thought: So she's just another girl from the Lower East Side like me. But I'm better at faking it than she is.

"We former countesses must stick together," Sarah said. She checked her reflection a second time to make sure her makeup was flawless. She turned to go, but before she left, she said to Katya, "What do they all say about me?"

"Only good things," Katya said, but by the look on the girl's face, Sarah could see the truth right there. She really was a hopeless liar. She wasn't going to last five minutes in this crowd.

33

Sarah had Nelson swing past Arlington Apartments after the Plaza, to fetch Libby. What is she wearing? Sarah thought as she came out. Could her hemline be any shorter? And what has she done with her hair? She must have gone out this morning as soon as I left, the little minx.

Libby climbed in the back. Sarah was hoping for a sign of contrition, but no, nothing.

"You've been with your stock lady friends," Liberty said.

Sarah saw Nelson glance at her in the rearview mirror. "Saks," she said to him, then slid the glass across so he couldn't hear any more of the exchange.

"Have you been drinking?" Libby said. "It's not even lunchtime."

"Made a killing on RCA."

"Well, good for you, Mama."

"What you done with your hair?"

"Do you like it?"

"You should ask me first if you can wear your hair like that."

"I'm sixteen years old, Mama."

"That is what I am saying. You are only sixteen!"

"It's a Dutch bob cut. All the girls at school have them."

"At Westover they will let you wear your hair like this? Is this a kiss curl?"

"It's the Louise Brooks pageboy look."

"You are too young to have a look. When I was your age, I did not have any look."

"You were never my age, Mama. Why are we going to Saks?"

"You must have something to wear for the Charlton party. Their eldest daughter is getting engaged."

A sigh. "If we must."

<hr />

The main floor of Saks was themed to the Graf Zeppelin flight. A huge papier-mâché zeppelin was suspended from the ceiling, and each department was styled on countries the aircraft would pass over on its way around the world: there were models costumed as German beer hall waitresses; metal gongs and red paper cherry blossoms coiled around the marble pillars in the Tokyo section; there were palm leaves to represent Los Angeles and cotton wool snow for Siberia.

The manageress of the fashion department recognized Sarah immediately. She invited her into her office to see the new season's catalog.

She turned around and saw Liberty. "Is this your daughter?"

Sarah saw the look on the woman's face, had seen that same look a hundred times before. "Yes."

The manageress gave her a tight little smile. "Oh, I'm sorry, I didn't realize. She's quite lovely."

And it was true, she was. When she was growing up, she had been all angles, all bones, but now she had bumps and curves in all the right places. Sarah's little caterpillar had turned into a beautiful butterfly with such flaming red hair and green eyes and looked not even a little bit like her.

Libby was oblivious, was staring at a sleeveless dress by Chanel in black crepe de chine. "What are you doing?" Sarah said.

"Can I have that?"

"This is not a dress for sixteen years old."

"Chanel says it's the frock that all the world will wear."

"All the world except you, bubeleh," Sarah said, and led her away.

In the end, she bought Libby a dress of shot silk taffeta, sleeveless, with a square collar and a two-tone taffeta flower at the hips. And a Lido cloche. Liberty acted like she had bought her a brown sack and a paper hat.

So, their first shopping expedition since Libby had gotten home from Westover for the summer. This was not how Sarah expected it would be. What a spoiled brat they had made of her at that school. She didn't appreciate nothing. Had she forgotten what it was like living on Cannon Street?

"Try not sleep so long tomorrow," Sarah said to her as they drove back through Manhattan and up Fifth. In her mind Sarah ticked off the stores she knew as they passed: Tiffany, where Dewey had bought her the engagement ring; Saks Fifth Avenue, where he had got the necklace she had asked for on their first anniversary; and just down there, on Madison, the Abercrombie & Fitch store, where she and all the stock market wives bought their mah-jongg sets. What a Wasp she had become.

"I thought maybe we will do something tomorrow," she said to Liberty.

"I don't want to go drinking shampoo with all your old face stretchers."

Sarah stared at her, didn't know what to say. Never would she have spoken to Mutti or her vati this way. It hadn't been like this before Libby went to Westover. What were they teaching her at this fancy school?

Or perhaps the trouble was something else. Before Sarah got remarried, it had been just her and Libby; no matter the poorness, she was still her mama, good and bad. But now, it didn't matter how many millionaire things they had, it wasn't the same.

Sarah even wished sometimes they could sit at the cluttered kitchen table in Cannon Street again, eating potato latkes and practicing her numbers on butcher paper, no bell to ring, no maid to bring coffee, no Nelson to drive them wherever in the shiny black Bentley.

Bit by bit, she was losing her bubeleh. Soon she would be all gone.

"I've arranged to see Frankie tomorrow," Libby said. "You know her mama's sick?"

"Mary? No, I didn't know this."

"I thought you did."

"Nothing bad?"

"I don't know. Frankie wrote and told me a few weeks ago. She was good to you, wasn't she, her mama?"

"Yes. A good woman."

"When was the last time you saw her?"

"I don't remember. It's been a while. It's hard to stay in touch."

"She still lives on Cannon Street. It's only downtown. It's not Wisconsin."

"Things are different now."

"Sure they are, Mama." And then, under her breath: "She doesn't know how to play mah-jongg."

34

"You're up early, young lady," Dewey said.

Eyes in the back of his head, that man, Libby thought. She went into the conservatory, where he was drinking his morning cup of coffee and reading the financial pages, ignoring the view over Central Park.

"I'm going out."

"With?"

"Some fast boy I met at a speakeasy. He has a red roadster and buys me champagne and cigarettes."

"Well, that's good. As long as you're not getting into any trouble."

"I'm meeting an old friend of mine downtown."

"I'll tell Nelson. He'll drop you off."

She kissed him on the top of his head. He had grown a bald patch the last couple of years, and it made him only all the more endearing. "Thanks, Dewey."

"Your mother says you've been talking back at her."

"Did she tell you to give me a dressing down?"

"I wouldn't dream of dressing you down, young lady. They don't pay me enough to take those kinds of risks."

"She's always telling me what to do."

"She's your mother, what do you expect?" He put down his coffee cup and folded the *Times* in his lap. He took her hand. "Take it easy on her, Libs. She means the best for you."

"I'll do my best," Liberty said, and slipped away into the bathroom before he could persuade her to apologize to her mother.

She didn't take up the offer of having Nelson drive her. Instead, she slipped out after Sarah had gone to the Plaza, and went down to Columbus Circle and took the Elevated instead. She didn't want them checking up on her; and besides, she liked to do things for herself.

The station was a riot of billboards, advertisements for Scotch tape, Welch's grape juice, Listerine mouthwash, Schick electric razors. God how she hated New York. Everything was buy, buy, buy.

She had written to Frankie before leaving school, had arranged to meet her outside the station on Grand Street. It was strange being back there after so long, after the washed-clean of Westover and the Upper West Side, being buffeted by the people crammed in the streets, the pushcart hawkers yelling so loud, the Jewish wives in their wigs, shoving her with their baskets. They were all still here: the men with side curls and white collars and shiny black suits; the Bolsheviks sitting in dark coffee shops, looking out at the world with their red eyes and fierce little beards.

She searched the faces, wondered if Frankie got her letter, if she would be there. Libby had worn her plainest dress, but she suddenly felt out of place. Hard to believe these were the same streets where she grew up.

She heard someone shout: "Hey, Miss Rockefeller!"

It was Frankie. Libby waved and pushed her way through the crowd to the other side of the street.

"Frankie!"

"Lib!"

They hugged each other. A whole term since they had seen each other, and it felt like a hundred years. Frankie never changed much;

she wore the same five-and-dime blouse she had on the last time they met, a pleated skirt, her hair a tangled mess. Liberty felt awkward, as she always did, in her Bergdorf frock, even though it was an old one, and with her new Dutch bob.

"Look at you," Frankie said, mussing her hair. "If it isn't the It girl. You're a sight to behold on Delancey Street. Don't get your new pumps muddy now."

"You stop that, Frankie. I can still give you a good hiding. Now where are we going?"

"Well, that depends. You're not too fancy for Coney Island, are you?"

<hr />

The people on the train were from the Lower East Side, most of them; the men worked down at the docks and the women in the sweatshops for pauper wages, like her mama had done. They came to Coney Island to escape the heat and squalor of the tenements, even though they most likely had just a few nickels in their pockets to spend. They couldn't afford the fifty cents for the bathhouses or a dime for a hot dog, so they wore their bathing suits under their clothes and brought their own food with them in big wicker baskets.

Liberty bought two hot dogs from a man in a greasy apron, and she and Frankie walked arm in arm along the boardwalk, past the groynes and dirty brown beach, the thrown-off clothes from Macy's basement or Klein's lying around in the sand or fluttering from the jetties. The tide was on its way in, the wavelets breaking over the sandcastles kids had built along the shore.

"How's school?" Frankie said. "Still hate it?"

"All the girls ever want to talk about is riding horses and whether they're going to Paris or Italy for the summer holidays. I feel like a duck in a henhouse in that place."

"Well, you've only another year till you finish."

"Then there's college. They're going to send me to Bryn Mawr."

"Where's that?"

"It's in Philadelphia."

"Thank God, I thought it was China."

"Dewey wants me to do history and philosophy."

"Why does he want you to do all that?"

"I've no idea. Mama just wants me to dress well and marry rich, but I don't know if there's a degree in that."

They went down one of the honky-tonk alleys, past the penny arcades and food stands. Such a din, Libby thought. All the mechanical pianos and girls screaming on the rides, the slam of bumper cars, and the barkers yelling in the shooting galleries or grabbing at the young men who tried to show off for their girls at the high strikers, two wallops for a nickel, five for a dime.

They lost themselves in the midway, everything smelled rich down there, like potato latkes and fried meat, or sweet, like popcorn and cotton candy. They went past the tattoo artists and the freak shows, women screaming as their skirts were blown right over their heads in the Blowhole Theatre, everything a shrieking commotion of mirrors and blinking lights and loud clanging music. Frankie kept offering to pay for the rides; but every time, Liberty said, "You get the next one," knowing Frankie didn't have the two bits to waste on the shooting gallery or fifteen cents to ride the Cyclone roller coaster.

But Liberty did, so finally they found themselves in two carriage seats on the Wonder Wheel, high above the holiday crowds and the deck chairs and the turrets and columns and mechanical scaffolding of the amusement parks. Down below they could see long lines of people queueing on Surf Avenue for the Cyclone. The wheel lurched to a halt, and they swung side by side, so high up, above everything. All the jangling and screaming and crashing was muted by the wind, so it was almost peaceful.

"How's your ma?" Liberty said.

"Still in the hospital. She can't work anymore. She's lost her job."

"How are you managing?"

"Didn't you know? Your mother sends us checks."

"Well, so she should."

"No 'should' about it. She doesn't owe us anything. She's a good heart, is what she has."

"Has she come to visit?"

"She doesn't have to do that."

"Your mama used to be her best friend."

"Well, bringing grapes to the hospital doesn't pay the bills. Don't know what we'd do without the money she sends us."

Libby stared out at the sea. The air smelled of salt and, faintly, even up here, of sugar and fried onions. "Still, she should make time for her."

"She's a busy woman."

"She's not busy, she's embarrassed."

"Well, that's no mind to me, Lib. She's done more for us than anyone else ever did. You go too hard on her."

"I can't help it, Frankie. She makes me so mad. Ever since she became Mrs. Sarah Dewey, it's like she's been someone she's not. And she's trying to make me someone I'm not too."

"What do you want from her?"

Liberty shrugged.

"You can't blame her for wanting a better life for you."

The Ferris wheel started up again, the carriages lurched, and Frankie laughed and Liberty screamed.

"Should we go and see the Swiss Cheese Man?" Frankie said. "They say he goes right up to the roof of the tent with hooks in him."

"No, I think it's sad."

They were in the Bowery, the long and crowded alley that wound through the heart of Coney Island from the Steeplechase to Feltman's Arcade. A wooden wall on one side rattled and shook when the roller-coaster ride went past.

"What about the Tunnel of Love?"

"With you?"

"I'll be the boy if you like and try and kiss you, and you can try and fend me off."

"I've never had a boy try and kiss me, so I wouldn't know how."

"It's easy," Frankie said, "you just turn your head away and pretend like you're not interested. It makes them try harder."

"When have you had a boy try and kiss you?"

"I've had my share. Haven't you?"

"Not at Westover. They're all girls."

"Just as well. Boys are no good for anything anyway; they only get you in the family way, like my sister. For the love of God, she's not much older than me."

"What are you planning to do?"

"I'll not spend the rest of my life making shirtwaists for a few nickels an hour, that's for sure. I'm planning to go back to school."

"Can you afford it?"

"Thanks to your ma, I can. I want to make something of myself, or at least, if I can't do that, I'll do something useful. Thinking of being a nurse, me."

"A nurse?"

"Well, it's not the most glamorous thing, I guess, but I'm no Jean Harlow, and I'm not clever enough to be a teacher. It means going to night school, and that'll be hard after I've been working all day. But it's that or end up like my ma."

They went to see Professor Bernard, Magician Extraordinary, and his star act, Bonita and her Fighting Lions. To finish, they went on the

Thunderbolt because the lines for the Cyclone still stretched halfway around the block.

On the train back into the city, they sat side by side on the hard wooden benches as the train rattled back through Brooklyn, and Frankie put her head on Liberty's shoulder. "Do you ever wonder," she said, "what would happen if you were born to another family?"

"How do you mean?"

"Well, I think about what I'd be like if my da had been one of those millionaire fellas. If I'd be different."

"I don't know, Frankie. I think we all make our own way. If we're strong enough, we find our own level in the end."

"It's nice to think so," Frankie said.

35

Dewey rolled away from her and onto his back, breathing hard. Sarah rolled with him, curled under his arm, ran a hand along the smooth skin of his chest, felt his heart beating against his ribs. "That was nice," she said.

She said it so soft, perhaps he didn't hear her. Was a woman supposed to like this? Some of the wives at the Plaza said they did, but they weren't good Jewish girls from the shtetl. He wasn't like Micha, her Dewey, not mister couple of minutes to do your business, then lie there snoring. So gentle, Dewey was.

When they were first married, he even asked her if she minded; and if she said she was tired, he wouldn't do anything, like she could have a say in such things. Her Dewey, such a character he was.

She felt him reach for her hand under the bedclothes. "I love you," he whispered into the dark.

They both loved her, her husbands, and she hadn't felt like she was enough for either of them. She wanted to say, I love you back, but she never could. Instead she said, "Wish I could give you a baby."

"Well, that's no one's fault."

"A good wife, she will give you a baby."

"It's God that decides these things, sweetheart."

"You sound like my vati," she said.

Maybe he was right, God decides. But her and Micha, they had tricked God, and now it looked like they would get away with it after all. Or at least, *she* would get away with it. How would anyone ever find out her secret now?

Well, there was still one way.

After the wedding, Dewey and George hadn't seen each other for a long time. Dewey knew how his friend felt about his new wife. Besides, George came to New York only two or three times a year, and when he did, Dewey kept him away from her, had lunch with him in his office or on Wall.

But she couldn't keep from seeing him forever. Seven years she had spent now—how did people say it in English? Waiting for the other shoe to drop.

It seemed to her as if every day she was waiting only for everything to come crashing down. How could she ever be happy, living in such a way? That was what you got from playing sneaky with God. Her vati had tried to warn her, hadn't he, before she left Haapvinni. *"Not for you to decide, Sarah. Is for God to decide."*

She closed her eyes, and she was ten years old again. She was lined up with her sisters in their yard in the shtetl. She could not even remember what it was they had done. Her vati stood in front of them. She could smell his moldy gabardine coat, saw his gray side curls hanging by his cheeks as he wagged his long and crooked index finger in all their faces.

"Now tell me the truth. Not how you would like it to be, but how it is."

How many times had she thought: I must tell Dewey how it is. But then she thought: What good is it for Libby now, knowing the truth? It made her feel sick. How could Libby ever be happy, knowing how her mother had lied to her all these years?

So much damage it would do.

No, her job now was to make things right for Libby.

Sarah waited until Dewey's soft, even breathing let her know he was asleep, and then she slipped out of bed and padded through the apartment to her study, turned on the lamp. The yellow light threw a pool of shadows over her writing desk. There was a secret drawer in one of the panels, and she slid it out. Inside was Micha's biscuit box.

She pulled off the lid. The newspaper cutting was thin as tissue now.

Her mother, Mrs. Clare Seabrook, was identified among the deceased, but no trace of the baby was found.

Burn it, she thought. Burn it, and it will be like it never happened.

Because I can't tell anyone now, she thought, not after all this time. I couldn't bear to lose my daughter now. I just couldn't.

She put the box back in the desk, snapped off the light, and went back to bed. Lay there in the dark for hours and never slept at all.

⇒✦⇐

Another sweltering New York summer's day. George Seabrook looked out the window of Bill Dewey's office on Wall and watched the crowds milling in the street with the sort of detached wonderment he felt when he looked at the animals in a zoo. On the radio that morning, they said the people were flooding into New York from all over America: Okies and hillbillies and crackers from the Deep South, all milling about on Nassau and Broad and outside the National City Bank headquarters.

A line of messenger boys shuffled through the crowds, carrying locked metal boxes filled with securities, each boy holding with one hand the handle of the box ahead and with the other the handle of the box behind. Armed guards were positioned front and rear. For all the world they reminded him of a prison chain gang he had seen as a boy down in Georgia. The crowds parted for them, staring in almost reverential silence, as if they were carrying holy relics.

"What the hell are all those people waiting for?" he said to Dewey.

Dewey shrugged. "Damned if I know, George. It's like being at a carnival, isn't it?"

"More like a racetrack," George said. "End of the day, there's going to be tears and a litter of torn-up betting slips."

"Not this meet," Dewey said.

"We'll see. Doesn't it scare you?"

"Scare me?"

"There are guys down there selling hot dogs and peanuts. It's not business, Bill, not real business. I heard on Friday, General Electric dropped twenty points in two hours. No one has control of this, Bill. It may not frighten you, but it sure scares the hell out of me."

"It's prosperity, George. It's the American dream."

"Is it? Only it looks more like hysteria to me. My hotel is full. There is not a room to be had. I heard someone has sublet the VIP suite. On the way here I saw people sleeping in the graveyard of the Trinity Church."

"Well, it's the biggest bull market in history, George. You can't blame them. Everyone wants a piece of it. Everyone wins."

"The way I've always understood things, where there's winners, there's always losers."

"Not this time. If you're smart, it's the chance to make a fortune. Don't you want to be a part of it?"

"Absolutely not. Some of these so-called securities people are buying aren't worth the paper they're written on. It's snake oil."

"I'll not deny the market has attracted some undesirables, but that always happens when there's money to be made. The market is fundamentally sound."

"Nothing can go on forever."

Dewey's face was thrown half in shadow by the shaded lamp on his desk. George's gaze was drawn to the vase of white lilies on the carved mahogany table in the middle of the office. Weren't they the kind of flowers you brought out at a funeral? Dewey flipped open the humidor on the desk and offered George a cigar. "From Cuba," he said. "Hand rolled."

George took one and lit it. He leaned back and watched the smoke curl toward the gold filigree on the ceiling. "You're not badly exposed yourself, are you, Bill?"

"No, of course not."

"You're not lying to me now?"

"Of course not. Why would I lie?"

"To get me off your back about it."

Dewey smiled and turned the conversation around, asked after Jack, how he was doing at Harvard. He didn't seem surprised when George told him he was sending him down to New York to learn the ropes at Davidson's when he finished his business degree.

"Throw him in the deep end," Dewey said. "It's what my father did to me. It's the only way to learn."

"I have high hopes for him," George said. And then, after a pause: "How's Sarah?"

There was a long silent moment. Sarah was a subject they had both studiously avoided for so long. "She's fine. She's a good wife, George, though I know you find that hard to believe. We've grown comfortable with each other."

"Do you love her?"

Dewey nodded.

"Does she love you?"

A shrug. "I guess she does, but . . ."

"But what?"

"Maybe not the way I love her. But what we have, it's enough for me."

George shook his head. "You could have had any woman you wanted."

"I'm happy with my choices, George. Perhaps Sarah is not your kind of choice, not a choice for many men in my position, but she's more than enough for me."

"Seven years," George said. "I didn't think it would last seven weeks." He dropped an inch of ash from his cigar into a thick onyx ashtray. "Always glad to be wrong."

"Water under the bridge. Why don't you swing by the apartment this evening for dinner?"

"I was supposed to have dinner tonight at the Waldorf. Business."

"Be great if you could make it. Time to bury the hatchet, George."

"I know," George murmured, and then the talk moved on to other things. Dewey tried again, with no success, to sell George on getting a piece of the market. As he was leaving, George said, "How's the girl? Liberty, isn't it?"

"She's not a girl anymore. She's sixteen. Got herself a Dutch bob and a hemline that gives her mother pink fits."

"Last time I saw her, she was giving Jack boxing lessons."

"She's still not the kind of girl anyone should mess with. Like her mother. Hope to see you tonight, George. Let me know, and I'll call ahead, get Cook to make something special."

"I'll let you know."

Dewey's secretary brought George his hat and cane and showed him out.

Dewey watched him walk out onto the street, two floors below. He smiled. He hoped he'd change his mind about dinner. He was sure George and Sarah could be friends, if only they gave it a chance.

It was stifling hot when George reached the street, and an assault after the ordered calm of Dewey's office. The peanut vendors and hawkers selling soda drinks were trying to outdo each other like barkers at Coney

Island. He was jostled this way and that by the crowds. If that wasn't enough, there was the construction hammering of all the new buildings going up, newsboys trying to shift their morning editions, cars and trucks beating their horns in the traffic. He jumped in a cab, eager to get away from it all. A circus was all it was. He had a bad feeling about it; Dewey was supposed to be the ringmaster, but George could not shake the ugly suspicion that his friend had jumped in the lions' cage himself.

Mary Donnelly was in a corridorlike ward that had fifty other beds in it. There was a screen around her bed, and Liberty knew what that meant, that she must be dying. A nurse brought a chair for her, and Liberty sat down and watched Mary sleep. She would not have recognized her if they had not told her it was her. Her cheeks were so sunken, all the flesh wasting off her. And her breathing, it sounded like there was a pair of broken bellows inside her, leaking and wheezing. A single tear had dried on her face.

She did not want to wake her, so she sat quietly and waited, shuddered at all the antiseptic smells, the person groaning in her sleep in the next bed.

At last, Mary's eyes flickered open. She blinked, and her tired face creased into a smile. "Libby."

"Hello, Mrs. Donnelly."

"What a surprise. Really, you shouldn't have bothered. I'll be out of here soon enough. How did you know I was in here?"

"Frankie told me. I saw her yesterday. We went out to Coney Island."

"Well, that's nice," Mary said, but the way she said it made Libby want to cry. What did she remember about what was nice, being so sick and so worn out like she was?

"Frankie said you've not been well, Mrs. Donnelly."

"It's nothing."

"I brought you flowers."

"Thank you, dearie. Oh, and look at you, all grown up. What a beautiful young woman you are these days. I remember when you were just a straggly young thing, proper fright you were. Now look at you."

"Had my hair bobbed."

"Is that what they call it? You look like a film star."

"Frankie says she's going to get hers cut just like it."

"Our Frankie always looked up to you. You've been a good friend to her."

"She's been a good friend to me as well."

"How's your ma?"

"She's fine, Mrs. Donnelly."

"You know she sends us checks every month, on the first, never misses a beat. She's a champion woman, your ma. I never took any of the money for myself, but it's helped out Frankie and her brothers and sisters no end."

"Frankie told me."

"That mother of yours, she's a heart of gold, she h—" She started to cough, couldn't stop. On and on until she was clawing at the air as if she could take the oxygen by the scruff of the neck and drag it into her. Her cheeks turned purple. Liberty shouted for the nurse, and two of them came, sat Mary up in the bed, and one of them hammered on her back to try and clear her lungs as she struggled and twisted on the bed. Finally, she drew in a long gasping breath, and after a few minutes she lay back, soaking wet and exhausted, on the bed. Her eyes had rolled back in her head.

"Is she going to be all right?" Libby said.

"You'd best be running home now," the matron said to her. "She needs to rest."

Liberty watched the nurses, how gentle they were with her, like she was their own. She could see now where Frankie had got the idea of being a nurse, and why she wanted to do it.

"You're very kind," Liberty said to them as she turned to go.

"It's our job."

"You do a good job, then," she said. Poor Mary. What a way to die. The world wasn't fair, how it took all the good ones. She remembered how many times she had slept at the Donnelly house, how many dinners Mary had cooked for her, how many times she had tucked her up in Frankie's bed when her mother was home late. Broke her heart to see her like this.

And her mama sent her checks! Why did she never come to see her? Her mama said she never missed being poor, but it seemed to Liberty there was something wrong with money if it made you hard.

36

Once, the world had crowded in on her with its smells and its people and the poorness of it. It was all so far away now; that New York was somewhere over there, through the haze. She was safe up here, in her private writing room of duck-egg blue, with its thick Persian carpet and macassar writing desk, its view over Central Park and the Manhattan skyline. That world over there could not touch her here.

Except, she thought, it does. It touches me through my Libby.

She turned away from the window and tried to concentrate again on the letter she was writing. She picked up her pen and stared at the blank pages in front of her.

Dearest Etta.

Seventeen years now since she had left, but it was not just a different time back then, it was a different world. Hard to remember sometimes what she was before she married Dewey, and almost impossible to think of herself as that young girl on the sled in the woods of Tallinn.

There were half a dozen crumpled balls of paper in the wastepaper basket at her feet. What was she going to say to them? The last letter from Etta said that her vati was sick, that she thought soon he would be in the world to come. Their poor sister Gutta was gone too, dead of a lung rot, leaving seven children and a husband. Gutta had always seemed so much older, it was hard to grieve for her. She had been like an aunt who came to visit sometimes, never like a sister. Vati had found her a husband when Sarah was still playing with her dolls, and Gutta had gone away to live with him before she even got to know her.

The only one of her little nephews and nieces she really remembered was Bessie, of course. In her letter, Etta reminded her that Libby was almost the same age as her Bessie now. Hard to imagine it. The last time Sarah had seen Bessie, she was still in swaddling, with a tiny heart-shaped mouth and a warm-milk smell.

For years, even before Sarah met Dewey, Etta had written in her letters how she and Yaakov wanted to come to America too, but then the Bolsheviks took over, and they couldn't get a visa. Now Estonia was its own republic, and she said things were so much better that they had changed their minds about coming to the Golden Medina. Tallinn was a good place for Jews now, she said. There were no more pogroms, and a person could live in peace. After what Etta said, Sarah had even thought about going back for a visit, but she could not imagine her Dewey walking on duckboards through the mud of her shtetl, getting mud spattered on his trouser cuffs.

Besides, it was always at the back of her mind, how could she go back? What would everyone say when they saw her Libby? While she kept her family world and her America world apart, she could hold tight to her secret. Ashkenazi eyes! Micha was no Ashkenazi, and everyone in Haapvinni knew it, and no Ashkenazi had hair *that* color red.

She unlocked the drawer on her desk and took out the leather-bound diary. It was so old, some of the pages were already faded and had worked loose. One of Libby's childhood drawings fluttered to the floor. Sarah picked it up, smiled at the three stick figures: her, Micha, Liberty, with their brown tenement in the background, a fierce red sun with a smile on its face.

She slid the drawing back inside the diary and shut it. It was the past, what was done, was done. She would not think about it anymore. That was the best way.

She looked down at the blank piece of paper on the desk. What can I say to Etta about my big sister being dead when I cannot really remember how she was when she was alive? What do I say about Vati when I do not even know if right now my sisters are saying Kaddish for him?

She heard Constance tapping at the door.

"What is it?" she said.

Constance peered through the door. "Sorry to disturb."

"It's all right. Come in."

"Mr. Dewey just rang me, ma'am. He said to tell you he is bringing a guest home for dinner tonight."

"A guest? Did he give a name?"

"A Mr. Seabrook, I think he said."

"What? But he can't . . . Ring him back, please, Constance. Tell him I am not feeling well. I cannot possibly receive guests at this late notice."

Constance looked confused and her face fell. It was the first time she had ever been asked to do such a thing. She licked her lips, thought about protesting, then fled the room.

George Seabrook, coming here? He couldn't. Sarah stood up and sat down again. She tried to think. This was what she had been dreading for years. Liberty as a child was nothing like Liberty as a young woman. She was so different now. What if he took one look and saw, not her daughter, but *his* dead wife?

She paced to the window, went out into the foyer, saw Constance on the telephone, snatched it from her. "Who is this?" she said.

"This is Eleanor at reception."

Sarah recognized the voice. It was Dewey's personal secretary. "I need to speak to Mr. Dewey. This is his wife, it's urgent."

"I'm sorry, Mrs. Dewey. I'm afraid he's left for the day."

"He's what?"

"He said he was meeting a Mr. Seabrook and then going home for the day."

Sarah slammed down the telephone and went into the drawing room, found a bottle of Dewar's Scotch, and poured three fingers into a crystal glass. It burned all the way down. Constance hovered in the doorway.

"Ma'am?"

"Where's Miss Dewey?"

"She's not here, ma'am."

"Where is she?"

"I don't know, ma'am."

"I thought she was in her room."

"She went out this morning, ma'am. She didn't say where she was going."

With luck, Sarah thought, she will stay out past dinner. But what if she doesn't? Constance was staring at her. Sarah looked down. She was shaking so hard, the whisky was spilling out of the glass onto the marble floor. "Thank you, Constance," she said. "That will be all."

<hr>

When she heard the door open, heard Constance hurrying across the foyer, Sarah thought Dewey was home. She rushed out of her study, thinking: I have to take charge of this. But it wasn't Dewey, it was Libby. She handed Constance her little burgundy beret and gave Sarah a look she didn't much care for. "Hello, Mama."

"Libby," Sarah said. "Can you come in here please?" She went back into her study. Libby followed her, and Sarah shut the door behind them.

Sarah crossed her arms. "Where have you been? I told you, you must not leave the apartment without asking me."

"You weren't here to ask, Mama."

"Do you know what I think? I think you stayed in your room until I was gone out so that you do not have to ask. Was deliberate. From now on, I forbid you to go out on your own. Do you understand me? You are only sixteen years old."

"You never worried so much when I was nine and you were a dancing girl. I managed pretty well then."

"How dare you say such a thing to me."

Liberty shrugged, all innocence.

"Do not call me dancing girl. And you will not talk back at me like this. You want the servants to hear us making such a fuss?"

"Of course, we mustn't let the servants hear."

"What is gotten into you?"

"Nothing has gotten into me."

"Where have you been?"

"I went to see Frankie's mom."

"How is she? I've been meaning to go and see her."

"You've been meaning to go and see her for seven years."

Liberty saw the diary on Sarah's desk, one of her old drawings peeking out of the top of it. Before Sarah could stop her, she picked it up. "What's this?" she said.

Sarah took it from her and put it back in the drawer.

"I didn't know you kept a diary about me." In her voice there was puzzlement, tenderness, suspicion.

"Every mother, she has a baby book."

"A baby book? Why didn't you ever show me?"

"Is just a silly thing."

"It's not a silly thing to me."

She went to the drawer, but Sarah stood in the way. "Not now. It's not the time."

"I want to see it."

Sarah locked the drawer and looped the key chain around her neck. "No," she said.

She heard men's voices in the foyer. Not now. Why does it have to be now? She wanted to scream, everything was coming apart at once. She heard Constance through the door, fussing over their visitor.

"Who's that?" Libby said.

"Stay in here."

"Why?"

"We have a guest."

"Who?"

"Don't matter who. Stay in here, don't move, all right? I am your mama, you do as I say." She wagged a finger in Libby's face, all the while thinking: Who is this shrew? What kind of woman did America make you?

She put on her hostess face, a big smile, and went out to the foyer. Dewey was standing there with Seabrook, Constance taking their hats and canes, Dewey about to lead his guest into the drawing room. Dewey gave her a peck on the cheek. "Sarah. Caught you out. What mischief have you been up to?"

"What?"

"I'm home early," he said, and grinned. He frowned, smelled the whisky on her, and realized that perhaps his joking had fallen a little flat. "Did Constance tell you? We have a guest for dinner tonight. You remember George?"

Seabrook gave a bow of the head, the perfect Boston gentleman. "Mrs. Dewey. I'm sorry for the late notice, but Bill insisted. Thank you for having me in your home."

Her mouth was so dry she could barely speak, put her hands behind her back so the two men wouldn't see she was trembling.

"You're the only man that's ever scared my wife," Dewey said, making a joke of it.

Then the door opened, and Liberty flounced out, all green-eyed charm and fire-haired bob, the deb of the ball. She smiled at Sarah, and the look in her eyes said it plain: Don't you tell me what to do.

"Hi, Dewey," she said, and kissed him on the cheek. Then she turned to George Seabrook, her arm out straight, offering him a handshake. "You must be Mr. Seabrook," she said.

"You must be Libby," George said, and took her hand and gave another little bow over the top of it. "How you've grown since we last met."

"How's Jack?" Libby said. "Is he over his black eye?"

The two men laughed. Sarah froze, watched George Seabrook's face for some sign of recognition, waiting for Libby's likeness to register with him. But there was not a flicker, nothing at all.

37

The moment seemed to go on forever. Sarah could hear the somber ticking of the ormolu clock on the sideboard in the drawing room. Then George laughed.

"You look quite lovely," he said to Liberty. "I never would have recognized you. Your father talks endlessly about you, of course. He says you've done rather well at Westover."

"I do my best," Liberty said with a sly look at her mother.

"She's very modest," Dewey said. "We get nothing but glowing reports. We're sending her to Bryn Mawr next year."

"Do they have a girls' boxing team?" George said, and the three of them laughed again.

"Would you like to have dinner with us, dear?" Dewey said to her.

Libby looked at her mother, and the corners of the girl's lips curled just so slightly into the hint of a smile. She is taunting me, the little minx, Sarah thought. "Thank you, Dewey, but you'll have to excuse me, I'm not feeling very well," Liberty said. "I think I'll go to my room. If you'll excuse me, Mr. Seabrook. It was nice to meet you." And then, in a loud whisper to her mother: "She's dying."

Sarah felt the blood drain from her face.

"Who's dying?" Dewey said after she had left.

"Frankie's mother," Sarah said.

"I'm sorry," Dewey said. "We'll send flowers." He and George went into his study for a drink before dinner and left Sarah standing adrift in the foyer, which suddenly seemed airless and dark.

⊰⧫⊱

The dining table was walnut, hand-carved; according to Dewey, it had been in the family for five generations. It was long enough for a dozen people, and sometimes they had enough people over for dinner to fill it, but tonight just three places were set. Constance had laid out the Lenox bone china, all raised gold and cobalt blue, on a freshly ironed Irish linen tablecloth. In the middle of the table was the silver menorah Sarah had brought with her from Tallinn; it was the only talisman of that former life that she had left.

The yellow light of the sconces and the glow of the candles danced in the silverware and the cut crystal. Dewey told Constance to bring out the 1921 Château Latour he had been saving for a special occasion.

As Constance served the consommé, George told Sarah how Dewey had been trying to get him into the market.

"Because you must be the only man in American not profiting by it," Dewey said.

"You see?" George said. "He is quite relentless in his pursuit. But I have told him, this market is not the place for a prudent business-man like myself. There are too many cheap bonds flooding the market, inflating values, and far too many uneducated investors dabbling with money they don't have."

"Dewey, he has a point," Sarah said. "Plus, the what-you-call-it money is back up to six percent," Sarah said.

"Call money," Dewey said, and smiled.

"And I read today about this board you are always talking about, what is its name, Dewey?"

"The Federal Reserve Board."

"That one. They are all moaning like I don't know what, but they sit on their tushies and don't do anything. You let the fox in the house, he will eat all the chickens. One day you got no chickens left, it's no big surprise."

George raised an eyebrow. "You know about the Federal Reserve Board?"

"She knows quite a lot about the market," Dewey said. "In fact, she does rather well at it."

"I make a few dollars. Not like Dewey, for fun only."

George gave her a tight smile. "I'm impressed." He dabbed at his mouth with his napkin. "But I'm afraid America is becoming too fast and too flashy for men like me. There's your Mr. Morgan on Wall Street, building himself the biggest yacht in the world, and he doesn't even have the time to go sailing. What's the use? I heard he's bought himself a Tintoretto, and he has no interest in art."

"Art is a good investment, George."

"You see, I thought it was culture. Call me old-fashioned if you like. Anyway, I'm sure J. P. Morgan can take care of himself. But to my mind, there's too many people getting loans from their banks to play this market. And they give it to them! What if I go to my banker and say I want a hundred dollars to put on a horse? It's the same thing."

"It's what banks are for, George, to lend people money so they can make money. People have a duty to invest. It's what makes America strong!" And for the first time in their married life, Dewey banged his fist on the table. The silverware rattled. Even George looked shocked.

The look on Dewey's face, how his eyes bulged in his head like a crazy man. He looked like one of the meshuggeners standing on their boxes on Wall Street, the ones he always made fun of. Something was changing in him, Sarah thought. Sometimes he was not her Dewey anymore.

"I thought it was hard work that made America strong," George said.

"People owe it to themselves and their country to get rich."

"But, Bill, surely, not everyone can be wealthy. Life doesn't work that way. Nations don't work that way."

"This one can!"

George took his time to answer, measuring out what he wanted to say inch by inch. "One thing that life has taught me, Bill, is that you can trust too much and believe too much. I've already lost too much to risk the things I treasure ever again. So whatever J. P. Morgan says, you can count me out of all this. Don't mind me saying, but it sounds to me like castles in the air."

Dewey pushed away his soup and leaned forward, pointing his finger at his friend. "They just put a new ticker system in at the Exchange because the old one couldn't keep up, listings and trades are growing so fast. What does that tell you?"

"Bill, you've been in this business your whole life, so I suppose you'd know better than me. But tell me this, what if you're wrong? There's all these people buying stock they can't afford on margin, but no one's selling. And all these profits everyone says they're making, it's all on paper. It's not real. And if it's not real, I don't trust it. Do you, Mrs. Dewey?"

Sarah stared at her husband. Look at my Dewey, she thought, that look on his face. What is wrong with him these days?

"If stocks do fall," George said, "there will be margin calls everywhere and no one able to pay them. People could get seriously hurt."

"That won't happen. It can't happen. There's people behind all this who won't allow it."

"What people?"

"You'll see."

Constance brought in a whole trout, slow-cooked. Everyone stopped talking while she sliced the fish off the bone and served it on their plates with asparagus and capers. Sarah felt George watching her.

He leaned forward. "You and Liberty," he said.

She felt her cheeks blush hot. Here it comes, she thought. Does he know something after all? She smiled and nodded, but didn't trust her voice to speak.

"You don't need to worry," he said.

"We don't?"

"Whatever happens in the market, your husband will take care of you. Won't you, Bill?"

"Of course," Dewey said, and raised his glass in a mock toast. The candlelight reflected in his eyeglasses. There was something about the way he said it that chilled her bones. He is lying, she thought, lying to me and to Mr. George Seabrook right here, who is supposed to be his good friend. He has a secret. I know because I know that look, I put on that same expression every day myself.

Cannot kid a kidder, like they say.

38

Sarah turned on the light on the bedside table, took off her eye mask, thinking it must be morning. A quarter past four. Her head ached, and her eyes felt gritty from lack of sleep. Had she slept at all? At the back of her mind was the vague remembrance of a dream, a lot of running, people shouting.

Dewey was snoring beside her, dead to the world. She went to the window, parted the curtain, and peered down at the sleeping city.

What would have happened to Libby, she wondered, if Micha had gone to George Seabrook back then, after the fire, and told him what had happened? He didn't have a wife, so Libby would have had a nanny first, then a boarding school as soon as she was old enough. What kind of life would that have been? This way, she'd had a mother's love, a happy family, and in the end, she had lost none of the richness she had been born to, had she? Sarah had made sure that Libby got the very best, in the end.

She squeezed her eyes shut and tried to imagine what it would have been like if Libby had been hers, really hers, if she had felt her growing inside.

She saw herself on the boat from Russia, Liberty sitting low in her belly, and her unable to keep her food down, not because of the rocking of the ship, but because her time was so close. Then hurrying back to the tenement, the baby coming quickly, in a rush, Micha having to fetch one of the neighbor women to help her through the labor. In her daydreams Tessie Fischer swaddled her newborn in a blanket and laid her in her arms. *"I am going to call her Liberty,"* she said as Micha beamed at her.

Sometimes it was all so real. If it wasn't for that George Seabrook, eventually that was the way it would have happened. That man. He kept getting in the way of a better past.

The world, it seemed to her, had gone mad. There were airplanes chasing each other through the concrete canyons downtown, buzzing the Woolworth Building, one had even flown under the Brooklyn Bridge. It boosted stock prices at Curtiss-Wright and Boeing, at least.

Then this madman—what was his name?—Babson, told a journalist that an eighty-point stock market crash was coming. One newspaper called him "the prophet of loss," and the name stuck. Soon everybody was talking about this *schlemiel.* For two nights Dewey did not get home until almost midnight. He said it was nothing to worry about, a market correction.

A few days later everything seemed to go back to normal, and no one talked about this Babson anymore. Dewey was right about things again. She stopped worrying.

Fall came and with it another heat wave with the mercury soaring into the nineties. She read about a rancher in Texas who hooked a radio to a loudspeaker and hung it on a corral post so his cowpunchers could stay up with the latest prices. She told Bill the next morning at breakfast, and for once he did not laugh at her.

"I heard that too," he said, in a way that made it sound like he thought it was a good idea.

Then late in September there was another drop. Dewey came home and told her not to worry herself. "Organized buying support" would steady the market; men like Morgan and Meehan, he said, had billions of dollars behind them; they would make sure any falls did not get out of hand.

Still, Sarah decided to stop going to the Plaza.

Libby went back to Westover, and Sarah went back to her old life again. But it was not the same for her anymore, all they talked about at the mah-jongg parties and the soirées was the market, always the market. Even Jane Pargetter knew about this organized buying support. Everything is going to be jake, she said. Nothing to worry.

Jane Pargetter was right. By the end of the month, everything was fine again, and Dewey seemed his old self. They were rich. The world was rich. Everybody was rich.

"But if things do go wrong," Sarah asked him one night, "how bad can it be? You are just a broker, right? You deal the hands, but you don't put money in the pot, you don't deal yourself in. Right?"

He patted her hand. "Let me worry about business, darling," he said. Then he went into his study and shut the door.

⟨⊶⟩

When had it started? Sarah was never sure. Was it that schmuck Babson, or was it that drop in September? Was that when they all should have known? One day she came home from one of her parties, and there was the *New York Times* lying there on the hall table.

YEAR'S WORST BREAK HITS STOCK MARKET

But maybe even that wasn't the start, because a week later the newspapers were full again of stories of cooks and cowhands and cab drivers who had gotten rich overnight. Dewey said the ups and downs of the

248

market, that was the way it was. It sold newspapers, but it didn't mean anything.

She even started going back to the Plaza again.

Then one Wednesday she got home late in the afternoon, a little tipsy from all the champagne, and she heard the radio in the kitchen, where Cook was making the dinner. She took a step closer, leaned in the doorway to listen. Prices were falling again, the announcer said, and he sounded breathless, like he was a millionaire type too. Over six million shares had been sold, he said, just today. It is the biggest crash in stock market history.

The mayor had sent four hundred policemen to Wall Street. Another reporter, speaking into a microphone outside the Exchange, said he had seen trader types with their collars and shirts torn off, flinging ticker tape and order pads into the air like it was a parade, but a parade where they had lost the war.

She went into her study and found the silver hip flask she kept in the locked drawer and took two long sips at it. Everything is all right, she told herself; it's all jake, like Jane Pargetter said. Dewey and her, they would be all right.

But what was it that George Seabrook had called the market? *"Castles in the air."* Perhaps that was what they really were, and now the castles were all crumbling down.

⟹

This morning there was no one at the other end of the breakfast table. Constance informed her that Mr. Dewey had left for work early, had told her to say that he would be home very late. Sarah told Constance she wasn't hungry either; just a cup of coffee, please. She felt a chill in the pit of her stomach. Is this how it all ends?

She stared at the letters on the table beside her empty plate and winced. Not so many party invitations these days. She picked up a plain brown envelope. The writing on it was an untidy scrawl, not the usual copperplate she was accustomed to receiving. She tore it open.

"Dear Mrs. Levine," it began.

Levine, not Dewey.

> *Dear Mrs. Levine,*
>
> *I am writing to let you know that our dear ma passed away on Friday last. She had the consumption as I suppose Lib has told you. I wanted to say thank you for all the money you sent her, it made her life and ours so much easier, you've a heart of gold, like Ma always said. So I wanted to let you know there's going to be a wake this Friday at our old place in Cannon Street, from four o'clock. It would be good if you could make it, but I know you're busy and all.*
>
> *Now she's gone, I was going to send back the last check, but Da said it was okay to use it to pay for the funeral and all. I hope that's all right.*
>
> *Sincerely,*
>
> *Frances Donnelly*

Sarah read it and read it again. No, she cannot be dead, she thought. I was going to go and visit her today. Look, it's here in my diary. Just had so many worries lately.

"Is everything all right, ma'am?" Constance said.

Sarah didn't answer. She let the letter fall to the floor and walked out, leaving her coffee untouched. This morning she'd need something a little stronger.

⟨⟩

Sarah sat in the back of the Bentley, her hands clenched tight on the alligator bag on her lap, Hermès and very expensive. She wished now she had left it at home. She remembered this ride only too well: Union Square, down Broadway, off on East Houston and into that other world, the pushcarts and hawkers and the brown tenements and struggle down in the shadow of the Williamsburg Bridge.

She felt a clutch in her stomach, a rush of panic. I don't want to ever come back here. I can't. Even the memory of it makes me feel sick.

Yet something made her lean forward, tap on the glass, made Nelson take her the long way, past the Jewish theaters on Second Avenue, and "Katz's That's All!" The old pickle shop was still there. Surely the old man in the yarmulke couldn't still be alive?

Nelson knew the way, remembered it from all those years ago. He pulled up across the road from the Florence Nightingale public school, parked at the curb, turned off the engine, and sat back. He didn't say a word.

Sarah watched the trolley cars and traffic crawling along under the girders of the Williamsburg Bridge, looked up at the tenement, found the window of the apartment where they used to live, just yesterday, just a lifetime ago.

I must go up, she thought. But she couldn't move.

Nelson watched her in the rearview mirror. "Everything all right, ma'am?" he said at last.

She nodded. "Wait here for me."

"I should come up with you."

"No, Nelson. I'll be fine."

She wasn't as nimble up the five flights of steps as she had been in her Follies days. By the time she got to the top, she was a little out of breath. She stopped outside Mary's apartment to compose herself.

She stepped up to the door. She could hear voices inside, steeled herself. She couldn't go back to the car, she was here now.

She rapped twice on the door with her knuckles.

She didn't recognize Dan Donnelly straightaway. He had aged a little. They all had, she supposed, but it was more than that. It wasn't that he was red-eyed drunk, though he was. It was the look of him. He stood there in the doorway, swaying, trying to focus. Over his shoulder, she could see the living room was full of men and women standing around with drinks in their hands, looking somber.

"Well, well, well. Sarah Levine. Or should I say Mrs. Sarah Too-Bloody-Good-for-Everyone Dewey."

"Dan, I—"

"Come to pay your respects?"

Suddenly Frankie was there beside him. When she saw Sarah, she grabbed her father's shoulder and tried to pull him away. "Leave it, Da," she said, but he shrugged her off. "I invited her! Now let her be."

"Invited her, did you? Without asking me?"

"She has a right to be here, much as anyone else."

"She does, does she?" He turned back to Sarah, so close she could smell the booze on his breath. "You know what really got to me?"

"Da, leave it, please."

"She never said a single word against you, not in all this time. 'She's just busy with her life,' she used to say. 'She'll be around one day to see us. She deserves her luck.' That was my Mary, never a bad word."

He took a step toward her, unsteady on his feet. "Get the fuck out of here."

Frankie pulled him back inside. Before the door closed, Sarah saw them all standing in the living room doorway, staring. She knew a couple of them, neighbors from the old days. They had the same looks on their faces that Dan had. "I'm sorry!" Frankie called after her, but Sarah had already turned away and was off running down the stairs.

"Are you all right, ma'am?" Nelson said when he saw her.

"Home, please," she said, and almost fell into the back seat.

She huddled in the corner, tried not to catch Nelson's eye; she didn't want him to see her cry. And what was it she was blubbing about anyway? She didn't want him or anyone feeling sorry for her. It was from shame, pure and simple.

They drove away from the dark, crowded streets, into the wide thoroughfares uptown, back to Central Park and the high world of the Upper West Side, where it was possible to breathe, and to forget. On the way she promised herself she would tell Dewey about this, and not about Mary Donnelly only, but about everything.

All this keeping secrets, it had twisted her out of shape, made her someone she did not recognize, someone she had never wanted to be.

She would tell him. He would not judge her; he would know what to do. After all, that was his business, taking care of things; making good decisions, sound decisions; never losing sight of what was important. She had to do it. She could not bear to carry this burden anymore.

If you tell the truth, then you can't go wrong. That was what Mary would have said.

She looked out the window. They were already back in that other New York, the New York of hotels and jewelry shops and money. This was not her New York, it never was.

"I must tell him," she murmured aloud.

She saw Nelson watching her in the mirror. She didn't care if he saw the tears running down her face, not anymore. She was done with pretending now.

⟞⟝

It was late when Dewey got home. His bow tie was askew, his suit rumpled, like he had been in a fight. His hair, always so slide-rule straight, was disheveled. He put down his briefcase, and they looked at each other. Then he walked into his study and shut the door behind him. She would always let him be whenever he was like this, but this time she followed him in.

Dewey poured three fingers of whisky into a glass. She heard the crystal tinkle as it rattled against the lip of the decanter. His hands were shaking.

"Are you all right?" she said.

"Bad day."

"How bad?"

"You should sit down," he said, and even those four words made her knees feel like Jell-O, and she collapsed into the nearest chair.

"Sarah, there's something I should have told you."

She tried to make light of it. "You've been playing the market, don't tell me."

He nodded.

"Really? How bad?"

He winced.

"Please, no."

"I didn't intend for this to happen."

"You told me once that you never play yourself. You said that was for schmucks."

"I know what I said."

"What will we do?"

"I'm sure everything will be fine. The market always recovers. It always has." He sat down at his desk and hung his head.

Never had she seen him like this. His shoulders heaved, and she realized he was crying. She got up and put her arms around him. Oh God, she thought, this must be really bad, worse than even I imagined.

"Whatever happens, I won't let anything bad happen to you," he said.

Sarah sat on his knee, stroked his head, put her arm around his shoulders. He sat there, slumped in his chair, like a boxer who cannot come out for the final round.

"Don't worry, Dewey. Whatever it is, nothing is that bad. We can get through this."

"You can say that because you know what it's like to be poor. I don't."

"Being poor is nothing. I can do it, anyone can."

"No, you were born to it. It's different. You don't understand."

She took his face in her hands. "Don't talk like this. You got me, you got Liberty."

"Have I? Have I really? The one thing I know about being poor, you can't borrow on credit." He eased her up off his lap. "I need to be alone for a while."

"Dewey . . ."

"Please, Sarah, let me be. We'll talk about all this in the morning."

Sarah went to bed, sat up reading, left the bedside light on for him. She couldn't concentrate on her novel, fell asleep she didn't know when, and when she woke, he still wasn't in bed. She looked at the clock beside the bed. It was after three. She crept out to the hallway. The light was still on in his study. She thought about going in, hesitated with her hand on the door. She took a deep breath and eased the handle, but it was locked.

She went back to bed. Perhaps he is right, she thought. It was easy to be rich, but to be poor, well, that took real chutzpah.

39

Tuesday, October 29, 1929

She was supposed to make nice at an afternoon tea at Jane Pargetter's, but she'd canceled, some little voice inside telling her to stay home. Instead, she sat in her study, trying to write a letter to Mutti and her father. The apartment was quiet. She wouldn't let even the cook have the radio on in the kitchen anymore. It was only bad news, and she didn't want to hear it.

In the middle of the afternoon, she heard Constance go to the door in the foyer and then heard her husband's voice. She was surprised. He had never come home so early before. She got to her feet and hurried out to see what was wrong.

Dewey was standing in the living room, swaying back and forth, staring up at the ceiling, as if he was deep in thought.

"Darling?" she said.

"Hmm?"

"What are you doing home?"

"Need some time off."

"But what's happened at the market?"

"The market? Oh, it will all work out." He smiled at her. "Everything will all work out now."

"You look pale, like nobody's business." He was still holding his shiny leather briefcase. She took it from him. "What can I get you?"

"Coffee perhaps."

"I will fetch Constance, ask her to make a fresh pot. Something stronger, you wouldn't like?"

He shook his head.

She put the briefcase by the door and went to find Constance, told her to make a fresh pot of coffee and bring it to them on a tray in the living room. But when she came back, Dewey wasn't there. The French doors leading out to the terrace were wide open, and the curtains were billowing in the afternoon breeze. Had the doors been open when Dewey came home? She couldn't remember.

Puzzled, she crossed the room to shut them.

"Dewey?"

She saw a pair of black lace-up Oxfords perfectly arranged at the edge of the terrace. They looked just the way he arranged his slippers before he got into bed at night, side by side, pointing outward.

She thought she could hear someone screaming down in the street.

Suddenly she realized what had happened. She felt sick. "Oh, Dewey," she said.

She dared a glimpse over the rail. Dewey was lying face down on the footpath, twenty-three floors down. A little crowd had gathered.

There was nothing to be done. It was all over.

40

The movers were carrying furniture out of the apartment to the elevators. Sarah and Liberty stood in the middle of the living room and watched them. Neither of them spoke. What to say? It reminded Sarah of those poor schlemiels getting thrown out of their tenement back in Delancey Street, their paltry things sitting on the sidewalk, so sad looking. A plate of pennies sitting there. She'd heard the tinkle of a few coins thrown in the plate, the shame of it. How much further could a person go and still be a person?

She felt light headed. She hadn't slept well, hadn't really slept at all since it happened; twenty minutes here, half an hour there, dressed on the sofa in the middle of the day. The rest of the time she had spent drinking coffee, wandering around the apartment, staring at the clock, the paintings, the floor, trying not to think.

She had a dull, throbbing headache. It hurt her every time she moved her head. What could she have done to stop him?

What could she have said? *"Dewey, I don't care if you lost it all."* In a way, it would have made them equals at last. It would have been him, with just the shirt on his back, and her, with a daughter she had stolen from one of his best friends. I wonder what he and the rest of the world would have said to that?

It would have made it easier to tell him about Libby. Now, because of what he did, she wouldn't have to. Life was funny.

Oh, Dewey, you didn't have to do *that*. Losing money is not the worst thing a person can ever do, believe me.

Finally, Liberty spoke. "So how much did he lose, Mama?"

"Everything, bubeleh."

"How much is everything?"

"I don't know. Three million. Four million. When it gets to be so many numbers, how can anybody count?"

"Wasn't there life insurance?"

"He thought there was life insurance."

"What happened to it?"

"He was so busy with his stocks, he forgot the premiums. He let it lapse, his secretary forgot to tell him, and now the company won't pay, not a cent."

"Could we take them to court?"

"If we had the gelt, we could get a fancy lawyer. But to get money for a fancy lawyer, first we got to take the insurance company to court."

Two men in overalls carried out their gold brocade chaise. Another had a walnut grandfather clock; Dewey had told her once it had been in his family since New York was still a colony, that was how old it was. Did they have clocks then? Perhaps he was making it up. Still, it was something all right.

"What happened to Nelson and Constance?"

"I had to let them go."

"Oh, Mama. How did all this happen?"

"I don't know. I said to him once, you got so much money, how much more do you want?"

"And what did he say?"

"He said: 'Just a little bit more.'"

The movers had even taken all the carpets, and with only the parquet floors, the place echoed like they were in a cave. Cherubs played on white clouds on the ceiling fresco over her head. They can't take those, she thought, but if they could, I would give them for nothing. Where does a fat baby get from flying in the sky? These goyim, she had been a part of them, but she never understood them.

"So now what will we do?"

"Look at the view, bubeleh. We won't see the world from up here again for a long time. From tomorrow, we start seeing the Elevated from underneath again."

"We'll get by."

"We always did before. But don't lose that hat. A long time before I can buy you another one like that from Saks."

Liberty took off the cloche and threw it over the edge of the balcony, the exact spot where Dewey had jumped. "That's what I think of Saks," she said.

PART 5

41

Greenwich Village, 1933

July in New York, and a sweltering sky, breathless and gray, like a blanket had been thrown over the whole grimy, sweating city. Sarah went down Bleecker Street, stopped by Zito's to get a warm-smelling loaf and pick up the spare keys to the walk-up on Cornelia. Zito, he kept spare keys, rings and rings of them, that all the people in the neighborhood left with him in case they locked themselves out. Like she had that morning.

Here everyone lived on top of each other, like on Delancey. It was only a few blocks except it was a different world, a place of row houses and coffee shops, grocers and fruit vendors, with sagging awnings outside and *Italienish* words in the windows, selling everything from pasta to pizza to headache powders.

It was like being back in the shtetl, an Italian one maybe, with cannoli instead of knish. But it was the goodness of people, that was what she liked. She never knew such goodness in Arlington Apartments or in Long Neck, even if she did see the sky every morning instead of a fire escape or the sooty girders of the Elevated.

They were selling corn and broccoli from pushcarts, a newspaper boy was calling out "Extra! Extra!" though this extra was all rotten as usual: Adolf Hitler and dust bowls and some gold standard or such business she didn't understand. Only thing she wanted to read was how they were opening a theater in New Jersey where you watched the movie outside, and you went in your car to see it. Good luck on such people in New Jersey to own a car. Whatever will they think of next?

She stepped into the gloomy hallway of their walk-up, evil smelling it was, stinking of old cabbage. She could hear that Brudebaker yelling at his wife, such a schlemiel that one, always drinking. They'd made the Volstead Act because of people like him.

There was a letter for her in the slot. She knew it by the handwriting and the kind of envelope it was, the row of lilac and pink ten-*krooni* stamps with one red one.

Etta.

She hurried up the stairs to their apartment, put the letter right there on the table, and went to the kitchen to see if there was any cream soda in the icebox. Days like this, she missed the refrigerator cabinet that Dewey had bought for her. She never minded so much before she was rich; that was the worst thing about losing everything: you remembered how easy life was. Dewey had told her that, before he died, and he had a point. When poorness had been normal, she never minded so much the mouse droppings in the drawers and listening to the jabber of everyone around, their phonographs and pianolas and the yowling of the cats down in the alley under the windows.

These days she never missed the fancy-schmancy mah-jongg parties at the Pargetters' or sailing with the Charltons on Long Island. What she missed were the easy-life things and never thinking, What if the rent man comes today, and I cannot pay? There was no one to say, you want eggs for breakfast, you want lobster Newburg for dinner? Such a life. Like a dream now.

What was so bad about the millionaire life was how it made you feel like you suffered when you were poor again.

But the worst thing was, every day, knowing she had let down her daughter.

But where was she? Sarah looked at the clock on the shelf. Should be home by now, she thought. She finishes at five o'clock, same like me. When should I start my worrying?

When, from the first day I held her in my arms, did I ever stop?

She sat down and tore open the letter from Etta; months since she last heard from her sister. She read through quickly, first for bad news, like she always did; and there it was, just under "Dearest Sarah."

My heart grieves to tell you that our vati is gone.

She read it again and again, wanting to feel like she should, like any good daughter should, waiting for anguish, waiting for tears. But nothing. It was like reading about some stranger in the newspaper.

Vati is gone. She tried to remember his face, or even his voice, but she couldn't do it. Like trying to remember a shadow, it was. She searched inside herself for something, anything, like rummaging through a drawer to find something she was sure she had left there. Where is it, why can't I find it? This is your father who is gone forever, she thought. Then she said it out loud: "This is your father who is gone." Why can't you cry for him, imp of darkness, you?

She looked out the window. Just a few feet away, through another window, an old man was shuffling around his apartment in his underwear, his hair awry. She felt so sorry for him, yet she could not feel sorry for her own father.

Try harder. She closed her eyes, tried again to remember what he looked like. All that came to her was the foggy memory of a stern man in a yarmulke with a gray beard and a threadbare frock coat, telling her: *"Send money when you can."*

She read the rest of the letter, more slowly this time: about his illness, about the funeral, how old their mutti looked since his sickness, gone to live with Zlota now. There was news about more people she couldn't remember. And then, at the very last, how Yaakov wanted to come to America. Life in Tallinn was good now, she said, not like you remember, not like when we were girls. But how long can it last, Yaakov says. A madman on one border, a crazy man on the other.

If anything should happen to Mama, God forbid,
he says maybe we should leave, before anything else bad
happens.

She turned and stared out the window again. The sun was setting, and the tiny patch of sky that she could see between the rooftops was brushed with pink. At last she heard Libby's footfall on the stairs.

Her beautiful daughter, she looked worn out. She wasn't anymore the talking-back girl from the fancy school, no time for bobs and nice clothes from Saks anymore, just a day frock, and her hair damp with sweat and sticky on her forehead. But still something about her, still men looked, no matter how tired and how little she cared about what she put on.

She took off her hat and flopped down on a chair, flushed from the heat and the ride on the trolley bus, fanned herself with the newspaper. "Hello, Mama."

"Bubeleh, you look all in. Are you all right?"

"Just so hot," she said. "What have you got there?"

Sarah pushed the letter across the table. "It's from Etta. My papa has died."

"Oh, Mama. I'm so sorry!" Libby stood up, put her arms around her, read the letter over her shoulder. "Did you know he was sick?"

"None of us lives forever. But you know, it's funny, I don't feel anything. I should feel something—he was my father—but I don't. So long since I have seen him, and, you know, we were never close."

"But still. He was your papa."

"He always used to look at us girls and say, 'Why did God do this? No son to say Kaddish for me.' That was only what we were to him, no Kaddish."

Liberty hugged her tighter, standing behind her chair. Something was wrong, Sarah knew. It was not just the heat and a grandfather she never knew being dead. She looked up at her. There was something in her eyes; she was looking but not looking.

"Something has happened."

"Nothing has happened, Mama." Liberty turned away, went to the icebox, got some ice, and put it in a tea towel, then put it on the back of her neck to cool down. She stood by the window, hoping for some breeze. "What weather. The sun is almost down and still so hot."

"Why were you so late?"

"I stopped to look in the Macy's window."

What a bad liar she was. "Since when do you care from Macy's? You don't like all that clothes stuff anymore."

"I like the clothes. I don't like the prices and the snooty people."

It was getting dark in the apartment. Sarah got up to turn on the lights, but the meter had run out. She went to the black box above the door, put a quarter in. She saw Liberty's hat lying on the table. She picked it up.

"Where is your hat pin?"

"I must have lost it."

"He tried it again, didn't he?"

"I can manage him."

"What happened?"

"The usual thing. He trapped me in the cloakroom after the other girls had gone."

"Did he do anything?"

"I didn't let him."

"This is the third time."

"Mama, I need the job. There's a hundred other girls he can get if he wants."

"Then he can have them. Enough, you don't go back there. Over my dead body, bubeleh."

"I have to go back. We can't afford rent and food on one wage only. Even together we don't earn the same as one man."

"I don't care. You are not going back, not even for your wages. You hear me? No one is going to take advantage of our poorness anymore."

"But how will we live?"

"I don't know, bubeleh. But we will find a way. I promise."

42

Liberty met Frankie at the White Tower on Greenwich Avenue, one-nickel hamburgers in a white brick medieval castle, right next to the big Kesbec Esso sign, "Cars Greased and Oil Changed."

The inside was all polished chrome and white tile, so clean you could eat off the floor, they said, though no one had ever tried. They sat at the five-stool bar and ordered cream sodas and jelly rolls from a Towerette waitress, and Liberty joked that it was what Frankie would look like in her new nurse's uniform. Frankie had finally finished her training and had got a paid job working in a hospital in Pennsylvania.

"Well, I can't wait. I won't be mucking out bedpans and being some sour-faced matron's unpaid slave. Although cutting up hamburger meat and working in an operating room are not that much different."

Liberty covered her face with her hands and told her to stop.

"Well, it means a postgrad certificate, which is another step up the ladder. I'll need all the bits of paper I can to stay out of the bread line."

"Pennsylvania's so far away."

"I'll come back every chance I can. You'll not get rid of me that easy. And what about you? You can't stay in that dead-end job forever. You're too good for that."

"Mama says I have to quit."

"He's not been putting his dirty paws on you again?"

"I had to stick him with the hat pin."

"I'd have put it right through his fecking eye."

"I'm not you, Frankie." Libby sipped her soda through the straw. "I don't know what we're going to do if I don't go back. We can't live on one wage, and there's no jobs out there. I'm no good for anything. That fancy school they sent me to, all I learned was to sit like a lady and say 'My postilion has been struck by lightning' in French."

"What's a postilion?"

"I had to go back for my final year for that. I suppose I'll never know now."

"Why don't you come nursing with me? Get yourself through night school and get away from here."

"I could never. My mama needs me." She watched the Towerette toss some rehydrated onions on the grill, shake salt and pepper over the patties. "Do you see the rest of them much? How's your little sister doing?"

"Pregnant."

"No!"

"Barely out of school, she is. I warned her. The boy she's been knocking around with, useless little gobshite, hasn't a job. I don't know how they're going to manage. If he doesn't stick around, she'll have to put the kid into a home. She can't afford to keep it. But that's what happens when you let boys mess around. And they all do; they can't help themselves."

"Are you still seeing that boy from the hospital?"

"Tony? Sure, and he wants me to marry him."

"Are you going to?"

"As if I would. He wheels stretchers around all day and mops the floors in the wards. I can do better, I reckon."

"You said you'd kissed him."

"Well, there's no harm in practicing. I even let him touch me a couple of times. I quite liked it. Like I told you, he's Italian, and those boys will do anything to a girl give them half a chance. The only time their own girls get down on their knees is when they're in church."

Liberty took a breath. Sometimes Frankie's talk startled her. Even when her boss at the sweatshop tried to make her do things, she hadn't known what it was he was saying. She had to ask Frankie to explain it to her afterward.

"Oh, Lib, you're the best-looking girl I know, like a beauty queen, you are. Take my advice, don't let a man fool with you until you've a ring on your finger, or else they'll leave you holding the baby, and they'll be gone. Happens all the time."

"A beauty queen? I am not."

"When we're walking out, men stare at you all the time. Have you never noticed?"

"They're looking at you."

"Heck they are. I have nice eyes and a bit of sass and not much else. But look at you. Even the clothes you wear. How you afford stuff like that, working in a sweatshop, beats me. Where did you get it?"

"Mama made it."

"You're skiting me."

"She makes dresses for everyone in the building. You know how she is. She gets scraps from work, hides them under her dress, and brings them home. Works Sundays and late most nights to make us a bit extra."

Frankie rubbed the material between her fingers, looked at the stitching on the hem. "I always knew she was good with a needle. I didn't realize this good. Where does she get the patterns?"

"She doesn't. Someone brings her a sketch or just describes something to her, she can make it."

"If you had a label on this, I'd swear blind it came from Bloomingdale's or somewhere." Frankie finished her soda, worked the straw around her glass. It made Liberty smile. For all her sassy talk,

Frankie was still like a big kid most of the time. "You know what? I have an idea."

"What idea?"

"My big brother Tommy works in the Garment District, pushing carts. Maybe he could help you."

"Not unless he knows the manager at the Saks fashion department."

"There's other ways. Why don't I ask him to steal you some labels?"

"How do you mean?"

"You know, some fancy fashion labels. That's what people pay for anyway, isn't it? They don't care about the dress as long as they think it came from Paris. He could tear a few off; no one would know it was him; your ma could sell her dresses for ten times."

"Isn't that against the law?"

Frankie looked at her as if she was mad. "Of course it is! Are you going to let that stop you?"

Liberty grinned. "I guess not," she said.

43

It was a Sunday. All the shops closed, Liberty stood outside the Saks window with Sarah, looking at the new season's fashion, a frown on her face.

"You could make that, Mama. What you make already is better than that."

"A lot of women can make as good."

"Not without a pattern and not so fast. And they don't have your sense of style. You make things with scraps, add little touches. You're a genius, everyone says so."

"Who is this everyone?"

"You know what Frankie said last night when she saw that dress you made? She thought it was from Bloomingdale's."

"What does she know from Bloomingdale's?"

"Mama, all the years you've spent working with schmatta, everything your papa taught you, you don't even know how good you are. All the women on our block want you to make them dresses. Every day there is someone coming around, asking."

"I don't have time. One or two I can do. Not everyone."

"Why not everyone?"

Sarah shook her head. "How much people will pay for homemade? The label and fancy-schmancy stuff on the collar, that is what they like. And look at this: the dummies they have in the windows."

"Mannequins."

"Still just a fancy name for a dummy, you ask me. I tell you, bubeleh, how many women you know have hips like a bar-mitzvah boy? Who's got a shape like that? No one got a shape like that. Well, you have, bubeleh; and maybe once, when I am in the Follies, I had that shape, all tall and skinny and no waist. But you and I, we are lucky. Look, now they make dresses with shoulder pads like a Green Bay Packer and big puff sleeves. Get a woman with hips in this, what does she look like? King Kong."

Libby laughed.

"My day, a girl could show her legs, bare backs, almost bare fronts even. And no underwear, God forbid. Now what have you got? Since all the millionaire types on Wall Street lost all their money, it's like the whole world should be sad for them. No more bee's knees, no more Charleston, and women dress like they are afraid what God will say if he sees them out. At least if they make women wear this stuff, they can make it nice, put a little oompa-oompa into it."

"What's oompa-oompa?"

"It's a word I just make up. But you know what I mean. You're twenty years old, oompa-oompa is all you got."

"What shall we do?"

"Maybe a walk in the Park. Such a lovely day. We can buy an ice-cream brick, celebrate. Tomorrow we will be living under the bridge with all the bums."

They walked up Fifth, past Tiffany and Bergdorf Goodman, all the shops that were once as familiar to Sarah as her own living room. They reached the big square Monopoly piece of the Plaza Hotel. Sarah lingered, staring at the comings and goings, remembering the days when she rode straight to the front door with her own chauffeur, didn't have to *schlepp* up and down with her nose pressed against the glass.

She saw Liberty stop and stare at something, someone. "Isn't that Mrs. Pargetter?" she said.

Oh yes, it was Jane Pargetter, no question. She looked like she had stepped straight out of the front window of Saks in her white wool frock and bolero jacket and white brimmed hat. She was coming from a soirée in the palm court, Sarah supposed, trying not to look tipsy as she stepped into the limousine, clutching a small white dog in her arms.

For a moment, their eyes met. There was a flicker of recognition, Sarah saw it in her eyes; then, just as quickly, she turned away and got into the shiny black Packard.

"Did she see us?" Libby said.

"She saw. Of course she saw. She is right there, I can spit that far. How can she not see us?"

"Weren't you two friends?"

"No," Sarah said, "but once we acted like we were."

The bell captain was staring at her, the same one from the old days, ramrod straight in his smart red uniform. He gave her a salute, even a hint of a smile. The help at the Plaza are so polite, she thought. Better than Dewey's old friends.

As the limousine pulled away, Sarah said, "Did you see her poodle dog? Was that in the *Vogue* summer catalog?"

"Autumn."

"That explains. I didn't see autumn."

⊰———⊱

Sarah sat in her kitchen and stared at the squashed bugs on the wall-paper, the slime of grease on the wall over the stovetop, the holes in the linoleum. What troubled her about such poorness was Libby; she was born for poodles and limousines and bolero jackets. It is because I love her so much that she must live with me here in my noisy linoleum world. This is all my fault.

She stared at the Sears catalog on the kitchen table in front of her. Everything now was ready-to-wear, with zippers not buttons. Sarah wrinkled her nose at the cheapness of it, and such sameness. Okay, they call them "town tailored," okay, silk or rayon. But if you buy from a catalog, she thought, you can walk in to afternoon tea or a matinee and there's another woman, dressed just the same.

What women want, she thought, is to look like Macy's front window for Hester Street prices; not only to look a million dollars, but to look like the only million dollars anyone ever made in their whole lives.

Libby walked in and peered over her shoulder. "Why are you buying a Sears dress, Mama? I thought you hated them."

"Never buy such sameness," Sarah said. "Such puffy sleeves, belts, big yoke collars. I can make twenty, thirty, before I get out of bed. Can make with my eyes closed and reading a book."

"You can't read a book if you have your eyes closed."

"Okay, Miss Smarty-Pants, but look you this one. Imagine, instead of rayon is cotton; and here you sew some pretty buttons, maybe a godet right here on the skirt, perhaps flounce of lace here. Whatever bits and pieces you can buy, cheap as scraps, but different every time."

"The ladies round here would snap it up."

"If they think it is by Jean Patou, they snap. If they think it is bust-your-door-down bargain, yes, they will snap. But if they think it is by Mrs. Levine from Cornelia Street, they will put up their nose and spit in the street."

"I have to go. I said I would meet Frankie at five."

Sarah didn't even hear her leave. She was still staring at the Sears catalog and wondering what she would do if she was this Mrs. Jean Patou. She wouldn't be working in a sweatshop. She would be making her own dresses, she thought, and sewing like nobody's business.

44

The long summer evening seemed like it would go on forever, the sun sitting plump over the roofs of Greenwich Village, and still it was no cooler. She could hear the *bup-bup-bup* of some kid throwing a handball against the wall down in the yard. The old man was still wandering around his apartment in his underwear.

Sarah stared at the spindle where she kept the household bills, then at the nut-brown Singer sewing machine between the window and the coal-black stove, golden scrolls painted on the black arm, the little drawers either side of the treadle, where she kept her needle and thread.

"What are you doing," it said. *"I can save you! Why are you ignoring me?"* It sounded like her mutti back in the *alte heim*: *"You are bleeding all the blood from my old heart."*

She got the butter out of the icebox and fetched the jar of rhubarb-strawberry preserve that old Mrs. Herzog had given her, sliced yesterday's bread on a wooden board. She could smell from somewhere fried liver and onions, and it made her stomach growl, but there was no money for such things until Libby found another job somewhere where the men didn't make her use all her hat pins.

She went back to the bedroom, unlocked the drawer where she kept the old biscuit box: a photograph of Micha, his soldier papers from the army, the newspaper clipping. Like parchment it was, so brittle. She thought, One day it will just crumble to dust.

She stared at it, wondered at how it could make her fingers tremble even after so long.

I should tell her, she thought. This life is not for her. What would happen if I found this Mr. George Seabrook, told him everything? Here, this is your daughter I stole. Look how beautiful she is! Here, take her. Do what you want with me. Only give her a life again, away from my poorness and bread and jam for supper.

She heard Libby on the stairs. She was running. Something must have happened. She fumbled the lid back on the tin and shut it away in the drawer.

Libby hurried in, face flushed, but this time not because her boss had been trying to touch her. She looked like she had found a diamond ring lying in the street. She grinned at Sarah and started to carve off a slice of bread, near the middle, reached for the jam.

"Bubeleh. Where have you been? Did you find a job today?"

Libby shook her head, but she had a smile on her, a smile like Sarah had not seen in a long time. She had under her arm a big brown paper bag, and she tipped it up and emptied everything inside it on the kitchen table.

"What are these you got?" Sarah said. Just scraps of material, that's how it looked. She picked one up, stared at it, puzzled. "Jean Patou," it said. "PARIS" in capitals in one corner. "Adaptecheune" in the other.

Fancy writing on silk. How many were there? Three dozen, four dozen. Another said "7. Rue St. Florentin. PARIS." Burgundy stitched on cream silk. Another, more simple, black capitals on white background: "CHANEL."

"Frankie's brother got them for us."

"He breaks the law for us?"

"It's not breaking the law, Mama. Well, all right, perhaps, if you call a little bit of stealing breaking the law. But Frankie said they owe you, all the money you sent them when their mama was sick."

Sarah sat down hard on the chair.

"But it is stealing. You say so yourself."

"It's a bit of fabric, Mama. Not a gold ring."

Sarah let the labels run through her fingers like they were gold dust.

"Well?" Liberty said.

"We'd better get to work," Sarah said.

Sarah went down to Orchard Street, to the remnants store, picked out what she wanted, and bargained with the owner until she thought he was going to cry, then bargained harder. Not until he screamed at her that he would fetch the police if she didn't get out of his shop did she accept his price. Then she went home and started work.

She plugged the lead from her Singer into the light socket in the ceiling. It was getting dark, and she would have to use a gas lamp to work by. "For everyone else, the day is finished," she said to Liberty. "But our day, it is just starting."

All night she spent sewing and stitching. Six dresses she made, like the ones they had seen in the window at Saks, but these she made from cotton and added her own touches, used the scraps she had bought from Orchard Street to make each one look individual: some lace here, flowers there, some godets in the skirt here, with a different color, different pattern. And then, a deep breath, and a quick prayer, God, please close your eyes and don't look. I wouldn't do this but I'm desperate. She stitched on the labels Frankie's brother had stolen for her.

The sun was coming up when Libby gathered the dresses, put them in a basket, and put on her shoes. "You keep working, Mama," she said. "I'll take them down Hester Street."

A mile and a half it was to schlepp them all the way over. If it works, it will be worth it. No more slave wages, and no more hat pins. And maybe next week, liver and onions for dinner.

By the time Liberty got there, the streets were already crammed with push-carts and hawkers, and just bedlam: herring smells, cheese smells, body smells. And everything waved in her face: towels, tablecloths, bananas, silk stockings, salt fish bundled in a Ukrainian newspaper, Italian sausage wrapped up in a picture of Mussolini.

You want a yarmulke, you want an apron, you want a pickle, you want, you want?

No sooner had she set her bag down on the sidewalk and took out the dresses, there was some mother fingering the material with her grubby hands. "What's that you got there?"

"Look at the label," Liberty said. "You'll never find anything this good anywhere in the street."

"What do I know from labels? It's schmatta only."

Liberty snatched it back, but now there was another woman grabbing at it, pointing at the label. "Lilian, you wouldn't know a brick from a pound of butter. How much?"

Soon Liberty had a crowd around her, and women were waving pennies in her face, and she was snatching back the dresses and bargaining. Three, four women at once.

"Because you got a fancy label doesn't mean I have to pay you a fancy price!"

"For what I'm asking, you can't get anywhere. You buy this good, you have to go to Bloomingdale's or Saks even!"

"I could make myself for a dollar!"

"You want to sew yourself, lady, and have everyone laugh at you? It's up to you." She snatched the dress out of the woman's hand and turned to her next customer.

She saw a policeman making his way through the pushcarts. She took back all the dresses and threw them in her basket. She ran off down a side alley.

"What's wrong with her?" one of the women said.

"Look, she's seen the officer coming."

"They got to be stolen," another woman said.

When Liberty stopped and looked back over her shoulder, three of the women had followed her down the alley. They were all holding out money.

By lunchtime, Sarah had made half a dozen more dresses. She was sewing the zipper on the last one when she heard Libby on the stairs. She came in, her wicker basket full to bursting still. She put her head on her arms, exhausted.

"Why are you back so soon?" she mumbled. "Couldn't you sell any of them?"

"I sold them all, Mama. You have to make more."

She sat up. "All of them?"

"You should have seen their faces when I sold the last one. I had a queue of women there. They made me promise to come back this afternoon."

"This afternoon?" She frowned. "But where is the money?"

Liberty hefted her basket onto the kitchen table. "I used every penny to buy more material. You have to keep going. Here, give me a needle and thread. I'll sew the buttons, Mama. I think we've got ourselves a business."

45

It looked lovely, this Washington Square, snow dusted on every branch, every bench, every wall, every gate, and all finely powdered on the grass. But it was not lovely, the winter, if you had no money to stay warm while you watched it from inside. Out there, the bums froze in the doorways or huddled in miserable rags by the drum fires under the Brooklyn Bridge.

Liberty climbed the steps to their apartment and clumped in, clapping her hands together to keep the blood moving, wrapped her arms around the boiler in the kitchen, closed her eyes, and sighed like it was a long-lost love. "So cold today," she said. "This New York. It is always too cold."

Out the window someone's gray shirts had frozen on the laundry line strung between the windowsills in the courtyard, like three startled ghosts.

"Soon it will be summer, and you will tell me it's too hot," Sarah said.

"Too cold, too hot. It is always too something. They should call it Too York." Warm in here, at least, away from all the busyness. The walls of their walk-up had disappeared behind piles of gingham and cotton, racks of dresses on wire hangers, baskets of fabric scraps. It was noisy with the clacking of two treadles on the linoleum floor. Sarah had hired another girl to help her; Irena, a Polish girl, still had mud on her boots from her shtetl in Miles-from-Anywheresky, which was what Sarah called her little village—even she couldn't pronounce the name.

"We need another machine, Mama," Liberty said.

"That means another girl."

"We can afford it."

"We got three girls, even four, it is still only pennies we are making."

"We can pay the rent, and we have plenty to eat. What do you want to be, Mama, Rockefeller?"

"Why not? This is not a life. What we had before, *that* was a life."

"I don't care about what we had before. That's gone now."

Sarah pushed back from her machine to stretch her aching back. "I want more for you than this, bubeleh."

"What we need is a shop."

"A shop! We cannot afford."

"You want rich? We'll never get rich working in this cramped-up apartment. It doesn't have to be big, somewhere with a shop window and a workroom. We could sleep in the back of it and give up this place, save on rent. I can't keep walking up and down the Bowery. Every week I need a new pair of heels. In a shop, the people would come to us."

"How could we ever pay for a shop?"

"I been thinking. We can make a lot more if we buy material straight from the wholesaler, cut out the middleman. That is where all our profit goes."

"Wholesalers won't do business with small fish like us." Sarah shook her head. "They won't make business because we are not big fish, but only way we can be big fish is if we make business with them. And this is supposed to make sense to a person how?"

"There has to be a way."

"You think of a way, you tell me."

Liberty had only just got warm. The thought of going back outside again made her shudder. But her mama deserved more than this. There had to be a way, and if there was, she would find it.

⎯⎯✦⎯⎯

There were derelicts sleeping in filthy piles of snow between the girders of the Elevated, empty quart bottles lying next to them. One, with three day's growth of gray stubble and an open sore on his bald head, was lying sprawled on his side with his trouser fly wide open. A hot-dog seller was pointing at him, making jokes about him with his customers. The poor man was wearing a suit, though it was smeared now with all kinds of unspeakable muck. Liberty supposed it was what he had been wearing for the last job he ever had.

I wish I could help him, she thought. One day I will, or people like him. It can't always be about me.

Away from Penn Station it was different. Suddenly she was in the Garment District, all of America had their clothes made right here, or so they said. There were deliverymen everywhere, banging around the street with their garment carts, delivering racks of clothes to the stores or loading them onto trucks—God help anyone who got in their way. She wondered if any of them was Frankie's brother, so long since she had seen those boys she probably wouldn't recognize them now.

She turned down a side street and found the place she was looking for in a row of three-story buildings, all with white pillars out front, stoops with stout enamel-painted doors. There was a single brass plate on the wall beside a door that said "Davidson's & Co."

She took a deep breath, squared her shoulders, and went in.

Under her coat, she was wearing a Liberté original, a burgundy suit that accentuated her sleek hips, menswear wool with silk fringe, decorative buttons, a faux flower on the lapel. She was proud of it, and proud of her mama for designing it. Maybe I live in a walk-up, she thought, but I still look like one of those women on Broadway that have to have something flashy when they get out of their limousine.

But if she was feeling sure of herself when she walked in, the look the receptionist gave her stopped her cold. The eyes behind the rimless spectacles reminded Libby of her teacher at the Florence Nightingale public school on Delancey Street. She had her hair in a tight bun, and she was wearing a shirtwaist that would have been fashionable twenty years ago.

"May I help you?"

"I have an appointment with the manager."

"At what time?"

Libby glanced up at the clock. "At eleven o'clock."

"And your name is?"

"Liberty Levine. Miss Liberty Levine."

"And what company are you from, Miss Levine?"

"Liberté Fashion House."

"Liberty Fashion," she said, scribbling on a pad.

"No, Liberté. The emphasis is on the third syllable. It's French."

The receptionist gave her a hard stare. Was it supposed to intimidate her? She might be Libby Levine from off Bleecker Street right now, but she still remembered what it was like to be Miss Liberty Dewey from the Arlington Apartments, and that was the look she gave her right back.

"One moment," the woman said, and moved away.

Liberty took in the office: a desk in the middle of the room with a pipe rack and a Remington typewriter, several bookshelves stacked with ledgers and thick-spined manuals, some filing cabinets. The men and women in the office were pretending to ignore her, but she could see them all smirking to themselves. Just another pushy good-for-nothing, who does she think she is?

She saw the receptionist whisper something to a woman sitting at a rolltop desk at the far end of the room. The woman checked the diary that lay open on the desk and shook her head. She heard her say, loud enough to hear even from the other end of the room: "Well, there's no Miss Liberty Levine in the appointment book for today."

The receptionist smiled triumphantly. She walked back to the reception desk. "I'm afraid—"

But right at that moment, a man walked out of the corner office. He was blond, young, and slick, exactly the sort of man Frankie had told her always to avoid. He wasn't wearing a suit jacket, and he had his shirtsleeves rolled up to reveal the thick fair hair on his arms. The red silk tie was tied in a Windsor knot under a patterned suit vest.

"Liberty?" he said as he came toward the front of the room. "You wouldn't be Liberty Dewey, would you?"

Everyone in the office looked up from what they were doing. She felt her cheeks burn, and it was an effort to keep her composure. How did he know her old name? "It's Levine now. Liberty Levine."

A cock of his head. "Is it? All right." He grinned again. "You don't remember me, do you?"

"I'm afraid I don't."

"Well, it was a long time ago. I guess we've both changed quite a bit. You have an appointment, do you?"

"At eleven o'clock," Liberty said.

"My secretary must have forgotten to write it down in the book. My apologies for keeping you waiting. Please come through."

Liberty followed him into his office. She spared the receptionist a quick backward glance. It was petty to enjoy such moments, of course, but the look of dismay on her face was a picture.

———

It was a busy office: folders scattered over the desk; a large black telephone; a full in- and out-tray; a glass ashtray, sparkling clean. The young man sat down behind the desk and leaned back, his fingers interlocked over his chest.

"Sit down, Libby," he said, and hearing him use the diminutive of her name startled her.

She stared at the carved wooden nameplate.

HENRY MURPHY
MANAGING DIRECTOR

"That won't help you. It's not my name."

"Should I be worried?"

"I'm filling in. I'm the assistant manager. Jack Seabrook." He tapped his nose.

Ah, the nose. There seemed to be a kink in it. She remembered now.

"I can't be expected to remember every boy I beat up when I was a little girl," she said.

He grinned. "I let you win."

"Of course you did."

"You've changed."

"So have you," she said. "I think you could take me now."

As they talked, she tried to remember if they had ever come across each other after that first meeting at the wedding; but she couldn't recall, it was too long ago. She remembered Jack's father had come to the apartment in the Hundreds once, but he hadn't brought Jack. She was surprised that Jack could still remember her, unless having a girl make his nose bleed when he was twelve years old had been such a mortal blow to his pride.

Jack Seabrook the man bore no relation to Jack Seabrook the whining, mealymouthed kid she held in her hazy memory. Although he looked every inch a lady's man, he had the sober demeanor of his father, someone who knew what he was about and had a stout checkbook to back him. Perfect teeth, perfect hair; she would have been wary even if she didn't know whose son he was.

"I can't believe you remember me," she said. "That was a long time ago."

"Ten years or so. A lot has happened."

"How's your father?"

"The same. The old man never changes; the world just revolves around him." There was a glint in his eye, something else lurking behind that charming smile. What was it? "I was sorry to hear about Uncle Billy. I was away at school at the time. I never found out what happened to you or your mother afterward. My father wouldn't talk about it."

"Dewey should have followed his own good advice about a man never investing more than he could afford to lose. He came up short on quite a lot of stock margins, and he'd forgotten to pay his life insurance premiums. An oversight in the office. We had to move out of the apartment, and everything was sold off to pay his creditors. I still don't think it covered all his losses."

"I'm sorry about that."

"Mama and I both went back to Levine. Pretended we were choosing a fresh start instead of having one dumped on us."

He nodded as though that made sense to him. "That was a bad time. Did the old man ever offer to help?"

"Your father? I've no idea. Mama never mentioned it. Even if he had, she would have been too proud to take anything."

Liberty felt his steely blue eyes appraising her.

"It's quite a surprise having you just walk in like this today. I couldn't believe it when I heard my secretary say your name like that. I thought: How many redheads called Liberty can there be in New York?"

"Only two, far as I know. Me and the old girl with the oversized candle out by Staten Island."

"She's a redhead?"

"She was, before the seagulls got to her."

He grinned. "How can I help?"

"I didn't know this was your firm."

"It's not, it's my father's. I finished business school last year, so he sent me here to learn the ropes. I think that was how he put it. Actually, he's testing me out to see if I have what it takes. Murphy reports back to him weekly, I believe."

"And Mr. Murphy is . . ."

"Away on business today, in Boston. You picked the right day."

"Did I?"

"I don't think you would have got past the fearsome Miss Riley otherwise. So tell me why you're here."

"I want to place an order. My mother and I are in the fashion business. We'd like forty cases of cashmere."

His expression didn't change.

"When do you think you can deliver them?"

Jack brought a yellow pad of paper toward him and unclipped a pen from his vest pocket. "First things first. What is the name of your company?"

"Liberté Fashion. Not Liberty. Liberté with an accent on the third syll—"

"I know how to spell it in French. How long have you been in business?"

"Six months."

"Six months. And how many people do you employ?"

"Three. Including Mama and myself."

"And your premises are . . ."

"In Greenwich Village. Where we live."

"And what is your annual turnover?"

"I don't know. We haven't been in business long enough to have an annual turnover."

He put down the pen. "You realize that Davidson's is one of the largest dyers and importers of textiles in the United States."

"That's why I came here. We don't want to do business with amateurs."

He ran his tongue along the inside of his cheek. "The thing is, we have never before sold to any company not listed on the stock exchange, let alone a shoestring operation in lower Manhattan. And you want me to give you forty cases of cashmere on credit?"

"I believe thirty days is usual."

He leaned forward, elbows on the desk. "You have a nerve."

"Yes, I do," Liberty said. "In my experience, you don't get far without one."

He said nothing. Liberty heard the clock ticking on the wall behind him and a freighter sounding its horn on the Hudson River. "I agree," he said. "Let's go to lunch."

"To lunch?"

"I'm hungry. When I'm hungry, I eat. What about you?" He was already on his feet and reaching for his jacket and coat, which were on a hook by the door.

She got a little clumsily to her feet, nonplussed. "What about the cashmere?"

"We'll talk about it over lunch. That's usual." He opened the door. "After you," he said.

Liberty thought he would take her to some fancy place with red plush and mahogany walls, where he would order lobster Newburg and French wine—no one cared about Prohibition anymore—and that he would then try to seduce her. Noblesse oblige.

So she was surprised, perhaps shocked, when he pushed open the door of the sandwich bar on the corner and swung up onto one of the stools at the counter. The countertop looked as if it had been wiped maybe once, back in the eighteenth century. He flicked yesterday's breadcrumbs on the floor with a casual swipe of his hand, then risked a laundry bill by resting the sleeves of his coat there.

He ordered a swiss cheese on rye with coffee. The heavily lipsticked girl behind the counter gave him her best smile as she took his order, for all the good it did her. Liberty shrugged and said that she'd have the same.

"The Ritz," Liberty said.

"Well, it doesn't seem right to be eating oysters when I know our bookkeeper feeds her kids baked onions stuffed with peanut butter."

"You are the best-dressed socialist I ever saw."

"The clothes are for the clients, the socialism is for me."

The coffees arrived in chipped mugs with no saucers. It was like drinking mud.

"I guess I'm one of the clients you don't have to impress."

"That's exactly right. In fact, I'm waiting for you to impress me. Why don't you tell me more about this little fashion business of yours?"

"Well, it's not mine, it's my mama's. The thing you have to know about her, when it comes to making dresses, she's a genius. She can run her hand over a fabric and tell you the thread count, the name of the manufacturer, and where it was made. She sews without patterns, and she can make something simple and make it look elegant, and not just if you're ten feet tall with hips like a boy, like the mannequins in Macy's window. She can make Mrs. Schmendrick from Hester Street look like Hollywood."

"Is that your pitch?"

"Don't got a pitch, just the truth."

"If you say so."

"You're making me want to hit you in the nose again."

He laughed and held up his hands in mock surrender. "Okay, okay. I'm still listening."

"We started out with a few yards of rayon plus a few rag ends and some lace, and with this, she made half a dozen dresses, gorgeous like you wouldn't believe. She gave them to me, and I sold them in an hour, down on Hester Street. So she made two dozen more. We were up all night, the both of us. I helped her sew the zippers and buttons. Next day I sold everything before lunch."

Liberty thought about telling him about the stolen fashion labels and then thought: No, perhaps not.

"We made enough money to buy more cloth to make another ten dozen. From that we had enough to buy another sewing machine, and then we hired a Polish girl, sixteen and straight off the boat. She works for room and board. She has nowhere else to go, and she can't speak a word of English."

"So you're a socialist too," he said, smiling.

"Listen to me. We sold those ten dozen dresses in two days. Two! People went crazy for them. They were fashion, but they were as cheap as you could make at home except they looked like they came from Saks or Bergdorf. That first couple of months, we cut and sewed day and night to build our little business. And here we are. These days we make enough to get by, but all our profits disappear buying new fabric to keep up with demand. Never can make real money unless we can buy wholesale. Then we can get a shop and not sell off a pushcart."

"Wait a minute. You sell from a pushcart, and you've come to us wanting forty cases on credit?"

"I know it seems unusual, Jack, but—"

"Unusual? Do you know what my father would say if he found out about this? And he would, because Murphy would love to tell him."

"So is that a no, Mr. Jack Seabrook?"

"It's a maybe." He took a bite from his sandwich and thought about it. "You really think you can make this work?"

"When I go down the Lower East Side, there's people following me, asking me what I've got. When I say we're sold out, they still follow me. They come to our apartment in Greenwich and bang on the door every hour of the day or night. We got customers from Brownsville to the Village. Even got our own label."

She fished in her purse for the label they had made and handed it to him. He shook his head in astonishment. "Liberté. Paris and London. Paris and London?"

"They are the names we give our sewing machines."

"Look, instead of coming to Davidson's, why don't you just raise your prices?"

"Jack, the people we sell to, they don't have a lot. People who can afford high prices, they don't buy off a pushcart, and they don't buy from people like me and my mama. To get our margin, we have to lower overhead. Specialize. Go for volume."

"Forty cases of cashmere."

"If you wouldn't mind."

⚓

They took the long way back to his office. He said he needed time to think, and anyway, the walk helped his digestion. Today there was even a little pale sun, though not enough to thaw the snow on the fire escapes and the black tar roof of the Elevated. A trolley car went past, churning up the yellow slush, bells clanging. She could smell onions frying at a hot-dog stand.

Jack was smiling.

"What's so funny?"

"When I heard Miss Riley say Liberty, I thought of this runty little kid with freckles and pigtails. I come out, and it's Greta Garbo."

"First time you saw me, you said I had a monkey face."

"I didn't."

"You did."

"Is that why you punched me on the nose?"

"I don't remember."

"Well, I'm sure whatever it was I said or did, I probably deserved it. I grew up without a mother. I'm told I was a bit of a brat."

"What happened to her, your mom?"

"I don't like talking about it."

They crossed the street. They were nearly at his office, and he still hadn't told her if she could have the cashmere. He was making her sweat.

"For what it's worth," he said, "I'm sorry about what happened to you and your mother. If it's any consolation, I think my father owes you."

"He doesn't owe us anything."

"Dewey was his best friend. He could have helped your ma out if he'd wanted to."

"He doesn't owe us a damned thing and neither do you. I don't want you or anyone feeling sorry for us. This is a business proposition, nothing else."

He stopped outside the office. She waited. If he went back through that door without giving her an answer, it was over, she knew it. She'd never get past Miss Riley a second time. He took off his derby and toyed with it in his hands while she held her breath. "Don't let me down, or I'll never hear the end of it."

"We can have the cashmere?"

"I'll organize it this afternoon."

"I won't let you down," she said. "In five years, we'll be your biggest clients."

"Come by tomorrow," he said. "There will be a shipment order for you to sign, and you can take the invoice. It will all be ready for you by eleven o'clock. Good-bye, Lib. It was great to see you again." He gave her his best smile and went back to work.

——◆——

Libby stood at the door and watched her mother work, the slight twist of a shoulder as she pushed at the wheel, the lift of a foot to free the needle when it caught on a piece of cotton. It was like a dance, and her mother knew all the steps without having to think about them.

Sarah was so engrossed in her work, she did not see Libby standing there. When she did, she gave a start, and the look of surprise was quickly followed by an impatient frown. "So behind on all these orders," she said, "and my daughter running around town like nobody's business, doesn't tell her mother where she has gone."

She was about to finish the hemline when she caught the look on Libby's face.

"What is wrong with you, bubeleh? You have found a million dollars in the street?"

"Better than that. I just got us forty cases of cashmere, wholesale." Sarah stared at her openmouthed.

"What kind of schmuck will give us wholesale?"

"Some schmuck at Davidson's. You know Davidson's?"

"Sure I know from Davidson's. Davidson's, Davidson's?"

"Do you know who owns the company these days? George Seabrook."

There was a long silence. Her mother stopped working, and the look on her face, as if someone had crept behind her and stabbed her. Okay, she never liked George Seabrook, but that was a long time ago.

Finally: "You talked to George Seabrook?"

"No, his son, Jack. Do you remember him? At the wedding? I gave him a bloody nose."

"That I should not remember such a thing. What are you telling me? He is in charge at Davidson's?"

"Assistant manager. What good luck for us! Mama? What's wrong?"

"You must tell him no."

"What?"

"You cannot take from such a man."

"Are you crazy, Mama? All afternoon I talked to him, I begged him for this. Forty cases of cashmere, wholesale! When will we get another chance like this?"

Sarah got up and walked out of the room. Irena looked up from her work, startled. "What is wrong with your mutti?" she said in Yiddish.

"I don't know," Libby said. She followed her into the kitchen. Sarah stood at the window, her arms wrapped around herself, rocking backward and forward, like she was praying or something, like the old men at the temple in their prayer shawls.

"Mama?"

"I'm sorry, bubeleh. You did good for us. You have done miracle for us. But promise me, after this one time, you won't ever go back."

"We have an account at the biggest wholesaler in New York. What are you saying? This will make us rich."

"I don't want any charity from that man."

"It's not charity. It's business. I told him we're going to be one of his biggest customers in five years. And we will."

"Don't care what you tell him. I say no, anyone else but him."

"There isn't anyone else, Mama! I only got my foot in the door over there because Jack Seabrook remembered my name, no other reason. Never will we get a chance like this again. What are you crying for?"

"Nothing."

"Then stop. Come on, Mama. Let's get back to work. We have orders to finish. You want to be a big-shot designer, this is our chance."

"All right, we take this order, this one time only. Then you don't go back there again!"

"Okay, if that's what you want."

"You promise me."

Libby thought about it. "I promise," she said. Well, kind of promise. Let's do this order, then we'll see. Let Mama get the crazy out of her system, and then they'd talk about it again.

46

"Tell me again how I was born, Mama."

They were lying in the dark in the kitchen. They had dragged out their beds and put them next to the stove to try and keep warm. It was so cold in the rest of the apartment, they used the second bedroom to chill the milk.

"I told you that story a hundred times."

"Tell it to me again."

"I was expecting with you when I got on the boat to come to America, but I thought you were a long way off, thought I would be a long time in this New York before you came. But as soon as I saw the Liberty statue, I had my first pains, and they came really strong on the way into the harbor. And I was so scared you would come before I got off the ship. And your papa, he met me on Ellis Island. I think I will collapse right there in his arms. He has almost to carry me from the ferry boat, then he puts me in the back of a cab. Well, not a cab like you have now, they were all horse carriages back then. And that very night, my first night in America, you came."

"And that's why you called me Liberty."

"After the first thing in America I saw, yes."

"You must have been so scared."

"Not so much. Your papa and a lady next door, Mrs. Fischer, they helped deliver. And anyway, I was there when my sisters had their babies, and like I told you, when Etta had her Bessie in the snow, when we were stranded in the forest, there was only me to help her. I remember I thought: If Etta can have a baby at night in the snow, I can have my baby in this big city in a big warm bed with all this help."

"I wish I could meet Etta and Bessie. You have talked about them so much, it is like I already know them. Do you think they will ever come here?"

"I don't know, bubeleh. Now go to sleep. Tomorrow is another big day. I must decide what to do with forty cases of cashmere!"

Four weeks later, Libby had in her hand a bank check for Davidson's and Co., the full amount they owed. Sarah said they should post it, but Libby said, "No, I am going to pay by hand, I want to see Jack Seabrook's face when I give him the money."

"Then let me do it," Sarah said.

"No, Mama, you have to let me do it."

"You don't like this boy?"

"What? No, of course not. This is just business."

Yes, it was just business, but Liberty could not hide her disappointment when she went into the Davidson's and Co. office, and Miss Riley told her that Mr. Jack Seabrook was not there. He had moved to London to open a new office. But she accepted her order for forty more cases of cashmere without demur.

As Liberty headed to catch a trolley bus back down Eighth Avenue, she knew she should feel elated. Who knew how their business would grow from now? But instead she felt curiously let down.

PART 6

47

Greenwich Village, New York, November 1936

Dearest Etta,
So, it is not long before I see you again, my darling sister!
I cannot believe the day has finally arrived. I am busy
making everything ready here for your welcome. You will
find things so different here, but I will do all I can to
smooth your move to your new life here in America. You
can live with us above the shop. There is not so much
room, but it will be like the old days, when you and me
and Gutta and Zlota all slept in the bed on the oven, do
you remember?

Everything has changed so much for me this last few
months. Business has gone strong to stronger. Our shop is
very busy, but now we have very rich and important cus-
tomers, big-name actresses and such. They come to me for
gowns and dresses, and they wear them at big millionaire-
type parties. Soon I think everyone will be wearing clothes
I have made right here at my dinner table! What seemed
just a dream even a year ago is now happening. We have
three girls working at the sewing machines, two Polish

and one from Vilnius. They work hard like I did when I first come here, but they are lucky, they do not have a boss who tries to pinch them on the bottom every day!

My darling Liberty has helped me so much. She is nothing for dress-making, but she is such a hard worker, she understands all the business things, and she is in charge of the shop and accounts and suppliers, and all the number things I cannot do, so I can concentrate on the making of dresses . . .

When she had finished, she put ten dollars in the envelope—as much as she could afford, not like the old days—and licked it shut. There was joy and dread in her heart. She was happy that Etta and her family were finally coming where it was safe. But what happens, she thought, when they see Libby?

Etta coming over now. It was going to cause trouble, just when everything was going so good. Soon they would be rich again: they would have a nice apartment, a nice life; she would get Libby a proper husband, a doctor or a lawyer. She wouldn't need a matchmaker when a girl looked like that. They would have a place in the world again, and respect.

But then, there never really would be a good time for the truth, would there? She couldn't put off this moment forever, she had always known that. Well, she had got through these messes before, she would get through again. Nothing was going to take her Libby away from her, not now.

⬥

When Libby looked up from the cash register, Jack Seabrook was standing in the doorway of the shop, his fedora in his hand, trying to look inconspicuous. It wasn't working. Several of her customers glanced his way, even two of the Jewish mothers who were old enough to know better.

His clothes alone set him apart, and of course the way he wore them. He had on a double-breasted overcoat with a gold silk fleur-de-lis handkerchief and matching tie, a suit that was hand-tailored—she could tell—and a pale-blue button-down shirt; costed by the yard, she thought, he was worth two or three weeks' wages for most people around here.

She felt a little flutter at seeing him, but waited until it had passed before going over, hoped she appeared unaffected. "Mr. Jack Seabrook. Come to have a look at where the real work is done?"

"Hello, Libby."

"I thought you were in London."

"I got back last week. My father has other plans for me, apparently. Thought I'd stop by and see how my little gamble paid off."

"Should I spot you a few bucks?"

He grinned. "You can keep it. It was a gentleman's wager. But you've done well."

"My mama has done well. I only cheer from the sidelines and get paid far too much for keeping her books and talking to salesmen."

He looked at the half dozen racks of dresses, the mannequins by the windows wearing Sarah's latest designs. "Who would have thought?" he said.

"You must have, I guess, or you wouldn't have advanced the credit back then. We have three girls working full time. We have our very own little sweatshop upstairs and two prominent Broadway actresses on the books. Mama is hoping to be back on the Upper West Side next year, but under her own steam this time."

"Good for her. Was it hard to find this place?"

"Rents on Orchard Street are cheap, even cheaper when you bargain as hard as my mama."

He raised an eyebrow at the photographs of Hollywood stars and starlets pasted to the bare walls, taken from magazines. "Are they all wearing your dresses?"

"I wish. Referred glamor."

"You're looking more beautiful than ever."

Libby felt herself blush—Goddammit—taken off guard, hated herself for falling for such a cheap line. "You look a little rumpled," she said. "Just got off the boat?"

"You should know I spent half an hour deciding which tie to wear to impress you. Can you get away for lunch?"

A customer emerged from behind the curtain that hung across the changing cubicle in the corner. She gave Jack a look of stern reproach for being there and brought her purchase to the register. Libby excused herself while she attended to her. When she had finished, Jack was still waiting patiently by the door. She put up the closed sign, waited for the last two customers to leave, then fetched her coat.

A cold November day. He turned up his collar and put his fists deep in his coat pockets. "Where shall we go?" he said.

"There's a really terrible place for coffee over on the corner. There's crumbs all over the counter, and the coffee tastes like mud. If I remember, it's the kind of egalitarian place you like."

"Sounds perfect," he said.

Everyone was walking with their heads down into the wind, and Jack had to keep one hand on his fedora to keep it on his head. They passed an Italian grocery with a picture of Mussolini in the window, frowning from under a feather-topped helmet, beside a color lithograph of the Madonna, her carmine heart luminous through the folds of her blue gown. A customer came out, and as the door to the shop opened, Liberty could smell the damp ripeness of the cheeses on the counter.

"How long were you in London?" she asked him.

"Three years."

"Has it been that long?" she said, though she knew exactly how long it had been. "How was it?"

"I couldn't wait to come home. It's so grim over there. The newspapers are full of bad news, day after day, and it's relentless. If it's not Hitler, it's Mussolini, and if it's not them, it's Franco. Before I left, there was a riot in the East End between the Jews and the Mosleyites. I don't know what the world's coming to."

"All we hear about here is the king and his American girlfriend."

"They say he'll give up the throne to keep her."

"What man would give up being king for a woman?"

"Depends on the woman, I suppose," he said, which surprised her. They stopped outside a diner on Bleecker Street, and she nodded to him, this was the place.

When they walked in, a man in a cap and an apron, which would have been white if he ever washed it, gave the counter a perfunctory wipe with a rag. Libby ordered coffee and a sandwich. "Just coffee, thanks," Jack said.

"Not up to your usual standard?"

"Too early to eat," he said. "Besides, if you can take the food in England, you can eat anywhere." He eased onto a stool. "So, Libby, your mom's done okay, then?"

"In her element. She still makes off-the-rack, but some of Ziegfeld's girls have had gowns made; plus she has two or three special customers, well heeled, they pay more than one thousand dollars for a single gown. A few months ago Gypsy Rose Lee—can you believe—she was in the Ziegfeld show, and she came to Mama as well. I'm gushing, aren't I?"

"A bit, but that's okay. You were right about your mother, then. She sounds like a woman of many hidden talents."

"All our customers have to do is show her something they've seen in a fashion magazine, doesn't matter if it's a Vionnet or a Lanvin or a Chanel, she can make it. Hand-turned hems, hand-sewn seams, work like hers you can't get in New York."

The mud arrived. Jack picked up the mug and sipped at his; she saw him wince.

"So long living with the Limeys, I suppose you drink tea now."

"I still drink coffee. But this is nothing like coffee."

"It was a big surprise to see you this morning."

"Well, I kept tabs while I was in London. My old boss at Davidson's said you were still on his books. I wanted to see for myself how things turned out for you. Seems George got it all wrong about your mother."

"We pay our bills."

"What about you? Do you have a beau?" He looked at her hands, but they were still hidden in her muff. "A husband?"

"It's been three years. I've been through two marriages and five engagements. Keep up, Jack."

They talked about the fashion business and movies they liked, and before she knew it, they'd been sitting there half an hour. She pulled his arm toward her, looked at his wristwatch: yellow gold with a brown leather strap. Expensive. "I have to go."

"So soon?"

"It was good seeing you again. I never got a chance to thank you for what you did for us. So . . . thank you."

A casual smile and a shrug. He reached into his pocket and slapped some coins on the counter. "Whatever he charges you for the coffee, it's too much."

"Good-bye," she said. So this was all there would ever be, after all.

"Come to dinner with me tomorrow night."

She tried to hide her surprise, pretended to think it over.

"I'll pick you up."

"You're asking me out?"

"It sounds that way."

"Tell me, is that the real reason you came by the shop?"

"Well, it wasn't to drink this guy's coffee."

"Three years it takes you to ask a girl to dinner?"

"It's only dinner. I'm not writing you into my will."

"Don't pick me up, I'll meet you."

"Okay." He reached into his pocket, took out a business card, and scribbled an address on the back of it with his pen, which was also gold, she noticed, to match the tie and the watch. "Seven-thirty," he said.

She watched him button up his overcoat on the sidewalk, replace his fedora, and head back toward Broadway with his collar turned up against the wind. What to make of him? Always so serious, but he loved the Marx Brothers; his father was her mother's greatest detractor, yet Jack had risked his censure to afford her credit; he was rich and good-looking, could have the arm of any deb he wanted, yet he came down to the Village to ask a girl he hardly knew to come with him to a— she looked at the back of his card—a Chinese restaurant on Doyers Street.

Well, better not let Mama find out.

48

Sarah took a deep breath, got herself ready. Here she was again at the kissing post, where Micha had come to get her, how long ago was it? Twenty-three years. Just a slip of a girl then. She was not a young woman anymore, but not a poor one either, in her fox fur and gauntlet gloves and blackberry beret, a proper businesswoman, and she had done it all herself.

Never was a woman so proud of what she had done, she thought, and so ashamed.

Through the window she saw the green goddess of the Liberty statue, her arm raised, looking out at the sea and all those shtetls on the other side of the ocean. Waiting, waiting for the rest to come, like she waited for me.

She looked up the stairs, and there they were, her family, these strangers she could barely remember.

A big smile she put on. Hugged and cried, shouted out how good it was to see them, ten times, a hundred times. Like a good Jewish sister, crying and kissing. And all the time thinking: What are they wearing? How old and plain they look. This cannot be my sister, cannot be my little niece whose life I saved!

And what about these boys, I have seen better-dressed creatures playing in the gutter on Orchard Street!

What a bad sister I am to have such thoughts. What is wrong with me that I could think such a way?

Yaakov was still handsome, but his beard and the wings of his long hair that stuck out from under his fox fur hat were gray now. And Etta, her beautiful sister, Sarah did not recognize her, so plump now, and chalk-white from sea sickness. And this one, this must be Bessie. The last time she had seen her, she was a babe in arms, pink and soft and hardly any hair on her tiny little head. Now look at her: dark pigtails and sad eyes and almost as wide as she was long in her heavy black coat and shapeless brown boots.

"This is Ruben," Etta was saying. "And this is Aron." She pushed forward the two surly-looking boys. They peered up at her from under their dark eyebrows, thin and gangly in their teenage bodies, like marionettes they looked.

This was how I looked when I first came, she thought, when I didn't know how to speak American, knew nothing of the schvartzes and skyscrapers and hamburgers and subways and Checker cabs.

They will survive like I did. We all survive, mostly.

But there was this dread in her. Suddenly she had these people from the alte heim watching her. In that moment, it was like she had a conscience again, like her vati and Elohim had arrived to take an accounting from her.

And next, they would have to all meet her Libby.

The children's eyes were like soup plates as they rode in the cab heading back from Battery Park. The two boys huddled in their seats not saying a thing. Yaakov was pointing and shouting in Yiddish. Bessie was shrunken up inside her coat, like a tortoise going into its shell.

"The children cannot speak any of this English," Etta was saying. "Only Yaakov can. He is learning for three years in Tallinn."

Another shout. Yaakov, mouth open, was pointing to the sky, peering up through the cab window at the high buildings, the Chrysler and the Empire State Buildings. It made her smile. For herself, she never looked up anymore. New York was New York.

Yaakov was like a little child. She remembered how once he had seemed so big and so manly, such love she had for him once. Now he was just another greenhorn.

"How are things at home?" Sarah said.

"It is so good there now, you wouldn't recognize," Etta said. "No one calls us dirty names in the street like they did when Vati was alive. Ruben and Aron can go to school with the other children."

"But how long will it last?" Yaakov said. "This meshuggener Hitler making trouble. Stalin is worse!"

Ruben shook his brother's arm and pointed. They gasped when they saw the Elevated thunder overhead, the winter sun and shadow flickering on the street like the end of a newsreel as the train went through the station. Etta shook her head at seeing so many people, all the men in fedoras and the women in gray and brown calf-length coats and suits, clicking along the sidewalks in high heels, everyone hurrying, everyone with somewhere to go.

"It is so crazy big here," she said, her nose pressed against the glass window. "However will we live?"

⟨―⟩

The apartment above the shop had just two bedrooms. They had the sewing machines for their three seamstresses in the living room at the front because it had better light, and their dinner table in the kitchen. After their walk-up on Cornelia Street, it had seemed impossibly big; now it would be too tiny and cramped for all of them.

Sarah told Yaakov and Etta they could have her bedroom, and she put mattresses for the boys and for Bessie in Libby's room. There were two more mattresses for Libby and for her; they would put them on the living room floor after the girls had finished work for the day. Only for a short time, Sarah told Etta. Soon she would have enough money for a lease on a new apartment. She and Liberty would move out, and Etta and her family could stay above the shop until Yaakov found a job.

Later, she took them all out to show them the city. Nothing would do but riding the Elevated up to Times Square, where they all stood around gaping at the billboards and the lights: Coca-Cola, Camel, Lucky Strike, Kool—"Even if you cough like crazy, Kools still taste fresh as a daisy." Etta could not drag the boys away from the fifteen-foot-high penguin in a top hat and a bow tie.

The boys pointed at the things Sarah no longer even thought about, like the little Mercury statues on all the traffic lights on Fifth. "What are they, Aunt Sarah?" "Why are they there?" But what could she tell them? They were just there, who knew why?

Bessie and the boys could have stood on the corner of Fifth and West Forty-Second all day, watching the streetcars rattling on their brass rails across the intersections, the live wires buzzing overhead; Ruben wanted only to go down into the subway and listen to the clatter of the turnstiles and gaze around at this subterranean wonder with its noise and its people and its advertising. "Chew Gum!" "Drink Beer!"

Another miracle: put a nickel in a slot for a slice of pie at the Horn and Hardart Automat. Who could imagine? Hot coffee spouting from the mouths of silver dolphins. Everywhere some new wonder for them. Towers taller than the tallest castles so that you could not even see the sky; caves that went on underneath the city forever; trains that flew in the sky; everywhere polished steel and mirrored glass and shining car hoods and clanging buses and tooting, impatient taxicabs, and people, so many people.

The boys loved it all, but it was winter now, and the afternoon was over before it started. By the time they got back to the Village, it was almost dark. They all huddled by the stove in the kitchen, and Sarah showed Etta the samovar. "Do you remember this, Etta?" she said. "This and a mattress and the menorah, all I brought with me from the alte heim. I have had them with me through thick and thin all this time."

She made some black tea, and they talked about when they were all young and Tallinn was part of Russia. The winters back there, everything frozen, you could boil the potatoes all day and still find ice in the middle of them.

"Is it cold here in winter?" Yaakov asked her.

Sarah nodded. "But somehow it seems warmer because of all the lights and the people. And because there is always hope here."

They watched the dusk fall and the lights of the neighboring tenements blink on one by one, and Sarah felt the fear tighten in her, like a knot in her belly, someone pulling the ends tighter and tighter. She would be home soon, her Liberty, her beautiful daughter with the red hair and green eyes that you could never see in a photograph. One photograph she had sent them, when Liberty was ten years old. What would they say when they saw her?

Sarah reached over the table and nudged Bessie's arm. "And how are you, little skinny bones?"

"I'm not skinny," Bessie said, without a smile. "I'm fat."

"You're not fat," Etta said, and the two boys giggled and nudged each other.

"Did your mother ever tell you the story of when you were born?" Sarah asked her.

"All the time," Bessie said, and raised her eyes to the ceiling.

"Bessie, don't talk to your aunt Sura in such a way! You put a knife through your poor mother's heart when you do that!"

"Let her be," Yaakov said. "It is her first day. She's missing her cousins."

"Zara and Bluma," Etta said to Sarah. "Inseparable, the three of them, since they were all little. Weren't you, Bessie?"

"I don't want you to talk about them," Bessie said.

"They are Zlota's girls?" Sarah said.

"She has three boys also, all grown up now."

"And Gutta's family?"

"We don't see them so much," Yaakov said. "They moved away."

"They came to Vati's funeral," Etta said. "Nice boys. One of them is married now."

"So sad he is gone. I cannot believe."

"Vati was so sick, for such a long time. It was a blessing. And Mutti so soon after."

"I wish she had never died," Bessie said, "then we wouldn't have to come here."

There was a hush then. Well, it was true enough, Sarah supposed. She poured more tea, added a little lemon. Yaakov drank it the old way, with a sugar cube clenched between his front teeth. The heat from the stove steamed the windows. One of the boys wrote his name on the glass.

And then she heard Liberty on the stairs.

The door flung open, and she was standing there, beautiful in her burgundy hat and her wool coat with the fur collar. There was a hush in the room when she took off her hat and they all saw her red hair.

"Libby, look, they are finally here!" Sarah said, jumping to her feet. I will be gay and enthusiastic, she thought, and this difficult moment, it will be gone.

Libby beamed and held out her arms, and waited for them to come to her.

"Oh *mein Gott*," Etta said, and put a hand to her mouth.

Silence.

"Is this our cousin?" Ruben said, finally. "She looks like a goy!"

49

"Did you know," Jack said, "that corner outside has seen more people die than any other street in America? It was a favorite place for the local Chinese tongs to ambush each other. They used hatchets in those days."

"You take me to all the nicest places."

"Thought I'd show you a little local color."

In fact, Libby was secretly delighted he had brought her here. Chinoiserie was in vogue. Elegant New York had discovered somewhere other than Harlem to slum it at night.

She looked around the dining room; half the Upper East Side were there. The only Chinese were the waiters, none of them much bigger than the two huge porcelain vases that stood on either side of the doors. A crimson screen with snarling golden dragons hid the patrons from the street, and the street from the patrons; so they didn't have to watch the blood running along the gutters during the next tong war, she supposed.

Tiny golden Buddhas, with joss sticks burning beside them, nestled in niches in the walls. The owner patrolled the room in a tuxedo, snapping at any of the waiters who weren't servile enough.

"So, before you tried to impress me with your knowledge of the Oriental underworld, you were telling me about Harvard."

"Not much more to tell. It's a stuffy place full of overprivileged brats like myself, but that's as good a preparation as any for the business world and for England, of course."

"Are you being groomed to take over from Pops?"

"Take over what?"

"Your father's business empire."

"It's not really an empire."

"It's not a kosher deli on the corner."

"I guess not. I was always being groomed, I guess. I'm his sole heir, the blue-eyed boy."

A bowing waiter in Mandarin pajamas brought them egg-drop soup in willow-pattern bowls and withdrew.

"Why are you the only boy?"

A flicker of a smile that suggested he had heard the question, but he didn't answer. He picked up his spoon. "Do you like the soup? It's not for everyone. They make the broth with chicken bones and drop an egg in."

"Does that mean the subject's off limits?"

"I guess so."

A waiter reversed into the swing doors at the back of the dining room, and for a moment she saw one of the chefs hacking up a chicken with a shining steel cleaver. Her eyes must have widened, because Jack glanced over his shoulder, but the doors had already swung shut.

"What was that?" he said.

"One of your favorite gang members was practicing his technique."

"Unlikely. They use machine guns, like everyone else, these days."

"Just to kill the chickens?"

Another smile. He looked utterly different when he smiled, a boy again.

"How long are you back in New York?" she asked him.

"That hasn't been decided."

"What are your choices?"

"The old man has promised me New York."

"All of it? Generous. But I'd hold out for New Jersey as well."

"I want the New York office. Davidson's. He said that once I earned my stripes, he'd make me the manager."

"And have you?"

"Have I?"

"Earned your stripes."

"I increased sales by twenty percent every year in London. He seemed encouraged by that."

"How was London? Did you pee on anyone's lawn?"

"I was discretion itself. I think I would disappoint you these days."

He told her about the monuments, the Lyons teahouses, the jellied eels, about cockney rhyming slang, the fact that there were no summers, the constant feeling that it was just about to rain or had just rained. "Though I didn't feel like that most of the time," he said, "because it actually was raining."

He tried to explain Marmite and Scotch eggs; his difficulties pronouncing Leicester Square and Holborn; and the intricacies of pounds, shillings, and pence.

"Everything is old there," he said. "All the buildings have turned black from the smog and smoke. Everywhere there's a statue of some dead king or queen or duke. The lawyers wear wigs. Nobody tips. And nowhere is open after six o'clock."

"So you stayed in your room and pined for lonely girls in Village clothes shops."

"Other times I went to the movies."

"Alone?"

"Only the westerns." He leaned closer so that their faces were almost touching. "There are some private pleasures you can only share with another aficionado."

Two waiters brought more bowls from the kitchen and broke the moment. Jack, of course, could use chopsticks. He chose a morsel from one of the steaming dishes and put it in her bowl.

"How do you like your chicken, Wild Bill?" she said.

He raised an eyebrow in surprise. "I like my chicken just fine," he said, in a perfect Gary Cooper drawl, and they both laughed out loud, and a matron in a diamond choker peered around one of the Chinese screens to stare.

⊰⊱

"I'd like to do this again," he said as they were leaving and waiting for the waiter to bring them their coats.

"Are you looking for another notch on your bedpost?"

"Is that what you think of me?"

"Am I wrong?"

He ran a hand through his hair, but a comma of it fell obstinately back across his forehead. It was the only part of him that was not geometrical, which made his choice in films and restaurants all the more interesting.

The waiter returned with their coats and hurried them out the door. She supposed he was anxious to get off work and start swinging cleavers at his colleagues. They stepped outside onto the street, and Jack found them a cab. After they were settled in the back, he said, "I'm not really a ladies' man, you know."

"As long as you're not a man's man, so to speak."

"I had a girlfriend before I went to London. We were about to be engaged when the old man told me he had other plans for me. She said she'd wait. She didn't."

"How did you find out?"

"She wrote and told me. Not even a letter. It was on the back of a postcard."

"Classy. What was the picture, don't mind me asking?"

"Statue of Liberty and Times Square. It said 'Howdy from New York' in red letters on a yellow background on the front. On the back it said: 'I'm sorry, I've met someone else, don't be cross.'"

"Did she write it, or have it printed?"

"Red ink. Quite jaunty. A nice touch, I thought."

"Well, that's women for you."

"Easier to climb Niagara Falls than to understand a woman," he said.

"Don't believe everything Wild Bill Hickok says. If it wasn't for Calamity Jane, he would have got himself burned alive by the Indians. You can drop me here on the corner of Minetta."

As she got out of the cab, he leaned forward and gave her the full benefit of the Jack Seabrook smile. She felt as if she had been caught in the headlights of an oncoming truck.

"Good night, Miss Levine. We should do this again."

She smiled back. "I'd like that just fine, Mr. Hickok," she said. She watched the cab drive off. Be careful, Libby, she thought. Remember, he hasn't told you how many women there's been since Little Miss Postcard, and you don't want to be the one to help him climb up Niagara Falls.

You're only a girl from the Lower East Side without a postcard to her name.

50

Liberty felt frozen through, numb with exhaustion. As she climbed the stairs from the shop, she stopped to take off her shoes. There were red marks on her heels, going to blisters. All day she had been schlepping the streets with her mama's Liberté portfolio, first to Federated, then Arnold Constable, De Pinna, finally S. Klein on Union Square.

Only an hour to get ready. She had to get freshened up and put on something nice. Jack had said he would pick her up in his car at seven. She had told him she would wait on the corner of Bleecker and Sixth. She didn't want him coming to the apartment. First, she would have to tell her mama about him, and she wasn't ready for that, not yet.

She hung back, her hand on the door. She really didn't want to go in there tonight. It would be crowded with Etta and her family, everyone staring at her: the boys with their lewd peasant eyes; Bessie, who could never look her in the eye and always dressed in black, like an old grandmother. So foreign to her, this family of hers. Once she had looked forward to it so much, having a real family at last. What a disappointment they were.

She took a deep breath and went in. The seamstress girls had gone home, but the living room was still taken up with the sewing machines and the baskets of needles and thread, the thimbles and pincushion dolls, with design patterns on the tables and racks and racks of finished and half-finished dresses.

Everyone was in the kitchen. The door to the bedroom where Yaakov and Etta slept was ajar. Liberty could see the bed neatly made, embroidered Russian peasant blouses and red velvet suits all hanging up neatly behind a curtain. How can Etta go out in those, she thought. On Orchard Street perhaps, but not here. Her mama had offered Etta some of her dresses, latest designs, and she had turned up her nose. How would she ever fit in if she walked around dressed like a greenhorn?

There was a white linen tablecloth set out on the kitchen table. She supposed Etta had brought it with her. The silver menorah had been brought out, freshly polished, and there was *challah* wrapped in something else that was new, a blue velvet cloth embroidered with gold Hebrew letters.

"What's this?" she said.

"*Shabbat shalom,*" Etta said.

"Etta has made the *seder,*" Sarah said.

Shabbas. Well, of course, but since they moved out of the Lower East Side, her mama had not made such a big fuss about it. When they had lived with Dewey, Sundays had been more important.

Liberty could smell broiled chicken and roasted meat. Sarah lit the candles on the menorah while Etta watched, then Yaakov took out a grubby prayer book and started to read the prayers.

He sang the "Shalom Aleichem" hymn to welcome the angels who visited every home at the start of Shabbat. He asked for their blessing, and then bade them farewell. Liberty fidgeted. What was all this, what was her mama doing? It was like inviting people from the jungle to have dinner with them.

"I made some of your favorite, gefilte fish, and Etta has made *cholent.*"

Libby felt a wave of panic. "But I have to go out," she said.

"But it is Shabbas," Etta said.

"Mama, what is happening? You never do this anymore. Not since Cannon Street have we done this."

Everyone was staring at her.

"You do not keep Shabbas?" Yaakov said to Liberty. He was looking at her as if she had said that she kidnapped babies and ate them.

"I'm sorry," she said, and went to leave the kitchen.

"But you will come with us to the synagogue tomorrow?" he said.

"I have to work."

"Work?" Yaakov said.

"I have an appointment at Altman's on Fifth Avenue. It's important. Isn't it, Mama?"

Sarah did not answer her, could not even look at her.

Liberty hurried out the door. Before she closed it, she heard Bessie say: "If Libby doesn't go to the synagogue, why do I have to?"

———⊰⊱———

Liberty had to find something to wear. She positioned herself behind one of the clothes racks and changed quickly, one eye on the door, nothing for those pesky boys to poke their head in here. There was no privacy even in their own place anymore. She put on a dark-red flared skirt with a lumber-jacket blouse. She had seen Claudette Colbert in the same combination in a magazine; then her best coat, black, with a Mendel fur collar.

At that moment the door opened. It was Sarah. "You are not going to tell me you are going out."

"I don't have to tell everything, Mama."

"Look at you, how beautiful you have grown."

Libby turned away, embarrassed. She set the cracked mirror against the wall for a better view of her own reflection. She supposed she didn't look too bad, in the right light.

"Where is it you are going?"

"The movies."

"Who you are going with?"

"Friends."

She felt her mother's expert eye take everything in. "A rather perky little hat you have for just going with friends."

"Because I have a mother who works in fashion. They expect nothing less."

"These friends, they got names?"

"I expect so. It helps when their mothers call them in for supper."

"Libby!"

"Jane and Emily."

"Never have I heard you talk Jane and Emily before."

"I don't have to tell you everything, Mama."

She made for the door. Sarah put out an arm to stall her, dropped her voice. "It's Shabbas. Stay here, for me, for your aunt Etta. Will it kill you, bubeleh?"

"When have you ever cared about religion, Mama? When have I?"

"Think on it not as religion, but family. They are new here. They don't understand."

"This is New York, Mama. They're the ones who have to change, not us. Why are you so scared of them?"

And she was scared, Libby could see it in her mother's face.

Sarah put down her arm and took a step back. Libby went out, closing the door behind her.

51

It was raining by the time they got to the Roxy. They hurried into the foyer, past the vendors waving souvenir programs and look-alike dolls of Robert Taylor and Carole Lombard and Jean Harlow. An usher in a tight red bolero pointed them to their seats with a flashlight.

The picture house smelled of perfume and the damp wool from a hundred coats.

They settled in. Two boys in college scarves sprawled over the seats in front of them, sniggering at their own silly jokes. They were perhaps not much younger than her date, she thought, and yet just boys to men, really.

"Why are you smiling?" he whispered.

"For me to know and you to find out."

They had come in halfway through a Betty Boop cartoon. Next they had to sit through the Universal Newsreel: aerial shots of Franco's warships blockading the harbor at Barcelona; the king of England out hunting in a tweed suit and heavy boots, interspersed with film of Wallis Simpson getting in and out of royal automobiles; in Chicago, ten people had been killed on the L after a collision at Granville station; finally, grim and dramatic music accompanied grainy footage of Adolf Hitler, his hand raised in the air in that peculiar salute of his, his acolytes clustered around him.

She was almost relieved when the red velvet curtain came down. Yaakov was right to get his family out of Europe, she thought. The world was going mad. Nowhere was safe, except America.

The Roxyettes chorus line danced onto the stage, blondes alternated with brunettes; the men in the audience started whistling and clapping, as did the college boys in front of her. She thought they were going to stand on their seats and wave their scarves like they were at a football game.

"Your favorite part of the show," she said to Jack.

"Let's go get a drink," he said.

⇥⊷

They sat side by side on a red velvet divan with their martinis. They could see their own reflections in the mirrors. "You look like a movie star," he said.

"Harpo Marx?"

"Carole Lombard."

"I bet you say that to all the girls."

"Only the ones who look like Carole Lombard."

"What made you choose this movie? Don't tell me Bing Crosby is one of your favorite actors? Not you, who likes Groucho Marx and Gary Cooper."

"I was curious about it. You can't get away from the damned song, every trolley driver in New York is singing 'Pennies from Heaven' like he expects the passengers to pass around a hat."

"He's not my idea of a leading man."

"What is your ideal man, Miss Levine?"

"I like them big and dumb," she said. "With blue eyes. And they have to like Gary Cooper and the Marx Brothers."

Jack just laughed.

⇥⊷

They went to Dinty's after the show. Jack's kind of place, Libby thought when she first saw it: linoleum on the floor and the only decorations were the black-and-gold signs hanging on the walls with pictures of oysters on them. But then she saw Eve Arden from the Follies at one of the tables and heard a man laugh behind her, turned around and saw the Yankees' rookie everyone was talking about, Joe something or other, sitting with a bunch of older men who were laughing at all his jokes. Clearly the "in" place to be.

So Libby was surprised that they even got a table, was even more surprised to find gefilte fish on the menu.

"I knew it was Shabbas," Jack said. "I thought you'd be pleased." He pointed to the Irish stew. "They use kosher beef and lamb."

"Serious?"

"Yes, seriously."

For all the hobnobbing going on everywhere, it was still almost Hanukkah by the time the waiter ambled over. Jack didn't seem to mind. He ordered a beer and corned beef and cabbage. She ordered the fish, though she doubted it would be as good as her mother's.

"What did you think of the movie?" she asked him.

"The guy playing the cornet was the best part."

"That Louis Armstrong. You like jazz?"

"Among other things."

"Your five favorite songs."

"That's a tough question. Okay. 'It's a Sin to Tell a Lie.' What's the guy's name?"

"Fats Waller."

"You know it?"

"It's my favorite song too. You just get better and better, Jack Seabrook. I'm almost sorry I beat you up when you were twelve."

"You didn't beat me up. I couldn't hit a defenseless little girl was all."

"Yeah, sure. Second favorite."

"'Summertime.'"

"Agreed."

"I saw Abbey Mitchell sing in Jazz Alley once. Third favorite: 'Minnie the Moocher.'"

"'Hi-de hi-de hi-de ho.'"

"Then . . . 'Stormy Weather.' Ethel Waters."

"You get one more pick."

"'Cross Road Blues.'"

"Robert Johnson? You like blues?"

"You know him?"

"You like the blues, and you know when it is Shabbas. Any more at home like you?"

"There used to be," he said, and she wondered if he was going to explain himself, but he didn't. "So what's your number one?"

"'The Good Ship Lollipop.' No question."

A waiter brought their dinners. The baseball deputation was laughing too hard at the next table. Jack shook his head.

"You don't want to go over and get his autograph?" she said.

"I'm a Dodgers fan. Tell me, are you allowed to dance on Shabbas?"

"It depends. Would you call it work?"

"You don't have to do anything. I could just hold you up and drag you around to music."

"I guess that would be okay," she said.

It turned out that Jack knew the guy at the door at El Morocco. The place had been a speakeasy during Prohibition, made its name with all the big-time celebrities who went there to break the law for the newspaper photographers. He had seen Babe Ruth here one night, he said. Another night, Clark Gable.

They held hands on a zebra-striped banquette under the papier-mâché palm trees, danced mambo and rumba on the tiny dance floor. The band played "Summertime," the perfect song for a winter's night in New York, he said, and they danced slow and close. She liked the feel of his hands through the cotton of her blouse. She held her glass in one hand, over his shoulder.

"Everyone is staring," she said.

"They're jealous."

"What are you doing with me, Jack?"

"Dancing."

"What we got in common? You're old money and I'm not any money. You're Harvard and I'm school of hard knocks. You ski in Switzerland and I don't know where; I can't even ice skate in Central Park without falling over."

"Does it matter?"

"If it is just a fling, it don't matter. That is what I am asking."

She sipped her martini and watched him over the rim of the glass. He held her eyes. That song kept going around and around in her head: One day this girl is going to "spread her wings." You see if I don't.

He seemed to make up his mind. "This isn't just a fling," he said.

"Is it for you?"

"I've never been flung, Jack. What would a good Jewish girl from Westover know from flings?"

"Lib, you're funny, you're beautiful, and you have—what do they say in Yiddish?"

"Chutzpah."

"I still think about that day you walked into Davidson's. If you'd gone in there on any other day, they would have thrown you out on the street."

"Well, like they say, good to be good, better to be lucky."

"We like the same music, we laugh at the same stupid jokes, you go to the synagogue as often as I go to church, we both eat Oreos the same way."

"When you ever seen me eat an Oreo?"

"You eat the top cookie, then the cream in the middle, right?"

"You do that too?"

"Not when anyone is looking."

"Cannot believe you do that."

"We could have been separated at birth, you and me."

He kissed her for the first time. It was only a touch of the lips, but they stayed that way, their faces almost touching, for the rest of the song.

"How did you like the kiss?"

"I liked it just fine, Mr. Cooper," she said.

Everyone else was asleep. It was just Sarah and Etta sitting in the kitchen, up close to the stove to keep warm, their shawls around their shoulders, waiting for Liberty to come home. Sarah had made them tea in the old samovar.

"How she has grown, your Bessie," Sarah said.

"Thanks to you, she is here. I would not be here either, if not for you. I still remember that night, how brave you were, Sura."

"Anyone would do the same."

"Such a girl you were. Bessie and me, we were lucky you were there that day. And you are lucky too. No husband, sure, but what a beautiful daughter you have."

"Yes, and such a help to my business. Do not know what I would do without her."

"You will have to do without, one day. Must be suitors queueing up in the street. Such a beauty she is. Such lovely . . . eyes."

Sarah nodded, waited. *I wonder when my sister is going to say what she really means.*

"And all that lovely red hair."

Sarah sipped her tea, scalding hot it was. She blew the steam, felt it warm her cheeks and nose.

"I wonder where it comes from?"

"Uncle Moshe, he had red hair."

"Was ginger, not like your Libby. Hers is beautiful. Like strawberry and gold."

Sarah nodded. If she does not say it, I am not going to say it. Maybe Etta will get tired of this game and let it be.

"Where can it come from, this lovely red hair? Maybe Micha's side."

"What do you want I should say to you, Etta? I don't know why my daughter is as she is. She is beautiful, what are you going to say next—'not like her mother'?"

"Don't fuss so. I was wondering, only."

"Don't wonder. Just drink tea."

A long silence. There was something else, she could feel it. Go on, Etta, say it, just say it and get it over with.

"Why did you tell her you were expecting with her on the boat from Russia?"

"What are you saying?"

"Liberty told me. We were talking. I asked about her recent birthday, and she told me how you had her the night you arrived here on the boat, how you felt her kick when you saw the Liberty statue, and that is how she got her name."

"Was a story, only."

"You were in America one year before your Liberty came."

"What does it matter? Better than, oh, you were born in some dirty hospital, I was screaming and sweating like every other woman in the Lower East Side."

"But it's not true."

"Must everything always be true?"

"Yes," Etta said. "Always. If we not got the truth, what we got?"

"Just a story," Sarah repeated. She finished her tea and put down the glass. "More better you go to bed now."

Etta shrugged and said good night and took herself to bed. Sarah pulled the shawl tighter around her shoulders, listened to the patter of rain on the windows, someone shouting down below them, on the second or third floor—arguments, always arguments around here. So hard to find a bit of peace.

It was exhausting, having Etta and her family here, when there was such little room. She had grown up in a house that was too small for everyone, no hardship in that, but somehow so crowded, all this. No room for so many questions in such a little apartment, that was the trouble.

It wore her out, all this pretending. What was it her father had said to her once? *"Always tell the truth, Sura, then never will you need a good memory."* She had thought about telling Etta the truth. But how could she? Because it wouldn't stop there; she knew what her sister would say: *"You must tell Libby."*

And telling Libby, it was impossible. *"Libby, bubeleh, sit down, there's something you should know. The story about how you were born on the ship? Well, it wasn't quite true."*

"What part of the story isn't true, Mama?"

"Any of it."

"So where was I born if I wasn't born in Delancey Street?"

"I don't know."

Sarah closed her eyes, tried to picture the look of betrayal and horror on her daughter's face as she understood the meaning, all the meanings. And that was only the start of it. Sooner or later she would have to tell George Seabrook.

"Mr. Seabrook, now I've come here, now I've told you everything there is to know, can you find it in your heart to forgive me?"

What do you think, Sarah? Can a man whose daughter you stole pat you on the back and tell you not to worry about it, we all make mistakes, never mind your husband knew he was Liberty's father right from the very first?

No, you cannot do it. Have to keep lying, there is no other choice. Cannot change your mind once you start down the road. Perhaps you and Micha didn't mean no harm when you started this, but no one will care about that, not now. When you do something that is just plain flat-out unforgivable, you cannot ever ask anyone to forgive, not later, not ever.

52

It was Bessie's birthday, and Sarah took them all out to dinner. After all the tension in the house, she told Liberty, it will be a good way to bring everyone back together.

She took them all to a swanky Schrafft's on Fifth, all dark wood paneling and Colonial furniture with bud vases on the tables. And the waitresses, in their black dresses with crisp white aprons and dainty collars and cuffs, even hairnets, carrying the food on trays balanced on their arms. Sarah was sure Etta and her family had never seen anything quite like it.

"You must have the cream cheese sandwich with the crusts cut off," she told Bessie. "Wash it down with the hot chocolate with whipped cream. For the boys, the hot butterscotch sundaes with vanilla ice cream and toasted almonds. Yaakov, you must try the chicken a la king."

Ruben frowned at his menu. "No knish," he said.

"I don't know this food," Aron said. "Can I have lox?"

"There is nothing wrong with this food," Sarah said. "It is all wholesome American cooking."

"I want knish," Ruben said, and earned himself a clip of the ear from his father.

"So, we're all together again," Sarah said. "This is nice."

"If only Zlota were here."

"And Zara and Bluma," Bessie said.

"Zlota won't ever leave," Yaakov said. "Her husband won't listen to me."

"You remember this day?" Sarah said to Etta. "When Bessie is born? I cannot believe it is twenty-four years."

Etta shook her head. "I was so scared."

"Such a beautiful girl you were," Sarah said to Bessie. "Such a tiny thing to survive such a fright."

"Tiny!" Ruben said, and snorted. Bessie elbowed him hard, and he howled. Yaakov jerked his son's elbows off the table and whispered sternly in his ear, which made Aron snigger all the more.

Such relatives I have, Sarah thought. She looked at her Libby for support, but she was looking out the window, in another world inside her head. What was wrong with her baby lately? Sarah was sure she had a gentleman caller. Whenever she said she was going to the movies with friends, she came home so flushed, so breathless. You didn't get that from watching a Bing Crosby movie.

"Such a beautiful girl, your Libby," Etta said, in Yiddish.

"She is the joy of my life."

"And for the longest time you thought you could never have," she said. "Such beautiful color in her hair."

Again with her hair, Sarah thought. You'll have red hair too, Etta, if I tip one of Schrafft's famous strawberry milkshakes all over it.

"How is she not married?" Yaakov said across the table. "She is practically a gray braids, like our Bessie."

Sarah felt her cheeks burn. Didn't he know Liberty spoke Yiddish almost as well as anyone at the table?

"She is a dark horse," Sarah said, in English. "I think she is keeping something from us. Aren't you, bubeleh?"

"Mama?"

"You're not fooling your mama. So many times you are out this week. You have a young gentleman, don't you? You should bring him home, let us all meet him."

"I don't have a gentleman," Liberty said.

"She thinks her mother is blind," Sarah said to Etta, and raised her eyes.

"Come on, Libby," Etta said. "Tell us!"

"The girl says nothing to tell," Yaakov said in his faltering English, "then nothing to tell. You should find matchmaker, Sura. She is too old for not married."

Sarah saw the look on Liberty's face. That was it, he had made her mad. "His name is Jack," she said.

"So I was right!" Sarah said. "You do have a gentleman. Why not we meet him?"

"You wouldn't like him, Mama."

"Who is to say what is to like, what not to like?"

"Believe me, I know."

"Is he Jewish?" Yaakov said.

"No, he's not Jewish."

"Where did you meet this Jack?" said Sarah.

Liberty turned and looked right at her. "At Davidson's, Mama."

They didn't understand, Etta and Yaakov and the rest. Sarah could feel them all watching her, but she couldn't hide the look on her face, too late for that. A wonder she didn't throw up all over this nice white tablecloth.

"*That* Jack? You said he was in England."

"Mama, don't get mad. He's not like you think he is."

"Not who you think he is either," she said before she could stop herself.

"I was going to tell you, I was waiting for the right time. I know you don't like his father. But he's not like him, he's so different."

Sarah felt the blood drain from her face.

"Wait till you meet him, you'll see."

Suddenly Sarah was on her feet. She had spilled glasses on the table. People were staring. She sat down again, tried to get control of herself. No, this cannot be happening. Her daughter, she would never do such a thing.

"No," she said.

"Mama?"

She felt Etta's hand on her arm. "Sarah, what is it?"

"This must stop," she said.

"Mama, you don't understand."

"No, you who don't understand. Anyone but this Jack Seabrook, you hear? You got to stop this now."

"It isn't going to stop, Mama. Not unless I want it to."

Sarah pushed back her chair and got to her feet again. Got to stay calm, she thought. Don't shout things, not here, not in public, not in front of your own family. "Talk about this at home, not here."

"I don't want to talk about it at home, Mama. I don't want to talk about it anywhere."

"Liberty!"

"I'm not a little girl anymore. You can't tell me how to live my life."

Everyone in the restaurant was looking, Etta's two boys openmouthed, Bessie too. "Such respect," Yaakov said to Etta. "Is this how girls treat their mutti in America?"

"I don't understand. What have you got against George Seabrook? What did he ever do to you that was so bad? You still hate him because he didn't help us after Dewey died?"

"You are my daughter, I don't have to tell why I hate, why I don't hate. You just do like I tell you."

"Maybe in Russia, not here."

"Please, bubeleh, we don't have this fight here, with the whole world watching."

"I love him," Libby said.

Sarah gaped at her.

"You've never loved anyone. You don't know what it feels like."

And she walked out. On her mother, she walked out. Sarah was about to run after her, but Etta put a hand on her arm to stop her. "Let her go, Sura. Let her be. Maybe better you talk to her later, when everyone is not so upset."

What else could she do? Nothing, nothing she could do. *Jack Seabrook.* It was punishment from God, that was what it was, punishment for her lies, for never telling her secret. This is what you deserve, she thought. What you deserve for being a bad wife, a bad sister, a bad woman.

You stole another man's baby. Did you really think you could get away with that? Now everything is going to fall apart, everything.

<hr>

Sarah walked blindly through the streets, needed to find somewhere to sit, sit and think. She had to talk to someone; could not talk to her daughter, could not talk to her sister. Who was left?

Micha! Micha was the only one who could understand this, show her the way through it.

She found her way to the park. She remembered there was a statue there, the Doughboy, they called it, one of those crazy statues they built for the soldiers from the war, as if they would care anymore from statues.

There he was, standing there so heroic. Is this how you looked? Is this what you wore, Micha, when they shot you? Doughboy had a big bronze flag folded around him, a gun in his right hand, and such a heroic moustache, like she never saw before. A cord tied a holster to his hip, and he had bandage things around his legs. She could almost smell the mud on him. A bandanna, too, under his helmet. He looked like a wild man.

Was this how you looked, Micha? Like a wild man?

Doughboy gripped the staff on the flag so tight, like he was braced for the bullet. Did you remember in that last moment that you did not have to be there, Micha?

She looked closer, at the stars on the flag, the edge of it brushing Doughboy's shoulder. Twigs had gathered there, blown there by the winter wind. Whoever made this statue, they must have been there, she thought, to make it so real. Perhaps the maker of this, he even knew you, my Micha. Perhaps this really is you.

She sat down on the wet wooden bench. Everything here smelled of damp like moss, nothing growing in these sad old earthy beds.

"Tell me what I have to do," she said, aloud. And why not? There was no one around to hear some crazy woman in a fur coat talking to a statue. "I cannot let her see this boy. How long this been going on, and right under my nose she does this? She says she is in love? What does she mean? What has she done? Cannot let this thing go on. So what to do? Tell her the truth about where she came from, then go to this Seabrook and tell him also? But then what? I will lose her, I will lose my Libby, and Libby is all I have. Maybe I will even go to prison.

"I have kept our secret, Micha, I thought this was all over, but sometimes it is like never will it be over. How did this happen? How did you get her? And why don't you ever tell me? Why get yourself killed for nothing and leave me here to fix? Because I cannot fix. You got to help me, Micha. Talk to me, tell me what I must do. Do I tell the truth? Cannot tell it. You got to show me some other way, Micha, before it is too late. You understand?"

53

Libby lounged on the leather settee, nestled into Jack's shoulder. She liked the feel of his arm around her, the smell of his cologne. The club was dark. She couldn't even remember the name of it, some anonymous place off Swing Street, a basement dive they had found, only half full, even when everything else was closed. There was a trio playing swing on the small stage at the back of the room; two enthusiastic regulars dancing the Lindy hop. The only light came from candles set in niches in the bare brick walls.

"I don't understand why she's so against you," Libby said.

"The old man never had much time for your mother. He thought she married Dewey just for his money."

"But that was years ago. And why would Mama still be sore at him? Dewey never listened anyway."

"I don't know. Maybe there's something else we don't know."

"You don't think he ever . . ."

"What?"

"Well, you know. She was a looker in her day."

Jack shook his head. "Say what you like about the old man, but he's a straight shooter. He would never try and steal another man's wife, least of all Uncle Billy's."

"So, what, then?"

"I don't know. I guess your mother knows, but she's not telling."

"What are we going to do, Jack?"

"She'll come around," he said. "She has to. When she sees we're made for each other."

She sat up. "What did you say?"

"You don't think so?"

"It's just that . . . I didn't know you thought that."

"Don't you think that too?"

"Yes," she said.

"I'm sick of sneaking around, Libby. We're old enough to know our own minds. They'll have to get used to the idea, won't they?"

"I don't know if Mama will ever get used to it. She talks about your father as if he's the devil himself."

"Frankly, I can see how someone might make that mistake."

"Will you talk to him?"

"He's coming down from Boston in a few days. He has a place on the Upper East Side. I'll go over and talk to him there, in private."

"What do you think he'll say?"

"What can he say? He could choose which college I went to, but I won't let him choose who I fall in love with."

Fall in love with. He made it all sound so straightforward. "You don't think this is moving too fast?"

"No, I don't. What about you?" He took her hand. "I know we haven't known each other long. But if we're going to get serious, we have to stop sneaking around like this is just some kind of fling."

"Well, Jack Seabrook, like I told you, I've never been flung, and I don't want to start now. What's that look? Don't you believe me?"

"I do, but—well, you're so damned pretty. I don't understand how someone didn't snap you up before this."

"I've had my share of snappers, baby. Only I haven't snapped back, until now."

"Well, then, we'll have to make a stand, or we lose each other before we've even begun."

She knew he was right, but she was scared. Something about the way her mother had reacted when she told her, she sensed this wasn't going to be as easy as he made it sound.

And going against George Seabrook? From what she knew of him, it might not be quite that simple either. The one thing she did know: her mama was keeping something from her. But what?

⟞⟝

The next evening Frankie was coming to town. She had written to Libby, saying she had some exciting news, and they arranged to meet at Penn Station. Libby's cab was held up in traffic, and she was late getting there. She was worried that she had missed her. She stood at the top of the stairs above the concourse, under its soaring girders and towering Greek columns, stared at the tide of fedoras and cloche hats pushing and shoving and hurrying on the platforms below. How was she ever going to find her among all these people?

"You're late," a voice said, and she spun around.

"Frankie!"

Libby barely recognized her. She was in uniform, a white jacket and skirt, a peaked cap with the navy's insignia. "Oh my God. Frankie, what have you done?"

"They want me to sort out that Hitler fella. I said I would, but first they had to give me a uniform and my own machine gun. I left it at home. They don't let you have machine guns in New York, only in Chicago." She looked down at her uniform. "Horrible, isn't it? White was never my color."

"Why didn't you tell me?"

"I wanted to see your face. It's a picture, and no mistake." She pointed to her shoulder tab. "And none of this 'Frankie' business. I'm

Ensign Donnelly now. Off to see the world, I am. Are you going to stand there gaping all day, or are we going to get some dinner? I'm starving."

They walked outside arm in arm and jumped in a rattling Checker taxi and drove over to Janssen's Hofbrau Haus, under the Chrysler Building. Libby had originally planned to take her to Jack Dempsey's, but it was a Saturday night, and she wasn't in the mood to fight the crowds. When they looked at the menus, Frankie made a face at the frogs' legs and partridge in *weinkraut*, so they settled for goulash and schnitzels and two glasses of wine.

Libby couldn't get over it. Frankie had changed so much since she had last seen her. It wasn't only the uniform; she had put a wave in her hair and taken a care with her makeup that she never had before. And there was something in the way she held herself; she had been brash on the Lower East Side, because that was what it took, but now the sharp edges had been replaced by a different kind of self-assurance.

Frankie appeared equally impressed. She weighed Libby over the rim of her glass. "Well, look at you, girl," she said. "You look like a film star. Where did you get that dress? Don't tell me your ma made it?"

"Of course. I told you, didn't I? We have our own label now."

"I suppose you'll be taking me to El Morocco after dinner."

"Just the '21.'"

"I'm not really dressed for it. I'll need to change into my civvies."

"When did you join up?"

"Two months ago. They're quite choosy. But there's not many nurses my age that have experience in an operating room, so I got the call."

"But why?"

"I want to see a bit of the world, Lib. I didn't want to live in Pennsylvania all my life. They're sending me to the navy hospital in Maryland first, but I've my name down for transfer to the Philippines when a place comes up. Can you imagine? I didn't even know where it was, I had to look it up in an atlas."

Their goulash arrived. They drank their Moselles and ordered another round. After she finished telling Libby all about the navy, Frankie wanted to know everything that Libby had been doing. She said she knew all along that Libby and her ma would do all right at the rag trade.

"You're going to be the new Coco Chanel," Frankie said.

"Perhaps Mama is," Libby said. "I've other plans. You know who I want to be?"

"Who?"

"Frankie Donnelly."

Frankie stared at her, her spoon poised halfway between her bowl and her lips. "Now what nonsense are you talking?"

"You're doing something worthwhile. You're helping people. A little angel in white."

"Get away with you."

Libby touched her glass to Frankie's. "The girl from Delancey Street made good."

"You're the one that's made good. Did you not just tell me business was booming? You have your own label and your own shop."

"But it reads better than it lives, Frankie. It's my mama's dream, not mine. Now eat your soup. I have a big night planned for us."

They drank manhattans at the Tap Room in the Taft on Seventh, then caught a cab downtown to the New Circle Bar at the Governor Clinton, where Libby said they could drink old-fashioneds all night for a quarter and listen to Jay Coe. They finished up at a club on Swing Street before sprawling into a cab in the early hours.

"What are you going to do about this Jack fella?" Frankie asked Libby as they headed downtown along Sixth.

Libby put her cheek against the cold glass of the back window. She felt as if she were burning up. Too much alcohol. "I don't know, Frankie."

"You can't let a good man go. Your ma will come around."

"What if she doesn't?"

"Then you can come join the navy and run away with me." Frankie was drunk, and it was just a stupid joke. But after she had dropped Frankie off at her hotel, Libby thought about what she had said and decided that perhaps it wasn't such a terrible idea. She even saw some sense in it the next morning when she was sober.

Anyway, what was wrong with wanting to have your own life? Perhaps the only sure way to make yourself unhappy was to let someone else live your life for you.

Sarah sat with her head down on the sewing-machine table. She was too tired to cook for everyone tonight, let Etta do it. The seamstress girls were finished for the day, and Liberty was out somewhere, but Sarah never had a moment alone anymore. She could hear Etta's brood in the kitchen. She couldn't get used to having so many people around, not like when she was little. In those days, she didn't like ever to be alone.

Tonight, she was too tired to do anything. Perhaps she would just sit here. Her arms and legs, how they felt, couldn't even lift them up anymore. Not the work that made her like this, it was this life, too complicated to live it anymore, and nobody's fault but hers.

She heard the door creak ajar, knew Etta was standing there, watching her. Let her watch.

"Sura?"

"What?"

"Are you all right?"

"Do I look like I am all right?"

"It's about Libby?"

"Sure, it's about Libby. What do you think?"

Etta sidled in another few inches, like Sarah was a bomb and any loud noise, any sharp move, it would level the whole apartment. And maybe she was right.

"You have to let her go, Sura, make her own life."

Sarah sat up. "You don't understand. It's complicated."

"Why is so difficult? Just let it be."

"Etta, I love you, you know this, right? You are my sister, my favorite sister in the whole wide world. I have missed you this last twenty years like nobody's business."

"I know."

"But you can't help me on this, believe me. Now please, I need to be alone."

Etta nodded and went out. The door clicked shut behind her.

Sarah closed her eyes. She thought about when she and Etta had been riding on the sled back from the market in Tallinn, how Etta had had her baby in the snow. What happened to that Sura? Perhaps one day she would come back, that girl.

But for now, this Sarah knew what she had to do.

54

A big expense, the telephone. It was Liberty who had insisted that they must have one. We cannot run a proper business without, she had said. She used it to talk to department store managers and wholesalers. A real Wasp on the phone, she was.

Sarah stared at it for perhaps half an hour before she finally summoned the courage to pick up the earpiece. She checked again that there was no one else in the apartment and then dialed the operator and told her the number she wanted.

An eternity before one of his flunkies answered, asked her name, told her to hold the line while he informed Mr. Seabrook that she wished to speak with him.

What if he refused her call?

Then she heard his voice. So strange, after so many years. "Mrs. Levine. How did you get this number?"

"It was in Dewey's diary. I kept it."

"I see. Of course. For a rainy day."

"You think I want your money?"

"I don't know. Do you?"

The money, always the money; that was what he had thought from the beginning. Well, she supposed that would make it easier to do what she planned. "I want to buy you lunch, Mr. Seabrook," Sarah said.

Union Oyster House, Boston

They were sitting in a wood-paneled booth, nice and secluded. She had seen him slip a note into the maître d's hand as they walked in, to make sure they were kept away from the hoi polloi. They talked about the weather and made small talk about the fashion business until their food arrived.

George regarded her over his plate of half a dozen shucked Virginia oysters. "Enjoy your lobster."

"It's a compromise," Sarah said. "They got no pickles."

"Long way to come to make jokes about the food in New England," he said.

"I get the bill at the end," Sarah said. "So I get the one-liners."

"But that's not why you've come up here. You're not fooling me, Mrs. Levine. You're dancing on hot coals."

"You don't chew your oysters?" she said. "Such good money I pay for those things, and you don't chew?"

"A good oyster I swallow whole." He gave her a tight smile and speared another with his toothpick. "What's this about?"

"What this is about, is my daughter and your boy."

He stared at her. "Jack? What about him?"

"Did you know he is romantic with my daughter?"

She let that sink in. He took a sip of his beer and straightened his waistcoat. "No, I didn't know that. My son has not mentioned this to me."

"He knows you would not approve."

"How did this happen?"

"A girl has to make her way in the world," Sarah said.

"What does that mean?"

"My Libby, she has a lot to offer. She don't want to work all her life doing rag trade like her mama. We're doing all right, but there's easier ways, if you get my meaning."

"Let me get this straight. Jack, you think, is the easier way. Old money, class, and privilege, there for the taking. Another Bill Dewey."

Sarah chewed a mouthful of lobster and smiled at him. Hold his eyes, she thought. Look convincing.

"So you took the train up to Boston today for what? For my blessing to the union, or a payoff?"

"You decide," Sarah said. "Me, I don't care which. I never did."

George took his napkin from his lap and threw it on the table. "I think these oysters are off," he said, and stood up. He signaled to the busboy, who ran over with George's hat and jacket. "I'm not for sale, Mrs. Levine. I'll bid you good day. Thanks for lunch. Don't forget to leave a tip."

Sarah waited ten minutes, and then left. She stood outside, under the awning, thought she was going to be sick. Someone stopped and asked her if she was all right, and she nodded and pushed them away. She had to get back to the train station, get back to New York. She wondered if maybe instead of getting on the train, she should lie down under it. You wanted to be a mother so bad when you were young, Sura Muscowitz. Could you ever imagine back then, this is the kind of mama you would be?

55

Upper East Side

Whenever Jack came to see his father, he always felt as if he had an appointment to see God, but wasn't sure he would get past his secretary. He admired him, respected him, sure, but he never fooled himself into thinking he knew what was going on in that great silver-haired head. His uncle Billy had told him once: "Old George's a good man, Jack. But he's lived all his life on that pedestal your grandfather built for him. One day he'll have to come down off that damned thing or spend his whole life alone, and I hope I'm around to see it."

Billy wouldn't see that day now. Jack kind of wondered if he himself would.

He sure couldn't fault the old man's commitment. He had practically raised him on his own—well, with the help of a housekeeper, a nanny, a tutor, and half a dozen house servants. But he would have had those anyway. He could have easily packed him off to boarding school, but he hadn't done it.

Instead he had kept Jack around, showed him how to fly-fish, box, catch a baseball, and read a set of ledgers. He made sure he went to the best schools, wore the best clothes, and had the best friends. But he wasn't the kind of father to wrap his arms around you. It's a man's job to run a business, he liked to say. It's a woman's job to spend the money and cry into her handkerchief over nothing.

Not that he'd seen his father with too many women.

He didn't come to town very much. Boston had everything he needed, he said: his club, a perfectly adequate golf course, and his mistress, who was penciled in for Wednesdays and Saturdays. He thought that coming to the apartment he kept on the Upper East Side was slumming it.

He didn't even open his own door anymore. His man, Harley, showed Jack through to the study. The room looked as if it had been engraved in sepia, was lined with books with gold lettering on the spines, mostly classics; some tomes on business practice; Thomas Hardy novels; nothing frivolous, and nothing American. There were oil portraits of his ancestors hanging on the walls. None of them looked as if they approved of Jack; he wondered if their expressions changed as soon as he walked in.

The room had been repaneled in mahogany; lamps threw a yellow glow on everything; a deer's head hung on one wall, looking moth eaten and miserable, as well it might. Shot and decapitated and stuffed, not even allowed to rest in peace. He wondered which of his ancestors had hunted the poor creature down, or whether his father had bought everything as part of a job lot in a mortgage sale.

"Jack."

"Father."

"Go ahead, sit."

He sat. "What was it Hemingway said? The 'road to hell is paved with unbought stuffed animals.'"

"I don't care much for Hemingway."

"You're looking well."

"Don't talk nonsense. I'm almost sixty and I smoke too many cigars and I work too hard."

"How's Jennifer?"

"My mistress is none of your affair. Unless you're sleeping with her as well, in which case, I'd have to shoot you."

Jack laughed.

"It amuses me that you think I'm joking."

"What brings you into town?"

"Business."

"Of course."

"Actually, I want to talk to you about your future."

"I was hoping you might. Is it Davidson's, or do you want me back in Boston?"

"I'm sending you back to London."

There was a long silence as Jack digested this. "But I've only just got back."

"True. It seems I have wasted the cost of two perfectly good first-class tickets on the *Berengaria*. But it was my error, so I won't be docking it from your not-inconsiderable salary."

"You promised me Davidson's."

"I have changed my mind."

"Mind telling me why?"

George didn't answer. This was always his father's way; he liked him to work things out for himself. When he was a child and asked his father a question—Why is the sky blue? Who was Homer? How do you spell *iniquity*?—he would simply look toward the dictionary or the encyclopedia on the bookshelf.

The silence in the room became oppressive; the ticking of an antique clock on the mantel made it even more so. Finally, the answer came to him. "Libby Levine."

"She doesn't use the Dewey name? Not even for the cachet?"

"It's her father's name. She took it up again after Uncle Billy died."

"Liberty Dewey, Liberty Levine. Whatever she calls herself these days, you are in over your head, I believe. London will help you see things more clearly, despite the fog."

"How did you find out?"

"I think the question should be: When were you going to tell me?"

"You can tell me how to run your business, you can't tell me how to run my life."

George got up and went to the macassar cabinet behind his chair. He opened the front panel and took out a decanter of brandy and two glasses. "Drink?"

"No, thanks."

Ice clinked into the glass. He poured two fingers of brandy and replaced the decanter on the tray.

"What the hell have you got against her?"

"She's not everything she seems, you know."

"Meaning?"

"She's a gold digger, Son. The apple never falls very far from the tree. I don't want you taken for a ride like your uncle Billy."

"You don't know Mrs. Levine married him for his money. Even if she did, what good did it do her in the end?"

"Yes, she had a run of bad luck. She seems to think her daughter will help her turn things around again."

"What?"

"I had lunch with her a few days ago. Did Liberty tell you?"

"No, she didn't."

"I didn't think she would."

"Well, perhaps she didn't know."

"Yes, perhaps."

"So what did you two discuss—over lunch?"

"The future. She has great plans. That was when she told me you and Miss Levine were romantically attached. She also said that if I wanted to end your budding romance, then she was open to offers. I politely declined."

"I don't believe you."

"What you believe or don't believe is up to you. But if you recall, I have always told you that *honesty* should be your byword, in business and in life. It is the only way a man acquires a good reputation. I may be many things, but I'm not a hypocrite."

"Libby had nothing to do with this."

"I'd like to think not as well. How did you meet her by the way?"

"She came into the office."

"May I ask why?"

The old man knew, or he wouldn't have asked the question. He just wanted to hear him say it: *"She was trading on our connection to get credit."* How much of a coincidence was that anyway?

"The truth is, you hardly know this girl, Jack. You met her five minutes ago, whereas I have known her for a very long time. Now, everything I ever suspected about her appears to be true. Believe me, I take no great pleasure in finding myself vindicated."

"To hell with you," Jack said. He stood up and walked to the door. He hesitated, then turned and walked back, put both his hands on the desk. "We both know what this is really all about."

"Be careful what you say, Son."

"Why? Because it hurts? If it didn't still hurt after all these years, we wouldn't be having this conversation now, would we?"

"It has nothing to do with Clare."

"It was just about the money for her too, wasn't it? It still burns with you. That's why there hasn't been any woman since, right?"

"You're going too far."

"Libby is not like her!"

"How do you know that? Are you saying that you're a better judge of women than I am? What about . . . what was her name? Emily. She married a senator's son in the end. Did you hear about that? Our money wasn't good enough for her; she wanted someone with a run at the White House as well."

Jack didn't want the Emily conversation. He went out, slamming the door behind him. He regretted it straightaway; the old man always said that petulance was weakness. The worst of it was, he supposed his father could be right. And anyway, he didn't have to prove it; doubt was like rust, it started small, but then ate away everything around it. Just like Clare; she'd been eating away at his father for years. "I don't want to end up like him," he said as he got down to the street and turned up his collar against the cold and the rain. There weren't going to be any Clares in his life. The next time he fell in love with a woman, he was going to be one hundred percent sure.

56

Jack was surprised to get a call from Art Woodward. They had never been especially close in college, had played on the football team together, but he had never been a great fan of the locker-room banter that was Art's specialty. But being at Harvard was like having chewing gum on your shoe, and he supposed it was true of all colleges: there were some fellows who you could never shake off, who clung to former college pals at their alma mater as if they were family.

He wasn't quite sure how Art got his number, but over the course of a few days, he left several messages with the doorman and with Miss Riley at Davidson's, and finally Jack felt obliged to call him back. They arranged to meet at the Harvard Club for a drink one evening. He supposed it wouldn't hurt.

The club reminded him of his father's study, magnified a couple dozen times. It had almost the same miserable dead animals on the walls, except the club actually had an elephant's head as well. He had wondered but never asked how it had got there. He supposed he didn't really want to know the answer.

Walking in, there was even the same fug of cigar smoke. He heard the clink of crystal tumblers, recoiled at the depressing glitter of chandeliers. It was everything he tried to avoid: old white men reading the

Wall Street Journal and sipping rye, the mahogany-paneled walls hung with the framed portraits of the forefathers who had blazed this same smug trail.

Art was already there, on his second bourbon judging by the unnatural brightness in his eyes. "Jack!" he shouted across the room.

Jack went over, ordered a single malt from the white-jacketed waiter. Art was effusive, started talking even before Jack had sat down, reminiscing about Harvard people Jack didn't remember, so-called good times he would rather have forgotten, football games he didn't recall winning.

Dutifully, he asked Art what he was doing these days. He said he had a job at Con Ed with his own office and a view of the Hudson. In his words, he was doing a-okay.

"That's great, Art."

"What about you, Jack?"

"Working for the old man. Textiles. He sent me to London to open an office over there. Just got back."

Art seemed to be in touch with everyone on their old college football team, knew what they were all doing, who had joined which company or got engaged to which girl. Jack expressed regret about a linebacker who had got himself shot in the Spanish Civil War, a wide receiver who had broken his neck skiing in Colorado with his father's mistress. Jack observed that they had died for the same cause, trying to put a Republican out of a job, and Art seemed to think that funny.

Inevitably Art wanted to talk about women. He had no problems on that account, he assured Jack; he had so many of them trooping in and out of his apartment, they had worn a track in the carpet. He'd even had complaints from the neighbors downstairs about the noise.

"What about you?" Art said. "Seeing anyone?"

"Too busy for that right now," Jack said.

"Really? I heard you were seeing that Libby Levine," Art said.

"Who told you that?"

"People talk. New York's the biggest village in the world. Someone saw you with her down on Swing Street, told Henry Devaux, and Henry told me."

"But I mean, how did they know who she was?"

Art wouldn't say. Jack had to press him.

"Look, Jack, you didn't hear this from me, okay?"

"Hear what from you?"

"Well . . ." A nervous laugh. "Look, a lot of guys know her."

Jack put down his glass. "What does that mean?"

"Well, she has, you know, a reputation."

Jack gripped the leather arms of the chair, tried to keep his expression flat.

"You didn't know? I mean, she's Bill Dewey's stepdaughter. Everyone knew Bill, God rest his soul. I guess that's how she knew some of the fellows. And she's a good-looking girl. No one's going to say no, are they?"

"Say no?"

Another nervous laugh. "A girl is looking for a good time, it's a gentleman's binding duty to show her."

"Bull crap," Jack said.

"Hey, she's great in the sack, right? You're onto a good thing there."

Jack stared at him.

"Look, you've been away in England. I guess you weren't to know. But I also heard that she was engaged to one of the brokers over at J.P. Morgan. Real high flyer. His old man owns an entire bank in California. Way I hear it, she got a nice little payday out of that."

No one had ever thrown a punch at another member in the Harvard Club, not to Jack's knowledge. If that was true, then he made history that afternoon. The ruckus certainly brought some of the old timers out of their chairs. Even the damned elephant raised its eyebrows, or perhaps he just imagined that.

He left as they helped Art off the floor and the steward ran to get him smelling salts. He didn't wait for them to throw him out, and he didn't give much of a damn if they banned him, because he was very damned sure he wasn't ever going back.

⸻◆⸻

Miss Riley peered at her over the top of her spectacles as she walked in. Her usual air of deference was gone. Something had happened.

"I have a luncheon appointment with Mr. Seabrook," Libby said.

"Yes, Miss Levine. Come through." Come through? Jack usually came straight out of his office to greet her. Miss Riley led the way through to Jack's office. As Libby walked in, his secretary shut the door behind her.

Libby waited for Jack to get up and greet her, but he just sat there behind his desk, tapping his fountain pen on the edge of it, like he was irritated about something.

"Jack?"

"Do you know a guy called Art Woodward?"

"What? No. Why?"

"Because Art sure knows you."

"Jack, what's wrong? Did you talk to your father?"

"Sure did. He said he had lunch with your mother in Boston a few days ago."

Still he hadn't asked to take her coat, hadn't found her a chair. What was wrong with him?

"Didn't know that either, huh?"

She felt herself getting angry and tried to bite it down. "Jack, you want to tell me what this is about?"

"The old man wants to transfer me to London, but I don't know. Maybe I don't want to go back there. Of course, if I leave the family company, it won't leave me with much. I'll have to get a job somewhere. I have some friends in brokerage and a degree from Harvard. Should count for something. I won't be exactly broke, but I won't quite be the catch I am now, I guess."

"What are you talking about?"

"You know as well as I do, the real reason your mother married my uncle Billy. Don't you?"

"Wait, wait a minute. You think . . . you think this is why I like you?"

"I'd love you to convince me otherwise."

Convince him otherwise? Perhaps she could have done so. Or perhaps his mind was already made up. Besides, why should she have to convince anyone how she felt? She didn't know what had happened, but whatever it was, damn him to a hundred different hells if that's what Jack thought of her.

"Well?" he said.

"Not inclined to convince you about anything, Mr. Seabrook," she said, and walked out.

57

Her mother and Etta were at the stove, shoulder-to-shoulder, making *kugel* and *matzo* ball soup for their dinner. All of Etta's family, plus the seamstresses, were crowded into the kitchen, listening to the radio. The king of England had just abdicated. Whoever heard of such a thing? Everyone was talking about it. He gave up the crown for an American woman. A *divorcée*, they all said, as if it was the same as being a dancer or a streetwalker.

Libby wanted to hide, be anywhere but with all these people in their apartment. Where was there to hide anymore? She took off her coat and put her arms around the stovepipe, trying to get the cold out of her body. She thought she would never feel warm inside again.

"What is wrong with her?" Ruben said.

So then they all started on her, her mother most of all, asking her if she was sick, why she looked so pale.

"It's her boyfriend," Yaakov said. "I will bet my shirt."

"That Jack?" Sarah said. "What is it he has done?"

"Nothing. Please let me be."

"Tell me, I'm your mother."

"He hasn't done anything. I don't want to talk about Jack anymore. Forget him! You won't ever have to worry about Jack again, all right?"

Sarah nodded, like this was what she had expected all along. "You don't see him anymore?" she said.

"I don't want to talk about it."

"I warned you from him!"

"Yes, you warned me. Congratulations, Mama. You always get what you want." She went to her room, pulled a suitcase down from the top of the wardrobe, started throwing her clothes into it.

Her mother appeared in the doorway. "Where are you going?"

"I can't stay here," she said.

"Where are you going?"

"I don't know. I guess I'll stay in a hotel for a few days until I get something figured out."

"Bubeleh!"

"What were you doing talking to George Seabrook, Mama?"

"Who tells you such things? To that man, I never talk, ever."

"Don't lie to me, Mama. Tell me what you did!"

"Anything I do, I do only for your own good."

"What have you done, Mama?"

"What do I do? I will tell you what I do. I do everything in my whole life only for you, work every day, my fingers to the bone to give you the life you should have had!"

"Life I *should* have had? What do you mean?"

"Just money and nice things," she said.

"Is that all that matters to you? What about Dewey? Was that for me, or for you?"

"How can you ask me such things?"

"Look, I don't care anymore. Whatever you said to Jack's father, it worked. I hope you're proud."

Her mother went to put her arms around her, but Libby pushed her away. She forced the lid down on her suitcase, snapped the locks shut.

"Bubeleh, you can't just go like this."

"Watch me, Mama."

She stormed out the door, never a look back.

⇌

Sarah stood there staring at the door, couldn't believe it. Not my Liberty, she wouldn't leave. Any minute she will come back. *"Sorry, Mama, all a big mistake, let's talk."* But she didn't.

Everyone was staring at her like she was a stranger. Even Yaakov shook his head at her. But what else could she have done? Impossible to do anything else.

She looked at Etta.

"What happened to you, Sura?" Etta said.

"You don't understand."

"No, you're right. I don't understand what happened to the sister who saved my life, who saved Bessie's life. No, don't touch me. Yaakov, he has a job now. We will move out tomorrow, day after, soon as we can. Let you be, just like you ask me."

She shepherded Bessie and the boys toward the door.

Yaakov went to follow them, stopped to look over his shoulder at her. "I still don't know how she got such red hair," he said.

One by one, they filed out. Sarah wiped her hands on her apron and went back to the stove to finish making dinner. She couldn't think of what else to do. Fats Waller came on the radio, singing "It's a Sin to Tell a Lie": "If you break my heart, I'll die." Never heard of Fats Waller in the shtetl, she thought. Only in America can a girl learn to tell such lies.

⇌

Libby took a room in the hotel Frankie had stayed in near Penn Station, and every day she went to the shop like nothing had happened. When her mother came in, Libby talked to her about business things, nothing else. Her mother seemed to accept it. Perhaps Sarah thought that she only had to give it time, that Libby would come around.

Libby waited for Jack to come by the shop, maybe leave a message for her, something. But three days and nothing. Lunchtime of the fourth day, she took a cab to Davidson's. By the time she got there, the rain had turned to snow.

Miss Riley looked up from her desk as she walked in. What was that look on her face? Like a cat licking cream off its whiskers. "I want to talk to Mr. Seabrook," Libby said.

"I'm sorry, Miss Levine. He's not here."

"Do you know where he is?"

"He is no longer working here, miss. He has returned to London to resume his duties with our office there. Would you like to speak to our new general manager, Mr. Elliot?"

"Oh. Oh, I see." She smiled at Miss Riley as if it wasn't much of a surprise at all. She wanted to scream; she wanted to drop to the floor and be sick; but instead she thanked her and went back outside to her taxi and told the driver to take her back to the Village.

On the way back, she resolved not to let this touch her. She wouldn't cry, she wouldn't think about it, not again, not ever again.

"Ma'am," the taxi driver said, "are you all right?"

"I'm fine," she said. "Just fine."

58

Libby got to the Sherry just after five, put her samples portfolio on the table. She peeled off her wool coat and beret and ordered a manhattan. She glimpsed her reflection briefly in one of the gilt wall mirrors, couldn't avoid it; the management seemed to think that all its customers wanted to look at themselves from every possible angle. I look a fright, she thought. Like I've been hollowed out with a spoon.

She was on her second manhattan by the time Sarah arrived. She watched her mother searching the lobby for her. She was wearing a caramel sable coat, had on the right amount of rouge, and her hair was in sculpted waves. She could have been an advertisement for *Vogue*.

I should be grateful, Libby thought, she's not your usual Jewish mother.

Libby raised a languid hand, and Sarah smiled and came over.

She ordered a martini from the white-jacketed waiter and took off her gloves and coat. There was snow melted on the fur collar.

"All this time since I have seen you," Sarah said.

"Two days, Mama."

"You're not still mad?"

"I don't want to talk about it, Mama."

"Three weeks now and living in a hotel like a girl with no reputation. Maybe it is time you come home. Etta and Yaakov, they are all moved out. You won't have to share the bathroom with half Russia."

Libby let that slide. "I went to Altman's for you today. You remember, I made the appointment last week."

"Altman's, yes. So, how it was?"

"They've agreed to take the entire spring range on sale or return."

"Libby, that's wonderful."

"I'm glad you're pleased."

"Pleased? I don't know what I'd do without you, bubeleh."

"They're your designs, Mama. You catch the fish, I wheel the cart down the lane and bargain with the housewives."

"You know that's not true. You have such flair for sales. Miracles you perform."

"It helps that all the buyers are men."

"Did I tell you I am looking at apartments all afternoon? On the Upper West Side. Near the Arlington, where we used to live before the crash. Like we always planned."

"Like you always planned. Well, good luck on you, Mama. You deserve it."

Sarah's face fell. Her martini arrived, and Libby ordered another manhattan, inviting a disapproving glance from her mother as well as the waiter.

"So, what are we celebrating?" Sarah said.

"I want to toast the future," Libby said.

"And what a future we have!"

"I hope you think so after I have told you my news."

"News? You have news?"

Libby took a breath. Her mouth felt suddenly dry. She finished her manhattan and prayed the waiter would hurry with the other. "I've enrolled to take a nursing degree at Yale."

Sarah smiled as if she had made a joke.

"Mama? You're allowed to say something."

"This is supposed to be funny, bubeleh?"

"Not to me. I've been thinking about this for a long time. It's what I want to do."

"No."

"I knew you'd say that. But it's too late. This time you don't get to decide. It's done. I called an old friend from Westover. Her father has some influence over there, and she got me in. So all the school fees Dewey paid, they didn't go to waste after all."

Her manhattan arrived, and not a moment too soon. Her mama just stared at her. Like a corpse she looked, still and gray in the face.

"Mama, please say something."

"How could you do this?"

"It's my life. It's what I want to do."

"But why would you do such a thing? This business, this good living we have now, it is all for you."

"Yes, that's the problem."

"What problem? How is there a problem of making a millionaire life for your daughter?"

"I'm sorry."

"You are sorry?"

"I don't want to sell clothes. This is not a life for me."

"Not a life? What do you know from life? I have been a good mother to you. Go ahead, tell me you wished you had another mother. Tell me."

"You are a wonderful mama. The best. But I'm twenty-three years old. You must let me be now."

"Let you be?"

"Let me make my own life. Loving is not just looking after, it's about letting go."

"I cannot let you go. Cannot."

"You have to. I know this is hard. But I've been thinking about this for a long time, ever since Frankie started nursing. Do you know she's in Manila now? The adventures she's having!"

"You think about this for so long? And you say nothing to me?"

"I knew you'd be angry."

"Yes, I am angry! Why not angry? I cannot believe what I am hearing."

She sat back in her chair, looked up at the crystal chandelier above their heads.

"A nurse? I cannot believe. You don't want a nice apartment, a motor car, nice things to wear? Instead you want to look at men's I-don't-know-whats and clean up other people's business all day?"

"I want to help people, Mama. I want to feel like I'm doing something worthwhile."

"What we do is not worthwhile?"

"You mean helping some society matron think she looks better than the bored lawyer's wife in the next apartment? It's not going to save a life, is it?" Libby immediately wished she hadn't said that aloud. It was just business, and there was nothing wrong with being good at it. "It's not what I want to do with my life," she said more gently.

"I won't help you," Sarah said. "I won't give you money."

"I didn't think you would. That's all right. I'll wait tables if I have to. Whatever it takes."

Sarah shook her head. "I cannot believe what you have done to me. Better I was dead."

"We both know what you did, Mama. I guess one day I'll forgive you, but today's not that day."

She realized she had drunk too much after all. It was as much as she could do to make a dignified exit without sprawling on the polished marble. Outside, the cold air made her head spin. Thank

God for the bell captain who found her a taxi in just a few dizzy moments.

The cabbie asked her where she was going. "I have no idea," she murmured, and then she fumbled in her purse for the card they had given her at the hotel and handed it to him. She had had enough of being Liberty Levine. It was time to be her own woman, whoever that turned out to be.

PART 7

59

Pennsylvania Station, New York, February 1942

How beautiful it was, this place, Libby thought; never mind all the noise, the announcements over the loudspeakers. It took her breath away, this great vault of girders, the crisscross shafts of light from the lunettes, the big clock with its hands creeping past eleven o'clock.

She sat down on one of the varnished walnut benches to wait. The whole world was going off to war down there—there were soldiers in khaki, sailors in white, kissing and waving to the women who would wait for them. Not all of them waiting, not in this war, some of them going off with the men, nurses in ANC khaki, the pretty WAVES all in white.

Libby had written to Etta, arranged to meet her at Penn Station and go eat someplace nearby. She almost didn't recognize her; she was looking for a dowdy Russian peasant woman, like the Etta she remembered from the last time she saw her. When was it? A long time, three years, maybe more, certainly since before she joined the army. Six years she had been away from New York, and how many times had she been back? She could count them on one hand. She and Etta had written to each other many times, but her rift with her mama had made things difficult.

She was taken by surprise when a woman in a long dark coat, her hair curled under her tricorn hat, came toward her and waved.

"Aunt Etta!"

Etta held out her arms. "Libby! Look at you!" These days she spoke English with a real New York accent. "Like a real hero, you look!"

"You want to buy a hero a cup of coffee?"

They hugged again, and Libby followed Etta out of the station to find the nearest diner.

Etta pulled her down in the chair beside her, gesturing to the waitress for coffee. It was steamy hot inside the diner; outside, New York was hunched and gray, wisps of steam rose from the grates in the street.

"How important you look in your uniform!"

Libby took her bag from her shoulder and loosened her coat. "Everyone is in uniform now."

"What a world we are having," Etta said. "So now there is war everywhere. Yaakov was right all along. Thank God we left when we did."

"Have you heard from Aunt Zlota?"

Etta shook her head. "Not for a year, maybe more. I worry so for her and her children. You hear these stories about what the Germans are doing. Once, I thought nothing could be worse than the Russians. Now look."

"It's good you are here, at least."

"I have such a smart husband."

"You look so well."

"You mean I look so fat! It is all this good American food we are having now. Too many cream cakes and candy bars, what they call." She laughed and put three spoons of sugar in her coffee. "So good to see you again. It has been so long. And the places you have been!"

"Only the Philippines, Aunt."

"But it all looks so romantic on the postcards. And warm!"

"Thank you for all your letters. They've meant the world to me."

"What else would I do? You hear from your mama lately?"

"Not so much," Libby said, and quickly changed the subject, warming her hands on her coffee cup. "How is Yaakov?"

"A proper *Amerikaner* he is. You should see him, manager of this big bookshop. You should see it over in Brooklyn. No pushcarts in the street. You want something, you have to go to a proper shop. We're modern now!"

"And the boys? Is Ruben still working with Yaakov?"

"Well, he's never going to do any good in school, that one. Shine a torch in one ear, you see the light coming out of the other one. But his little brother, he does okay. Like I write to you. God willing, he will start college next year."

"And Bessie. Has she had her baby?"

"A little boy, praise God."

"A rich husband, you said in your letter! Who would have thought, Aunt Etta?"

"Rich, but a face like a pickle that's been run over by a truck. Still, you can't have everything. At least she has a husband. What about you, bubeleh? We are all so worried for you when we hear on the radio about the bombing."

"I was never near Pearl Harbor. I was in Manila until the summer. Lucky for me I got transferred back to San Fran."

"Someone up there is looking out for you."

"I got sick. It didn't seem like luck at the time. I spent two months in the hospital. Funny how it's all turned out. You remember my friend Frankie? I wrote you about her."

"She is all right?"

"She's okay. She has a baby girl now, lives in San Diego. But her husband was on the *Arizona*. He's lucky to be alive."

"Well, at least you're safe."

"Nowhere is safe in a war, not when you're in uniform. I'll see action sooner or later. Hopefully I can make a difference to someone."

"Your mutti must be worried sick about you."

Two young soldiers burst in, bringing an arctic blast of air with them. Outside, the rain had turned to sleet. The waitress came over and refilled their coffee cups.

"She sent a telegram to the base to make sure I was all right, after Pearl Harbor. She thinks Pearl Harbor is in California. I wrote back to her, but she didn't answer. She barely ever writes. I don't think she's ever really forgiven me for leaving."

"She never was this way when we were growing up. It is America does this to her. Will you go and see her?"

"Of course. But I'm scared about it. It's always difficult between us now."

"You should try and mend this thing."

"I don't know how. And anyway, perhaps I haven't forgiven her either."

"That she should come between you and this Jack, I can't believe."

"I'll try and sort things out with her. With the war and everything, this might be our last chance."

"Don't say such things!"

Libby stared into her coffee. "The best days, you know, they weren't those years on the Upper West Side, with the maids and the view of Central Park and the chauffeur. It sounds grand, I know, but the times I loved best were when it was just me and her, living in that broom cupboard in Greenwich Village, building our little business, finding a way to survive every day. It was hard, but it was fun too."

"When they made your mama, God took away the mold and used it for making tigers."

"Yes, she's tough. That's her greatest strength and her biggest weakness."

"She loves you, Libby."

"I would give anything to start over, you know, go back to Cannon Street with her and Frankie and Frankie's mom, eat potato pancakes, and play in the mud in the street, and buy pickles from the old guy on Willett Street. They were good days. Mama wasn't so damned complicated then. And what about you and her?"

A gloomy shrug. "What to do? I thought that one day she will let it be, but you know, it is like she doesn't want to have anything to do with the past anymore. And me and Yaakov and Bessie, we are her past. Still, when you see her, will you tell her . . ."

"What, Aunt Etta?"

"Tell her I miss her. Tell her that without her, my life is just a sled stuck in the snow. Yes, tell her that."

⊸⊷⊷⊸

Mama has done well, Libby thought, as her cab pulled up outside the red-and-white canopy of the Barrington Apartments, and a uniformed doorman stepped out to open the door. Twenty people working for her now, a factory in Brooklyn, and such a list of customers, with Bloomingdale's at the very top. As her mama reminded her in the few letters she wrote, she could have been a part of it. But Libby was happy with how it had all turned out. If only her mama could be as happy for her, if only she could let go of the past, like Etta said.

The elevator opened on to a marble foyer and a pair of dark-blue Japanese cloisonné vases on wooden stands. Her mama stood between them with her hands folded, as if she was waiting to greet an exiled monarch. She was almost fifty years old now, but she looked at least ten years younger. She was wearing a tangerine collarless top with a nipped waist over a gored skirt.

"Well," she said, "look at you in your blue, very blue, uniform."

"Hello, Mama. I see your lips moving, but I see your eyes redesigning it."

Sarah plumped out the shoulders, pulled at the buttons at the waist. "Perhaps I would have made it so it brought out your figure a little more."

"They don't care about my figure in the army. Not the generals anyway."

"And what is that you have on your head? And is it a tie you are wearing?"

"It's called a forage cap," Libby said, and handed it to a maid who was dutifully standing by to collect it. "And yes, the tie is part of the dress blues."

"Ah well, thank God you're safe." A brisk hug. "Dressed like a janitor, but safe. How long will you be in New York, bubeleh?"

"Just tonight. They're sending us to Washington tomorrow. I have twenty-four hours' leave."

"Washington you're going?"

"For military training. I've only been in the army two years, and now there's a war. They're panicking because we don't even know how to salute properly."

"Where will you go after that?"

"Who knows? It's the army. They never tell you; they just do it."

"You want to stay here tonight?"

"Thanks, but I'm staying with a friend, we have a hotel near Penn Station."

Sarah's eyes shot wide. "A man?"

"No, another nurse from my unit. She gets in tonight."

Sarah showed her through the apartment. She said she had bought it eighteen months before—Is it that long since I have seen her? Liberty thought. It was a classic six, with three bathrooms and more marble than the Parthenon. The living room, with its views over Central Park, even had a frescoed ceiling. She had almost outshone Dewey.

After the tour, Sarah asked the maid to bring them coffee and arranged herself on a tapestried sofa, as if she was posing for a *Vogue* photographer. She is making a point, Liberty thought, letting me know what I could have had if I had stayed.

Unopened novels were scattered about a glass-top coffee table— D. H. Lawrence, James Joyce—along with several copies of *Vogue* and the *New Yorker*.

They talked about business. Liberté Fashion was all over New York now. Bloomingdale's stocked her entire catalog, and a young Brooklyn actress called Gene Tierney had bought several of her dresses. She was charging private customers thousands for one of her creations.

A maid brought coffee on a tray.

"The suit you're wearing, is that one of your creations?" Libby asked, nodding.

"You like it?"

"It's beautiful. I always thought you were a genius. Even after what you did, I still thought that."

It was like a shadow passed over Sarah's face. "Still you talk about that man."

"Yes. Still think about him too."

"It is all such a long time ago. I don't know how you remember such things. Don't you have a beau now?"

Libby answered with a shrug.

"You won't always be so young and beautiful. How long you going to be this old-maid nurse?"

"Is that what I am?" Libby sipped her coffee, almost amused. "There's been a couple of close calls, but it never turned into anything."

"What is wrong with these boys, that they don't want to get married with you?"

"It's not the boys, it's me that's the problem. Whenever something looks like it will get serious, I get cold feet."

"I don't understand this cold feet. You get a boy, he's not so terrible, it don't matter about your feet, you make children. What is so hard?"

"It sounds so romantic when you put it like that."

"Romantic, you don't need. Romantic just for movies. Real life, you want a serious boy with a job and everything down there working right."

"Like you and Papa. It was an arranged marriage, right?"

"Yes, whatever you want to call, arranged. But I get to love him, like an old pair of boots."

"I haven't found an old pair of boots that fits me yet."

"You are impossible, impossible!"

"Oh, Mama, enough about all that. Show me what you've been working on for the spring catalog."

There was a studio with windows all along one wall. It looked right over Central Park and the Upper West Side, flooded with light. There were wire half mannequins, some bare, some hung with partly sewn scraps of unfinished designs; a large table with pencil designs and sketch pads scattered over it. Sarah sorted through them. How far she's come, Libby thought, from everything piled on the kitchen table of a leaky tenement.

"This new War Production Board, what can you do? First they ban anything with cuffs, then the only cotton you can buy is black or brown, now they say a dress cannot be more than twenty-five inches here to here, like we will win this stupid war everyone wearing short brown dresses."

"Well, it's worth a try," Libby said, but Sarah didn't even smile. "It's called rationing, Mama. We have to preserve resources."

"What resource?"

"Cotton, for example. You can make uniforms with it."

"If this you are wearing is the kind of uniform they make, let Japan win. This is our big chance. No more fancy-schmancy stuff from Paris in the shops anymore, now here in America at last we can have our own look."

"The war is not about fashion, Mama."

"Obviously," Sarah said, and tugged at Libby's collar. "Well, okay, if this is what Mr. Roosevelt wants, then Sarah Levine will be the greatest patriot type ever. Look, five dollars of this denim stuff; with this I will make a dress you can wear anywhere, either to make cake or make whoopee, whatever you call it. Libby. *Liberty*. You're not listening."

"No, Mama, not really."

"What is wrong with you?"

"I was wondering why you didn't write to me."

"What are you saying? Of course I write to you."

"Birthdays and Pearl Harbor. Are you still angry at me?"

"Why not angry, bubeleh? I should be happy with this life you are living, doing dirty stuff, cleaning bedpans, and wearing this uniform, clothes that don't even fit?"

"My job is about skill, kindness, and compassion. I don't see any dirty stuff."

"You could have a good life here."

"I like my life just fine."

"You could die in the army! What then, what then if you die, bubeleh? How can I ever live?"

Libby tried to hug her, but she pushed her away.

"Bad enough to be a nurse, but the army, that you don't have to do."

"It's my life, Mama."

"Only some of it."

"What's that supposed to mean?"

"Enough. Enough. You want a manhattan?"

"I guess."

"I'll get Charlotte to make them," she said, and hurried out of the studio, but not before Libby saw that she was crying.

They sat in Sarah's living room, staring out the French doors at the shadowed city. Under the army-ordered "dim-out," the neon signs in Times Square had been turned off. There were hardly any lights above street level now. Even down there in the street, the restaurants and bars along the Park had just a few lights on, and the cars and taxicabs had hooded headlights.

For the first time since she was a child, Libby could make out stars in the sky over the city. A dull sheen of ice glittered on the footpaths.

Libby sipped her manhattan. "Are you okay, clunking around in this big apartment on your own?"

"Once, I think I will have grandchildren to play with."

"Bessie has a boy now. You could play with him."

"I heard. You know what, I never even seen him."

"Whose fault is that? Go and see Etta, Mama, make amends with her. It's been too long."

Sarah didn't answer. Charlotte came in and said that dinner was ready.

As they ate, Liberty told Sarah about Manila and the Sternberg Hospital and the friends she had made. Most of her old unit were still out there, she said. She hadn't heard from them in months. One had got out on a hospital ship before the city fell. She had heard the others had escaped to other parts of the islands or been taken prisoner. "Only lucky I got sick when I did," she said.

Charlotte had brought them lobster bisque and exquisitely tender lamb cutlets cooked with thyme. Sarah listened to everything Libby said, but offered very little in return. For dessert there was coffee and handmade chocolates, and Libby ran out of things to say. She stared out the window, at the black rim of ice on the terrace, thought about another Upper West Side apartment, another terrace, and wondered what would have happened if Bill Dewey had not jumped off it.

"You're going to be twenty-nine years old this year," Sarah said.

"I know."

"Don't you want to have a home, a husband, a family?"

Not this again, Libby thought. Didn't we just do this? "Perhaps you could arrange a husband for me."

"If you want me, I can."

"I was joking."

"Marriage is no joke, bubeleh."

"I know it isn't, Mama. That's why I'm not married. I take it very seriously. If you hadn't interfered, perhaps I would have married Jack Seabrook."

Sarah worried her linen napkin between her fingers. Libby saw how pale she had gone.

"Why did you put Etta out?"

"I didn't put her out, she put herself out."

"She misses you. She says you haven't spoken to her in years."

"She hasn't spoken to me either."

"Mama, it doesn't matter anymore who was right, who was wrong. Etta said to tell you that her life without you is like a broken sled in the forest. You know what she means, right?"

Sarah shook her head, as if she was trying to brush the memory aside. "You see Etta before you come to see your mother?"

"Mama, never mind that. You have to mend this."

"Don't have to do nothing."

"You're so damned stubborn," Libby said, and looked at her wrist-watch. "I have to go. Good night, Mama."

"God keep you safe, bubeleh."

"Not even God can keep everyone safe. There's too many of us, even for him."

They waited in the foyer while Charlotte fetched her coat and for-age cap. Please hurry, Libby thought. I can't stand this damned silence any longer. There was so much she wanted to say, but she had given up trying.

"There's something I have to tell you, bubeleh."

"Tell me, then."

But then her mother stepped back, shook her head. "One day, another time. This is not a good time."

"When is there going to be a better time? They're probably sending me to Europe soon. Perhaps, you know, this will be the only time."

Sarah shook her head. "I can't. Not yet."

"When, then?"

Libby kissed her on the cheek. Sarah held on to her as if she was drowning. Libby felt a lump in her throat and that wouldn't do. She had promised herself there would be no tears until all this war was over; not for herself and not for anyone else. She had to cope.

Charlotte came back with her things, and Sarah broke away.

"What if I never see you again?" Sarah said.

"You will, Mama."

"Liberty, I'm sorry."

"What for?"

"For everything."

"Sorry won't bring Jack back."

"You don't understand," she said. "I did it for you." She blinked away tears.

To hell with it, Libby thought. Her mother had had all night to tell her why she had done it, instead they had talked about hemlines and the War Production Board. Well, it didn't matter anymore.

"Go and see Etta, at least," Libby said. "Please." She heard the elevator bell, and she kissed her mother on the cheek and stepped inside. The doors closed. That was it, she thought. Our last chance, gone.

Jack saw his father sitting in the lobby bar, impeccable as always, the only serge blue suit in a forest of khaki. He was drinking Scotch and smoking a cigar. The other soldiers crowded into the bar had somehow formed a perimeter around him, like he was a five-star general. You had to admire the old boy, the way he managed it.

"Drink?" George said when he saw him.

"Too crowded in here. Let's find someplace else."

"Suit yourself," George said, and finished his Scotch. They walked down East Forty-Second, found another bar with not quite as many uniforms, and took a table in the corner.

George went to buy the round. Jack asked for a beer, but George came back with two Scotches and a tumbler of water, no ice.

"So you joined up. Didn't think about asking me first?"

"For your permission?"

"For my advice."

"Which would have been?"

"I could have got you a better posting."

"You mean a safer one."

"Would that have been so bad?"

"I'd rather do it my way for once and take my chances." He touched his glass to George's. "Bottoms up."

"May I ask what brought on this sudden rush of patriotism?"

"All the posters said Uncle Sam needed me. It's good to be needed."

George looked at the flash on Jack's epaulette. "So which outfit are you with?"

"Sixteenth Infantry. New York's Own. They made me a captain on account I have an Ivy League education. They probably think that means I won't swear in front of any five-star generals."

"Swear at them all you want. I don't care if they put you in the stockade. Better than being blown to bits."

"You don't have to wear a uniform to get blown to bits. Goering's boys didn't get me in London. I'm kinda hoping my luck will hold."

"I brought you back here to get you out of the war, not so you could walk straight back into it."

"I march these days. Walking is for civilians." Jack took a swallow of the Scotch, watched his father over the rim of the glass. There was a diner across the street, and he realized it was the one where he and Liberty went for lunch that very first time she showed up at their office, brazenly begging for credit.

"Why the long face?" Jack said.

"I would have thought that was obvious. You're all I have."

"I wouldn't say that. You have a mistress, and the Harvard Club."

"Son, please."

"Look, Father, I know you think I'm ungrateful, that I've always had everything laid on a plate, and I guess you're right. But the reason I'm not grateful is everything I got for free cost so damned much, end of the day. It cost me my self-respect and my ability to think for myself and to make my own mistakes. I stayed in London when you wanted me to come back because I was my own boss over there. I stayed when the war started because I was doing a damned good job for you and because I would have felt like a coward running away once the bombs started dropping. The people we employ over there, they couldn't run away. Why should I?"

"Anything else you want to add to my list of sins?"

"Such as?"

"The real reason you're so goddamned sore is that you never forgave me for the Levine business."

A shrug. "Can't really blame you. That wasn't your fault. You're just an old truth teller, right?"

"I thought you'd get over her quicker than you did."

"So did I, I guess. We both got a nasty surprise."

Jack finished his Scotch. He thought he could use another one.

"The worse thing," Jack said, "was it took away my faith. I don't trust women anymore. I look at them, I wonder what it is they really want, and I always come up with the same answer. I've wised up, I guess, but I've become a little remote, if you know what I mean. More like you. A chip off the old block. You should be happy about that."

George had a strange look on his face. He put his empty glass down on the table, so hard the ice rattled in the tumbler. "Let's go out to dinner," he said, "get a few drinks at the club. We'll both get good and soused before you leave."

"Can't, my train leaves at eight o'clock. I have a new commanding officer now. He even outranks you these days."

"Is that how you saw me? Your commanding officer?"

"It's not how I saw you, it's how it was. You ran my life, and I guess I let you do it. I didn't want to let go of all my privileges. I'm as much to blame."

The taproom smell and the heating in the bar were suddenly too much. Jack needed to go outside and get some air. They went out, stood on the sidewalk.

"Do you know where they're sending you?" George asked him.

"There's talk that after basic training, we're headed back to England, fight the Germans for Mr. Churchill."

"Just don't get yourself killed, all right?"

"Is that an order?"

"Look on it as an urgent request."

"I'll send it through to my CO. I'm sure he'll consider it."

Jack headed back down the block to his hotel. He looked back once, when he was turning the corner, was surprised to see the old man still standing there in the street watching him. Damn if he didn't wave good-bye.

60

Sarah rehearsed her speech silently in the cab all the way to Brooklyn.

"Etta, I'm sorry it came to this. You and me, we are sisters, and our vati and mutti would be turning in their graves if they knew we were not speaking. But you have to understand that none of this was my doing. I didn't make you leave, was your idea only. But I'm prepared to forgive and forget if you are."

"Did you say something, ma'am?" the cabbie asked her.

"Nothing, nothing. Just drive," Sarah said.

No, that wouldn't do. *"I didn't make you leave, was your idea only."* That wasn't right, she couldn't say that. She tried again.

"Etta, my darling sister. I think you owe me an apology. All that time not speaking, you were the one who left, so angry and puffed up, after I give you and your family food and shelter when first you come here. But it was all a long time ago. If you will apologize, so will I, and we can try and put this behind us."

Already they were on the Brooklyn Bridge. Sarah felt the panic rise. They would be there soon, and she still could not decide what it was she should say.

"Etta, I have had a long talk with Liberty. She said I should come and see you about what has happened. It is still difficult between us, as you know. I still cannot forgive what you did, but at least you and I should be

like sisters again. She says you have missed me, and I have missed you a lot also. I still think that none of this was my fault, but can we at least be friends again?"

Yes, that was it. She rehearsed it over and over until she was sure she had it right, word perfect. Soon, too soon, they pulled up outside a two-story brownstone just off the parkway, a proper *alrightnik* neighborhood. She paid the cabbie his fare and got out.

A cold day, ice in the wind, a paper scrap tossed and bounced along the street, the sky gray as a winding-sheet. She pulled up the collar of her coat and repeated her lines one more time.

She stood on the sidewalk, got herself ready, staring up at the stoop and the black-painted front door, then took a deep breath and went up, rapped three times with the brass knocker. A part of her hoped Etta would not be home, that she could go home, come back another day when she was feeling better, stronger, about this.

She waited. No one came. She turned to go.

The door swung open.

"Sura," Etta said.

Oh, the look on her face. *Mein Gott,* she is going to cry. Sarah lurched forward and threw herself into her sister's arms. What was it, the speech she had? She didn't remember a word. "Oh, Etta," she said, "I'm so sorry. I've been such a fool. This is all my fault. Please forgive me."

61

Sarah sat in Etta's parlor, her head down, staring at the green carpet with the big pink roses, listening to the ticking of the big clock on the mantel. Etta had made black sweet tea, just as she liked it, but she had not touched it, left it there on the table to grow cold. More important things to do today than drink tea.

Sarah looked around the room, saw a photograph of Etta and her family on the mantel: Yaakov; the boys, so grown now; Bessie.

"Bessie is having the *bris* for her baby this weekend," Etta said.

"She is married now? A nice boy?"

"A nice Irish boy."

"She married a goy? Etta, how could you let such a thing happen?"

"That I should get in the way of what makes her happy?"

"But Etta . . ."

"She was never like your Libby, not a Rembrandt. I figured she wouldn't get that many chances. She liked him, he liked her. It took a long time to persuade my Yaakov, but in the end he saw the sense of it." She brought another photograph from the mantel to show her. "Look you, how happy they are." She sat down, took her sister's hands in hers. "You will come?"

"She won't want me there."

"Of course she wants her aunt Sura there. If not for you, Bessie will not have a life to make a life. Remember?"

"You think so?"

"I know so, Sura."

Sarah brushed the back of her hand impatiently across her face. This was a good thing, what was there to cry for? She thought about that day in the snow, when Bessie was born. That Sura, she was so different. She was brave, and she had no secrets from anyone, least of all her favorite sister. It was plain to her, the only answer was to get her back, if she only could.

Only you got to do it now, Sarah, before you got time to think, got time to be scared. A deep breath. "Etta, before you decide if you want me at the *bris*, maybe there is something I should tell you first. Something I never told another soul."

"Well, I am your sister. You can tell me. Whatever can be so bad?"

"What can be so bad? I will tell you. Imagine the worst thing a person can ever do. The worst. Now imagine ten times that."

"You have murdered someone?"

"Worse," Sarah said. "I stole their baby."

Etta looked confused. "What baby?"

"What baby you think, Etta?"

"You stole Libby?"

"I didn't know I was stealing. I swear it. When I come to America, Micha has this little baby, gives her to me. He says, Sura, this is ours. He says she is a foundling; someone has left her in the street. Well, you know, I think, this is America, it happens. We bring her up. We love her to bits and pieces. Then just when everything is nice, my crazy husband, he joins the war, says he wants to fight Germans. What does he know from fighting Germans? Nothing, it turns out. He gets himself killed. And that's when I find in his stuff, this thing he has torn from the newspapers. It is from after we arrive in America, this man is looking for a baby that everyone thinks is killed in a fire. A fire at the hotel where Micha is working."

"Which man? This Mr. George Seabrook?"

Sarah didn't answer. They looked at each other, and Sarah waited for her sister to work it through. "So Libby is this Seabrook's daughter," Etta said.

Sarah nodded.

"And Jack is his son?" Etta's eyes widened. "That is why you wouldn't let her see him."

"Yes. That is why."

Etta took Sarah's hands in hers.

"Did your Dewey know this Mr. George Seabrook?"

"Sure he knew him. That is how my Libby knows his Jack."

"But she is his sister. They nearly make romance. And she doesn't know? You don't tell her?"

Sarah couldn't raise her eyes from the floor. She just shook her head.

"Oh, Sura!"

Sarah shook her hands like they were covered in something foul and she could not get it off. "You tell one lie, then you have to tell another because of that first lie. Before you know, everything has gone *bopkes*."

Etta got up and paced the room, her arms folded across her middle as if it was hurting her. She went to the window, parted the lace curtains, looked out at the street. "Look at this America," she said. "All these brick houses and bigness and nobody talking. Look what it does to us."

"It is not America does this," Sarah said. "I did it. Nobody else."

"Oh, Sura, Sura."

"One thing I wanted, what I promised. I would never lose my Libby. And what happens? She is like a stranger to me now. She is polite, she writes letters, but my daughter, I don't think so. Nothing like before. She hates me. And now, now she is going off to some stupid war, like my Micha."

Etta stared out the window for a long time, not saying anything. Finally: "You have to tell her."

"I can't. Not now."

"You must, Sura."

"I will lose her for always."

"And that is different how? Do it, Sura. Do it before it is too late. Don't do it because you will lose her or you will not lose her. Do it because it is the right thing, and because she deserves to know."

Sarah nodded. Etta was right. She was always right about such things. Even if her Libby never forgave, at least Sarah would not have to live with this burden anymore. And how could Libby ever forgive? For being a possessive mother, for meddling, maybe. But to forgive for not being her mother at all?

How could she ever do that?

A gray, grim day outside. Isn't it supposed to be spring? Sarah thought. It was like the war had affected everything. The man beside her in the café had the *New York Times* open on the table in front of him while he drank his coffee. Sarah read the headlines over his shoulder.

Wainwright had surrendered Corregidor, and the Germans were still attacking Russia, somewhere called Kharkov. The newspaper said the Russians' sixth and ninth armies had been encircled. That sounded to her like a lot of armies.

There was another whole column about Jews in France and Belgium having to wear a yellow Star of David wherever they went. She thought about their Zlota. Still no word. She wondered if they were making all the Jews in Tallinn wear yellow stars as well. Hadn't she tried to tell them all? Doesn't matter if it's Germans or Russians, none of them like us.

She watched the crowds hurrying to and from Penn Station, so many uniforms now, even the Camel man in the poster in Times Square had a flying helmet and goggles on. Everything was war, war, war, just what they had come to America to hide from. Seemed to her, you tried to run away from badness, but in the end, it came after you.

She felt again for the package on the seat beside her. Most days she came out with just a clutch for powder and her purse; today she had with her a large leather bag, not her usual show-off thing from Bergdorf or Saks, a cheap thing, but big enough to put the parcel in, and Libby couldn't sneer at her for being too hoity-toity.

The waitress brought her coffee, and she stirred sugar into it, then let it go cold. She felt like she was going to be sick. All these years she had kept what she had in her bag hidden away, under beds, in secret drawers in desks, and these last few years in a safe-deposit box in her bank.

But Etta was right, it was time to stop with all the hiding. This might be her last chance to do things right.

"Mama."

Sarah looked up, and there she was, her Libby, standing there in her blues and forage cap. "Wasn't sure you'd come to see me off. It was good to get your message."

"Sure I'm coming, what else am I going to do?"

Libby sat down. How beautiful she looks, Sarah thought. A new perm in her hair, her eyes shining, excited or afraid, maybe both. She saw two sailors look over at her daughter from another booth, and she glared back at them until they looked the other way.

"Leave them be, Mama," Libby said. "They don't mean any harm."

"You have men look at you like this all the time now? Is because you are nurse, doing I don't know what."

"I can look after myself, Mama."

The waitress brought Libby coffee.

"I still don't understand why you want to go fight Germans like . . ." She was about to say, like your father, and stopped herself. "Like my Micha."

"I'm a nurse, Mama. The war is where young nurses are needed the most right now. Word is they're sending us overseas on the USS *Wakefield*, bound for Scotland. After that, no one knows."

"Scotland? They got Germans in Scotland now?"

"Field training, I think."

"I thought you already got training in Washington."

"Combat training, and other things you won't want to know about. What's that you've got there. Is that for me?"

Sarah didn't answer. No, she thought. No, I can't do it.

"Mama?"

No, you got to, she heard Etta say.

Sarah picked up the bag and put it on the table between them.

"You're trembling, Mama."

"Open it."

Libby unzipped the bag and looked inside. She took out the biscuit box.

"You bought me biscuits? The army does feed us, Mama."

Sarah nodded at the bag, and Libby reached in and took out an old leather-bound notebook. A child's drawing, scrawled on yellowing butcher's paper, fell out of it onto the floor. Libby picked it up, frowning.

"Your baby book," Sarah said. "You asked me once about it. Well, here it is, all yours now."

"Why are you giving me this now? You're being very mysterious, Mama."

Libby opened the book. There were diary entries in Yiddish, written in Sarah's careful Hebrew letters.

"You remember your Yiddish?"

"I remember it."

"Then you can read for yourself. You see the dates? It begins 1913, the year you were born."

Libby flipped through the pages. "Why are there two columns? I don't understand."

"Open the box."

Libby pulled up the lid. She peered inside, sorted with her forefinger through the medals and papers inside.

"Read this newspaper here," Sarah said.

Sarah unfolded the yellow scrap of newspaper very carefully. It was worn thin, as delicate as a butterfly cocoon. Libby brought it closer to her face to look more closely at the photograph.

"Micha cut it out of the newspaper."

"It's from the year I was born."

"I didn't find this newspaper until after he died, I swear you."

Libby read it quickly, and the color drained out of her face. "This is me? I'm the baby?"

"That is why the two columns in the baby book. One side is what is real, the other one is what I tell my vati and mutti and everyone. So they think you are really mine."

Libby looked as if she was about to say something, then shook her head. Sarah took Libby's hand, but she pulled it away. "Micha said you were a foundling girl. I didn't want my vati to know. At the time, I think, what else I can do? I cannot write: Oh, when I get to America, I find this baby on the street, be happy for me. Micha said it was better this way. He never told me about the newspaper, about George Seabrook. Not a word."

Libby stared out the window. A flurry of rain whipped against the glass. Finally, she put both hands to her throat. She was wearing a locket on a gold chain. She slipped it over her head and opened it. Inside the locket was a grainy black-and-white photograph, the picture of Micha that Sarah had given her all those years ago. "This man is not my father?"

Sarah shook her head.

"He did it for me," Sarah said. "He was not a bad man, Libby, please believe."

"Let me get this straight, Mama. You're telling me George Seabrook is my father. *That's* why you stopped me seeing Jack."

"I was scared to tell you. I think maybe you will never forgive me." She waited for a denial, but there wasn't one. She put her finger on the newspaper cutting. "I don't know why this Mrs. Seabrook came to be in the hotel, alone, with you. Maybe only George Seabrook knows the answer to this."

"He doesn't know about me either?"

"Until now, no one knows. This morning, I go to see Etta, make better with her, like you said. And then, it just comes out of me, I cannot stop it. And Etta, she begs me, she says, Sarah, Sarah, you got to tell her."

"This"—Libby stared at the newspaper cutting—"this Clare Seabrook was my real mother?"

"I am still your mama."

Libby looked away.

"I raised you from when you were a little nothing. I fed you; I brought you hot soup when you were sick; I been there for you, always. Tell me, how am I not your mother, bubeleh?"

"When did you find out, Mama? When did you *know?*"

"Only when my Micha didn't come back from the war, I found this box hidden under our bed with his private things."

"And you still didn't tell anyone?"

"I tried so hard to be rich for you, make sure you do not have the poor life, you do not suffer because of what we did, Micha and me."

"You have to tell him. You have to tell Jack's father."

"I can't, bubeleh."

"If you don't, I will."

Oh, the look on her Liberty's face. Sarah knew she was right, like Etta was right. How had all these secrets ever helped for anything?

"Promise me!"

"I promise," she said. She tried again to reach for Libby's hand, but she pulled away.

"I have to go," Libby said.

She walked out, left the notebook and the biscuit box on the table where she'd dropped them. Sarah crammed them back into the leather bag, threw some money on the table, and went after her. She almost lost her in the crowd, buffeted this way and that by all the people.

Finally, she caught up with her, tried to catch her arm, but Liberty shrugged free.

"Libby!"

"I'm sorry, Mama. Please just go home. I can't bear to even look at you right now."

She turned away and was soon lost in the crowds milling about the station entrance. Some people stared at the crazy woman in the Chanel coat who was shouting "Come back, come back!" with her mascara running down her face. But then, there were a lot of people crying outside Penn Station that day. There was a war on, and everyone had their own problems.

62

Two Miles off the Coast of Oran, Algeria, November 8, 1942

Liberty felt the hull dip and lurch on the ocean swell, heard the dull thunder of guns from the beach. The scuttlebutt was the French wouldn't fight, but that's not how it sounded to her. It looked like she was going to war after all. They had been told to expect to come under heavy fire when they got to the beach.

This waiting was the worst part. She knew she should be scared, like everyone else, but all she could think about was the same thing she had thought about ever since she left New York, that thing her mama had told her in the diner across the street from Penn Station.

You're not who you think you are.

She had been in a daze when she left the diner, couldn't even remember catching her train at Penn. It was all a blur. Every day since, she had thought about next to nothing else. When she rejoined the other nurses at the surgical unit, they thought it was all because of a man.

"Levine's got herself a beau. Still thinking about mystery man, dreamy head?"

If only it was that simple.

Everything her mama had said kept churning over and over in her mind on the long voyage over the Atlantic and on the train down from Scotland. They had finally ended up in a barracks in some place called Shipton Bellinger in the south of England. She had never heard of it, and neither had any of the other girls. She didn't even know exactly where she was. Nothing seemed real, not her past or her present. It was like she had been cut adrift from the world, from everything she had ever known. Was she Liberty Levine or No-Name Seabrook, missing, presumed dead since 1913? Perhaps neither, perhaps she was just the number on her dog tags.

Once they got to England, they had been loaded with field packs and sent tramping through the hills every day on long hikes. She had loved it because, by the end of every day, she was too exhausted to think anymore. For two months it was just walk and sleep. Before she knew it, they were on a train back to Scotland. They boarded a troopship called *Monarch of Bermuda* in a damp, gray place called Greenock. No one told them where they were going. They were just a handful of nurses surrounded by a wolf-whistling Ranger battalion and some boys from the Sixteenth Infantry. New York boys, one of the girls had said. *"Hey, Levine, you're from New York. You can make the introductions."*

Joking around. Only it wasn't funny.

Months now, and she couldn't make her peace with this. So many things that seemed at odds in the past made sense to her now; but there was still so much that didn't. Too many questions she should have asked.

"Did you ever love Dewey, or was that whole marriage about me?"

"Didn't George Seabrook ever once guess? Don't I look even a little like my mother?"

I must look something like her, Libby thought, because I sure as hell don't see anything of me in George.

At least she knew why her mama had gone so far out of her way to come between her and Jack.

Jack.

396

A few days ago, she had been standing on A Deck, watching some GIs exercising on the deck below her, and she thought she'd seen him, for a moment. Her mind playing tricks, because Jack Seabrook was in England the last she had heard, still running Daddy's business. Even if Jack was in uniform, George Seabrook would have found a way to keep him out of all this, get him posted to a cozy headquarters somewhere, leave the real fighting to the guys and girls from Orchard Street.

An artillery shell landed close off the starboard side.

It was still dark outside the porthole. She looked at the luminous dial on her watch. Five fifteen, and all the tables in the mess were crowded. All the officers and nurses in combat fatigues, no one talking much, a few whispered conversations, everyone getting ready.

"It's started," someone said, and they went up to A Deck to watch the first wave of the Sixteenth Infantry Division getting ready to board the landing barges below them.

One by one the barges pulled away from the ship and headed for the shore. It was getting on to dawn, but the navy destroyers were lobbing smoke shells into the water to provide cover for the GIs. It all looked almost ghostly in the sparse gray light.

"We're next," someone said.

63

The day vanished in an instant, though there were minutes of it that seemed to last an eternity. The front line moved five miles inland, and a captain assured them the last of the French and Arab snipers had been eliminated.

The Forty-Eighth Surgical had been moved into a shack back from the beach, behind the command headquarters. Libby opened her C rations and stared at the glop inside with little enthusiasm. Something made her think about the pickle man on Delancey Street.

She peered out through the shattered window. The LCI were being unloaded on the shore, a chain of GIs ferrying boxes of supplies from the small boats to the shore. She heard the nerve-wearing metallic clanking of the bulldozers working the beach, compacting the sand for the half-tracks.

The blackout was scheduled for 1800. All the lights went out on the LCI, and they were plunged into the dark.

She curled up on the cold tile floor and stared at the ceiling, watched the artillery flashes play along the sky through a hole in the tin roof. The army was engaged in a full-scale assault on Oran.

North Africa, it was supposed to be hot. She had expected palm trees and a blazing sun. Instead she lay there shivering with cold. Her fatigues were stiff as cardboard from the salt water. There had been hardly any sun to dry them. Her eyes were still smarting from seawater, where she had gone under while wading onto the beach. There was sand in her underwear and in her boots, and she was too tired to do anything about it.

She heard one of the other nurses crying in the dark. They grow them tougher on the Lower East Side, she thought. Frankie would be proud of me.

Libby closed her eyes, thought about Micha, the man in the black-and-white photograph, whose likeness she had kept around her neck for so many years. She felt for the locket, remembered yet again she had left it on the table in the diner, next to the biscuit box and the leather-bound diary. She wished she still had it, for luck.

Was this how it was for him, she thought, on his first day in a real battle? Was he brave, or was he shaking and terrified, like I am now? What did he think about on his last day? If only I could go back and ask him, so many things I want to know, most of all—what really happened the night he made me his daughter.

She couldn't even remember what he looked like anymore. One day, perhaps, Jack would fade into the shadows too. She had to put aside everything she thought she once knew. The beloved papa of her memories never really was her father; and Jack? All the feelings she had for him must be forgotten, and forever.

⚓

She woke up with a start, a corpsman shining a flashlight in her face. She looked at her wristwatch, it was almost midnight.

"Message from the colonel," the corpsman said. "All the nurses we can spare are wanted up at Arzew. Bring all your supplies with you."

Libby shook herself awake and followed him out the door in the dark.

Arzew

The jeep bounced over ruts and jolted through sandpits. The sounds of the battle were getting closer. Just before they reached Arzew, Liberty saw the blink of gunfire very close and heard the slap of bullets in the air, and the two soldiers on the Thompson gun behind her opened up. The sound of the gun deafened her. She put her hands over her ears and closed her eyes, slid down the side of the jeep, would have burrowed into the cold metal if she could.

By the time they reached the town, her ears were still ringing. She peered ahead, made out the silhouettes of palm trees, a huddle of square-roofed buildings. The staccato of gunfire over the rooftops sounded very far away now, though it could be she was still deaf from the Thompson gun.

The jeep stopped in front of a high fence, their driver shouted a password to an unseen sentry, and a wire and timber gate swung open and they drove through.

"Out," someone shouted, and she and another nurse tumbled out of the jeep and followed the corpsman across a shadowy compound.

There was a squat building directly in front of them, and they ran toward it. Someone inside must have been waiting for them. The black-out curtain that served as a door was pulled back, and they ran through.

The stench alone was worse than Delancey on a hot day, a miasma of filth and muck mixed with the coppery stink of blood and stale ether. All around them in the dark, men were moaning. A corpsman turned on his flashlight, and Libby gaped at the rows and rows of men lying on stretchers. Most of them looked as if they had been left as they were when they brought them in, God knows how long ago, abandoned to their pain and their blood.

A captain told her she was on triage. She had done her training at Walter Reed, thought she knew how to do it, but nothing could have prepared her for this, crawling around in the dark with a flashlight, tying labels on bleeding young men, deciding who would live and who would die, who could go to the operating table and who had to suffer longer. Some of the men begged her for water, and she couldn't even give them that, knowing that the surgeon wouldn't thank her when the soldier choked on it when they gave him the ether.

A medic went around with her and, on her orders, went to find stretcher-bearers for the ones who couldn't wait for surgery. Libby tried to focus on the job, fought to keep down waves of panic. She had never seen anything like this, not at Walter Reed, not in the Sternberg in Manila; the injuries were horrific—under the blood-soaked dressings were bright shards of splintered bone, raw red meat, green and gray viscera spilled and dried onto the canvas stretchers.

She had been working perhaps an hour, perhaps two, shone her flashlight into the agonized face of yet another young soldier. "Where are you hurt?" she said to him.

"I can't feel my legs."

She knew that voice, though it had been years since she had heard it. She held the light beam on his face until she was sure, then moved it back down his body to the blood-soaked fatigues. So she hadn't imagined seeing him on C Deck.

"Lieutenant?" The corpsman was staring at her. "Lieutenant, are you all right? Your hand's shaking. Perhaps you need a break."

"I'm all right." She tried to get a better look at the wound. Treat him like any other casualty, she thought. "Are you in pain, soldier?"

"Captain," he groaned.

He hadn't changed one bit. "Are you in pain—sir?"

"My back. Nothing else."

"Let's roll him," she said to the corpsman.

She turned him on his side as she had done with others countless times before, the corpsman helping her, on her count. She found what looked like a crater wound from a shell fragment. The dressing was useless; blood had soaked right through it. She peeled it off, trying to assess the damage. Some of the muscle looked to have been punched out, but it was impossible to tell exactly how bad it was.

"Get him up to the OR," she said.

"But, ma'am, it's a spinal," the medic whispered. "We got a possible pneumothorax over here. This guy can wait."

"There could be renal compromise. The OR. That's an order, Corporal."

"Yes, ma'am."

After the corpsman had taken him away, Liberty took a moment to compose herself before she moved on to the next soldier, but then someone tapped her on the shoulder. It was the captain.

"We need you in the OR," he said.

"I haven't finished here."

"The nurses up there have been working twelve hours without a break. It's an order."

"Yes, sir."

There was barely any equipment in the operating room, most of the Forty-Eighth's supplies were still on the beach or had yet to make it off the ship. There was a wooden table in the middle of the room that had been scrubbed with disinfectant, the only light they had was a corpsman holding a flashlight. There was a single rusty spigot in the corner, and a metal hand basin to use as a scrub sink.

A blanket had been hung over the single window as a blackout.

As she walked in, the draft from the open door made the blanket blow back from the window, and Libby heard something zip by her face and she ducked instinctively, even though she knew it was already too late. There was a sharp ping as the bullet ricocheted into a kidney dish and sent it spinning across the floor.

There was a moment's silence as everyone in the room looked at each other.

"Everyone okay?" a surgeon said, with exaggerated calm. "Anyone who is unable to answer, please step forward." There was tense laughter. He looked up at Libby. "Can we all take a little more care with that door, please?"

"I'm sorry, sir," Libby said.

"That's all right, Lieutenant. But let's not do it again."

Liberty washed her hands under the dribble of water coming from the spigot in the wall, her heart still hammering in her chest. Life turns on a dime, she thought. Ever since that fire in 1913, I've been riding my luck.

64

It was just after four in the morning when the doctors finished operating on their last patient. She was exhausted. She ached to find somewhere she could curl up and rest. She sat down on a box outside the OR and immediately fell asleep. It felt like only minutes later when another corpsman was shaking her by the shoulders, telling her she had to make the rounds of the post-ops, and she sat bolt upright. "Yes, I'm fine, I'll do it."

The soldiers who had survived the operating table—and there weren't nearly enough of them—lay on stretchers in the unlit room next to the OR. She got on her hands and knees and went around with a flashlight, checking pulses and airways, giving a little water from her canteen to those who needed it, reassuring them as best she could.

It was pitiful. Even the most terribly wounded had been redressed in their combat fatigues to keep them warm because they did not have enough blankets. All of them were shivering, from shock or from the cold. Some of them were crying for their mothers, big men twice her size even. Some were in terrible pain, but she had to use her syrettes of morphine sparingly; the captain said they were almost out.

There were sticky pools of blood around some of the litters, but they didn't have any plasma to give the wounded. They would have to get those boys back to the ships as soon as they could. Most of them wouldn't make it.

She crawled around in the muck, was almost done. He was one of the last. She knew him by the captain's bars on his shoulder, though he looked so pale in the torchlight, she barely recognized his face. His breathing was so shallow, she wasn't sure if he was even conscious, even if he was still alive. There was a corpsman sitting by his feet.

"Give us a moment," she said to him.

"You know this guy?"

"An old friend."

"Captain told me not to leave him. He can't feel anything below his belt. He's worried the rats will eat his feet, and he won't notice."

"I'll call you back when we're done. If you want to smoke, make sure you're under cover. There's snipers."

"Yes, ma'am," the corpsman said, and slipped away into the dark.

After he had gone, she shone the flashlight on Jack's face, was surprised to find him awake.

"It is you. I thought I was dreaming."

"Wish . . . you were. Christ . . . any morphine?"

"We're running out. Can you hold on?"

"Guess."

She found his hand. He squeezed so hard, it hurt.

"What . . . doing here?"

"I volunteered. What about you? I thought you were in London."

"Old man . . . hauled me back Stateside when . . . war started. Wanted me . . . out of harm's way." A grimace that was meant to be a smile. "Showed him, right?"

"You sure did."

She unscrewed the top of her water canteen, held it to his lips. He gulped at it, most of it spilled down his chin.

"Married?" he said.

"Why?"

"Yes or no, Lieutenant."

A shake of the head. "You?"

"There was only ever you." He blinked at the ceiling. "Still . . . hate me?"

"I crawled through the sick and the blood to find you when I'm so exhausted it's as much as I can do to breathe. What does that tell you?"

His face contorted as another spasm of pain hit him. God, he was squeezing her hand so hard it was like she could feel the bones breaking.

"You know, when my mama went to see your father in Boston," she whispered, "it was all an act, a show. Everything she said to him, she made it all up. Even your father never knew the real reason she did it."

"What reason?"

"Did he ever tell you about your mother, what happened to her?"

"Clare? . . . Yeah . . . what about her?"

"You know about the little girl who disappeared in the fire?"

He nodded.

"That was me, Jack. I'm your long-lost sister. My mama didn't want anyone to know. That was what it was all about."

The guns started up again, artillery rumbling in the distance, the distant flashes glimmering through the top of the blackout curtains and dancing along the rafters. She waited for him to say something, but he didn't. Instead, he started to laugh, but it was cut short by another spasm of pain, and this time he squeezed her hand so tight she gasped aloud and tried to pull her hand free. His whole body went stiff with pain. It took forever for the spasm to pass, and when it did, it left him breathless and soaked in a grease of his own sweat.

"Libby," he said.

"Don't talk. Enough now. Rest."

"No," he said, his voice cracking. "Something . . . you should know."

65

George Seabrook had sent a limousine to pick Sarah up from the station. As it turned through the gates of the estate, she tried to steel herself for what she was about to do. She had spent most of her life trying to avoid this very moment.

Don't think any more about it, she told herself. Walk in, say the words, then what will happen will happen. Then you don't have to live with this weight anymore.

Sarah had never imagined anything quite like this, not all the wrought-iron gates and great, flat green lawns like Yankee Stadium and blue hydrangeas in the garden beds and sweeping gravel driveways lined with American elms. And the house, with its gray-white stone and Greek pillars, it reminded her of that *Gone with the Wind* movie she had seen. There were brown ivy branches all over the façade, like a green curtain it must be in the summer. So there was a little bit of all-for-show in this George Seabrook after all, wanting everyone to see his millionaire-ness.

The limousine pulled up under the white portico. Like Penn Station it was, with lunette windows high above, like walking into God's living room. The chauffeur got out, came around the car, and opened the door for her. She hesitated, took a deep breath, and got out.

She had expected stiff, she had expected formal. Instead she saw George Seabrook waiting at the door to greet her himself, just in his shirtsleeves. She could not have been more shocked if he had come out in his pajamas and slippers.

"Hello, Sarah," he said. "Been a long time."

Not nearly long enough, bubeleh, she thought.

She followed him past a breakfast room and a library and a drawing room, everything in muted grays and greens, veined marble on the floors, all polished like nobody's business. There were blue-and-gold Sèvres vases in niches along the walls, a grandfather clock in a walnut case, and a chandelier hanging halfway down the stairs, so big you could light Broadway with it.

She fought the urge to run away. No, I promised my Libby I would do this. As the doors to the study opened, she felt her heart hammering in her chest so hard, she thought: I am going to have a heart attack and drop dead right here on this nice silk carpet.

There was a mahogany-paneled study with a stone fireplace, just the right height, something a Yankee gentleman could rest an elbow on while expounding on the state of the Union or when he was telling some silly Russian Jewish girl she was going to go to prison for what she had done, and while he was about it, he would ruin her business too.

"I'll have Winston bring us coffee," he said.

Outside, the sun went behind a cloud, in sympathy with the position she found herself in. It started to rain. George Seabrook stood by the French doors, watching the water puddle on the terrace. "Would you like to sit down?" he said.

Sarah shook her head. I only want to get this over, she thought.

"Will try not to take up too much time," Sarah said.

"Oh, that's all right." George went to his desk, took a cigar from the humidor. "Do you mind?" he said, holding it up.

"It's your house," she said, "your cigar."

He lit a match, held it at an angle over the flame, rotated it slowly. After it had toasted, he put it in his mouth and puffed on it. His eyes creased, and he gave her a small smile. "Nothing quite like a cigar."

"Me, I still like potato latkes."

"Well, we all have our little vices. Never thought I'd ever see you in Boston again, Sarah. You don't mind me calling you Sarah? After all these years."

"You call me whatever you want."

Her eyes fell on the photographs on the desk, one of a much younger Jack on a skiing holiday, another in sepia of a woman in a long dress and high collar, very formal, posed in a photographer's studio.

"My first wife," George said. "Jack's mother."

That threw her for a moment.

"It's one of a very few we have of her. Let's go out on the terrace."

He eased open the French doors. The air outside was frigid, the lawns a glitter of moist and vivid greens. Gray clouds swept away toward the city, dragging a veil of icy rain behind them. Almost one in the afternoon, the sun weak and yellow through the scarecrow trees.

"Of course, I am wondering why you're here today."

"It is about Liberty."

"I assumed it must be. How is she?"

"She is a nurse now, would you believe?"

"A nurse?"

"Even worse, she broke my heart and joined the army. Now I don't know where she is. They sent her somewhere, I don't know, Scotland, she said. Are there wars in Scotland?"

"Not since Culloden, I believe."

"Well, if Culloden is anything like this Hitler, I wish them good luck with him. Anyway, Mr. Seabrook, Liberty is why I came, something I have to tell you, should have told you a very long time ago."

He rocked on his heels, savoring the cigar, smiled, like he was remembering some good joke. Maybe he had been drinking before she got here. Never trust these rich types, they are drunk before breakfast and think it is sophistication.

The butler appeared in the study with a tray, a silver coffee pot, and two bone china cups. He poured the coffees and left them on George Seabrook's big walnut desk.

"Shall we?" George said.

"First, there is something I have to tell you."

"Very well. Whatever it is, you look like you're in a hurry to get it off your chest."

Sarah took a deep breath, but suddenly the little speech she had rehearsed on the train all the way from New York went right out of her mind. "Maybe first I will sit down after all," she said to him. Her knees were shaking, she couldn't stop it.

They went back inside, and Sarah dropped into the chair on the other side of George's desk and took a deep breath. She felt light headed. Say it, Sarah. Get it done.

George sat down opposite her and pulled an onyx ashtray toward him, tapped the ash from the end of the fat cigar. He took a lump of sugar from the sugar bowl with a pair of small silver tongs and raised an eyebrow. Sarah shook her head. He popped two of the sugars into his own cup, took a sip.

"Mr. Seabrook—"

"You can call me George."

"No, I will call you Mr. Seabrook. In a moment, you will see why. I only ask that you wait until I have finished before you say anything. Then you can decide what it is you want to do with me."

"Do with you?"

"Do you remember, Mr. Seabrook, the fire that burned down the Grand Central Hotel in 1913?"

It was like she had dashed a glass of water in his face. All the blood went out of his cheeks, and he sat back so hard, she heard the leather squeak in his chair.

"Of course I remember."

"My husband worked in that hotel. He was the janitor."

"Wait a minute. I met the janitor one evening. The concierge, Max something or other, he took me to meet him. That was your husband?"

Now it was Sarah's turn to look confused. "You met my Micha?"

"I don't remember his name, or even his face. But Max assured me he was working in the hotel the night it burned down."

"My Micha, he never told me anything about that. He died in the war a long time ago, and there are a lot of things he did not tell. But I know what he did that night."

"And what did he do?"

"He got a little baby from that fire and brought her home with him."

Sarah watched the play of emotion on the man's face; it was like watching a statue come to life. George Seabrook, always so proper and so formal, sat there with his mouth open, trying to find the right words. But there were no right words.

He got up, very slowly, and went back out onto the terrace. She watched him staring up at the sky, his hands in the pockets of his pin-stripe trousers, blinking at the drizzle of rain. Finally, he seemed to shake himself, and he came back in, closing the terrace doors behind him.

"I don't know what to say."

Sarah stared at the polished floorboards.

"That was Clare's baby," he said.

"Clare?"

"The woman who died in the fire. She was my second wife."

There was a long silence. Their coffees grew cold on the table.

"When your husband came home with a baby, I mean, what did you think, what did you say?"

"It is my first night in America, Mr. Seabrook. My first night! What do I know from hotel fires? He said he found the baby in the street. Mr. Seabrook, if you ever lived on Delancey Street, you would know, finding a baby in the trash round there, well, it is not such a big deal that you would write the papers about it."

"That's what he told you? That he just found her?"

"Yes, that is what he told me."

"How did she get her name?"

"From the Liberty statue, the first thing I ever saw from America. 'Come to me,' she said, 'I will make all your dreams come true.' And she did. She gave me a baby when Micha cannot give me a baby, you know, the usual way."

"He was . . ."

"He thought he was. Turned out it was me all along. Just Life, having its little joke."

He nodded, slowly. "I see."

"So, the little baby, we raised her like she was our very own daughter. But she wasn't, was she, Mr. Seabrook? She was your daughter. Mr. Seabrook, we stole her from you."

His hands were shaking. He reached for his cigar, but it had gone out. She waited for him to say something.

Finally, he said: "Does she know?"

"Only I tell her before she went off to this stupid war. I don't know how she will ever forgive me. Perhaps never. Maybe, too, I will go to prison. I do not know what crime they call it, but I am sure it must be a crime, yes?"

"How did you find out, about Libby, about me?"

"After my Micha died, I found this." Sarah reached into her purse and took out the cutting from the newspaper, the one she had found all those years ago in Micha's biscuit box. She unfolded it very carefully and put it on the blotter on the desk between them. George pulled it toward him with his forefinger, recognized the faint and grainy photograph of himself as a much younger man. He picked it up and the tissue-thin paper tore. He had to hold the pieces together on the desk while he read through the article. When he had finished, he sat back again.

"After I find this, I didn't need to be that Mr. Einstein to work it out."

"It's a long time to keep a secret like this," he said.

"A lifetime."

George nodded. He looked down at the cutting and shook his head. What was his expression? Not angry, like she thought he would be, just sad. "Is there anything else?"

"One more thing, I got to tell you. I loved my Liberty like nobody's business, and maybe if I had my time over, I would lie to you and to everybody all over again. Maybe if not for my Libby meeting your Jack, I would go to God never telling. Who knows? But it is up to you now. Anything you do, it is okay. You got a right."

He was quiet for a long time. She waited for him to reach for the telephone, maybe jump up and go crazy and hit her with his fist, and what could she say, anything he did she would deserve. What she did not expect was that he would sit so quietly, with his head bowed; she certainly did not think she would ever see a tear run down the big Yankee nose of George Seabrook.

He wiped it away brusquely with the back of his hand when he was aware of it and stood up, went back to the French doors, his unlit cigar clamped between his teeth.

"You understand what I told you?" Sarah said, after the longest time.

"Yes, of course."

He came back to the desk, fiddled with a box of matches, fumbled it onto the carpet, gave up, and tossed his cigar back into the ashtray. "It's my turn to tell you something now. Dear God, the past never lets us be, does it?"

She nodded. No, never.

"You're not the only one who knows how to keep secrets, not the only one who thinks they're the worst person in the world. You've just told me something you didn't want anyone in the world to know. Now it's my turn."

This, she had not expected.

"My first wife died soon after Jack was born," George said. "She drowned. Some people say it was an accident, and perhaps it was. I hate to say this, but it was a little convenient for me. You see, I had a young mistress named Clare at the time, and my wife was not too long in the ground when I married her."

Sarah watched a muscle ripple in his jaw. He turned and looked at her as if he was wondering if she could work out the rest and save him the pain of saying it aloud.

"Have you ever had an affair, Sarah?"

"That I should think of such a thing."

"Probably wise. For myself, I discovered that those things that are exciting inside an affair are much less so in a marriage. I regretted marrying Clare almost immediately. She was much younger than me, and in many ways, we were not suited. We overcame our difficulties, as many couples do, through distance. In those days, I traveled frequently on business. When I came home from an extended visit to London, and Clare declared herself pregnant, well, I had my suspicions, of course, but I chose to ignore them. Then one night, during an argument, she told me to my face that the child was not mine. So I threw her out. That is how she came to be living in the Grand Central Hotel in New York six months later."

"Liberty is not your daughter?"

"Her father, I believe, had reddish hair and green eyes. He was a rake, as we used to say in my day, very handsome, very charming, but about as faithful to Clare as she was to me. As I understand it, having a mistress with a small child soon proved tiresome for him, and he soon found a replacement. He paid up on the room in the hotel and left her there. He died in a brawl over a gambling debt two years later in San Francisco, and the world mourned such a loss. But I shouldn't judge, my behavior was scarcely better. I had been unfaithful to my own wife. So we all got our comeuppance, as they call it. It so very rarely happens, but life made exceptions for us."

"But you put this advertisement in the newspaper."

"Well, I regretted my anger and my pride, and besides, it wasn't the child's fault. But I could hardly tell the newspapers, or the police, that the infant was not mine. I would look like a fool."

"And Jack?"

"He is very clearly mine: stubborn as a mule and uncompromising as all hell."

They looked at each other for a long time, these new versions of their different histories playing out in both their minds. "So, what happens now?" Sarah said at last.

"Your behavior, I have to say, has been reprehensible. Should it ever become public knowledge, you'd be pilloried for it, and your business will crumble overnight. Socially and financially, you would be ruined."

"Is that how you will punish me?"

"Why would I want to punish you? I am in no position to judge you. Something else I've never told anyone. There was this young fellow called Art Woodward, an old Harvard pal of Jack's. I had him do a little dirty work for me to make sure Jack did what I wanted. Bribed Art with the offer of a job in my Boston office. You think I am going to condemn you, Mrs. Levine? We all do things we regret, and sooner or later, life catches us out. We can all only hope that there is something or someone that will offer us some measure of mercy in the end."

"But I stole your baby."

"You stole nothing from me that I had not already tossed aside. If Jack is to be believed, I am a tyrannical and unbending father. Seems to me Liberty was assuredly better off with you. As you have pointed out, you loved her like your own. I suspect I would have been too busy and too bitter to have treated her with much more than a sort of distracted sense of obligation. Sarah, let's forget about the coffee. Warm your bones with some vintage port, and let's talk about what we can do to make all this better."

He stood up and poured two glasses from the decanter on the mantel, held one of the glasses out to her. "It's time we both laid the past to rest, don't you think?"

"Let God bring them both home safe," she said.

He smiled. "If we sinners dare to ask it," he said.

⊷

The sun was still not up, dawn just a dirty orange stain in the eastern sky. A truck pulled up outside the hospital, and the most seriously wounded were carried out on litters and loaded into it. Libby heard one of the wounded men moan as he was maneuvered into the back.

Jack was one of the last to be loaded. She squatted next to the stretcher, reached for his hand in the dark. He was so cold and still shivering from shock and pain. "They'll get you morphine when they get you back to the beach."

The men couldn't even smoke cigarettes because of snipers. The sooner they were out of here, the better. They had patched the wounded up as best they could, but they all needed to get to a proper field hospital.

Jack had asked her last night how bad he was hurt. What could she tell him?

It didn't seem right, didn't seem fair, to find him again, to finally know the truth, and then have it end like this. She put her lips close to his ear. "I never forgot you, Jack."

"I never . . . forgot you . . . either."

"I'll see you Stateside."

"Like that . . . just fine," he said. Would he make it back to New York? He might not even make it back to the beach. If he did make it, would he want to? A wound like that.

She bent toward him to kiss him good-bye, but then two corpsmen shoved her aside and hefted the stretcher into the back of the truck. He was the last.

She watched the convoy rumble back toward the beach. They were barely out of sight when a medic came and told her she was wanted in the OR.

She went back into the aid station, up to the OR on the second floor. They were still in blackout, but a corpsman had jerry-rigged an operating lamp by suspending a flashlight from a rope hanging from the rafter. As she walked in, the draft from the door moved the blackout curtain in front of the window.

She didn't hear the crack of the sniper's rifle, just saw a blinding flash of white light. One of the nurses screamed, and then a surgeon shouted: "Sniper!" But Liberty was already flat on her face on the floor of the OR and didn't hear either of them.

66

Walter Reed Hospital, Washington, DC

George Seabrook sat by the bed and waited for his son to awake. Jack looked pale and wasted, the skin taut under his cheekbones. Seabrook remembered how handsome he had looked in his officer's uniform the day he left, how indestructible.

But nothing was unbreakable.

What was worse, it wasn't even the Germans who did this to him. They told him that this had happened fighting the damned French. Weren't they all supposed to be on the same side?

The nurse had offered to wake him, but George had said no, let him rest. Just time now, the doctors all said, time and healing.

Will he walk again? he asked the doctors every time he saw them.

We don't know, they said. We hope so. We have to wait. His spinal cord was bruised, but not severed. We have to wait for the swelling to subside.

"Knowing my son, he'll be playing football again in six months," he said, staying bullish. At least he was alive.

He took the chart from the rail at the foot of the bed, flicked through it, but none of it made any sense to him. They had told him all there was to know, done all they could. They couldn't perform miracles. These days, mothers and fathers praying for miracles were everywhere.

Jack's eyelids fluttered. There was a moment of panic on his face as he tried to remember where he was.

George reached for his hand. Jack squinted against the light, the merest flicker of a smile. "If you're here, this must be bad."

"Not a bit of it. You'll be fine."

"Can I have some water?"

There was a glass beside the bed. George held it to Jack's lips, and he sipped through the straw.

"How long have you been here?" Jack said.

"A little while. I didn't want to wake you."

"Have you spoken to the doctors?"

He nodded.

"When I'm out of here, will I be able to play tennis?"

"Sure, you will."

"That's great. I could never play it before." He looked down at his feet. "See that? I can wiggle my toes."

George swallowed back the lump in his throat, dared himself to hope.

"Liberty's mother came to see me a few weeks ago. We've stayed in touch."

The shadow of a smile on his son's face. "So you know what happened?"

George nodded. "I wrote you a letter. I guess you never got it."

"Maybe it got shot to hell, like me."

"Well, it doesn't matter now. You found out the truth the hard way."

"So did you," Jack said, and smiled and closed his eyes. "Will you do something for me?"

"Anything, you know that."

"Find out for me if she's all right, will you? That she didn't get herself hurt over there."

"Sure. Like I said, Sarah said she'll keep me posted."

"Sarah now, is it?"

"I think I might have misjudged her, Jack." The fact was, she had already rung him to tell him what had happened to Liberty. But he wasn't going to tell Jack about that right now. When he was better. Another secret, but this time he had a good reason for keeping it.

"I'm so tired. I might rest for a while now," Jack said.

He closed his eyes and slept. George Seabrook sat and watched him, even prayed a little, though it was perhaps a little late to bargain with a God he had never had much time for before.

An irony to all this. He had always thought himself a good man, a man who knew right from wrong. It had occurred to him lately that he had counted himself too high in his own reckoning.

But he was hoping for a fresh start, for him and for his son. You never knew; stranger things had happened after all.

＝⇒◆＝

The grave was at the top of the hill with commanding views of the bay. Not many of the mensch out here today, Sarah thought, too cold to mourn. There was ice along the sedge on the shoreline, like the day her Micha left Tallinn for America, the northerly wind raising whitecaps on the bay. This wind, it cut through the skin, right through the heart. It was nicer in the summer, when the maples were in leaf, but she supposed no one out here minded the weather much anymore.

She made her way up the hill, watching for the ice; that would be real slapstick, wouldn't it? Real W. C. Fields, break your neck in a cemetery.

The marker stone was near the top of the hill, a thick chunk of snow-dusted granite, the best money could buy. No cross, of course, that was just for the religious, who believed in such things.

She knelt down by the grave, took the dead flowers out of the little vase. She supposed an hour from now, these fresh ones would be curling up in the wind as well.

A handsome stone, it was. She had to hand it to George. He had dug deep for this. She had had nothing for headstones like this back then, not after she had paid off all the creditors.

WILLIAM THEODORE "BILL" DEWEY
1881–1929
ONE OF LIFE'S GENTLEMEN

Sarah looked up; a winter wren was watching her from the twisted, bare branch of a maple. He cocked his head, like he was surprised to see her there. Why so shocked, little bird? I have been coming here the same time every week for thirteen years.

She touched a finger to her lips and laid the finger on the cold stone.

"I love you, Dewey," she said, and then got to her feet and went back down the path to catch the train home.

67

Pier 12, North River, New York

Sarah wondered how her Libby would look, had imagined her in a wheelchair or coming down the gangplank on a stretcher with a bloodied bandage covering her head. But no, there she was, waving even, not even a nurse holding her arm. She had on dark glasses under her ANC cap, had a walking stick, though it looked to her she wasn't using it too much.

Sarah ran to her, hugged her, felt her stiffen in her arms. "Not too tight, Mama. I lose my balance real easy."

Sarah backed off, held her at arms' length. "Thank God, you are alive. Those Germans, they were better shots in Micha's day."

"Not even Germans, Mama. The sniper was French."

There was a small dressing on her forehead. Sarah had expected much worse. She touched the edges of it with her finger. "This is not so bad. How are you feeling, bubeleh?"

"I'm okay."

"This is all you have?"

Sarah went to take the cardboard suitcase from her, but Libby stepped back. "It's okay. I've got it."

"I have a room made up for you in the apartment. You stay with me, yes, long as you want."

"Thanks. I'd like that. But let's walk for a while first."

Sarah looked at the cane in Libby's right hand.

"I lose my balance sometimes. Mostly I'm okay. I just want to take a look at New York for a while."

Much of Battery Park was closed for the new tunnel, so they walked into the wind along the promenade. Libby found a bench and sat down, looked up at the sky, her eyes closed. "So good to be back," she said.

"When they told me the wound you had, I cannot tell you what I was thinking."

"The bullet was bouncing around inside the OR like a pinball, knocked me off my feet, and put a dent in my head as it went past. Didn't even break bone. The surgeon on the ship told me I was lucky. I said to him, if I was that lucky, it would have missed me completely."

"But you are okay?"

"I have some blurred vision and ringing in the ears. That's why they sent me home. I have to have another medical exam next month."

"Good luck with that. You won't pass it, not in a hundred years."

"You don't think so?"

"Not after I break both your legs with a baseball bat. Never going back to this stupid war."

"Thanks, Mama."

A sailor walked past, arm in arm with a brunette. She saw Libby follow them with her eyes. She guessed what she was thinking.

"I hear Jack is doing okay," Sarah said. "He wants you to go see him. He's home now. His father has hired a nurse, every day he practices his walking."

"I hope the nurse isn't too pretty."

"*Pretty* is not the word I would think of. What I think when I see her is, this girl will punch your lights out if you mess with her."

"Just the kind of girl he needs, then."

"I am sorry, Libby."

Libby didn't answer her right away. She looked up at the sky, like she was thinking about something else. "When we got to Africa," she said, "we landed at a place called Oran. That first night we had to triage the wounded in the battalion aid station. We had no proper light, just flashlights. And suddenly, there was Jack, lying on a stretcher, this huge hole in his back. And I said to the corpsman, take him first, and he said, but there's this other infantryman, I think he has a lung shot, and I still said, take this one. It was the wrong thing, I knew it was the wrong thing, but I did it anyway. I guess you know that feeling."

"What happened to the other soldier?"

"He lived, but no thanks to me."

Libby took Sarah's hand, squeezed it, and put it in her lap under hers. They sat for a long time in companionable silence.

So, is this how my forgiveness comes, Sarah thought, not with floods of tears and rending of clothes, but a simple shrug of the shoulders, a rueful smile?

In the distance, Sarah could make out the Liberty goddess. She looked so small under the lowering sky. She had heard so many immigrant songs over the years. Now, she thought, we are playing the final notes to just one more.

"I think we're done here," Liberty said. "Let's go home."

ACKNOWLEDGMENTS

My heartfelt thanks once again to Jodi Warshaw at Lake Union. I'm lucky to have you as my editor. Also to David Downing for once again bringing your prestigious talents to bear on this one, and to the wonderful Nicole Pomeroy and Elisabeth Rinaldi, for checking and double-checking absolutely everything. And last, but not least, to Lisa: for all the late nights and red eyes and insight. Can never thank you enough.

BIBLIOGRAPHY

Allen, Hervey. *Toward the Flame: A Memoir of World War I.* Lincoln: University of Nebraska Press, 2003.

Birmingham, Stephen. *The Rest of Us: The Rise of America's Eastern European Jews.* New York: Little, Brown, 1984.

Bonk, David. *Château Thierry & Belleau Wood 1918: America's Baptism of Fire on the Marne.* Oxford: Osprey Publishing, 2007.

Brown, Jay M. "From the Shtetl to the Tenement: The East European Jews and America, a Social History 1850–1925." Yale–New Haven Teachers Institute, February 2, 1979. www.yale.edu/ynhti/curriculum/units/1979/2/79.02.02.x.html.

Coan, Peter Morton. *Toward a Better Life: America's New Immigrants in Their Own Words, from Ellis Island to the Present.* New York: Prometheus Books, 2011.

Cunningham, Laura Shaine. "Ghosts of El Morocco." *New York Times,* September 5, 2004.

Ewen, Elizabeth. *Immigrant Women in the Land of Dollars: Life and Culture on the Lower East Side, 1890–1925.* New York: Monthly Review Press, 1985.

Fessler, Diane Burke. *No Time for Fear: Voices of American Military Nurses in World War II.* East Lansing: Michigan State University Press, 1996.

Friedman, Harold, and Louis Borgenicht. *The Happiest Man: The Life of Louis Borgenicht as Told to Harold Friedman.* New York: G. P. Putnam's Sons, 1942.

Galbraith, John Kenneth. *The Great Crash 1929.* London: Penguin Books, 1975.

Gordon, George Vincent. *Leathernecks and Doughboys.* Pike, NH: Brass Hat Publishing, 1996.

Kazin, Alfred. *A Walker in the City.* New York: Harcourt, Brace, 1951.

Klein, Maury. *Rainbow's End: The Crash of 1929.* Oxford: Oxford University Press, 2001.

Mendelsohn, Adam. *The Rag Race: How Jews Sewed Their Way to Success in America and the British Empire.* New York: NYU Press, 2014.

Miller, Greg. "During Prohibition, Harlem Night Clubs Kept the Party Going." *National Geographic Magazine,* April 2017.

Monahan, Evelyn, and Rosemary Neidel-Greenlee. *And If I Perish: Frontline U.S. Army Nurses in World War II*. New York: Anchor Book, 2004.

Munger, Sean. "Throwback Thursday: A Night Out in Manhattan . . . in 1930." SeanMunger.com, May 7, 2015. https://sean-munger.com/2015/05/07/throwback-thursday-a-night-out-in-manhattan-in-1930.

"New York City—Café Society or Up from the Speakeasies." YODELOUT! New York City. Accessed August 31, 2018. http://new-york-city.yodelout.com/new-york-city-cafe-society-or-up-from-the-speakeasies.

Rosenberg, Jennifer. "Flappers in the Roaring Twenties." Thoughtco, updated March 21, 2018. https://www.thoughtco.com/flappers-in-the-roaring-twenties-1779240.

Salkin, Allen. "Fading Into History." *New York Times*, October 22, 2002.

Schanberg, Sydney H. "Dinty Moore's Reflects Opulence of a Bygone Era," *New York Times*, June 4, 1964.

Stanton, Jeffrey. "Nickel Empire" Westland.net, 1997. https://www.westland.net/coneyisland/articles/nickelempire.htm.

Sterner, Doris. *In and Out of Harm's Way: A History of the Navy Nurse Corps*. Newport, RI: Navy Nurse Corps Association, 1996.

Theeboom, Sarah. "A Brief History of Orchard Street's Oldest Stores." DNAInfo, April 14, 2015. https://www.dnainfo.com/new-york/20150414/lower-east-side/brief-history-of-orchard-streets-oldest-stores.

Thomas, Gordon, and Max Morgan-Witts. *The Day the Bubble Burst: The Social History of the Wall Street Crash of 1929.* New York: Doubleday, 1979.

ABOUT THE AUTHOR

Photo © 2017 by Lisa Davies

Colin Falconer has written over twenty novels, mainly historical fiction and crime. His work is enjoyed by a wide audience and has so far been translated into twenty-three languages. Though his roots are in his native London, he now lives in Australia.

When he was nine, his primary school teacher said he was a dreamer who was always making up stories and he would never amount to anything. He still thinks that was a bit harsh.

If you think so too, you can follow Colin on BookBub to receive notices about his new releases and sales. You can also visit his website at www.colinfalconer.org or connect with him at his Falconer author page on Facebook for news, advanced reading copies, and contests.